The Fisherman's Child

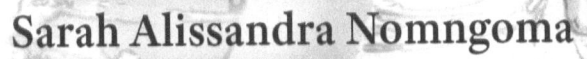

Sarah Alissandra Nomngoma

FLOWER *of* LIFE PRESS

FLOWER *of* LIFE PRESS

Published by Flower of Life Press
www.floweroflifepress.com
Jane Ashley, *Publisher*

Flower of Life Press books may be ordered through booksellers or by contacting: support@floweroflifepress.com

Cover and back cover photos by Sarah Alissandra Nomngoma
Interior rock art paintings by Sarah Alissandra Nomngoma
Cover and interior design by Jane Ashley

Library of Congress Control Number: Available upon request.
ISBN: 979-8-9987870-6-5

To my beautiful daughter
You are my inspiration and my joy
I will always love you

Until you've found pain
you won't reach the cure
until you've given up life
you won't unite with the
supreme soul
Until you've found fire
inside yourself, like the friend
you won't reach the spring
of life

—Rumi

"This is the year of the woman. A time when we focus on the dangers and difficulties women have been forced to go through. Women have had to make enormous sacrifices and fight to survive. All these challenges have come to mothers. Mothers have had to stand up and fight for everything that is right, for their children and for their families. A mother is a mother no matter what happens. A mother is a woman who carries so much on her heart and in her hands. All things come from the womb where the child is created. The child that comes from a womb comes from a very sacred medicine that will heal them for a very long time. Women do not understand how powerful they are, especially when they believe and pray to God. God made a woman for a man. Someone who would remind him of all that is right and wrong. She assists him in developing greater understanding, compassion, and kindness. A woman brings deep healing through her words and life."

—*High Sangoma Gogo Viginia Mutwa (Wife to the Honourable Baba Credo Mutwa)*

"Set in Africa's southernmost tip, this story pages us through the challenges that forge in us the insight and spiritual growth needed for our Soul's development. Tinged with poetry and the wisdom of folklore, it tells of Africa's mysteries. The Fisherman's Child *is truly a story of love.*"

—**Desia Faith Weaver, South African Author of** The Art of being a Divine Human: Inspirational Insights, Vol 1-12

"Riveting and intriguing. I am unable to stop reading. The content is so familiar with what I know and have experienced in South Africa. The alcoholism and violence experienced in homes, the apartheid laws, the evictions. The genocide of the Khoi San people has not stopped... they are still enslaved by alcohol. The 'dop system' still exists today. The Khoi San youth are being shot daily, on their way to or from school, or while playing in their backyards. All by design so that they never get to know who they are, who their Ancestors are, and the deep spiritual connection with their Ancestors that needs activation. So, I'm forced to stop and reflect, touched deeply by the rawness of the memory. This is an amazing and deep love story. I shed so many tears, yet in the end Lisa chose 'wisely.' Her special friendship and journey with the bushmen is so deep and spiritual, her amazing and special journey with UBaba Credo Mutwa, the great iSanussi. Our Holy Wise Teacher. SA did not understand. The amazing Bushmen artwork, I stop and study it and see so much being said from the world of the Ancestors. This is really the Hero's Journey of a single mother, a warrior spirit, self-empowered, and an inspiration to any woman who has had to raise a child or family on her own. By reading this book, I had the inspired opportunity to visit my own 'Hero within.' Wonderful ending." Gaitses/Gure

—Dr Chief Krotoa-Smith, Integrated Spiritual Healer

"The mother's love is indestructible, and this beautiful work proves that a mother's love never dies. The challenges of motherhood, being a single mother, and bringing new life to form in this world is not a task to be taken lightly. The author weaves a beautiful story of how soul mirrors, unconditional love, compassion, grace, and humility are true superpowers of the mother. These superpowers have the ability to change our world for the better, and this beautiful story will make you laugh, cry, and evoke emotions of everything in between. A walk through the holy fires, back to Love."

—Stellar Fairbairn, Co-author of Magdalene Unveiled, Musician~The Magdalene Codes Vol. I and Vol II

"The Fisherman's Child is a captivating and magical tale that begins when fated lovers meet, and a dream of love is devastated by addiction. A single mother follows her dreams and finds family within the sacred indigenous peoples of South Africa. How will they come together to keep dreams and ancient wisdom alive, despite opposition from every side? The Fisherman's Child takes us on an intimate journey through the sacred medicines, and the wisdom keepers who keep these traditions alive. How will Lisa respond to the mandate to write about it all? A powerful read not to be missed."

—Mari Dreamwalker, Author of Keeper of the Sacred Shawl

CONTENTS

Introduction

Song-lines sung about our lives
Forever
Connect heaven with earth

If you look out to sea from the coast off the Cape Peninsula, on a clear day, you can just make out the gentle contours of West Africa, gradually fading into a mauve and hazy distance. It is here at the north-facing tip of the Cape of Good Hope that my story begins... A story so deeply etched into my being that it has forever changed and shaped my perspective on life.

Before the encounter, I was, like so many human beings, mostly unaware and disconnected from the possibility that there could be any other way of seeing "homeless people," other than people who are not like us. As vagrants, tramps, and those who have completely lost their way. It is an interesting and especially narrow point of view coming from those who live on the African continent, where many original tribes people have always lived lightly on its red soil, as nomads, pilgrims, refugees, adventurers, and travelers on foot.

As an artist and poet, I've seen much through eyes that search for beauty beyond the surface... and couldn't have known the journey experienced by the homeless until it touched me in a personal way. A way that broke open my heart from the safety and conformity I was used to. A way that allowed me to see into the heart of an individual, suffering and longing for a place in the world. Perhaps this depth of compassion and understanding would have arrived eventually through research or the work I did in the field with the Bushmen people or with disadvantaged and abused children. But nothing could have prepared me for the experience that will unfold with the telling of this story. It's a story that connects all of us, every single human being, to the ancient legacy of our past and to the choices we must make for ourselves in the context of our rapidly changing environment and future world.

The African continent has seen far too much conflict and political upheaval, especially in recent decades. During the years of Apartheid, before 1994 when Nelson Mandela became the President of South Africa, young men over the age of eighteen were conscripted into the National Defense Force. They were sent to army bases across the country and even to neighbouring countries, Namibia and Angola. These young men, who grew up tough on the outside, were forced to keep the painful truth of their experiences in the army locked deep within their souls. Young men who, after their military training, were desperately in need of healing and the kind of depth and unconditional love that is rarely found among humans today. These were my childhood friends. South African brothers, family members, children growing up together in a country filled with xenophobia, violence, racism, discrimination, division, and iniquity. I understood very early in life that I would have to make some difficult choices. Choices that would often seem completely at odds with my family and societal values, and at times with those who knew me. Even as I accepted the world as it was, a quiet determination grew within me—a resolve that, no matter how many times I tried and failed, I would do everything in my power to live with greater compassion, love, and peace. This conviction became my guiding force, urging me to move beyond resignation and to seek out a way of being that honored both myself and the world around me. Each experience, no matter how difficult, only strengthened my commitment to discovering a gentler and more understanding path through life.

If I could only speak to my younger self now. I was such an adventurous, passionate, and naive young woman. Living in a dream world where love, idealism, and goodwill belong. How I would love to gently put my arms around her and tell her this: "Lisa, no matter what happens, you will always be the visionary you were born to be. No matter what people say or do to break you, they will never take away your essence. Don't ever give up on your dreams and remember, your love truly matters."

This is the story of how I fell in love with a homeless man and bore his child. It is the Heroine's journey. The adventure of Lisa, my younger self, and my evolution into wisdom through my experience as a single mother. A journey that found me, at times lonely, often broke, but always faithful to myself and my beautiful daughter.

Dawn

That's where we began
in the womb of a humble woman
We've done it all backward
The curved ball has returned
On its way home bringing
light, warmth, and sound

Poem child
eyes that can speak
You are a testament
Life lived not to seek
You have taught me
with every breath
I'm alone

being you
The Divine spark
sparkles
the plain truth rankles
all prideful discipline
cracks
and shards expose
a nude and half-formed acolyte

daughter
The honour is mine
to free you
exquisite, winged soul

may those who try to make you unwholly
through your tears
be brought
to the heart blood
of their own painful fears

And may simplicity
be your beauty
unmasking many who know not their own

sister soul
belonging not to me
may our lives describe
ever wider circles of love

CHAPTER 1

THE WAR WITHIN

When the heart breaks, it bursts open like a rose.

The human heart is an instrument of fire and ice and of every other emotion in between. All my life, I have felt the effect of these two extremes, but today my heart burns with anguish from missing my daughter Kathleen. This exquisite young woman who has grown up and flown away. Every day, I am accompanied by the ghostly, intense longing just to see her sweet face again, to hold her in my arms, and to hear that silvery voice that belongs only to my child. Nowadays, she never calls me or comes to visit. And no matter how much I distract myself or embrace my feelings of grief and longing, they follow me everywhere I go like a shadow. She was so much a part of my life for 19 years, and then one day she was gone. Sometimes it felt like I was keeping an eagle in a cage, especially those last few years of her schooling. Of course, I knew that she needed to soar, explore, and find a life of her own, and so I let her go. It was causing both of us pain to experience the beating of her full-grown young wings against a cage that was our home. We both knew it was time, and so I drove her down the road, released her, and watched her fly away.

At first, there were promises to come home and visit, as most kids will do, but later the date was extended, and then the messages started to rain in. "I've been offered a little cottage on my boyfriend's farm, and we are going to be doing it up. I'm too busy, Mom. Sorry, we are on our way out. Can't talk now!" And then slowly but steadily, the criticism and heartbreaking words began. Words that attack and blame and shame for all kinds of things to do with the way I am as a mother and how she grew up. Telling me that her boyfriend and his wealthy family considered me financially and mentally unstable. Insult after insult came raining in, making me feel quite breathless, and as though my heart could barely beat another beat. Not a single word from her was spoken in gratitude or love. Nothing at all said about missing her home, her special cat, and our friends. The peaceful sounds of nature, the forests, and the gentle, warm oceans where she had spent so many happy afternoons swimming. All forgotten. Slowly, she had begun to blank me out of her life, using hatred as the wall from behind which to hurl her rage at me.

"I don't want to come home and visit you. I don't want to see you or talk to you on the phone. There is nothing you do and nothing you offer that I need anymore. I just don't need you in my life anymore, Mom. I never had a real family, and I never knew my dad because of you."

Kathleen's words pounded and wounded my soul, and I felt my mother's heart break a million times beyond all limits of grief. Even now, when I remember that morning, I can still see myself as if from a distance… Lisa, hunched on the veranda, her head in her hands, staring at the phone in disbelief. She had been sipping tea, lulled by birdsong, when her daughter's message arrived.

"Who wrote these words? We've shared so many moments of joy together in the past. Yes, of course, the years of single parenting have been immensely challenging, but this can't be the young woman I raised with so much tenderness and love… What has happened to her to make her say these cruel things? Oh, I just don't know what to believe anymore," she whispered to herself, shaking her head.

She smiled softly as her imagination rolled back the years and memories, to pictures of herself and her child bent over magical story books, of happy times drawing and making paper dolls together, of adventures with their dog and beautiful days at the seashore, building sandcastles and swimming with snorkels and goggles. Of picnics with friends, planting vegetables in their garden, easter egg hunting, and gathering wild berries to make jam. Kat's first attempt at baking a cake for her mom, which had made her smile so when she was feeling ill. Tender memories of the two of them, singing, hugging, and laughing together in their old car with a snow woman melting on the bonnet, as Lisa drove them through snowcapped mountains. Hikes and swims in forested waterfalls. Wonderful trips to pick cherries, wild apples, and tangerines from farmers' orchards. Christmas holidays with their family in Cape Town and their trip to London, exploring the River Thames and the mysteries of the magnificent old city.

Memory after memory and adventure after adventure filled her mind. "Was it all so bad? Was I really such an uncompromising, uncaring mom and terrible person?" she thought aloud. "It's been tough raising Kat on my own, but I certainly couldn't have done more for my daughter. By choosing to become a single parent, I broke the cycle of abuse and set a new pattern of self-empowerment for future generations. I brought Kat up to be a fiery, free, and independent young woman with a mind of her own, and I have let her live her own life. God knows, I was a good mother to her. I suppose, more importantly than anything else, she knows unquestionably that I love her. Despite all the challenges and arguments about boundaries and financial difficulties, there was always honesty, laughter, and the spirit of love in our home," Lisa sighed.

"How I wish I could show Kat the truth, but she won't understand until she is a mother herself someday. All the vicious insults and criticism from folk who do not understand the first thing about single motherhood. Only I know that these labels do not fit and that I'm nothing of the sort.

"If only my daughter could see the influence that such people have, and the million voices enticing her to listen and do what they believe and say. Nothing, absolutely nothing will ever replace the love of her own mother. Surely Kat does know this? I know she is angry at me because she grew up without a dad and for putting my foot down to her boyfriend. But to banish me from her life because I dared ask for respect and kindness at home is craziness. I never expected Kat might continue a senseless family pattern of intimidation, exclusion, and cruelty." Lisa absently wiped tears of frustration and hurt from her wrinkled cheeks.

For some time, there had been a constant and strained sense of impatience from Kat and her boyfriend. She couldn't quite put her finger on what it was or where this was coming from, but intuition had told her that the two young people were planning to start a life together. Lisa had been kind and frank with them both about the reality of taking such steps. She assured Kathleen of her support, especially regarding her studies, but for some reason, David seemed irritated by Lisa's encouragement of her daughter's independence. He appeared determined to disregard her role in her daughter's future. "Why on earth is this young man so overwhelmingly protective of Kat? Hmmm, I'm not imagining it! There's something else going on here," she thought silently to herself.

Lisa remembered the polarizing rancour and the rain of acid verbal abuse during his last visit and how she'd had to put her foot down with Kat's boyfriend. Her mind took her back to the scene of confusion that still ripped through her heart like sheet lightning. Kat and David were standing in her kitchen, roaring accusations at her. "Don't tell me what I can and can't do. You are not my parent." Lisa had stood her ground. The situation had escalated, and despite Lisa's best attempts to be calm and ignore their youthful arrogance, eventually she couldn't take it anymore. "David, you are welcome to have a respectful conversation, but if this is how you insist on speaking to me in my home, then I think it's best that you pack your bags and leave, please," she said in an angry but firm, clear voice.

For a while, there was a silent standoff, and then David left. "Fuck your mother! Just cut her off completely, Kat. You don't need her in your life anymore." Lisa overheard Kat's boyfriend growl as he carried his bags to the car. Kathleen had never been the same again. Then what had always been the inevitable evolved into a hastened and icy departure. Kathleen had made up her mind that she would go and live with David and his family on the farm. Somewhere where her mother could never interfere with them again. Her daughter's betrayal had touched an ancient wound, triggering a hot lava of outrage and pain in her. This wound was a raw place where women, mothers, and all that is sacred about motherhood and the bond between mothers and children had been desecrated in recent generations. As she sat in the stillness of her thoughts, Lisa felt the roar of heartbreak and grief exploding out of her womb and heart in aching sobs.

"There is absolutely not one thing I can do to change this!" she whispered through her tears to the clouds and the swallows flying overhead. "I can't call Kathleen on her cell phone because she doesn't answer, and the rare times that she does, she finds reason to go off on yet another angry rampage. Ah, if only things had been different. If only Kat had not grown up without her father. Perhaps if Kat had known the wonderful sense of warmth, belonging, and protection that having her own loving father and family entails, she would not have wanted to leave home like this," Lisa sighed. "I am paying a heavy price for my choice to be a single parent. Now there is nothing I can do to resolve my daughter's inner battle. It's up to her to make peace with who she is and to accept the turmoil within herself. Although this is a heartbreaking situation, in some ways, I'm grateful it has happened. I'm so tired of justifying myself, of fighting through people's judgmental, self-righteous attitudes for the tiniest drop of understanding. I'm weary of the endless hum of criticism that comes with the territory of single parenting. Mostly, I'm just tired of going above and beyond to please everybody, my daughter, her friends, and her world. I've had enough.

"Go ahead, Kat, do your worst. Cut me off if that is what you intend to do. Close the door and walk away, my beautiful child. Of course, it's your life and your choice to make. May God protect you and guide you home to what is real, to truth, and to a deeper understanding of your mother's love," Lisa whispered to the wind.

She leaned back against the cushioned armchair and closed her eyes. Very soon, she was asleep.

Dreaming of Lions

Magic rarely happens to people who are afraid.
It's only in unguarded moments when we let
go and are completely ourselves that the power
and Majesty of Life takes us into the deeper current
of its flow.

A lone black eagle soared, catching the updrafts and circling in slow motion across the highest peaks of the Cederberg mountains. A few streaks of cloud stretched lazily across the vast blue of an African sky, and the golden sunlight infused the landscape with life. Lisa sat on top of an ancient sandstone boulder, her arms hugging her long legs to her chest. She was transfixed, looking out at the vast mountain landscape littered with lichen-covered rock. A brack river snaked its way between the bushes and rocks far below her. She had come up here, both for the silence of the mountains and in search of the exquisite and elusive San rock paintings that called to her soul. These mountains of the west coast of South Africa, the Koue Bokkeveld and the Cederberg, were covered with the ancient rock art of the San or Bushmen folk. She felt a sense of peace and completeness in the mountains among these deserted ancient ancestral spaces once inhabited by the Bushmen, the original people of Africa. Behind her was a wide rock shelter that was protected from the elements by a sprawling and gnarled old Ficus Africanus tree. The kind of tree that the Cape Leopard use as their perch and to sharpen their claws. Painted inside and on the smooth rock face were the most beautiful rose ochre eland with full bellies and white dewlaps. Each delicately depicted antelope was about the length of her arm; the entire frieze of magnificent eland bulls was breathtaking in its enormity. These ancient visual signatures left behind on the rocks were the first form of symbolic communication, possibly preceding the runes and hieroglyphs and all other forms of contemporary writing— exquisite letters from our human ancestors across time and space. The entire rock shelter, although not deep, was lit by this incredible painting. Many now faded, red-ochre figure paintings were overlaid by these Eland bulls. On the floor of the overhang, the sand and red-tinted soil were powder-fine and soft to the touch. It was a sacred place for the return of a Bushman family group to find safe shelter and one where they could sleep. Lisa had been hiking and exploring in the Cederberg for many years, but this "Cave of the Eland" remained her favourite temple of the soul. She had questions about the Bushmen, humanity, and her life purpose in relation to all of this. Questions no one seemed to have answers for. Perhaps it was the voice of her quest, but she knew that something and someone was calling her. She sought her answers alone, deep in the silence of the mountains.

Lisa knew that she couldn't stay in the present situation. It was a good place. Nothing was wrong with the small town of Aurora in the Western Cape mountains of Southern Africa. It was beautiful and ideal for an artist like her, especially one who loved solitude and nature. She had lived in a comfortable, spacious old farm cottage amid a fascinating community for almost five years. There was a gorgeous guest cottage attached to the farmhouse, often filled with friends or paying guests. Even her Bushman friends from the Kalahari had come to visit her here on their way back home to the desert. Local folks would drive up the West Coast to see the spring wildflowers or just for a quiet getaway in the fynbos-covered mountains. Folks loved the old farmhouse with its sunny courtyard and wild garden and would come back regularly to visit. There was a quaint little restaurant just down the street from where she lived, run by an elderly French chef and his South African wife. They were both excellent cooks, offering their cuisine especially in the holiday season when the restaurant was open every day. Bouillabaisse, made with local crayfish and fish, beef bourguignon, fresh garden artichokes with hollandaise sauce, quiche Lorraine, beautiful Cape wines, olives, home-baked bread, freshly ground coffee, and croissants. Delicious smells would waft gently over the little town from their kitchen. The restaurant served as a watering hole for the locals and for frequent travelling visitors.

There was always something exciting happening in Aurora. It was the place where the sunsets over the West Coast were the most spectacular she had ever seen. International visitors and interesting friends would come from far away to see her painting studio and to talk about the Bushman people and their rock art. Lisa's reputation and career as an artist were thriving. But on the inside, the direction of her life felt ethereal, unreal, and incomplete. Her soul strings kept tugging at her with a powerful wind at her back that was taking her through the fynbos veld of this lovely place and drawing her onward. The question haunted her every day. What was it that her soul was asking for?

She knew it wasn't because she longed for bright city lights and entertainment. What she loved most was the silence and the peace of the remote Cape mountains. Looking back, the feeling of stability and sanctuary was slowly suffocating her. Her soul needed more than this. She fought a difficult inner battle because in the quiet, secret space of her guarded heart, she knew what was to come.

Sometimes we experience life in reverse. Our souls seem to know what must happen. A sense of the inevitable draws us towards experiences and people. And this was the way it was for Lisa.

She had been dreaming about lions. Every night when she closed her eyes, a recurring dream would be waiting for her. It was a dream about future meetings and facing her inner fears where she found herself surrounded by prowling, pacing lions. After a while, she began to feel more relaxed, playful, and even at one with these lion beings. In her waking hours, Lisa continued with her paintings, with everyday chores and routines, pretending that everything was the same and that life would go on as it always had. She tried to feel contentment with her peaceful existence in the beautiful mountain village of Aurora. But in her heart, she was already in this world of lions and lionesses. Then one night, the most vivid dream came to her about a meeting of souls. She dreamed that a lion had transformed into a man and had flown with her over the wild Atlantic shores. She had smelled the sound and soft, velvet, brine smell of the ocean. She and the lion-man were dancing together. Above the milk woods, they soared and floated. The dream was an ecstatic experience like none she had ever had before, and she knew this was a premonition of something more to come. It was a dream so powerful and had moved her so deeply that shortly after Lisa had this dream, she began to pack all her worldly possessions and prepare to follow her heart on this journey to meet the soul her dreams spoke of.

Mantis Mother

Mantis moans softly like a changing wind
Take me to your bosom dear friend
Let me shelter there for just one more night
And the emptiness echoed back at Mantis. . .
One more night, one more night
When the warmth of summer became the chill of storm
Mantis flew far, far away
Searching for warmth she could not find
Her body grew and outgrew its purpose
Still, she found no human warmth
and little understanding
and yet she grew
larger still
Bigger than her body
Then Mantis spirit
gently said
who will rock me now that my body's dead
No mama and no lover can embrace my
evolving form
And the wind blew lightly into Mantis spirit's face
while the ocean carried her body
into its deep embrace
"Surrender, Mantis Woman,
become the lover and the mama, too
Give understanding and human warmth to all.
Don't wait!" Wind said.
"No, don't wait until your spirit's dead."

It was early in April 2003. Lisa would always remember when they met because it was a most ethereal, special time of year. Autumn, when the seasons are in flux and the heat of the summer is over, when, in the mornings and evenings, cool mists envelop the Cape coasts.

Lisa woke early that morning when the bay was still shrouded in mist. She didn't bother to brush her thick mop of auburn hair or to brush her teeth. She pulled on a bathing costume and grabbed a beach towel, intent on taking Baloo, her happy-go-lucky dog, to the beach for a swim in the sea.

It was one of those haunting, magical days when you can feel the elements, the swirling mists and turquoise ocean, the soft white sand, and the bold, grey-gold-granite boulders that stand silent sentry to ancient times. Lisa ran through the shallow water, slowly gaining the courage to dive into the icy Atlantic Ocean while her beloved dog padded down the beach behind her.

He was sitting smoking a cigarette on a rock that jutted onto the beach when she first saw him. Something deep within her knew that it was him, the lion-man she had dreamed about. Lisa kept running until she got to the same spot on the beach, and she noticed him standing on the sand, smiling at her dog. "He's got the right idea," the stranger said, bending down to stroke the smiling spaniel. She ran past them laughing, an incredible lightness of being in her soul, in her feet, in her hair, and in her heart.

The sun slowly made its way over Lions Head and up over the Karbonkelberg mountains, spreading its warm rays through the mist. Lisa swam in the clean, cold ocean, diving between the crystal blue waves, and emerged feeling whole and renewed. All the signs were presented to her to show what lay ahead. While she was swimming, she had found a giant, green praying mantis floating in the foam of the seawater. It was the most magnificent, surreal "Praying Mantis" she had ever seen, almost 14 cm long and with a wingspan of the same length. Yet, as she gazed at the delicate creature cupped in her hands, she felt a lingering sense of sadness. There was no sign of life from the mantis that had fallen to its watery fate.

In Africa, and particularly among the Kung! Bushmen of Botswana, the Praying Mantis is the oldest symbol and an incarnation of God. The Mantis was also known to be an embodiment of Kaggen, the Trickster, and a divine messenger. In many indigenous cultures throughout the world, the Mantis is a reminder to remain calm, prayerful, and observant. Lisa had been shown repeatedly by her Bushmen friends that when a mantis appeared at a significant time in one's life, it was most often a sign that presented a message from the "Great Creator." Lisa didn't fail to notice that the drowned mantis from the sea was a most unusual sign.

It was early, and the mist still enshrouded the beach. The stranger re-emerged as if from a reality that was part of a dream. "You know this beach well," he said, taking a deep draw of his cigarette. Lisa looked up and beamed at him. He leaned against a granite rock while Lisa wrapped herself in a dry towel. She didn't feel at all uncomfortable in the stranger's presence as she sat warming herself in the early morning sun. Finally, the mysterious man began to speak in a quiet, slow drawl.

"I grew up here. This beach, this part of the coast, is where I learned to fish. I come here quite early in the mornings when there's hardly anyone around. Love it here," he said with a half-smile, looking out at the ocean.

Lisa was quiet. They both were, for a long while. It was as if they were communing with the sea and one another in silence. She could feel the energy of his presence intensely. It seemed to her that he was the kind of person who could completely blend into the environment. Clearly, he belonged to the ocean and nature. He seemed so naturally detached from the human experience that it obviously took an immense amount of effort for him to engage on a normal or "social level." Lisa was a loner herself and had spent most of her life either painting or exploring nature, and she instinctively understood his detachment. "You live around here?" he asked, breaking the silence.

"No," she answered, shaking her head. "I'm visiting at my folks' place for a while. And I'm thinking about moving back to Cape Town again," Lisa said with a shy smile.

"Ah, then no wonder I haven't seen you here on the beach till now. You must have grown up on this coastline, though?"

Lisa nodded her head, smiling at him.

"So, you've seen the dolphin pods that frequent these shores at this time of the year chasing shoals of silverfish," he said. Lisa looked at him in recognition of his words.

She nodded. "Yes, when I was growing up here, I sometimes would go swimming with the dolphins. I wasn't afraid of them. They always seemed to me to have incredibly shy, gentle natures. Once, an entire school of dolphins surrounded me, leaping over my head and swimming beneath and around me in a vortex of ecstatic energy. I could feel their amazing sense of extra-sensory perception and how the dolphins were communicating with me in some inexplicable way. After some time had passed, one of the larger dolphins gently nudged me with his soft rubbery nose, encouraging me to return to the shore. I was shivering with cold and exhilaration by that stage. This same gentle dolphin swam with me all the way into shallow waters."

"Dolphins are our friends," he said, smiling now, too, and the words began to flow out of him like the soft turquoise waves lapping onto the beach. He spoke about the different cetaceans that visited this coast, Southern Right (baleen) whales, humpback and sperm whales, porpoises, and dolphins. His obvious passion, knowledge, and understanding of sea life in this vast area fascinated her. As he spoke, Lisa began to feel not only his sense of detachment but an aura of sadness and shadow that surrounded him. He seemed to disappear into the mysterious realms of his imagination, into the silences between his words. For a long time, they both sat looking out at the ocean as he pulled deeply at his hand-rolled cigarette.

The Fisherman wore an old, stained khaki sweatshirt like a second skin. He carried a canvas knapsack to keep his fishing gear in. His faded jeans were torn and scuffed at the ankles and his well-worn leather boots, used to hard wear and strenuous walking. His face was covered in the downy, soft fuzz of new beard, almost that of a young adolescent. The whole of his being was otherworldly, as if he walked here but did not belong. The Fisherman's spirit was already free of the physical realm. His body stuck on this plane, beyond the ages of time. He was a being born into a world that he could make absolutely no sense of. That is, until Lisa came along and peeked at the light under the crack of his well-guarded and metal-plated soul gate and saw his light.

He was a poacher by trade. He fished for Lobster, crayfish, or "Kreef." He fished at night and watched the moon. He knew all the nuances of tide and current and when to take the optimum chance to throw a line and bag his prize. This was his love, his passion, and his joy. He danced from rock to rock as waves and surf crashed in the dark. His silver movements were a surreal blur of light and liquid focus on the sea. The Fisherman knew the freedom to live and pass undetected by hordes of humans who live by codes regulated by the clock.

Lisa found herself sitting spellbound beside this unique and magical human being that misty day in April. And before she knew it, she was utterly absorbed, listening to the lonely fisherman tell incredible stories about the sea, about his adventures fishing on the South African Marine research vessels, about whales and sea monsters and huge schools of flying fish. Hours slipped by, and the rising sun had evaporated most of the mist. Suddenly, she remembered her own world, family commitments, and the day. Lisa gathered her things. "I must go. It's already getting so late." She told the Fisherman goodbye with the kind of wordless, wistful smile that said, "I hope we will meet again."

Her move away from her home in Aurora had not yet been consolidated. Lisa had simply packed all her nonessentials into boxes and paid for a place to store these few pieces of her furniture. The happy, old farmhouse now seemed so empty without all her things to decorate its beautiful wood and terracotta tiles. Then, Lisa left the little town with her old truck piled with essential personal belongings. She still hadn't made any fixed decisions about where she would live or what she would do. For the past few weeks, she had been staying in the tiny guest cottage at her mother's home on the Atlantic coast. She knew she had to make that decision and let go of her old life, surrendering to whatever came next.

Eventually, she and her mother took the drive up to the town of Aurora together. She had not much left to pack, only to fetch her remaining belongings and arrange with the farmer to hand over the farmhouse keys. It was also a good reason to say a last goodbye to the friends she had made in the village, the lovely couple who ran the French restaurant, and the Khoikhoi community surrounding Aurora. Lisa and her mom stopped along the road for lunch at a quaint farm "padstal" on the West Coast. They bought a few basic groceries—some locally made mebos,[1] farm eggs, boerewors[2], sticks of dried meat or "biltong," and some golden "Hanepoot" grapes to take along with them. Slowly, she began to feel a sense of peace and direction again. The heaviness of the move and saying goodbye to her beloved cottage and friends became the lightness and release of what was simply no longer meant for her.

Her mother had always been a compassionate and understanding woman. A fountain of wisdom and her "Rock of Gibraltar" at times like these. She came from old "Rhodesian" pioneering stock and was a practical farm woman at heart. In the days that followed, she and Lisa spent wonderful moments sitting under autumn leaves of the huge oaks on the farm in Aurora, drinking tea and chatting.

---

1 Sugared dried fruit
2 Spiced sausage

"I am afraid for the future, Mom," Lisa said simply, looking at the tea leaves at the bottom of her mug. "As special as this little village is and as lovely as the people are, I must admit to having had moments of intense loneliness here. As you can see, there are not many younger people in this town. Sometimes I long to relate with other people my age, and perhaps someday, I hope to find love. It has become crystal clear over the past few months that it's time to leave Aurora." Lisa closed her eyes with a sigh of resignation. "This place has been my home and safety for so long, and its people have become like my extended family. Leaving here makes me feel so uncertain. What will I do next? How on earth will I manage in the city on an artist's salary?" Lisa said, sighing.

Her mother reached out her hand and lightly brushed her daughter's cheek.

"My darling, you know more about rock art than anyone I know. You have lived and loved your Khoisan rock art paintings," her mother had said, a smile in her warm brown eyes. "Whatever you choose to do and wherever you go next, just keep on painting for the summer exhibitions in Cape Town. You must remember that your work brings people a profound sense of peace and serenity. I am so proud of you, my child." Her mother knew that Lisa would always walk an unusual path in her life. She also knew that her daughter had a fiery and independent spirit. One that would never be tamed.

My mother and I had not always been on the same page about my chosen career and the fact that I had not married Mr Right, the boyfriend my parents would have approved of. Growing up, I had been a challenging and independent young woman. One who chose to go on frequent walkabouts in search of the disappearing Bushman communities of the Kalahari and to explore the magical cave art of the Cederberg mountains. My mom believed in a career and relationship that would bring stability and normality, but I wasn't looking for a safe life of conformity. I was searching for truth, fulfillment, and the kind of love that brought growth to one's soul. For a while, her disapproval became extremely difficult to bear, and we had almost drifted apart. Then one day, my mom had a breakthrough. She wrote me this beautiful poem:

Your love shines through like a steadfast light
A beacon so brightly familiar
Taken for granted, scoffed at and ignored
You're sometimes so immature

Now these painful looks and thoughtless words
A darker side invoked
Your anger and your hurt lashed out
And in the night, I woke
A sudden jolt, I felt the lash,
Of God's Divine insight
Forgive me child, no not a child
It's me who never grew!
God that her light should dim my way
For my heart would surely break
A lonely and a blind old fool
Who chased her friend away
So let my love shine back my child
I'll be your beacon too
I respect, admire and have gratitude
To a shining soul much higher

So always be yourself my dear
And love no matter whom
Your love you give is so precious
Yes, your love really matters!

Lisa didn't see the Fisherman again for a long time afterward and had almost forgotten about the meeting until one steely, gray winter's evening, she noticed a sky-blue VW motor home parked in the corner of the beach parking lot. It was his vehicle. Lisa was just on her way home from a walk on the beach when she recognized the Fisherman getting out of his van.

"Jeepers! That's a perfect vehicle for an adventurer like him," she thought to herself. The Fisherman looked up briefly and greeted her in his usual detached manner. He was busy at the back of his van, packing stuff into his knapsack.

"Hey, it's you," he casually tossed the words and a quick smile backward.

His vehicle practically gleamed; it was clean, polished, and obviously very well-loved. "Wow! That's a beautiful camper," Lisa remarked, walking over to say hello. The Fisherman stood up and smiled at her with pride.

"Yes, she's a beauty," he said, touching the shining metal gently. It was almost sunset, and he had been preparing for a walk down onto the rocky promontory. His canvas knapsack was bulging with bags of snacks and a lemonade bottle. He was all set for sundowners. "Well, do you want to come along and join me then?" he asked, looking at her with a rakish smile.

"Okay," Lisa smiled shyly. "But only for a short while, though. I must get back to feed this hungry mutt," she said lightly, looking down at her adoring dog.

There was a chilly, early winter breeze blowing, making their hair tousled in the wind. Lisa shrugged a warm jacket over her shoulders as they walked down the rocky path together. "I forgot to ask you your name the last time we met. I'm Lisa," she said shyly.

The Fisherman glanced at her and smiled. "Hi, Lisa," he murmured, "I'm Ian."

They made their way through the labyrinth of granite boulders and found a comfortable, sheltered spot where they could watch the sunset. Lisa remembered how he had produced a joint, an oily newspaper parcel of fish and chips, an ice-cold bottle of lemonade, and cane spirits from his knapsack. "Like to join me?" he asked, taking a metal camping cup out of his bag and offering her some.

Lisa smiled with bemusement at his quirkiness. "No, thanks," she said, smiling shyly and shaking her head. "But I'd love some fish and lemonade, though. I'm hungry, and your food smells really good."

Ian poured them both drinks and they sat in companionable silence, sipping sun downers, munching fish and chips, and watching the vivid, fiery colours fade as the sun set over the Atlantic horizon. The Fisherman seemed far more relaxed in this setting, with a drink in his hand. Thinking back on events as they unfolded, Lisa remembered how utterly golden those moments were. There was no judgment, guilt, or bravado, just the natural ease of two souls connecting. To Lisa, it felt like being with a kindred spirit. They spoke easily together about random, simple things like the mood of the sea and their experiences. Lisa listened, fascinated by his thoughts about how the moon and weather affected the ocean. She could see by his calloused hands and tough physique that he was a man who lived very closely with nature. It never occurred to her to see him as most people did, as a social outcast. Lisa was an artist, a poet, and philosopher, and in many ways, by nature of her lifestyle, she was an outsider, too.

Before Lisa left that evening, she scrawled her cell phone number onto the greasy paper bag and gave it to Ian. But in the days that followed, he didn't call her. She hadn't expected him to, as he had told her that he had no cell phone and did not like technology. He was too different from the mainstream kind of person whose life is centered around telephones, computers, and TVs. Ian was a wild man and clearly wanted to stay that way. Living under the radar, free and unencumbered by societal chains. Only the fact that he was human with the need for companionship and warmth allowed him to stay loosely connected with other people.

Between leaving her last home in Aurora on the West Coast and trying to find her feet in the city again, Lisa took long mountain walks with her dog, Baloo, and swam at the beach near her parents' home. Occasionally, if she was up early in the mornings, she would catch a glimpse of the Fisherman, sitting with his back to the world, smoking a cigarette, preoccupied on a rock at the sea water's edge. He was never with companions and seemed utterly detached from the rest of the world. Lisa began to wonder why he was always so alone.

LOST

We're in cages
every particle of space
measured by distances
that keep us all at bay
you turn a cage into a place of wildness
Where does "society" hide you?
Lost
utter your unexplored space
every particle
keeps you away from the rest of the world
It's what "they" make you do
what "they" turn you into
wild man
Do the millimeters keep anyone safe?
The Dream that frees you for a while
The substance opens doors so wide
the cages melt into the snow
All knowledge is yours to know
Arms of loved Ones open wide

In the dream there's no Divide
What do the millimeters mean anyway?
Lost in cages, more and more
Our children
are looking for
a bridge from broken homes
lonely lives
burned out existences
and overused lies
Where will our children find their bridges
If there is only emptiness and fear
Lives built on broken parentage
On anger, blame, absence of
Love and care
As long as we miscast
As long as war rages
As long as there are no places
for hidden human faces
As long as we're disconnected
It's our weakest link
As long as we think there's no solution
Addiction lies buried
Far beneath
A refusal to grow and think
There is a way to end all suffering
as hard as it is to hear
A Simple Solution
The way out is in
All it takes is to face the fear

One step becomes a bridge
One hope
Becomes a dream

The heart that once was hidden
Reconnected and is seen
beyond
Abandonment and tears
What was Lost
and precious, suddenly will reappear
It's up to us

The way we choose
will make the future crystal clear

It was a cool, misty evening on the Cape Peninsula coast. Earlier that morning, there had been rain—mist rain, the kind that gentles one back to sleep. A man slipped out of the shadows and walked across the street towards a small cluster of restaurants and bars that lined the coastal road to Chapman's Peak. He carried a heavy canvas knapsack, worn and stained with sea salt and age. He walked into a small bar-restaurant, ordered a brandy and Coke from the waiter at the bar, then asked to see the manager. A burly guy with a beard and a leather apron stepped out of the kitchen. With a glance at the full canvas knapsack and a broad grin, he slapped the Fisherman on the back and took the canvas bag from him, disappearing into the kitchen with his prize. He reappeared a few moments later, carrying a small bank bag filled with orange South African Rands. The notes were folded neatly into a tight bundle. The two men exchanged a few words, and then the burly restaurant owner gestured to a small candle-lit table in the corner of the room with a smile.

The Fisherman took his brandy over to the table and sat sipping his drink while the delicious smells of food wafted gently from the kitchen. An attractive, portly waitress wearing the traditional Khoisan "doek" on her head emerged from the kitchen, carrying a plate of food for him. It was an enormous steak, well done to perfection. Potato chips on the side and a few steamed vegetables. She set the plate down in front of him, and the Fisherman looked up briefly to thank the large, kindly woman. This meal had become a tradition for him. The manager knew exactly what he wanted and how he liked it done. The Fisherman knew this restaurant well, and the manager and staff knew him and liked him. They trusted him to bring them what they needed without any fuss or trouble. The prize crayfish fished off the Atlantic coast. These "Kreef" were off-limits to most fishermen and highly illegal to catch without a permit.

Most crayfish caught from the local fishing trawlers in Hout Bay were processed and packed for export to foreign countries. Usually, the only crayfish restaurants could buy were the commercially grown lobsters and sometimes the excess of export quality kreef—but at a heavy price. Crayfish poachers and fishermen like these were extremely valuable assets to the restaurant trade here on the Cape Town coast.

The Fisherman ordered another double brandy with Coke and sat quietly, sipping his drink and enjoying his meal. He spoke to no one and hardly looked around as he ate. When he was finished, he thanked the waitress for his meal and silently disappeared the same way he had come. Back into the misty street carrying his now empty canvas kit bag, back to the beach, back to the sea, to the element that had always welcomed him, nurtured him, and had provided for him like a mother.

CHAPTER 2

POETRY AND MUSHROOMS

I write poetry about love and about the beauty and chaos of
life. . . about everything that I don't understand, and that leaves
me feeling empty and lost. It often feels as though I take a short
journey to visit an eccentric, wise old sage with a long, gold-white
beard and plenty of deep, insightful wisdom. Often, this wisdom
left written on the pages of poetry shocks me, and very often, it
leaves me rocking with laughter at a situation that I had thought
was an unbearable impasse. I'm so grateful for the gentle voice of
poetry to guide me through the maze of life.

The change of environment had brought challenges and
questions. Lisa was painting and writing, floating, and wondering
about the strange Fisherman who had captured her imagination.
She would wake in the middle of the night thinking about her
conversations with Ian. The vision of the Mantis kept coming back
to her whenever she thought of him. Lisa lit a candle when she
couldn't sleep. She picked up her pen and her journal and began
to write. The sentences she wrote seemed to blur together into the
form of a poem about the drowned Mantis that she had found in
the ocean. Then she made a copy of the poem on a fresh white
piece of paper and tucked it into a manila envelope, meaning to
give it to Ian at the next opportunity. It was evening when she next

saw his VW camper parked at the beach, but Ian was nowhere to be found. "He's probably gone fishing," she thought pensively. Lisa folded the envelope with her handwritten poem into the door handle of his van. She sensed that the Fisherman would read her poetry and relate to the message, but she had no idea how much or how deeply this would affect him in the future.

The next time Lisa went for an early morning run on the beach, Ian was there waiting for her. She had her towel over her shoulders, and her hair was still dripping wet from a dip in the icy ocean. Lisa smiled widely when she saw him.

This time, he walked up to her with a smile in his eyes. "Thank you for your beautiful poem," he said, looking unusually focused. "Your words struck a deep chord in me, Lisa." She could see by the way he spoke that he meant these words sincerely. Ian wasn't a man given to idle chit-chat. He was a hermit by nature and carefully chose whom he interacted with. "Would you like to come for a walk with me this morning?" he said quietly, looking over at her. Lisa nodded. "Okay," she said, looking at him with surprise. They ambled along the rocks overlooking the bay. Lisa was acutely aware of Ian's rough, masculine appearance. He still wore the same khaki sweatshirt that seemed to be his favourite item of clothing. Everything he wore was old but looked clean. His shock of thick, wiry, blonde hair was uncombed and wild, and he had a mischievous, leonine way of surveying the world through all this wildness.

They sat together on a wide granite shelf overlooking the ocean. Ian fixed her with his sea-green eyes and began to speak very frankly about himself as if telling her not to expect more of him. "I'm a fisherman at heart, Lisa," he began. "I love boats, but I don't have a boat of my own or a skipper's license. As an independent fisherman, I don't qualify for the legal fishing quota necessary to make fishing a full-time business," he said. "Up to recently, I've been doing the hard labour, line fishing onboard the South African deep-sea Research vessels. They don't pay extravagantly well, but I bought the vehicle I'm driving with what I've saved over the past few years. I hope to eventually save enough money for my own boat and a fishing license. Like any business, you've got to own one to really make money. Anyway, I've just finished a three-month stint onboard SA Marine. I'm thinking perhaps about joining the next research team again this winter. I've already made several trips with West Coast Marine in the last few years and absolutely love it. I love the ocean, the people, and this work. The problem is that there isn't permanent work with the team unless I am fully qualified in Marine Conservation, and I don't have the money to complete my studies right now. So, I'm just camping out, fishing, considering my options, and taking stock of my situation. Could even join an ocean-going vessel for Greenpeace," Ian mused almost as if to himself.

Lisa sat listening to him speak, nothing to say, nothing to do, just to be and listen.

They sat in silence for a while, listening to the seagulls wheeling and calling above them. The sea spray wet their faces. "Your life sounds like mine at the moment, Ian," Lisa said eventually. "I think you just have to trust that what you're looking for is just around the corner."

Ian smiled a wry smile, "Ah, that's easy for a beautiful, sensual woman like you to say," he said, glancing at her with that mischievous grin. "I'm sure you can use your seductive charms to your benefit. But I'm a man, and it's different for us in the workplace. It's far more competitive among us men. The only time I've ever really enjoyed work was when I was out deep-sea fishing and when I was catching kreef off the rocks. It's rough, hard work, but I don't mind it. I'm in my element on the sea."

Lisa could sense while Ian was speaking how lonely he was and how much he appreciated the company and the chat.

She saw Ian quite often after that. Sometimes they would take long walks along the coast together or just sit on a rock and talk. He would always bring along his knapsack with necessary stuff, penknife, water, and tobacco and sit with her and smoke his hand-rolled cigarettes.

Then during the cold winter months, Ian disappeared. He hadn't said anything to Lisa about going away. One day, he was gone, and there was no way of keeping in contact. She had accepted that this wild lion-man had migrated in his motor home to where the fishing was best or perhaps had joined the deep-sea fishing crew.

Out upon a wintry sea
The fishing boats trawl along
Lazing across the hushed morning sky
Bands of blue and silver
Shimmer to the west
The boundless ocean calls
Here in today's domestic peace
The soul travels on
My thoughts skip from horizon to horizon
Not hugging the coast
where the fishing boats lie
But in the depth, they travel still
Canceling the current of
Conscious choice
Until
They find themselves in light and power
Ignorant of where I am it forms
Heaven in this place
And radiant purpose
Lights my face

With a tender, most exquisitely perfect movement, the Fisherman's rough claw of a hand prized the precious mushroom from its earthy hiding place and placed it softly in a cloth-lined canvas bag with the others that he'd collected on his mornings foraging sortie. This was almost a lost art, the art of living off the soil and understanding the bounty that the earth provided. After the rains, at the change of the seasons were when the Fisherman would begin to forage in the forests. He would change his entire living and sleeping schedule around to suit the emergence of this precious resource, waiting a few days for the dampness to saturate the ground and begin to reach and catalyze the underground mycelial network of delicate, microscopic filaments and mushroom spores. Then, like magic, the Cape storms would arrive, leaving a flowering of fungi in the damp earth. Each time he walked into the forests after the gentle rain, he would find them there, these forest floor treasures, great pine rings, porcine in the fields, and fairy rings of the tiny brown toadstools that he used to dry and give flavour to his stews.

The Fisherman was not only an urban Bushman, he was also a druid without a master, lost in time, lost in a country where such skills could only be understood by the African traditional healers—learning his magic craft from the earth herself. He was born into a time when souls like him were rarely understood. A man of natural magic, the wild, free magic born of a life lived utterly at Her whim. This was wild magic, and he knew how this worked, yet he did not have the wise ones to assure him of his path. The Fisherman was undoubtedly born to become a sorcerer, a druid, and magic man. The invocations he knew were powerful. His hand and eye, so deft and accurate that they were far beyond the sleight of hand tricksters' art. His movements were so definite that only a man trained by life's art of survival could have learned them. And yet, because he was lost in a time when magic had all but ceased to exist, the Fisherman had become invisible to most.

His magic and the land's magic had long become a lost art. And all respect for this skill had almost been completely lost, as well.

The Fisherman trudged comfortably down the rocky forest mountain paths, his weather-beaten canvas bag filled with loamy soft mushroom treasures. He was dreaming about the mouth-watering flavours of the delicious mushroom stew that awaited. He glimpsed another cluster of voluptuous forest fungi, bulging out of the ground, but these he did not stop to pick. Instead, he softly growled under his breath, "Got enough." He bent his wild mane head towards the earth, leaving his knapsack beside him on the ground and throwing out his arms in one wide earth's embrace. Then he lay down and smelled with a long bliss-filled breath, the loam and leafy tender mushroom funk, the damp and cloistered loveliness of the earth. This earth that the Fisherman had always so adored.

He had tried once to take his skills into a productive way, to grow, produce and harvest mushrooms for the hospitality and domestic market. But this was not his way and went so against his grain. The Fisherman was precisely what this name connotes— the man who casts his net or line and lives off the bounty that the ocean and Mother Earth provide, no more, no less. And in this simple way, he was happy.

It was early one spring morning when Ian came back.

His hair was cropped short, and he was wearing a smart, fresh denim jacket and an olive-green T-shirt. The Fisherman had walked down the path between the dense milk wood trees to find Lisa on the beach. He looked elated as he waved at her.

"It's Ian." Lisa caught her breath when she saw him, and her heart skipped a beat. She walked towards him, and he greeted her with a simple brotherly squeeze of her shoulders and told her that he'd been away these past months on the deep-sea fishing boats, then for a short while, up the coast looking for oysters and mushrooms. He had been hoping to work on the charter boats in the Eastern Cape. They chatted happily as they walked back up the path to the parking lot where his camper van was parked.

Lisa noticed that the dashboard of his camper was even more strewn with dried mushrooms and lichens of all kinds. "Look!" he said. "I have something special I want to show you." He took a piece of invoice paper out from his notebook. On it, Ian had neatly handwritten in block print what almost looked like a numbered shopping list. "I wrote this for you," he said, shyly passing it to her. Lisa read the list silently, feeling bemused and a little bit embarrassed. *Ten reasons why Lisa is an angel*, it read. In the space on the other side of the page were detailed drawings of local mushrooms. "I'd almost given up completely," Ian said in a soft voice. "There was a moat and a metal gate in front of my heart, and these gates had almost completely shut before I met you," he said with his head bowed. "Tell you the truth, I'd given up on life."

Ian's words fell like leaden sheets of ice around her feet, melting as they landed. Lisa searched the silence for evidence of deceit or any emotional maneuvering. She saw none, just a bare and sincere sharing from a lonely human being. She also saw the courage it had taken him to share this with her and for him to live a life as it had been, in isolation from others and even from kindred spirits. As she held this simple gift of love in her hands, she felt tears of compassion pricking her eyelids. She shook them back and smiled back at him in gratitude.

"Come with me for coffee in the village," he said. "I need supplies, and there's bound to be a few field mushrooms for the picking after the recent rain." Lisa shook her head. "No, Ian, I don't have anything warm to change into, and I'll freeze to death if I stay in these wet clothes," she said. It was still cold in September. The Cape mountains were often sprinkled with snow, and when the wind blew in from the mountains, it was icy cold. Ian dived into the back of his motor home and came out with a pair of thick mountain-climbing socks and a dry sweatshirt. "Here," he said with a chuckle, holding them out to her. "Sit down and I'll dry your feet." Before she knew it, he had wrapped her cold feet in a towel and was rubbing them to get the circulation going. Then he put his thick thermal socks onto her feet. "Hmm, I think what you need is someone to give you some good old-fashioned TLC," he commented in a matter-of-fact sort of way. Lisa blushed with embarrassment, quite taken aback by his gesture of affection. Ian had been the perfect gentleman in her company, in his rough, shy way and this was the first time she had ever heard him say anything suggestive of his feelings for her. She smiled at him gratefully as he warmed her feet with his calloused hands. "Alright, I'll come for coffee with you," she said, smiling.

As Lisa climbed into Ian's vehicle and looked around at the interior space, she realized that this was home for him. Despite the small space and his limited resources, he had made this an organized, comfortable, and well-equipped sanctum. Ian was an intelligent, altogether capable and interesting person. He had immersed himself so deeply into nature that it was woven into the fabric of his life. Mushroom specimens, dried bracket fungus, geodes, handbooks on mycology, sea life, and all sorts of interesting artifacts lined his vehicle dashboard. He had created a comfortable living area at the back of the camper with wooden shelves for storage all around the sides. Piles of books and magazines were stacked on safety shelves. Ian clearly loved this motor home and knew how to maintain it well. His carefree lifestyle was fascinating to an artist like her.

It was raining as they drove into the village. The raindrops scattered on the windscreen as they cruised lazily downhill. After coffee at a local cafe, they stopped at the shopping center for supplies. At the time, she'd thought nothing of the fact that along with his grocery shopping, Ian had stopped in at the bottle store and bought a large bottle of cane spirits.

"I suppose he's a typical South African and a fisherman," she trolled her eyes and thought naively.

The shopping center was close to the coast. It was still raining gently, and Lisa remembered shivering and feeling quite cold. Ian parked at a road siding, turned off the ignition, then looked at her with that already familiar, mischievous grin on his face. He reached into the back of his van and opened a drawer where he kept a few odds and ends and cooking utensils. Then, taking out two plastic cups, he poured them each a stiff shot of cane spirits with Coke. "Here," he said, "This will warm you up. In my family, we start drinking early in the day."

Lisa's eyes grew wide as she felt the first chime of alarm bells ringing in her soul, but she went along with things as they were. "Thanks, Ian, but I'm not much of a drinker," she said, smiling at him and shrugging. "I suppose a sip to warm up won't hurt."

"I drink this stuff to steady my nerves," he said. "Come on, let's have some breakfast." Ian cut them some fresh bread, tomato, and cheese, and they sat munching sandwiches and sipping their drinks in the rain.

They ended up in each other's embrace that day. The pull of physical attraction was too strong, the cane spirits too heady, and the atmosphere in the early spring rain, too romantic for there not to be love that blossomed between the two of them. Ian had put one strong hand behind her shoulder and pulled her body towards his warmth. She closed her eyes as she felt his breath on her face. Then she felt his bearded skin brushing hers and his lips melting all her defenses. It was a kiss that brought her into the ecstatic realms where she had danced with the lion-man in her dreams. He drew her gently into the back of his motor home cave and cleared a space for her on his bed. Then he pulled his well-worn sweatshirt over his head, revealing his broad, furry chest. Neither of them spoke. Nothing else mattered. He looked at her for an eternal moment, and she, at him. And then he bowed his wild head like a beautiful bird drinking from the flower cup of nectar and kissed her again. Together they opened love's rich, fragrant petals to reveal themselves in all completeness to one another. On that fateful day when their two souls met, the whole world merged into the harmony of angels and the beautiful song of love: a fisherman and an artist.

Ian was a few years younger than she was, unemployed, a smoker, and as far as she knew, a heavy drinker—everything that pointed her in the other direction. But there was something else between them that went far beyond the ordinary. It wasn't just physical magnetism. There was something even more potent than that. It was almost as if by grand design, fate had orchestrated that they meet and had created extraordinary circumstances for both of their benefit—a simple opportunity for their highest potential to flower. It was exactly as her vision had described it. Her dream of lions and her soul's deep desire to explore, grow, learn, and expand, had manifested as a simple fisherman named Ian.

Seal skin soul skin
Back in my skin
You see no one
Lost in the sea
My skin swimming with me
Here in this place, I came out for a while
To talk with the man who would capture
My smile
Strange beauty that hides
with the outward forms of disguise
Back in my skin
A seal again

I want to paint the way the Earth feels
at the way I touch her with my feet
The way she sighs and closes her eyes
at my body leaning against her rocky surfaces
for comfort
I want to feel her joy and tenderness
as she bends her leafy earthiness around me
and my lover
an eternal witness to our kiss
I want to know her heart and reflect
the depth of her wounding
every time she sees me crying
understanding the imbalance
that has become human law
I want to express the way the Earth
trembles with happiness as I stand in her salty waters
Grateful and overcome by her beauty
The gentle breeze of her magic
Between-ness playing on my skin
I want to feel the feeling she feels
at every footstep and touch of heritage
To marvel at the impression my feet
have made in her and how she treasures them
I want to know that
I am in Earth
And she is in me

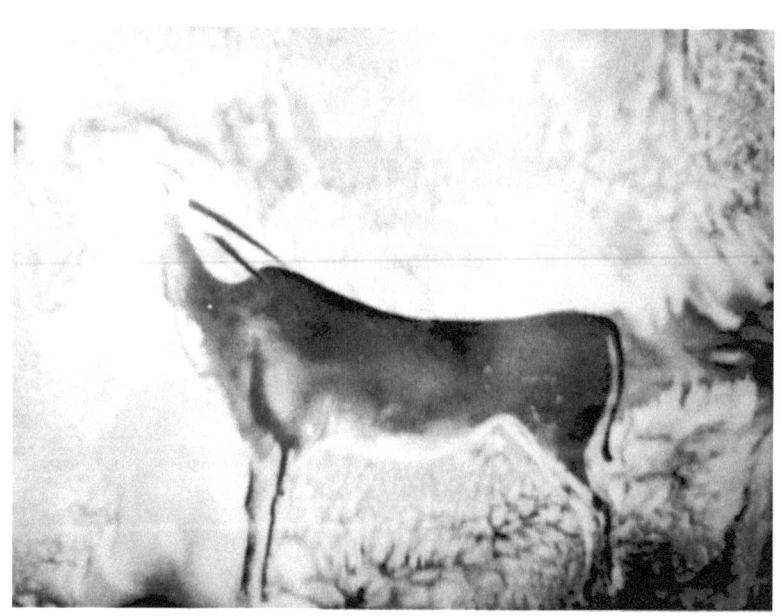

CHAPTER 3

THE FISHERMAN'S SONG

The Fisherman lived by no man-made rules but by the moon, the tides, and the sun. Lisa sensed his pulse, his warm sea animal breath. A real earth being, a wild creature, more alive than any she had ever known. Rough unpolished, as real as the rain. And living on this planet, utterly isolated from others of his kind, by his lifestyle, his deep sadness, vulnerability, and shame.

They began to see one another often after that. It was a wild love affair that had swept her up in its damp, loam moss and autumn leaf swirl. She rested in it and the soft, often inebriated arms of her lover. Ian had the face of an angel and the physical strength of a lion. His second name was Richard, and Lisa would often laughingly tease him, calling him "The Lion heart." It was sad that her lover suffered from so much insecurity and anxiety. He had nothing to fear and everything—absolutely everything and more—to his benefit: the looks, the creative talent, strength, resilience, a brilliant, inventive mind, and photographic memory. There was so much to love about Ian, and as she got to know him better every day, she discovered more about him that made her smile and love him even more.

Ian had grown up on the slopes of Table Mountain in Higgovale, one of the oldest, historical, and most beautiful suburbs of Cape Town. Back in the early days when Ian's father first bought their home, there were still small vegetable farms in the higher reaches of the city. Ian's parents had purchased a small plot of land near what used to be a local dairy farm. From their home, one could look out over the entire expanse of Table Bay, and they had the Table Mountain fynbos, the wild guinea fowls, cape chacma baboon, mongoose, genets and dassies in their back garden. He had grown up exploring the mountainside, fishing for tadpoles in the nearby streams, and later, fishing in the sea with his father.

Ian had wanted to be a Marine Biologist more than anything in the world when he was young. Both parents supported his dream but unfortunately for Ian, his father passed away long before he completed his studies. This left his grieving and widowed mother without financial support and means of helping him achieve his dream. Instead, he spent eighteen months stuck in an isolated South African army base on the Caprivi strip border between Namibia and Angola, conscripted to do his National Military service. It was sweltering hot in this environment. Ian never forgot the impressions that the wild African bush had made on his memory. The sounds of hyenas calling to one another in the night and the effect of thunderstorms and drenching desert rain on the landscape.

One fateful day, a terrible accident happened which was to affect him for the rest of his life. Some of the young artillery men had been using the weaponry building as a secret hideout where they could share an illicit smoke. A sign on the door said, "Highly inflammable, No Smoking"—but they had ignored it. One of them may have dropped a match or carelessly stubbed out his cigarette too close to the drums of nitroglycerin. Perhaps some of the chemicals had spilled onto the ground and had instantly ignited or perhaps the building had been the target of sabotage. Within a few seconds, the whole building was engulfed in flames, and before the men could escape, it exploded. Ian wasn't the only one in his regiment who suffered from post-traumatic stress disorder long after witnessing the horrors of the accident on that day. He'd been resting from the heat of the day in the army barracks when he heard the explosion and tortured screams of his army buddies. He grabbed a wet towel and rushed half-naked into the flames to help them, but it was already too late. Not one of Ian's friends made it out of that explosion alive.

The shock, his burns, and the smoke inhalation had brought on a severe anaphylactic attack. Ian was flown back to Cape Town Military hospital and spent several months recuperating in a psychiatric ward. Thankfully, he was never sent back to that Namibian border post again and spent the remainder of his National Military service happily serving as chef at the Naval base in Simonstown.

Ian was brilliant both as a fisherman and a chef and could prepare the most heavenly seafood braais,[1] serving up an entire seafood platter, mussels, harders, or snoek, and kreef or crayfish caught himself, fresh from the sea. These were his gifts of love to Lisa, his way of offering gratitude for the sense of belonging that he felt with her. That sense of numbness in his heart was beginning to thaw. His prize, a bag of crayfish and a fish or two, would wait in the refrigerator for someone to wake up and open the door to a whole load of treasures. A huge thank you from his soul.

They both enjoyed the simple things in life, good food, laughter, poetry, conversation, making love, walks in the Cape fynbos mountains and the sea. They would spend hours together at night beside the ocean, watching the sparkles on the waves from the rocks. Ian was like an ecstatic puppy dog when they first became lovers. He would do absolutely anything for Lisa. Sometimes late at night, he would bounce up and down the beach, intermittently lying in the sand and making sand angels and then racing up and down in the waves splashing Lisa and laughing as he showered them both with the luminescent glowing phosphorescence in the sand and seawater. Ian was always happiest when preparing food

---

1 Barbecues

for them, especially seafood dishes. It was a partnership made in heaven. For a time, nothing else existed as they explored the new dimensions that opened through one another's eyes.

He took Lisa with him to catch crayfish only once. "It's too dangerous, Lisa," he said, looking at her seriously. "I don't want you to get caught poaching with me. I know how to handle any trouble, but you don't." Lisa knew that he'd already had a few run-ins with the police for catching crayfish without a permit, out of season.

One evening, after sunset, they walked down to the edge of the rocks. She sat watching him in the twilight from a flat rock overlooking the coast. The Fisherman moved quickly, leaping with confidence, right out to the furthest boulder at the very edge of the sea. He bent to unravel his line from the wooden fishing reel, taking out a bucket of bait he had collected earlier, he hooked up. Lisa watched him in the haze of twilight softly singing the refrain of the Fisherman's favourite song under her breath. It was a love song that he often sang to her in those halcyon days.

"Whichever way life goes, I will always love you.
However our love flows, I will always love you.
No matter if you stay or go, I will always love you
I will always love you; I will always love you."

She watched Ian leap like a dancer through the briny spray onto the rocks where the crayfish had taken his bait. Then once he had pulled the kreef out of the water, he turned and threw the clawing spidery sea creatures onto the rocky ledge where Lisa sat watching. To her horror, Ian yelled at her to grab each of the crawling, scrabbling kreef! She didn't know how she did it, but somehow, each crayfish made it into the bag. It had taken little more than an hour to fill an entire canvas kit bag and felt like no time had passed at all. It struck Lisa powerfully then how Ian walked the very knife-edge of life, leaping from each slippery, kelp-covered, granite rock to avoid the crashing spray of the waves. His was a dangerous, harsh life though quite exquisite and magical in its way. Watching him, the skill of his craft seemed like wizardry in Lisa's eyes.

Sometimes Ian invited her to have dinner at one of the gorgeous seafood restaurants on the Cape peninsula coast with his wealthy European patron. His elderly friend was an international swallow, a retired businessman who lived abroad and only returned to South Africa for the summer. Uncle Otto, as Ian would affectionately call him, reminded Lisa of "The Godfather." A man's man through and through. He relied on Ian to maintain their summer beach home throughout the winter season while he and his wife were away. This kindly Swiss gentleman served both to provide employment and as a father substitute to him. Uncle Otto treated Ian as though he were an adopted son, spoiling him with gifts and lots of manly advice and keeping Ian busy fixing one or the other of his properties during the winter months. In the summer, Ian would be kept busy catching crayfish and catering to their expensive, seaside holiday homes. There was always plenty of part-time work and enough money to ensure that Ian could run his motor home and travel. Ian had the world at his feet. When Lisa met the fisherman, he was in the prime of his life and had so many opportunities open to him. And if he had put his mind to it, he could have traveled, studied and become anything he wanted to.

Whenever the tide and the moon were right, he would go fishing, sometimes for a few days at a time. On one of those occasions while Ian was away, Lisa woke early just as the sun's rays lit up her tiny flat on the Atlantic coast. She grabbed her car keys and a towel and ran down the stairs on her way for a run on the beach. As she rounded the corner to the road, she stopped abruptly and gasped in surprise. She stared in shock at the empty off-street parking place where her vehicle was usually parked. A sinking feeling began to spread through the base of her stomach and up through the whole of her body, making her limbs feel paralyzed. "Oh no! Where's my car?"

she gasped. Her battered, old, faithful farm bakkie had been silently stolen away in the dead of the night. A thief had come to her street and hot-wired her vehicle while she slept. Lisa remembered how her dog, Baloo had woken her with his whining and barking inside the flat. At the time, it hadn't occurred to her that somebody might be stealing her truck. Her farm cottage in Aurora had been so safe and her neighbours so friendly and trustworthy. Living in the city was not at all the same. Here it seemed that there were covetous eyes everywhere. People in the cities were hungry in ways that filling the belly would never satisfy. Even Ian had asked her recently if she was willing to sell her old truck. "Well, sure, if you have a brand new one, I could trade it in for," she'd laugh, light-heartedly. Never once had she suspected that somebody would want her beat-up old farm "bakkie" enough to steal it.

When Ian came over later that morning, Lisa was still sitting on her bed, hugging her knees to her chest and wearing the T-shirt and shorts that she'd thrown on that morning to go to the beach. Her eyes were puffy and red from crying. "Hey Lisa, what's up?" Ian asked, sitting down beside her.

"My vehicle has been stolen," she said flatly, looking at him.

"Hmm, probably one of the criminal gangs that work this area, noticed your vehicle," he muttered angrily. "Have the police taken a statement yet?"

"Yes, they were here earlier, but I don't suppose that they will ever catch these "tsotsis,"[2] she said with a shrug. "It was entirely my fault. I didn't have the door lock mended. Whoever it was, they just opened the driver's seat door and cut the gorilla lock with a bolt cutter. It was so stupid of me to think that this sort of thing would never happen in Cape Town. I have been saving money to buy a new car, but I don't have enough, not even with the trade-in value of my old one. Damn! Why did this have to happen now, just when I needed a vehicle most to get around town?" Lisa shook her head slowly and sighed.

---

2 African word for thieves or bad people

"I'm so sorry, Lisa, and I'm here if you need me to take you anywhere, okay?" Ian said with genuine compassion and gave her a warm hug. "Remember, we're a team now. I've got your back." He smiled at her with such genuine warmth in his eyes and that hurt, stolen place in her heart began to fill with Ian's kindness again.

It wasn't long before he started to spend more time at Lisa's place. After a while, she became quite dependent on Ian without even realizing it. Overnight the whole dynamic of her relationship shifted from an exciting, interdependent, beautiful exchange to a situation where Ian was her chauffeur and the one who made all the decisions. Her frustration at not having a vehicle anymore made her feel resentful. She was so used to her independence, and it wasn't long afterward that Lisa and Ian had their first heated argument.

It happened early one Sunday morning when a cold South Easterly wind had begun to blow. Ian had woken up feeling extremely ratty and on edge.

"Hey! What's got into you this morning?" Lisa said, frowning. She was sitting at her dressing table, brushing her hair. From her bedroom mirror, she could see Ian pacing up and down, looking at the clock on the wall and muttering under his breath.

"Nothing, I just need to get going. I must get to the Loop Street bottle store as soon as it opens," he growled. "You wanna come for the ride?" He was clearly in a terrible mood.

"No way, Ho jay! I'm not going into town today, especially not with this wind blowing. See you later. I'd like to read my book for a while and maybe take a walk along the coast with Baloo later," Lisa said, gently stroking her dog's silky head.

The Southeast wind had been blowing all night long and it was still blowing hard outside. The trees were bent low with the force, putting both of their nerves on edge. This cold wind was often called a "Black South Easter" and commonly known as the "suicide wind" because of how it made so many Cape-Tonians feel.

"Ian, what's making you so jumpy this morning?" she said, looking straight at him. "Does it really make a difference whether you go into town today or tomorrow morning?"

"Who are you to ask me, Miss Sanctimonious," Ian snapped back at her harshly. "You clearly don't get it. You don't know what I need or why I need it. And whatever you think of me, no one is without their faults. I'm pretty sure you've got a few skeletons of your own in your closet, Lisa. In fact, I heard a few strange stories about you from your brother last night. Not sure what to believe these days," Ian snarled at her.

Lisa sat still for a moment, shocked into silence by the accusing tone and the cruel words she had just heard her lover say.

"What are you talking about, Ian? What on earth is going on? You're behaving like Dr Jekyll and Mr Hyde," she said, frowning. "I'm not trying to change you or judge you. And it's obvious to me that something is bothering you. If it's so wrong that I care about you, please let me know because the way you are speaking to me this morning is making me wonder exactly where I stand." Lisa's face was flushed, and she looked at Ian with sparks of fury in her green eyes.

There was leaden silence between them for a few minutes as Lisa finished brushing her hair. Ian didn't say anything. His face looked swollen and blotched with the anger that had risen in him, too.

"For heaven's sake, Ian, it's Sunday," Lisa said, putting her brush down and shaking her head. "I was really looking forward to spending time with you."

Ian was quiet for a long moment and had stopped pacing. After a while, he came in, sat down heavily in Lisa's armchair, and put his head into his hands.

"Look, Lisa. I know I'm being an absolute idiot." He exhaled and looked up at her. "It's my fault, not yours. I have moments of extreme anxiety, to put it mildly. 'Post-Traumatic Stress Disorder,' the military psychologists called it when I was in the army. At the time, they gave me a prescription for anxiety and told me the attacks would probably wear off. But they didn't and nobody ever told me what I could do about it. The medication is expensive, and I don't like the side effects, so I've had to learn to cope with the condition myself over the years. When it happens, my heart starts to race, and I feel completely out of control. It's been like this ever since the days when I was posted to the Angolan border." Lisa was watching Ian's face intently. "It was a rough experience, and I still find it hard to talk about it. Anyway, we all had to sign a non-disclosure statement when we went into the army. Geez Lisa! We were only kids, hardly eighteen, fresh out of school. What did we know then, dressed up in that flipping SADF khaki soldier kit, pretending to be men? We were all just cannon fodder for the military. Those days when we were stuck out, in that God-forsaken hell hole, have left their indelible mark on me. Basically, the easiest route I know of stopping the waves of anxiety from coming on is to get quietly drunk or stoned and pretty much stay that way until the attack wears off. I've no idea why the feeling gets so bad sometimes. When it does, I get jumpy and irritable and my chest starts to close in, especially if I run out of alcohol or don't have any 'zol' or cigarettes to help me calm down." He paused, narrowed his eyes and took a deep breath. "By the way Lisa, last night, at your parents' dinner, your brother, Mark cornered me and started asking me a million questions about the army, my background, my education, and private life. I'm sure he was just doing his brotherly duty, checking up on me. I suppose they just want the best for you. But then he began telling me all these little family secrets."

Lisa rolled her eyes. "Oh God, no!" she exhaled.

Ian continued undaunted. "I suppose he meant it as 'man-to-man talk,' but I don't even know him properly yet. I must admit, I felt a bit overwhelmed and claustrophobic, and after a while I made an excuse and went outside for a cigarette. If you don't mind me saying so, your brother seems to have a bit of a chip on his shoulder.

And for some reason or other he's really got it in for you. From my perspective, you two are poles apart in your outlook on life."

Lisa was staring at Ian with surprise on her face. She had dreaded another outburst or a personal attack and a million questions about her past. Instead, he looked back at Lisa with compassion in his eyes. "It's okay, Lisa. I get it; I understand more than you think I do. Your life is none of their business. My own family has been judgmental of me, too. They have no idea what I've been through, and I really don't care about telling them either. In fact, it's my own family's attitude to me that has turned me into a recluse. As you know, I don't do the social thing very easily," Ian shrugged as he spoke.

Lisa listened to Ian with her heart on fire. Tears had sprung out of nowhere and glistened in her eyes.

"Wow, thanks, Ian. I really appreciate you sharing this with me." Lisa got up from her dressing table. She took his hand and placed it on her heart. "You have mine, entirely," she said, smiling through her tears into his eyes.

"And you have my heart too, Lisa. But please, always be gentle and take care of it, okay?" Ian said in his rumbling voice. She nodded and he pulled her towards him and kissed her. All the tension between them softened and melted like magic in his bear-like, solid arms.

"How about I take us both for a meal later at Chappies seafood restaurant," Ian said, looking at her.

Lisa smiled at him. "That's a great idea. Perhaps we could go for a walk with Baloo before we do? I'm keen to explore that beautiful melkhout forest kloof with the waterfall on the higher reaches— the one we stopped to look at the other day, on Chapman's peak road?" Ian smiled back at her and nodded.

"Ja, I remember the place. Okay, I'll just stop off at the cafe on the way and get some tobacco."

Lisa nodded soberly then hesitated. "Ian, I want you to know where I stand regarding your drinking. I won't ever judge you if you keep it in check and never compromise our safety or well-being while you are under the influence. Promise me, please?"

Ian shook his head slowly and affectionately at Lisa. "Fine, my precious Lisa. I promise you," he reassured her, laughing at her seriousness.

When I think back on that heated moment, I remember how even though I laughed with him, I was left with a strange, ghostly feeling. It was as though there was a stitch left undone in the weave of our conversation. While my younger self swept these feelings away and hid them in the furthest part of my mind, I knew, even then, that Ian had serious emotional damage to heal. Although I was still not ready to admit it, I was aware that I couldn't trust the Fisherman's word when it came to alcohol. There were so many issues around Ian's drinking in those early days. Naively, I still believed that we would work everything out and that love could conquer all. It also bothered me immensely that I didn't have my own car. And I knew that I wasn't ready to move in with Ian until I was independent again. Those quiet warning bells were still ringing in my heart.

Later that evening, Ian and Lisa sat at a restaurant table on the beach side terrace at the Chapman's Peak Hotel, eating delicious grilled yellow tail fish, sipping glasses of crisp white wine and chatting about the future. Glorious sunset-gold colours lit up the outline of the Sentinel mountains like wildfire. Despite the discomfort of the icy Southeast wind and that morning's heated argument, it had been a beautiful day, and they were both feeling happy, positive, and hopeful.

"We could build a home of our own, you know Lisa. Something so extraordinary and off-grid that no one would even know we were there."

Lisa grinned at him and nodded her head. He was speaking the quiet dreams of her own heart out loud.

"Few people know about the Karatara hills of the Wilderness mountains. They say the last of the wild coast elephants still roam these forests. Maybe we should find a plot of land in the forests and build a house and an art studio for you. A tree house or a cob house or something even more way out. Hey, how about a house built entirely out of hemp or straw bale? Who knows, technology might have advanced so far by then that we might be able to pre-order a completely self-sustainable, 3D printed home, someday." Ian was getting completely carried away with the ideas in his head.

Lisa laughed at his enthusiasm. "Oh, Ian, you come up with some zany ideas sometimes. Yes, I think planning is good and, in the meantime, we could drive out there and get a sense of things. What do you think, my crazy fisherman?"

"Think? I know that I want to be with you for the rest of my life, my beauty."

Lisa smiled. Her turquoise eyes were shining, and her hair was alight with the colours of the sunset. It glowed like a halo that danced with life as she moved. Ian got up from the table and bent over to kiss her and give her one of his gentle hugs.

"I love you, my forever woman," he whispered simply in her ear. "I think it's a great idea. Let's take some time out and drive up the Garden route along the coast in the camper. Then we can have a good look at the area. There is a strong possibility that I could find a permanent job at a hotel around there. You know, Lisa, if you like the idea of us building a cottage together in the future, this might be the perfect place and time for us to start looking."

Despite her misgivings, Lisa nodded. She pushed back her hair and nodded with a brave smile. As the days passed, she began to look forward to the trip with Ian.

In the early spring, they left Cape Town and camped at beach resorts along the Tsitsikamma coast. Ian took Lisa to visit all his favourite secret forest haunts. They moon-bathed under a full moon in quiet pirate coves. Swam together in the golden brack waterfalls of the Tsitsikamma rivers and explored the forests for rare ferns and mushrooms. They hiked the fynbos mountain trails along the back hills of Karatara and Wilderness among the enormous old Stinkwood trees where the last of the mysterious Knysna mountain elephants are said to live. Lisa had brought her painting kit along, and while Ian was fishing for Kabeljou and Stompneus, she sat on the beach painting sparkling water colours of the ocean. It was their honeymoon time, and at first, it had bonded the two of them more closely together. They were flying in utter ecstasy at having found one another and fallen in love. The world had opened wider, and everything had become possible to the two lovers. They lived in a bubble of beauty, sweet, exotic and so heady. They slept under starlight skies and traveled into the places of their dreams together.

The Fisherman had lit a cigar-sized joint and was puffing contentedly on this while steering his motor home along a deep, forested, green winding road, down to the small fishing village of Buffalo Bay. He had a glazed look in his eyes and was smiling like a cat that had got the cream. Lisa had all the camper windows wide open as they drove and was singing along at the top of her voice to a recording of the song, "The Age of Aquarius." Her copper hair was flying in the wind, and her face was alight with the widest and happiest smiles. It was one of the most sublimely happy moments of their time together. They were both "high," in their different ways. She, on love and the beauty and ecstasy of life. Him, with the happy sense of belonging, being in love, and the intoxication from his smoke.

Ian pulled over into the parking lot where there was a lookout point onto the rocks and good fishing to be had. "See you just now," he said, flashing her a happy grin. He took some bait out of his fishing bucket at the back of his van, grabbed his fishing tackle and equipment, and strode out onto the distant rocks. Lisa squeezed some sunblock into her hands and rubbed it all over her freckled skin. Then she grabbed her wide-brimmed sun hat and a towel, closed and locked the vehicle, and walked down onto the beach. It was low tide, and as she walked further out onto the rocky spur that led into the sea, she saw the flat rock on which she was standing was littered with a scattering of small, exquisitely shaped stone tool microliths. The ground at her feet looked like a magical treasure trove of ancient history. She bent down to pick up one of the delicately shaped stones and examined the precisely shaped edges. These were the fishing tools that the original ancient African "Strandlopers," the Hottentot or Khoi-Khoi fishermen, had created with their hands thousands of years ago. The small stone tools had been flaked with such even precision, forming the perfectly sharp edges needed to cut open a fish and clean the scales away for cooking on the open fire. Close by to the scattering of stone microliths was a distinctly hand-grooved indentation in the rock where stone tools, fish spears, and knives had been sharpened on the rock surface. Lisa felt as though she had fallen through a time warp into a space where only herself and the Fisherman existed in parallel with the earliest African fisherman and inhabitants. She bent to pick up a handful of the stone tools and noticed the tiniest glimpse of red ochre-stained bone stuck into a fissure on the flat rock surface. Carefully, she prized the small, polished piece of bone from between the rock. It took a while to jiggle and ease it out, but when it finally released, she gasped in surprise. Then she saw it! Carved into the smooth polished surface of the bone was an image, a rough, crude almost, engraving of a whale.

Lisa heard the rich, unmeasured voice of the Fisherman just behind her. "What have you found, my beauty?" He crouched down beside her, touching her hair with his calloused hand, moving it aside so he could see what it was that she was so intent on. "Wow, you've found the real thing, hmmm," he said softly, as fascinated as she was.

"I know this is a valuable artifact, but I'd like to keep it for a while. It's such a unique treasure and reminds me so much of you, Ian." There was no need to explain everything to the

Fisherman. That was what Lisa simply adored about him. He felt the beauty and history of this place to be a profound living thing. It wasn't just a piece of bone or old, boring information to him. It was brought alive by his love of fishing and the wonder and awe at how these ancient Hottentot or Khoikhoi fishermen had fashioned such useful tools and carving, using only elements of the natural world. He understood what she saw and how she felt about this mystical and magical entry point to another time where the African ancestors once dwelt; fishing, living, loving, and sharing, just like they were. He stood up. In his hand were a pair of freshly caught silver Kob. They gleamed with green and blue iridescence in the sunlight. "Come on, let's get some supper on the go," Ian said and turned to walk back to the camper.

Soon, the Fisherman had their meal sizzling on the "braai" fire that he had made beside the rocky beach. He had poured himself his customary double cane and coke and sat sipping beside the fire while Lisa went for a dip in one of the rock pools. When she got back from her swim, Ian presented her with the whalebone amulet he had made into a necklace. He had carefully threaded a length of strong leather through a small hole in the bone and created a delicate clasp using his fishing tackle. "Don't ever take this off, Lisa," he said, looking at her. "Remember me, no matter what. Remember the sea and how we met." Lisa smiled and touched the whale amulet at her throat.

Later that night, as they lay wrapped in each other's arms, listening to the crash of the surf on the rocks nearby, the Fisherman asked her sleepily, "Tell me, my beauty, have there been many before me?" Lisa hardly gave his question a thought. "I can't remember exactly, Ian. I've often been disappointed in love. But there's been no one I have loved like you." She murmured simply and truthfully. Afterward, she realized that she had made a big mistake stating the truth so flippantly to this solitary and intense man. Perhaps she ought to have given more consideration to his question. She hadn't known the extent of the pain that he had suffered from his previous relationship. Her answer would come back to haunt them both. It would eventually become the trigger that caused her beloved Fisherman to show a side to his nature that she could not ignore. Thankfully, they were both still steeped in the bliss of their honeymoon time and were so in love that her comment was brushed away for a while as she snuggled closer into Ian's warm, soft embrace and fell asleep.

The red ochre-stained piece of bone was palm-sized. It was smooth with wear and weathered by the salt and sea. As graceful and elegant as a woman but as strong and sturdy as a man. The image engraved onto its surface was of a whale. It was a gift from the ancestors of the Khoikhoi and the Fisherman who loved her. It connected the two of them, the Fisherman and Lisa, binding them both to the spirit of the Great Mother. The amulet was the symbol of the Ocean Mother and a powerful reminder that "Truth is the mother of us all."

It had been softly raining all night, the kind of rain that creeps up so softly that you hardly know it's there until you feel the moisture on the grass and in your hair. "Look, Ian," she murmured to the Fisherman, who lay in half sleep beside her. Lisa had been awake for some time, watching the raindrops catch the light and slide down the glass windows of the camping van. It had begun to rain that evening, and they had both fallen asleep to the comforting sound of the rain drumming on the metal roof of the motor home. She awoke in the early hours of the morning and found herself mesmerized by the slow, sliding, heavily laden raindrops as each created a path like handwriting on the vehicle windowpane. The lights of the distant town and passing cars lit the raindrops gently and sparkled like multi-faceted diamonds. Lisa could see the patterns they made and the glow they cast as they trickled slowly down the front windscreen of the van. She pushed her thick mane of disheveled hair away from her face and blinked her eyes to make sure she was seeing clearly.

Ian sat up sleepily to look at the rain and see what she was watching so intently. "Ian, it looks like the rain is writing something," Lisa said softly. Ian rubbed his eyes and stared. She wasn't exaggerating, nor was she seeing things. The trickling rain had spelled out a vaguely visible word. Ian squinted and began to read out the letters of Lisa's name.

"Did you write on the glass before it started raining last night?" Lisa asked, looking at him bemused.

"Mmmm," the fisherman murmured, shaking his head. "Maybe it's some kind of trick? Look, the letters are all mirror image letters because we can read them from the inside of the windscreen." Ian made a scary face and pulled the sheet over his head like a ghost. "Ooh! It feels eerie but, at the same time, magical. As if somebody were trying to scrawl a message onto the wet glass of the windscreen just for you," Ian said, wide awake now.

"I bet if I told anyone else about what just happened, they wouldn't believe it. But there it is," Lisa said. "And even stranger, Ian. I just woke up after a vivid dream where I saw my grandmother, Kathleen, sitting in her garden, underneath her papaya trees. She was waiting to give me a message. Granny was always so proud and dignified when she was alive. She was sitting there in her wise way, with her hands folded on her lap, looking at me. I looked at her and she smiled and said in her straightforward way, 'My darling Lisa. Make sure that your young man is a gentleman.' That was so like my grandmother. I can't help wondering if both these happenings are coincidences or if the message in the raindrops is linked somehow."

The Fisherman smiled at her and drew her into his warm arms. "Lisa," he said slowly, savouring each sound. "I love the ring to your name. My Queen," he said, kissing her hand and laughing. "You know what I think? I think your name will give you power for what is to come in our future world. All the old patriarchal systems are all going to break down very soon. And from what I've seen, human-un-kind have already removed themselves so far from nature and from the original way of life where folk could survive in a more natural world. People will need strong leaders. Those who have the courage to live from their hearts and trust the law of nature, just as you and I do. But first, the old systems, everything that no longer works, will break down and become obsolete. We must be strong, Lisa. I am here for you, but you never know what tomorrow will bring. You have to know your own strength to survive."

Oh, I remembered our conversation that night, for a long time after we parted. And it broke my heart to know the softness like the rain that was the Fisherman's true nature. This truth would gradually become so obscured by his addiction and self-abuse.

The following day at low spring tide, Lisa and Ian went down to the rock pools. The Fisherman gave her a basket and showed her how to look for sun oysters. She was soon utterly enraptured by the hidden treasures in the emerald and azure sea pools. As she bent down to peer deep into the shadows, she saw a dark, murky shape move from one rock into the small crevice of another. Dark tendrils drifted after the shape had disappeared. As Lisa watched, she noticed the tendrils that looked so like kelp had the delicate suckers of a tentacle on the other side. And then she saw it. The dark gray, ghost-like shape of an octopus. It was standing upright on the rocky seabed on all eight tentacles, staring straight at her in fright. The creature was trapped. It couldn't swim away because the tidal pool was too shallow, and it could not risk climbing onto the rocks. The octopus tried to swim around to the back of the rock and disappear underneath it, but there was simply no space. Suddenly, it revealed teeth that looked much like a parrot's beak and lunged at her. Lisa hurriedly stepped back, leaving the poor creature in peace and continued to forage for her basket of shellfish and sun-oysters.

It was a beautiful morning, and she was feeling blissfully warm and contented as she combed the tidal pools and rocks for sea treasures. The Fisherman had been scouring the rocks close by her for abalone and oysters when suddenly she heard him shout behind her. There stood the Fisherman, with a dripping, oozing shape in his gloved hand. He had caught the octopus. "No, Ian, don't. Please let the poor Occi go!" she implored. But he had already turned the octopus inside out and bashed it against the rocks. Lisa felt a cold, numb horror watching him kill this beautiful sea creature. "It's good food, Lisa and I can use the rest for bait," he said pragmatically. In that instant, she realized what it took to fish for a livelihood. Watching Ian deftly catch and prepare the octopus brought home the reality that she would never want to share this part of his world. Ian left the prepared octopus tentacles in a bowl on the camping table to soften and marinate in spirits overnight. The next day, their bowl was gone. When Lisa walked over to the campsite shower the next morning, she caught sight of a ragged, old Khoi man sitting on a rock, a way off with their enamel bowl in his hands. The wrinkled old grandfather of the streets was hungrily finishing up the raw octopus mixture for breakfast.

Ian's motor home was more than a traveling vehicle for the two of them. It was a cocoon and their private inner sanctum. Much like a hermit crab occupies its shell, the Fisherman had become a part of his blue camping van. He took care of his vehicle exquisitely, looking after its engine immaculately and building a comfortable interior at the back of the vehicle. He had crafted beautiful wooden shelving and built this into the upper interior space, and more underneath the futon mattress at the back of the vehicle. Fishing equipment was stored under the bed and in airtight buckets. In addition, he had secret storage spaces under the floorboards of the motor home where he kept cash, a small bank bag of Ganga,[3] and a spare hip bottle of cane spirits or brandy.

At first, Ian's secretive behaviour did not occur to her as anything out of the ordinary, just quirky. This fisherman was a unique man indeed. But, as they traveled and spent more time together, Ian's habitual use of alcohol became more real for her. She gradually understood his need for secrecy and his unspoken expectation that she become complicit in his addiction to alcohol and mind-numbing substances. This requirement was to become a challenge and a point of conflict between them because Lisa had never been a drinker, smoker, or drug user in any way at all. All her joy and exhilaration were in her connection with nature. Her weakness was the adoration she felt for the Fisherman and all the exceptions and compromises she had made for him. He knew it, too. At first, he would encourage her to loosen up a little and to share his drink to warm her in the cool of the early evening beside the braai fire, especially after a day of swimming in the sea. This was a harmless enough invitation, but Lisa felt wary. They were two unique souls, both free and unfettered by the stuff that most humans identify with. But there was one clear difference. Lisa had already realized the trap of addiction a long time ago. And she was far too independently minded to become a part of Ian's drinking habit.

The Fisherman's mind was like a fine sponge. With his photographic memory, he remembered every tiny detail of his life and the ocean and coastline where he used to fish. This capacity perfectly served his ability as a survivor, but not so when he became drunk and negatively charged, for then all his memories of shame and hurt would surface, and he would turn these viciously onto Lisa, using every nuance, every flaw he could find to break her and make her clay in his hands. It was such a ridiculously unnecessary

---

3 Marijuana

ploy and so clearly an unconscious pattern that surfaced while he was under the influence. He already had her hook, line, and sinker. He only had to ask, and she would have done almost anything to please him. But what the Fisherman asked of her when on his drunken rampages was too much. He had found her weak spot. It wasn't so much the verbal abuse that would follow when he became drunk that was hard to witness. It was watching his tormented soul emerge. First, his own beliefs about himself as a failure would erupt. His failure as a man, as a provider, and his inability to fit into mainstream life. And then he would begin to project his anger outwardly at her. This was aimed at all the women in his life who had betrayed him and whom he, too, had betrayed.

In these moments, he would growl at her, lifting his leonine head and looking vaguely out at the world, "I thought you were my angel until you told me that you had slept with a rugby team of men—what a waste of time, what a joke. Now I know what's wrong with you. Here I was thinking that this time was something so special and that I was special to you, special to someone on this entire fucking planet. But I suppose I've been fooled again, and I am just one of your conquests." And he would rage on and on and on like a wounded lion roaring his pain and anguish into the night. It was pointless to try to speak to him when he became like this. Lisa would quietly leave him raging and slip away, feeling sick to the pit of her soul. She knew he would feel better in the morning and that it would all blow over. But what she wasn't sure of was how she would make a life with a man who was so unconscious of his insecurities and negative behavior when he was drunk, unless he was willing to find healing.

Hidden deep in my heart was a sense of shame for not having found a soul mate in my younger years. I had fallen in love a few times, but it hadn't taken long to realize that it was infatuation and not the kind of love that was lasting. Like the Fisherman, I was a recluse by nature—a quiet soul—one who thrived on introspection and being a part of the stillness and rhythm of nature. I wore natural, comfortable, practical clothing and was not defined by my appearance. I loved all things sensory and ethereal—not loud public statements of physicality. The experience of love for me was a subtle continuation in every word, in every single ordinary movement, in every awakening to the day, the beginning, middle, and end. It was all a part of one exquisite, magical cycle that began again at every moment.

In those magical honeymoon days, the Fisherman had revealed the same tender qualities that meant everything to me, the sacred and the profane about love. "It's all about soul connection and simple things like the rich, natural smell of you!" he would say whenever they were together. He was right. Much of the beauty of intimacy between us was simple. Ian and I had found one another in this holy place of being, in the exquisiteness of touch and the connection between our hearts. But whenever issues or doubts arose, the sanctity between us would dissipate, and my sense of shame would begin to surface again, triggering inner conflict and emotions that felt completely overwhelming to me. I was an extremely sensitive soul, and this sensitivity had been heightened every time I was mistreated or betrayed. I had felt abandoned and heartbroken every time a love affair ended, and I had so wanted this love between Ian and me to be different. We were perfect for each other, but whenever Ian started drinking too much, he would become rough, cruel, and callous. I didn't feel safe with him anymore when he was like that.

I was a wild thing. A creature filled with the honey of wisdom and gorgeous treasures. Each treasure was meant to be explored, found, and reclaimed as some ancient and magical relic. Like an ancient story in an ancient scroll saying, "Here I am, explore me, find me, create me, awaken me. I am a mountain, a river underground. Tap into my fountain. But heed well. No water and no treasure, not one word will I ever share unless you have the sensitivity to hear, feel, sense, and see me."

*As a younger woman, I could sense but didn't yet understand
what my soul longed for. But as I matured, the truth became
plain. It was just as my dear grandmother had shown me in the
dream, "Make sure your young man is a gentleman, Lisa," she
had said. I hadn't realized the importance of her message then. Of
course, I needed someone gentle in my life. Someone who would
be prepared to walk with me across the song lines of my broken
heart. Oh, in those days I had hoped so much.*

There was a time while they were travelling that she left Ian
alone to his anger and had gone to sit beside the dying embers of
the fire they had shared earlier that evening. She found a quiet
mossy pillow where she could lay down and watch the canopy of
stars and the Milky Way shining above her. When Lisa moved to
stir the coals, she felt her own hot tears spill and fall with a quiet
hiss onto the embers of the fire. Her thoughts began to travel back
to a time in Namibia's deserts when she first heard the story about
the little wood ash girl who created the stars in the heavens. Lisa
imagined she could hear the faint, reed-like, rhythmic voice of a
young bush girl in the distance, singing alone beside the fire. The
memory of the wrinkled, old !Kung woman who had told this
story came back to her clearly:

*"A long time ago, there was a beautiful young bush girl who
waited beside the fire for her beloved hunter to return. Her
betrothed was still an inexperienced hunter and hadn't come
home that night after the hunt because he was lost in the vast
Kalahari Desert. She had sat up waiting and waiting until she
knew in her heart that he could not find his way home. That
night, the girl had reached into the dying embers and, taking
out handfuls of the warm, wood ash, she flung the glowing*

coals so high into the dark night sky that they had remained there, glimmering and shining where she threw them. And somewhere deep in the desert wilderness, the lost hunter saw these glimmering embers that now lit up the night sky. The young hunter was able to follow the source of the stars to find his way back to his village and the wood ash girl who had guided him home."

When the storm of her tears was over, she returned to the sleeping Fisherman. Somehow, Lisa had found the strength to continue in a lighter way, to support Ian and steady his mind. To help him see the good in his life and appreciate all their blessings and to accept the contrast of his chosen, natural path with that of the mainstream world.

They were already back in Cape Town when something happened that Lisa hadn't expected. She was sitting in the passenger seat with Ian, driving along the Cape coast road, when suddenly they heard a car hooter behind them. Somebody leaned out of their car window and called Lisa's name. Ian pulled over into the parking lot and stopped the car. A silver BMW pulled up next to them. Lisa got out of the car and went to greet the driver. A tall, elegant, middle-aged woman with beautifully styled, ash blonde hair alighted and greeted them both warmly. It was Lisa's friend, Charlie. They had met through her circle of friends from Aurora on the West Coast. Although Charlie lived far away on a farm in the mountains of Tulbagh, she and Lisa had become good friends and had stayed in touch.

"Lisa, my darling friend. It's so lovely to see you again," she said in her large and polished English way. Lisa gave her a warm hug. "And who do we have here?" Charlie indicated to Ian, who was gingerly standing on the curb, rolling himself a cigarette. Lisa smiled. It was still a new relationship, and both Ian and Lisa were very shy and private people.

"Charlie, this is Ian," Lisa said, bringing her over to meet Ian.

"We all wondered where you had disappeared to," she said with a secret smile. "It seems that big changes are in the air for this new millennium. I am moving to Cape Town with my daughter, Dana. Hopefully, we can see a bit more of each other now. I'm in the process of finding a comfortable flat where Dana will be close to her new school."

"That's wonderful for you, Charlie," Lisa said. She knew that Charlie had been unhappy living on the farm and had been looking for a way to resolve the challenges she faced as a single mother.

"Yes! Dana is so much happier here. I think we will both be better off here in Cape Town." She looked a little sad when she said this, and Lisa knew that Charlie was leaving her partner and life with him behind. "We must move beyond our limitations, Lisa. All of us must realize at some point that if it doesn't work, we must move on." Again, she flashed Lisa that whimsical smile. "And you two?" she asked, looking over at Ian and Lisa. "This must be a very new thing and very special for you both. You must both treasure and protect the love that you have found. It is a rare and sacred flower. And if you won't mind me saying so, I sense something imminent between the two of you," she said, laughing mischievously. "It's as plain as daylight! I wouldn't be surprised if you two were to become parents to a beautiful child in not too distant a time."

Lisa blushed and looked at Ian. He had blushed too and was looking at her. He reached over and squeezed Lisa's hand, and without words, they both acknowledged that what Charlie had just said was true.

"Well, you two love birds. I'd better be on my way. I have a meeting with an estate agent, and my daughter is waiting for me to collect her from horse riding this afternoon. Let's get together for lunch. I'll contact you once I've settled into my new apartment, Lisa. We'll see one another soon. Bye for now." Then, with a wave and a swish of BMW tyre dust, she was gone, leaving the couple feeling startled and very exposed.

Ian and Lisa were intensely aware of their feelings for one another and the unexpressed hope they both shared for a life together as a family. Ian had already given voice to his desire for a daughter someday. He dreamed of building his own home and starting his own fishing charter business. They had both agreed that they were far from ready for this. She had been so careful right from the very start, but even so, it seemed the stars that had brought them together had a divinely preordained plan. Not long after the chance encounter with Charlie, Lisa missed her period.

The marmalade mermaid whispered to you
it was a sound as soft as the sea
couldn't make out if you were asleep
or if you were pretending to be
world news rattled on
the drums and the guns
they were all tuned into what had begun
to the spoken word on a blank space
to the sound of a voice with nobody's face
sometimes at night
like when the moon shone
so bright that my stomach began to swell
and somebody phoned to tell me
you wrote and said someone else
said all's well
then my God He came down from a hole
in the sky
from the place where they point
when they call him a lie
and the place that he came from

THE FISHERMAN'S SONG

was ringed by a word
the word was mercy
God alone knew why
and I believed him at last and
understood the lie
so my darling when illusion takes you
by surprise and even while the green
mermaids threaten to capsize
your boat of inspiration
Remember that song you once heard on the shore
and that truth is precious to few
The sounds of the sea may always be heard
to understand it is not easy to do

CHAPTER 4

LITTLE HOUSE IN THE FOREST

Come, Fisherman, and heal your soul. Wash away all the pain and sorrow. Let the salt pass through your warm brown skin. Let your sea-blue eyes gently understand and retrieve the treasures of your heart. Fisherman, know that even though I left, I loved you whole.

The days following Lisa's discovery became a blur of events. Ian was euphoric when Lisa showed him the thin red line on the home pregnancy test. It was as though all the lights had gone on inside of him, and he jumped into action.

"Let's go over and tell my mom. Come on." He smiled with undisguised delight shining in his eyes. So later that afternoon, Ian and Lisa drove over to his mother's Higgovale home on the slopes of Table Mountain to tell her the happy news about becoming a grandmother.

"Hmm," his mom had said, taking another sip of her cup of tea and nodding. Lisa could see that Ian's mother was holding back far too many words. "Well then, the two of you should start making plans for the future," she said kindly.

He and Lisa stayed to chat with his mother for a while, and as they got up to leave, she called her son aside to speak with him privately. "Ian, I want you to take special care of Lisa now that she is pregnant. Take all the pressure off her and make sure she gets plenty of rest, please. It might not seem so, but these first few months are the most critical, and she will be at her most fragile and tired then. Alright, my darling. And good luck to both of you," she overheard Gwyn say to her son.

Lisa spent her days feeling alternately queasy and elated. She threw up whenever she smelled brandy on Ian's breath and when she thought about him being drunk again. A secret part of Lisa knew that had she not fallen pregnant at that point, she might have considered giving him an ultimatum about his drinking and separating from him.

Soon her pregnancy became a matter of family business. They were both swept up into the current of family dinners, meetings with the midwife at the clinic, and chats with well-meaning brothers, sisters, cousins, uncles, and aunts about child-rearing. It was all too much and too soon for Lisa. She felt utterly adrift with all the comings and goings. Her soul longed for a serene and peaceful space simply to be with her unborn child and to feel her pregnancy in the quietness of being alone. Ian's mother came over for supper to discuss the future of their grandchild, and both parents offered to help pay for a wedding at the beautiful Mount Nelson Hotel. Lisa began to feel that this time with Ian and their expected child had become about social responsibilities, commitments, and saving the family's reputation. Although she was very grateful and prepared to accept that this was important to a certain degree, the level of family involvement was overwhelming. Ian clearly felt the same way. He wasn't the kind of man that would ever settle for a traditional marriage and a life of compromise. Eventually, Lisa reached breaking point. She called the phone number of a private agent on the Garden Route and accepted the lease for a cottage near the little town of Wilderness. Then she made a bank transfer for the deposit of the cottage, using some of the money that she was saving to buy a new car. Within a fortnight, they had packed up and filled the back of Ian's motor home with their most essential possessions, his fishing gear, and

Lisa's painting materials. They left Cape Town and their respective families and drove onward into their future together, to their new home on the Garden Route.

The little cottage overlooking the slow, winding Wilderness River was an idyllic place for a young couple starting out on their own. Built onto the gentle slope of the hill above the sleepy little village, it had a comfortable, cozy lounge with a fireplace, and outside there was a sunny veranda where they could sit and enjoy morning coffee or a "braai." Lisa's dog, Baloo, had a huge meadow to romp in with plenty of nature walks close to the cottage. The rooms were comfortably furnished and from the wide bedroom window, they could watch the meandering river and hear the distant rumble of the ocean and the calls of forest louries, robins, and wood hoopoes. One of the first things Lisa did when they arrived was to flop down, with spread-eagled arms and legs, onto their comfortable double bed in the sunlit bedroom and take a nap. She could just imagine a child being born into this sunny and happy environment.

Arriving at their new home in the Wilderness was a blissful time. They were starting a new life together and bringing their child into this beautiful, forested world. Lisa felt the tiny baby within her womb beginning to take form and grow.

Not long after their arrival, Ian returned from grocery shopping in the village. He was grinning from ear to ear and shining. "Hey! Lisa, I have just been asked to work at the Wilderness Hotel restaurant as a chef," he crowed as he walked through the door. "The manager called me just as I was going down to the village this morning to get the groceries. He invited me for an interview at the hotel, so I went there immediately. The hotel management took a liking to me and immediately hired me."

"Holy Moly, that's fantastic!" Lisa enthused. "When do you start?" she asked.

Ian shrugged. "Looks like they need me to start tomorrow on a trial basis. Will you be okay on your own here, my Lisa?"

"Sure, I will, Ian," she said, putting her arms around him and smiling into his eyes.

Everything seemed to be going so well for them both. She felt sure that the arrival of their little one in this beautiful home would be so perfect. Lisa was feeling positive and glowing with the joy she felt in their new future. Now that Ian had a job, she would be able to get on with her painting quietly at home. Their financial situation could only get better, and she was ecstatic about spending time alone, making a home for the two of them.

Slowly, Lisa began to unpack her art equipment, paintbrushes, pencils, and jars filled with colours ready for her to begin her inspired creations. Every day while Ian was away at work, Lisa would paint and wander the nearby paths with Baloo, exploring the farm and forest nearby. Often, she would gather armfuls of flowers, wild herbs, and sometimes a few wild mushrooms for Ian to identify when he got home. Her life was full, and she was content. This aspect of their lives was blissful, but underneath all of this, Lisa still held her reservations about Ian. She could sense that although he seemed sure about this baby, their new life and his new job, something didn't feel right about him giving up his freedom so suddenly.

It seemed to Lisa as if Ian were living a life that was not entirely his own, as if he were making an enormous sacrifice to be with her. He was not a mean-spirited man and was always generous with her. But it was his drinking that caused anguish in Lisa's heart. She had noticed that whenever he would shop for food and other necessities, he would find a reason to buy bottle after bottle of expensive, strong spirits. Lisa was now sure that Ian was an alcoholic. They argued about him wasting money on the way home from a shopping trip to the nearest town. She usually tried her best to express what she needed to say to Ian in the gentlest way, but this time she failed miserably. And it was from that point onward that the wheels started to come off and their relationship began to flounder. They had been chatting happily about the preparations they needed to make for their child when Lisa tackled the subject of his drinking habit head-on.

"Ian, I know it's your business and that you are earning good money now. That's not the real problem here. I've noticed you have been dipping into our grocery budget to buy liquor." There was an icy edge to her voice when she raised the subject, and she could sense how he stiffened when she mentioned his spending. "You do remember that I promised to accept your drinking on condition that you kept it in check and that you would never compromise me in any way."

Ian closed his eyes momentarily as though to brace himself for an onslaught of her condemnation. "What now, Lisa?" he sighed.

"Ian, if you think about it," she said pointedly. "I have put so much of my own resources into this move and into setting up a life for us both. Of all people, you should understand that I need to save money to buy another car. Luxuries like brandy are not the commodities we should be spending money on right now. Anyway, you have a responsible job at the Wilderness Hotel that you cannot afford to compromise."

"In what way am I compromising my job or you, Lisa? Come on. You're completely overreacting. I'm the one who is bringing home the bacon. And I'm not complaining am I, nor am I compromising my job in any way," Ian blurted out, on the defensive now.

"But you are," she retorted. "You're not only compromising yourself when you drink so heavily. Your drinking has reached a level that is not healthy for either of us."

Ian was stone silent. But she could see that his face had become dark with anger. Still, Lisa continued unfazed by his cold demeanor.

"Ian, I'm carrying our child. Surely this is not the kind of father you want to be. Right now, we both have to think about the future for all of us and not about self-gratification anymore. Honestly, I never thought I would say this to you, especially not so early into our relationship, but here it is. Your drinking lifestyle is incredibly selfish! You need help, Ian, proper counseling, and medical assistance. You simply can't keep on drinking like this!"

Ian reacted with fury, and so suddenly, it was as though a fuse had been lit and detonated internally.

"Fuck, Lisa! Can't you just leave it alone?" he yelled at her. "It's not as though I haven't given you my all. What more do you want? Do you want to destroy everything, everything about me and about us, too, while you're at it?"

Lisa couldn't help herself. She completely lost it with him. "So now you're shifting blame onto me! Oh, you are totally off track, Ian. For God's sake, how can you think only about yourself when it's not just about you anymore? It's about this baby and us. We have a child to consider now!" she screamed at the top of her lungs.

Ian's answer to her challenge was to put his foot down on the accelerator of his vehicle and frighten her into silence. The image of the drowned Mantis she had found when she met Ian flashed before her eyes. Lisa quietly asked him to stop the vehicle and pull over so that they could both calm down and drive home safely. A cold and painful reality had begun to dawn in her heart.

Later, as Lisa sat outside their cottage watching the stars and listening to the night jar's call, she thought about the wood ash girl once more. She could hear Cape Eagle owls hooting in the woods nearby and the gentle live hum of the cicada beetles all around her in the evening silence. She put her hand onto her belly and felt the sense of roundness growing in her belly as her little one began to take form.

Life in their little cottage would have been the most blissful experience imaginable without the tensions. Both Ian and Lisa loved the beauty of the place, the hikes, the nature, and the simple abundance of living there. But when Ian started drinking, he would begin a downward spiral of negativity that, despite Lisa's best intentions, she could not change. Instead, Ian began to pull Lisa down with him. Lisa was a plain-spoken person, but she was not abusive. She found herself thinking how ridiculous and pointless it was that he would waste so much of his time trying to find reasons to fault her. At times, he would find Lisa painting and spend hours tearing her apart until she had to put her work away and leave their little cottage to take a walk with her dog, Baloo. His usual reason for being upset with her was scary. When Lisa had met the Fisherman, she was in her early thirties. In his negative state of mind, he would blame her for the fact that she had left a trail of previous partners and that he had not been her first, her one and only love. His arguments were so utterly insecure and unreasonable that, at times, they bordered on being psychotic. "If you're so Goddamn perfect, Lisa, then why were you behaving like such a whore!" He would throw insult after insult at her until she couldn't take it anymore.

Ian began to scare Lisa. Her body reacted to the stress of his verbal abuse. He wasn't giving her the necessary space to rest. Her pregnancy was being tested to the limit by his frequent bouts of drinking and argumentative benders. At times, Ian would get into his camper and storm off, and Lisa would be left not knowing whether he would ever be back. When he finally did come home, drunk, often in the middle of the night, he would fall into bed, smelling strongly of tobacco, marijuana, and things that Lisa didn't know about but that smelled and felt terrible to be near. Lisa would wrap herself in a sleeping bag and curl up on the couch beside the fire. She would never know where he had been, and he would not tell her. Lisa knew in her heart that the situation could not and should not continue. Something would have to change if they were to stay together. She had been painting throughout that terrible time, with the radio playing next to her to keep her sanity. The words to Christina Aguilera's latest song, "Beautiful," would come floating across the airwaves straight into her bruised and confused heart. *You are beautiful, no matter what they say.* The song kept playing again, speaking to her soul and to the unborn little one in her womb.

Early one morning, after another of Ian's late-night benders, Lisa began to bleed heavily. She knew exactly what was about to happen, but she was beyond caring. At that point, Lisa was almost three months pregnant and still feeling very fragile. She brewed filter coffee for them both and then carried the steaming coffee mugs into the bedroom. Ian opened one bleary eye when he felt Lisa sit down on the edge of the bed beside him. He propped himself up on one elbow. "What's up, Lisa?" he asked. Lisa looked at him wistfully, with pursed lips, "Ian, I've started bleeding and it's not stopping. I think I'm having a miscarriage," she said, looking down at her coffee cup. She had a towel in her other hand, and she teared up as she showed Ian the deep red stains. "I've already called my doctor this morning. You're going to have to take me to the hospital as soon as possible, please." Ian sat up, looking alarmed. He took a sip of his coffee and then reached for his warm, green sweatshirt. "Okay," was all he said. Lisa felt saddened that it had taken this level of shock to make him realize how fragile she was and how desperately she needed his support at this time.

Lisa was given a bed in the maternity ward at the general hospital. It was so peaceful lying there alone, looking out of the hospital window at the view of Knysna Heads. She remembered being glad to be there, away from the craziness that had been going on in their home. At first, she had fought the reality, hoping against all odds that something could be done to save her pregnancy. But later, as things progressed, she felt something come loose deep in her womb, and she knew she was losing their child. The miscarriage had made her feel utterly helpless, but relieved that the suffering was all over. There was no question in her mind that this pregnancy had its perfect timing and that this had simply not been the right time for their child to be born. Ian came over at visiting hours the next morning, smelling of brandy, and sat next to her bed. He laid his head on Lisa's womb for a long, long time. She felt no blame or judgment, and she didn't argue with him about what had happened. She knew that he felt remorse but couldn't express his emotions. And though Ian had been so abusive, she felt only deep compassion flowing in her heart. Even then, she knew that his alcohol addiction was his only way to deal with confusion and the pain of his grief.

Compassion... come
gently alight
softly on my fingertips
touch my heart with love's delight
Come passion now
the world is twisted so
better to remain awhile
until the hurt is gone
Compassion deep
let the grass and flowers wildness
grow into the cracks where once
gravestones were piled
pour into the recesses
of the deepest wound
Never cease your filling
Until the world heart is unbound
come passion come
from every place in the universe
join hands and minds in
Understanding
how

This cold ice
can be reversed
Let it tell you
Let it heal you
Let compassion be within you
compassion
Light and gentle carefully
Let it rebuild and realize us
Into a loving world
we share

Blue Moon

Not long after her stay in the general hospital, Lisa had another vivid dream. In her vision, she saw a tall, dark-haired woman dressed in the magnificent robes of a Priestess. The beautiful woman was standing beside a pool of natural spring water in the darkness of night. Instinctively, Lisa recognized her as a holy woman. It felt as if she were beckoning her to come and be cleansed in the clear spring water of the pool. The Priestess spoke to Lisa with her eyes, showing the deep, clear water and telling her that she needed to bathe in the living waters to cleanse herself of the past and begin anew. She stood proud and tall and raised both her hands to the sky, and as she did, she showed Lisa the full moon. Lisa followed her gaze and saw there was not only one but two moons shining in the night sky. And when she looked down at the reflection on the surface of the mountain pool, she saw that the moon was a sparkling azure blue. She glanced up to ask the Priestess more about the moon and where to find the water, and noticed that the holy woman was gone.

Lisa woke up startled at the early dawn and wondered about this dream for a long time. She knew that it was a message from Spirit to help her heal from the loss of her unborn child.

"Ian," she said one peaceful morning while they sat together having breakfast in the sun. "Do you think we could plan to go to Cape Town sometime, please? I have something important that I need to do." She told the Fisherman about the dream that she'd had.

Ian listened quietly.

"The strangest part was that I was shown a clear mountain pool and two moons, and I saw a blue moon. That part of the dream I don't understand. The message was clear. 'Cleanse yourself on the night of a blue moon.' But what could that mean?" Lisa mused.

The Fisherman began to smile and then chuckle at the dawning of his realization. Then he looked up at Lisa with the first truly radiant smile he had shown in a long time. "This coming month in July is the month when a rare two full moons will occur. They call this the time of the Blue Moon. I will take you to a pure, mountain spring I know of on the slopes of Table Mountain in Cape Town, where you can cleanse yourself," he said, touching her face. Ian was such an attentive, understanding, and caring lover and a beautiful jewel of a being without any mind-numbing substances in him. These sober moments when Ian was his authentic self were all that was left to her, all that was left between them, and the only thread left of their precious love. Lisa smiled back at him in gratitude, and for the first time in weeks, they embraced, holding one another gently for a long time and rocking to heal all the hurt between them. It was one of those rare moments of true clarity, revealing the love that they felt for one another.

It was in these mythic and beautiful realms where pure magic and nature exist that Lisa had met the Fisherman and where they both belonged. The long embrace between them felt like coming home. Lisa wept in her lover's arms that morning. Not at the loss of their unborn baby but at the many times they had lost themselves and the pure and exquisite magic of their fragile love. Now they both stood at the edge of a choice, to begin again and allow the healing and this love to grow again. The Fisherman said nothing; he just held her gently and let Lisa weep into his old, green sweatshirt.

Ian drove Lisa to the mountain pool on the Table Mountain contour road. It was a freezing cold night in early winter, but he was waiting to wrap her in a warm, dry towel and help her into dry clothing. Afterwards, Ian wrapped her in his arms, resting his chin on the top of her head. The two of them stood silently, complete and at peace, looking out over the edge of the mountain at the magnificent jewel-lit Cape Town, the mother city at night.

Argonaut Shell

After the miscarriage, Lisa began to have a completely different attitude towards Ian's drinking problem. The brief stay in hospital had given her time to rest and reflect on what was happening and what she had to do to improve her situation. She would sometimes pack a picnic and go with Ian when he went fishing, but she never sat on the beach with him for long. Lisa would take herself and Baloo for long walks, beach combing, collecting shells, and letting her mind heal. On one of these walks, she found a beautiful and delicate Argonaut shell. It was as large as a dinner plate, translucent white, and tipped with brown at the spine of each spiral. Lisa carried her treasure back to the beach, where Ian was packing up his fishing gear. She showed him the treasure that she had found.

"Round like the moon, and so white," he said. She could see that he had been weeping. "Ian, I am still here," she said gently. "After all, it is our love that is so precious. It's as delicate as this exquisite nautilus shell. Please let's both try to be gentle with one another from now on." She carefully put the Argonaut shell into their picnic basket and reached up to kiss him tenderly on his bearded face.

Sally's Advice

Ian was very busy running the hotel kitchen on the river in Wilderness. He was often away at work all day and sometimes until late at night. This gave Lisa the time she needed to relax, make decisions, and heal after the miscarriage. She'd just sold a valuable piece of art, and although she needed her independence and a car, she had made up her mind to spend part of this payment on the support and counseling that she knew she needed. Lisa's doctor had given her his recommendation for a good psychologist in the village.

When Lisa finally sat down in Dr Sally Malevich's comfortable consultation room, she was desperate to share her heart. There was a knot at the base of her solar plexus as she walked across the street towards the building where the psychologist had her practice, but as soon as she entered the door and met Sally, all her nervous tension began to melt away. She felt immediately at home in the company of this salt-of-the-earth professional. Sally smiled at her with a kindness that showed in her warm brown eyes.

"So, what brings you here to see me, Lisa?" she asked gently from her comfortable leather armchair. Gradually, Lisa began to describe to her therapist what had happened before her miscarriage. The psychologist listened carefully and then nodded.

"Lisa, you know, so much of what happens to us, these catalytic events are often a reflection of patterns that started a long time ago when we were children. I can see that you already understand this and care deeply about your life. I know that you care about your partner too, but let us start at the beginning so that we can address the problem at its root," she said sensitively.

Long after I left the therapist's consulting room, I recall thinking about what had happened in my childhood. I had grown up privileged to live in one of the most exceptionally beautiful places in the world. It was a wonderful, healthy environment, growing up near the sea and with a beach nearby. The coastal stretches of the Western Cape in South Africa were known for their breathtaking scenic beauty. International films and commercials were often shot on these beaches and along this stretch of the

Atlantic coastline. I knew that while affluence and the beauty of a place could bring great inspiration and peace, it certainly did not teach anybody about living with compassion and emotional intelligence. In my understanding, these qualities of empathy and compassion originated in those who had suffered immensely and who spent time contemplating what it meant to be an authentic human being: I was in a desperate state at that point. I felt confused and lost. I did not fit into the world of the privileged, nor did I feel safe or confident to be my authentic self, given the situation with Ian.

These were the questions that Lisa sought answers to whenever she went to see her therapist. As she began discussing her thoughts, perspectives, choices, and opinions, her attitude began to change drastically. Lisa felt increasingly empowered with new understanding and greater trust in her own judgment. Ian saw her overall well-being improve and began to sense her shift. As she grew more confident, his insecurities increased, but it no longer mattered to Lisa. She no longer allowed him to buy alcohol when they went shopping, and she refused to accept his drinking at home. Lisa knew that Ian desperately needed emotional support, but right now, she could not help him. She had begun talking with him about attending the Alcoholics Anonymous twelve-step program and finding professional support for PTSD. At first, Ian was resistant, but he did not want to lose her. Occasionally, she would pack up her Art equipment and find him back at the bottle after work. Ian just couldn't help himself and was so sensitive about his drinking habits that her silence would set him off on a tirade of words. Lisa got it; she understood that Ian's drinking had medicated his fears and emotional pain. She also knew that his behaviour was not about her in any way. She understood that his dependency had everything to do with unresolved emotional issues—unexpressed feelings of shock, grief, abandonment, shame, and inadequacy. But at the same time, the way that Ian was dealing with his issues was damaging his life and negatively impacting those closest to him. Every time he began to drink heavily, his rage would spiral out of control, and Lisa would have to get out of his way.

Gradually, Dr Sally Malevich became an anchor in her life. Lisa looked forward with enthusiasm to her regular weekly sessions with her therapist. After the first few consultations, Lisa was ready to delve a little deeper as she peeled back the layers of her life.

"So, I understand that your family comes from Cape Town, Lisa. How did you feel about your parents while you were growing up?" Sally asked at her next session.

Lisa's face blanched. There was a long silence as she collected her memories and thoughts. She didn't like to speak about her family to others. She was extremely loyal to those she loved and especially to her family. Also, she knew that just like many South African families, they too had their own problems.

"This is strictly confidential, Lisa," Sally assured her. "This space is entirely for you. It is a safe container where you can share your memories and pain without anyone judging you. Sharing your challenges will give you a chance to reflect and eventually heal these patterns, my dear."

Lisa nodded thoughtfully at her therapist. She liked the dark-eyed, attractive, middle-aged lady and instinctively sensed that she could trust her. "Okay," Lisa whispered. She could feel the palms of her hands sweating with nervous tension. Lisa closed her eyes for a moment and felt the shock waves as she remembered Ian tormenting her in his drunken state. She couldn't help the thoughts that shouted out in her mind. *What had she done to deserve his criticism? Why was she the object of his rage? Was it her fault? And if so, what could she do to change this and bring her lover back to his senses again?*

"I am curious to hear about your family, Lisa," her therapist patiently repeated.

The steadiness in Sally's voice brought her back from her reverie, and Lisa began. Once she started speaking, the words felt like a powerful natural spring opening in the ground. All her memories of childhood began pouring out of her.

"I think it was the conflict with Ian that has made me remember this," she said hesitantly. "It's brought back all these old memories and emotions. Both my parents were intelligent and refined people, but I remember terrible domestic battles at home when I was a child. My father was a distinguished academic and scientist who sadly passed away several years ago. Although devoted to my mother, my father's primary commitment was to his work and his research. I remember how so many arguments in my childhood home stemmed from my father's frustrations at not achieving recognition in his career, his sense of limitation, and his irritation at us, especially at my mother. I must admit that it feels as if the current situation with Ian is a replay of what I went through as a child. I remember my father's bouts of drinking and the scary events that used to follow. Sometimes, home just wasn't a peaceful or safe place to be. Alcohol consumption was so much a part of the fabric of our South African lifestyle that everyone in our family and around us just accepted it. You know the old jingle, *Braai vleis, rugby, sunny skies, and Chevrolet.*

"If you remember, back in the 1970s, it was an image that most South Africans felt familiar with. My father was no different in this regard. But I think the real problem was that most men of this generation just were not equipped to handle life's challenges." Lisa sighed deeply and looked down at her lap. Her hands were no longer so tightly clenched, and her body began to relax as she spoke. As Lisa began to share her memories and experiences, her hands relaxed, and the rigid set of her shoulders softened. There was a sense of release as she allowed herself to speak, the weight of unspoken worries gradually lifting as Lisa found herself more able to express feelings that had long been held inside.

"How did all of that make you feel, Lisa?" Sally asked her kindly.

Lisa looked up at Sally. Tears were beginning to well up in her eyes as she released the painful memories of her childhood. "I felt sad, lonely, and unworthy a lot of the time. We grew up walking on thin ice, desperately trying and failing to meet the pressure and the unrealistic expectations set by our career-driven father. I distinctly remember my father's rage and his consequent remorse, and I remember my mother's deep depressions, her silences, and how she tried to build a protective wall to isolate us and herself from the rest of the world. We lived in a bubble for many years. My mother said she did this because of her sense of shame and powerlessness at what was going on in our home.

"At first, when the violence began, it was because both my parents were quarreling about money and my father's drinking. Then, when my mother began to withdraw, his emotional outbursts started to affect my brothers and me. My mother didn't know what to do. She tried turning to a religious support group, but that wasn't the answer. Prayer had always been a personal and private time of sanctuary for her. Eventually, she went to see our family doctor, who listened quietly to her suffering and concerns. He prescribed some over-the-counter, calming medications and suggested in his fatherly, bedside manner that my mother find a day job to bring in much-needed income. Whether he was right or not, I don't know. All I know is that my father's drinking carried on until the day he passed away," Lisa said.

"It must have been an extremely difficult time for your mother. She must have loved you all very much to have stayed the course in her marriage," Sally said gently.

"Yes, her family still means everything to her. When she was younger, my mother used to enjoy home crafts, and she was good at them. She knitted, sewed, did macrame and weaving, and was also a fantastic cook. Although she very rarely had the time to paint, I remember what a gifted artist she was and how she loved painting animals and wildflowers. It was such a tragedy that my mother could not follow her dream of becoming a graphic artist. Professional training would have helped her break out and become completely independent. She would have been brilliant at it and so successful. But instead, my mother decided to save up the fare and travel overseas by ship. In this way, she could leave home and live in London, as far away from her autocratic father as possible. London in the 1960s must have been her dream come true, and my mother loved it! She loved the freedom to be herself, to meet young people who, just like her, were spreading their wings and enjoying all the vibrancy and colour of the time. It was the age of 'Flower power,' miniskirts, house parties, Jamaicans, the Beatles, and a whole new era of music and fashion. And it was where my mother met my South African father. My parents eventually returned to South Africa to face political sanctions and the isolation, restrictions, and conflict of the apartheid era in the 1970s and 80s. I'm quite sure that had quite a lot to do with my parents' frustration," Lisa paused, thinking.

Sally nodded at her. "And how did your parents' frustration affect you at the time, my dear?" she asked with a gentle smile.

"As a child, I was constantly fraught with the same sense of powerlessness that my mother had—experiencing and seeing my parents arguing and things being smashed and broken. I remember how desperately unsafe it often felt in my parents' home. I remember trying to scream to stop my parents from fighting, but I was so frightened that no sound would come out of my mouth. And how, as a child, I would often become frozen with fear—in fact, I still do when arguments and violence happen. I didn't know what to do to help my mother or siblings when my father got into one of his rages. Sometimes, no matter what the weather was like, I would grab a warm jersey and just get out of the house. I would walk in the mountains or on the coast and sit inside the caves where the Khoikhoi fishermen used to go. It's interesting how even now, after all these years, I feel comforted when I am in these natural spaces. I still have deep wounds from all the conflict at home. I believe that is where my greatest trouble lies, Sally, but I still don't know how to change my reactions and responses to life."

Sally noticed that Lisa had begun clenching her hands again, and her head was bowed low in deep reflection. "How do you feel about your mom now, Lisa?" she asked.

"Well, I've certainly repeated all her mistakes," Lisa smiled wryly, shaking her head. "I grew up pleasing people, just like my mother, always the rescuer, the peacemaker, trying to avoid conflict at all costs. I was the little parent in all my relationships, constantly putting up with abusive and emotionally unavailable partners. None of these relationships ever worked out in the end, no matter how hard I tried. I was in such deep pain throughout my early adult years. As children, we were never allowed to speak out about what was going on in our home or to rock the boat in any way. We all just had to pretend everything was okay. Nobody said anything or tried to talk to me about what was happening. All my pain was bottled up inside me for years. I didn't know how to express my feelings or value myself in any way. Of course, my father provided us with a good home, and he was a loyal father, but he seldom acknowledged or encouraged us for our achievements. He believed that 'children should be seen and not heard.' So, we simply got on with our lives in the best way we could, and I became very independent as a result. We couldn't speak with my father about anything, especially not our hopes and dreams, and we dared not challenge him in any way. My mother dared not challenge him either. She would always discourage us from breaking the mold or doing anything that might not meet with my father's approval. Once I left home, I became the black sheep of the family because I refused point-blank to conform. Even so, I still wasn't listening to my inner voice; I was just angry and rebelling, I suppose. So many years have passed, but I am still unable to speak up for myself confidently. My ability to express my needs and make firm, healthy boundaries was utterly shattered in my childhood. This is still my deepest and most difficult emotional hurdle. Even though I have strong intuitive abilities, my childhood wound prevents me from recognizing dysfunctional relationships and responding in a normal, healthy way."

Lisa stopped at that point and looked directly into Sally's eyes. "I hope you don't think that I'm being unfair about my parents."

Sally smiled, and her warm, intelligent eyes behind her glasses looked kindly at Lisa. "No, my dear, there is no judgment here. It is entirely understandable that you've had a challenging time with relationships, considering your childhood background. When one is not shown much support, protection, or nurturing by one or both parents, it becomes difficult to attract healthy relationships into our adult lives. Then our priority is to heal the most important and valuable relationship we have, which is with ourselves. It may take some time before you begin to feel a sense of ease and forgiveness for what has happened. But once you have made peace with all of this, the memories will begin to fade and heal. And some day, all that will be left of your emotional wounds will be the scars to remind you of how much you have healed and of how strong you truly are."

"Thanks. Yes, Sally, you are right. I understand that both my parents were simply doing the best they could at the time."

When Lisa finally stopped speaking, she found that tears had begun to flow softly down her cheeks.

"I think that is enough for one session, my dear Lisa." Her therapist got to her feet, smiled at her, and passed her a box of tissues and a glass of water. "We can continue next week at the same time. In the meantime, please take things very easy. Do you keep a journal?"

Lisa smiled and nodded.

"If possible, I'd like you to write down your thoughts and even your dreams. If you have some rescue remedy at home, keep it close at hand. And be gentle with yourself, okay?" Sally Malevich said.

One evening, soon after Lisa's counseling session, Ian's drinking and negative behaviour began to get out of hand again. "What is it that makes you need to act like such a whore?" he roared at her. Lisa walked quietly over to the bedroom wardrobe and took out her warm sheepskin boots. Mechanically, she sat down on the bed, put them on, and wrapped a warm jacket around herself. Her handbag was at the front door. As she reached for her bag, Ian lunged towards her with his powerful fist, but she had already opened the door and slipped away before he could reach her. He was too drunk to react fast enough, anyway. She found herself running with her handbag and coat for the safety of the main road and the nearest bed and breakfast accommodation. That night, she lay awake wondering, feverish with the knowledge that once Ian had begun being physically abusive towards her, there would be no stopping him. There was no longer any question about it. Lisa knew that she had to leave him, come hell or high water. After this bout of anger and projection, he was there to fetch her the next morning and to take her for breakfast, but he absolutely couldn't own his behaviour, no matter what had happened or what Lisa said.

Not long afterwards, Ian got back from work early. He would not admit it, but the truth was, he had lost his job because of his drinking. Alcohol had become such a critical part of his life, his way of medicating himself, and a deeply entrenched habit. It had become his only coping mechanism. Ian firmly believed that it made him calmer, but he didn't realize that he was constantly crossing the threshold of no return. In this state of unconsciousness, Ian's actions and reactions had become extremely irrational and violent, and he was no longer safe to be with.

That same week, Ian asked Lisa to take him with her to see her therapist. He must have known that it was his last straw. Although he knew that he had his own problems, he still clung desperately to his excuse that what was affecting him was Lisa's past and her fiery, independent spirit.

"Exactly what is it that Lisa does to make you feel this way, Ian?" Sally Malevich had gently asked him when they sat down in her consulting room. Sally listened carefully for some time, and when Ian couldn't find any other answer than what little he knew about Lisa's past, Sally carefully explained the dynamics of projection to him.

"All of us have a past, Ian, and we can all learn from our mistakes. It's not who we were ten years ago that truly matters. It's who we are right now, our choices, how we respond to life, and how we treat others," she said pragmatically. "If you think about it, most of the triggering we experience comes from our childhood and traumatic events in our own past. I would like to recommend that you explore these feelings a lot more. Of course, you would have to be completely committed to your own healing process and be willing to have some therapy yourself so that you can manage your feelings of disappointment and distrust. In the meantime, I highly recommend that you join a support group. You will find that there are many ordinary men and women, just like you, who are addressing the same challenges at Alcoholics Anonymous."

When Ian left the therapist's consulting room that day, he looked deeply shocked. The psychologist had made it impossible for Ian to deny his addiction and the issues that lay beneath the surface of his behaviour.

The next time Ian began acting out his rage in her presence, something in Lisa snapped. "That's it, Ian. That's enough. I'm leaving you, and when I come back to the cottage, I want you gone!" she said firmly. "I mean it. This time, you have pushed me too far! I want you to pack all your stuff and leave tomorrow, and I don't want you coming back." Lisa took her raincoat and handbag and walked out of their cottage.

It was almost nine o'clock at night and pouring with rain. She waded through the mud and crossed the forest into a neighbor's property in the dark. When she got to their house, she knocked on their big wooden front door. She was too tired and traumatized to care about what they might think of her. There was a flicker of light as she saw two old people open the curtains and peer out to see who was out there in the rain. When the tiny, grey-haired woman opened the door of their house, she gasped at Lisa in surprise and exclaimed, "Oh, my goodness, what on earth has happened to you, my dear?" Lisa was dripping wet and shivering.

"Good evening. I'm so sorry to bother you both so late," she said bravely. Her teeth were chattering as she spoke. "There has been a difficult and dangerous situation at home, and I have needed to walk away from it. I hoped that you were home and that I could ask you for shelter just for tonight, please." She was completely drenched to the skin, and her face was white with shock.

"Yes, of course, lovey, come in. I've often seen you walking on the farm gathering mushrooms and flowers, and I wanted to invite you around for some supper or coffee," the old lady said as Lisa stood dripping in their front entrance. "Come in, come in, and dry yourself beside the fire. I will find you a towel and something warm to change into."

Old Mrs Harris busied herself around her farmhouse kitchen, warming up a bowl of soup while Lisa dried her dripping hair and changed into dry clothes. When they asked her what had happened, she briefly told them about Ian and his drinking problem. "I can't thank you enough, Mr and Mrs Harris. I could think of no other way to deal with this situation. I just needed to stay somewhere safe, away from him tonight until he has gone," Lisa explained to the kind old lady and her husband as she sat shivering beside the fire.

"Yes, you have done the right thing, my dear," Mrs Harris said, nodding her gray head in understanding. "And you absolutely must never go back to this young man ever again."

The very next morning, Ian packed up in a fury and left.

When she finally stood in front of their gutted and empty cottage, she felt only a flood of relief.

Seems there's little to bind us
Now the child is lost to us
Your drink is like solvent
Dissolving our new love as it flourishes
Your smoke-like clouds that
Hide my gold and your gold
Turn my sea-green eyes grey
in your gaze
My past masks delight
In our present
Of each other's presence
Of each other's exquisite loveliness
And our anger
Blows holes in strategic places
Where the spirit of our heart's truth enters in
How can this love survive
When all is lost like this
When I am labelled, past and pain
And liar
No value in my truth
Which is me, utterly me
the one you love
Surely you love the truth.
The me that shines with gold
Moves like soul
The me whose eyes sparkle sea-green
with laughter at you
With love and joy and freedom
not disillusionment
Am I not good enough?
To be treated with utmost respect, adored, and comforted
Am I second-rate to cigarettes and drink?

Less important to you?
Is my respect and love and nurturing not enough for you?
Seems there's little to bind us now
Except the child in you and the child in me
That wants to come through all of this
And be loved, really loved
Without anger, resentment,
smoke clouds and liquor
Like a delicate flower
Our love will try again and again to be born

CHAPTER 5

Journey into the Kalahari Desert

"The Bushmen in the Kalahari Desert talk about the two 'hungers.' There is the Great Hunger and there is the Little Hunger. The Little Hunger wants food for the belly; but the Great Hunger, the greatest hunger of all, is the hunger for meaning..."
—Sir Laurens van der Post

In late winter, Ian had gone back to Cape Town through the driving rain, sleet, and snow that fell on the mountain passes. He had returned to his family home in the heart of Cape Town, where his widowed mother lived alone. In some strange way, his mother was relieved at the turn of events, which now left her son with no choice but to face his addiction. By that point, Lisa knew she did not want Ian back in her life. She'd received several text messages that were most unlike him. "Lisa, please give me another chance. I'll go to AA meetings, to a therapist... whatever it takes," his messages read.

She knew that many promises had been made, but so far, none had been kept. Lisa no longer had any expectations or confidence in Ian's word. She had far too much in her own life to consider. Her next art exhibition was in just a few months, and without a vehicle, it was clear that she would soon have to give up the little cottage in Wilderness. Before Ian had left, she made sure that she had bought enough food and provisions for the house to continue with, and then she set herself the task of completing her paintings. Every day, Lisa lit a crackling fire in the cottage fireplace, and then she painted through the sleet and the rain and the cold of winter. She painted through all her feelings of loss at the recent miscarriage and the shock and trauma at the terrible way she had allowed herself to be treated. It wasn't a long walk to the little town of Wilderness, but even so, the kind old neighbor who had given her shelter called in from time to time and offered to take Lisa shopping. She continued her weekly sessions with Sally Malevich, and in the weeks that followed, her resolve became firmer and clearer. She communicated with Ian rarely, and then only to settle their affairs and make boundaries clear. She finished most of the paintings that she had set out to complete before the third month had passed. It was September and the beginning of Spring. Lisa arranged a lift back to Cape Town with her paintings carefully rolled into a tube, her few belongings, and her dog, Baloo.

Ian met Lisa on the beach when she returned to Cape Town. He hugged her and held her hand, but that was as close as Lisa would allow him. "How are things going with you, Ian?" Lisa asked him gently. There was no malice or bad feeling between them, only a sense of sadness and disappointment. She could feel his heavy heart as he shared with her the victories and difficulties of his path to quitting drinking. "Oh, I'm okay," he said with a wry half-smile. "Things have been a little tough with quitting, but it's going well so far. I've been fixing holiday homes for international friends and working part-time in a local restaurant. And I've put some money aside for the deposit on a flat," Ian enthused. "Lisa, I've made up my mind to start seeing a psychiatrist every week." Lisa smiled and nodded her head in encouragement. She didn't have much to say, and she was still feeling hollow and drained. The stormy time in their relationship and the miscarriage had brought up so much of her pain, and Lisa knew she could not handle any more conflict between them. He knew she still loved him, but as much as Ian wanted to see her again, she wasn't ready, and so she kept her distance.

She tried to distract herself from the dull heartbreak that followed her around like a shadow—spending time with her mom at home, cooking meals, drinking tea in the sun in the lovely courtyard at her parents' house, and preparing her work for framing. But the sense of emptiness and loss haunted her, gathering like stormy weather and often bringing her to silence and stinging tears. It left her feeling a longing for compassion and love beyond anything she knew. Lisa would sit for hours leaning against the damp, salty granite rocks down at the beach where she and Ian used to go. And there she would let her loss, longing, and the burden of her miscarriage rise and form like a crashing winter storm wave.

During this time, Lisa was invited to attend a "Family Constellation" therapy session in Cape Town. She went along to observe and was fascinated by the visual aspects of the process. Constellation therapy reminded her of healing methods she had seen used by the !Kung Bushman medicine men in Namibia. These Bushman trance healers worked with the realignment and clearing of energy within a field. Lisa had been witness to the exquisite, rhythmic, hypnotic singing, clapping, and dancing around the communal fire that induces the shamanic trance. She'd seen and felt for herself how the medicine man would begin to shake and become highly energized or potent. And how, in his heightened trance state, the shaman could locate the blockage and draw the poison out of the afflicted. She'd also seen during the trance dance how the Shaman touched and shared the healing potency that he carried. The !Kung people believed that suffering reflected a bad spirit or sickness carried within the entire group and often in the wider environment. This innate understanding enabled the Bushman medicine man to heal and cleanse the entire community.

Soon after Lisa returned to Cape Town, she received a phone call from a good friend.

"Hey, hey, Lisa, honey. How're you doing?" It was Sissy Taylor, an ex-South African who had just flown in from America.

"Sissy. Wow! It's so lovely to hear from you. It's been such a long time since we saw each other. How is sunny California these days?" Lisa asked, smiling at the sound of the friendly voice on her cell phone.

"Oh, things are okay. But divorce hasn't been easy. I need this break so much, and I'm keen to get into the desert and meet with our Bushman friends again, darlin'! How 'bout a lovely get-together with all the Cape Town gals? What do 'ya say? Can you meet me tomorrow morning, at around ten thirty, at the Company Gardens restaurant in Cape Town, under the old rubber tree? You know the one?"

"Sure, I'd love to." Lisa chatted happily with Sissy for a few more minutes on the phone and then said goodbye with a promise to meet the next day.

Her women friends, Anna Blinkman, Charlie Douglas, and Sissy Taylor, were all women known for their involvement with the Bushman First Nations people. Sissy had created the Khoisan First Nations Trust, which she ran from her home in Los Angeles, America. Charlie had a lifelong fascination with all African indigenous heritage through her experience with Somali and Kenyan culture. Lisa had become friends with Cape Khoikhoi, Anna Blinkman, through her earlier explorations into the Northern Cape, researching rock art and the contemporary art and craft of the San. Anna, a determined and well-connected young Khoikhoi woman, had fallen in love with the Khomani people and their desert ways, and she had made the Kalahari her home. Anna met her Bushman artist husband, Raaikat Blinkman, while working with the Khomani people as a facilitator for the African San Institute. Raaikat and Anna were married and living in the Kalahari bushveld.

Travelling to the Kalahari was always an uplifting and rejuvenating experience for Lisa. The landscape seemed to widen as the road travelled North. She watched the arid Karoo bush and scrubland gradually metamorphose into acacia thorn tree vegetation. Giant sociable weavers nests hung from the Acacia trees and red soil anthills as tall as a man marked the desert bushveld. Lisa felt a huge surge of release and freedom as they entered the Kalahari wasteland. Recent events and her separation from Ian had been extraordinarily intense and draining. Lisa felt emotionally torn between her love for him and the numb feeling of loss. She needed space to think clearly, to be with her soul sisters and the salt-of-the-earth Bushmen who, through the years, she had grown to love as an extended family.

When the bus finally arrived in the town of Upington, the three women were met by Anna's friends. They were taken to a hotel on the banks of the Orange River, where they were to stay for the night. It was wonderful to be in this arid environment, so dry yet strangely fluid. Watching the powerful flow of the wide, perennial river was incredibly affirming. Lisa and her friends ate their supper on the hotel deck while watching the sunset. The next day, while Sissy arranged a rented car, Charlie and Lisa walked down the busy street to the local grocery store. They would need to stock up on some basics for the journey—fruit, greens, coffee, milk, dog food for the Blinkman's hunting dogs, and other basic foodstuffs to take with them and deliver to the Bushman family where they were staying. Once their shopping was finished, Lisa walked over to the tobacco stand to buy a few pieces of "Kudu biltong"[1] and some packets of loose tobacco. Gifts for several of their Bushman friends. Lisa dreamily watched the dusty Kalahari Street scene outside the grocery store window while waiting for the assistant to finish weighing out the "biltong." Colorful street vendors outside on the pavement were selling bananas, oranges, cabbages, and locally dried fruit in economy bags. Another was peddling Chinese goods, watches, socks, and cell phone accessories. A taxi drove past with music pumping

---

1 Traditional dried game meat

from its crammed interior.

Dignified Tswana women with elegantly braided hair and traditional bright "Shwe Shwe"—cotton attire walked past on the street outside the store. Lisa had been absently leaning against the shop counter, utterly absorbed, watching the people of the Kalahari going about their daily business, when she noticed the price on the biltong scale rapidly escalating until it registered over ten thousand rand!

"That absolutely can't be!" Lisa exclaimed. The shop assistant frowned with confusion. He looked perplexed and tried weighing the biltong again. Then Lisa stood upright and began to giggle with embarrassment as she realized that she'd been leaning with her full body weight on the edge of the biltong scale.

Later that evening, once they had arrived in the desert and were all gathered around the fire for supper, Lisa brought out the prized traditional gifts of Kudu biltong and local tobacco leaves to honour her Bushman friends Raaikat, Oom Haasie, and Surrikat. She told them her tale of how she almost paid R10 000 for Kudu biltong. The crinkled, smiling faces of her Bushman friends erupted into raucous laughter. "Dit is hoeveel n mens moet betaal vir Wit Vrouw Biltong,"[2] they cackled. The Bushman's humour and their earthy fondness for their friends always warmed her soul.

Earlier that day, they'd driven into the desert in the car that Sissy had hired in Upington. Lisa knew this road well and had driven here before, but only as far as tourist destinations and guest camps along the tarred roads. This time, they were headed for Blinkwater and the red sand dunes. Sissy drove them through the hot scrubby desert landscape and turned off onto the long stretch of dirt road that led to the Guest Lodge at the Twee Rivieren Parks board resort. This was the gateway to the Kgalagadi Transfrontier Game reserve. The Blinkmans had taken their four-wheel-drive truck in for repairs at the mechanic's workshop at Twee Rivieren, and it was almost ready for collection. Anna was planning to drive

---

2 That was the price of white-woman Biltong.

them on the last leg of the journey to Blinkwater in their truck. To their surprise, Anna's husband Raaikat was already waiting at the workshop, sitting on an old oil drum with a wide grin on his face.

Raaikat was a fascinating Bushman. His slanted eyes were deep, moist pools hooded within his golden-skinned brow. He was both "maer en skraal,[3] and tall for a Bushman. And he had a constant quizzical look on his face—half-amused and half-listening. He wore western clothing almost as one might carry a bright flag to announce their presence, always with a strong pair of "velskoen"[4] and Khaki workman's pants or denim jeans. In addition, he wore a leather bracelet decorated with delicate ostrich shell beads on his wrist, while a single pendant of engraved bone hung around his neck.

Raaikat was an artist but also a true craftsman. He filled his hours beside the fire, carving and engraving exquisite scenes of Bushman life onto ostrich eggshells and bone. Whenever there were visitors to their hearth, he would take out his treasures: ostrich-shell bead necklaces and bracelets. His engraved ostrich eggs and drawings were kept aside and sold to higher-paying clients and shown at the galleries in Cape Town to generate income for his family. Raaikat was determined to buy his wife a little house in the small desert village of Welkom. He was a man who was never idle. If there was ever a moment when he was not crafting a necklace or pendant, he would take up his battered guitar and entertain his visitors and family for hours with his amusing and simple "Liedjies," played in the Bushman's traditional half-key tones. His favourite tune, "Bokkie, bokkie, bokkie, ek is lief vir jou," would echo around the fire and into the world. It was a well-known traditional South African song, and he sang it with affection and warmth. Raaikat was a master at collecting good memories and friends.

While they waited for Anna to collect her truck, Lisa and her lady friends plunged into the lodge pool to wash off the travel dust.

---

3 Lean and wiry
4 Leather shoes

The temperature in the desert was already a blistering 38 degrees, and that was only at mid-morning. After some last-minute curio gift shopping and the purchase of a large bottle of Amarula liqueur for Charlie, they were on their way with Anna at the wheel beside Raaikat, Sissy, Charlie, and Lisa in the back. Driving over the red dunes was like surfing the desert ocean. Anna followed a rough desert track that none of them except their driver could see.

The road to Blinkwater was a mysterious experience of endless red dunes to a distant oasis. Before the Blinkmans left Twee Rivieren, they had filled a 500-litre plastic water container for the trip back to the farm. Anna told her friends that the farm water had an extremely high lime content, too heavy in minerals to be drinkable. She explained that they could use it to wash or cool off in the heat, but that it was not for human consumption. The local water was only used for the goats on the farm.

Once they arrived at the tiny settlement, Anna and Raaikat took the travelers down to a cement brick storeroom to sleep and safely keep their bags. It was the only weather-proof brick building on the farm except for the windmill and livestock dam, and had been Raaikat's art studio space. However, Raaikat and Anna chose to build a small grass "skerm"[5] to sleep in at the highest part of Blinkwater dune. It was closest to an enormous, old "Witgatboom."[6] Here, they were protected from the wind and could be much cooler in the heat of the desert.

That night, they all made supper on the fire and sat around the dying flames sipping liqueurs until very late. Sissy and Charlie had both gone to sleep in the brick storehouse. The full moon was bright that night, and the fire was almost out. The ripple of shadow cast by the moon on the dunes slowly melted as Lisa watched the moon rise. Everything was silent and still around her. She lay spread-eagled, arms open, under the moonlight on a blanket that she had thrown down beside the fire. Her soft belly

---

5 Shelter
6 Shepherd's thorn tree

slowly filled and expanded with breath and became round like the full golden moon.

Their Bushman friends had long ago crawled into their grass "matjies huis" to sleep. Raaikat looked at her and laughed as he said goodnight. "Jurre maar die blerrie maanbefok vroumens is mal om onder die volle maan te le," he commented sleepily to his wife. Lisa could hear Raaikat and Anna in their "matjieshuis" laughing softly to one another about their crazy South African friend, sleeping fearlessly beside the fire in the moonlight.

As Lisa watched the moon that night, the old San/Bushman folk story about Mantis danced through her thoughts. She remembered Raaikat telling a story once that went like this:

"The moon is not to be laughed at. In Khoisan folklore, the moon is alive and never dies. It grows large and disappears but is always born again, coming back slowly in a matter of days. We can talk to the moon and ask for anything, children, rain, luck in the hunt, and the moon will answer by sending a sign. This is one of our stories that tells how the moon was created." He smiled mysteriously and began.

"One day, Mantis and his beloved Eland friend had been ill-treated by the Meerkats. And so, Mantis pierced the sun and caused the sky to become dark. He jumped into the darkness, and then because he could not see, he took off one of his shoes and threw it into the night sky so that it could become the moon. Now, the reason why the moon was red was that the shoe of the Mantis was covered with the red dust of Bushman land, and it was cold because the shoe was only leather. The angry sun followed the spoor of the moon as the moon travelled in the sky because the sun intended to fight the moon. The moon was pierced by the rays of the sun. In pain, the Moon set slowly and died, but was reborn the next night when it lit up the darkness. A part of the moon remained in the sky and lived while its decaying and wounded part died. The part of the moon that lived was joined to its head, face, and thinking strings. And as

the moon grew, so did its stomach, which became full and gave light
to the people on the ground."

Lisa had brought a down sleeping bag with her, and as soon as she felt the night cool, she climbed into her warm bag and fell gently asleep. Upon waking before dawn to the sound of distant goats bleating and their bells clanking in the morning dust, she drank some water and rolled up her sleeping blankets. Then she walked quickly into the red dunes behind the settlement. The cool morning was such a lovely time to explore and experience the sunrise over the red dunes of the expansive Kalahari Desert.

Lisa sat with her back against a dry kameel doring tree stump and gazed into the distant horizon. She could just make out the hazy form of a large Eland bull, grazing peacefully on the dunes. As she sat daydreaming, thoughts about this graceful antelope drifted across her mind. The Eland, most beloved of the African antelope to the Bushman people, was the favourite of their Bushman God, Kaggen. Not only was the Eland meat tender and sweet, but it had a fatty dewlap underneath its throat and a layer of belly fat that was always cooked and eaten and used by the Bushmen during rituals and in many other ways. The fat was mixed with herbs and ground ochre to make salves and medicines, to cook and store food, soften animal skins, and grease sinews for bows. The Eland was symbolic of all that was good, potent, sacred, and plentiful about their lives. This majestic large antelope was frequently the subject of Bushman rock paintings because of its quality of potency and magic.

"That must be Namibia," she thought, gazing west. She could also see North past the dry riverbed into Botswana's vast Kalahari Desert lands. She squinted into the distance to where she imagined she could see massive African Baobab trees. Called "the upside-down tree," these baobabs could grow from fifty to sixty meters high and nine meters in diameter. They have great thick branches that sprout haphazardly from the sides of the trunk and reach like stretching arms into the sky.

According to San folklore, the Great Spirit gave each animal a tree to plant. Last in line was a hyaena who received the final tree, a baobab. Unfortunately, the hyaena was so disappointed at what he received that he angrily threw the baobab onto the ground, planting the tree upside down.

The bark of a baobab tree is smooth and thin and sags like the skin of an elephant's leg. Its waxy, bulbous trunk is soft and pulpy, and if you lean against a baobab, you will find it warm from the sun. One almost expects to hear a great heart beating in the tree trunk. Most living baobabs range from around 125 to 200 years old, and there are very few younger trees. The reason for this strange phenomenon is largely due to the close relationship of elephants with the African baobab. Elephants have a considerable impact on the land, opening forests as they uproot shrubs and debark trees, depositing enormous, fertile dung piles which provide baobab seeds with the perfect growth opportunity. At sunset, after the first spring rains, these giants of the Kalahari Desert landscape put out huge, sweetly scented, white flowers resembling gardenias that are as white as the moon and as fragrant. These beautiful, heavy blossoms droop downwards towards the earth, beckoning pollinators with their scent. Soon, bats arrive to feed on the big blooms, and, as they feed, they pollinate the flowers. Then, after just one night, the blossoms start falling to the ground. The trees continue blooming until December, but this first flowering is the most spectacular, and there is nothing to compare with the sight of a giant baobab standing on a carpet of white. In summer, they bear pods shaped like pears, commonly called "the cream of tartar fruit" because of the cooking ingredient, cream of tartar, which is produced from the Baobab seed pulp.

Lisa sat quietly, scanning the vast desert that opened before her. Most of the Kalahari landscape she could see was encompassed by the Kgalagadi Transfrontier Park, the largest game reserve in the region that begins in the Northern Cape Province of South Africa and spreads right across southwestern Botswana.

She listened to the early morning desert sounds and watched the round sun disk climb over the horizon, shedding its rays like warm fingers over the red dune landscape. She checked her cell phone for messages. There had been zero connection down on the red dunes of the farm. A message from Ian had blinked onto the screen. "Lisa, I have some really good news for u?" the message read. Lisa hesitated for a while, then wrote a short text to Ian. "Not much connection in the desert. xox." and pressed "send." She put her phone away in her pocket and walked slowly back through the sparsely vegetated thorn and grassy landscape, stopping to examine the filigree patterns of wildcat footprints in the desert sand and the patterns that the grass makes when the wind blows. All these tiny observations were the secret language of the seasoned Bushman tracker.

The desert river flows deep underground
Across vast sand expanses
The desert river snakes its way deep down
Stopping every now and then
to shimmer its graceful blue in between valleys
as an oasis
Just enough to keep love and hope
The caravan of thought traveling
Bringing sustenance to you on the other side
Of the desert
And keeping me alive in the wasteland
without you

When she arrived back in the camp, the fire had been relit, and an old coffee can was bubbling on the fire. This Bushman coffee is called "Moer koffee"[7] because it is brewed on the fire until it reaches its fullest strength. Raaikat was busy making a loaf of "asbrood,"[8] kneading the dough and leaving it to rise in the early morning sun. As Lisa approached, climbing the dunes behind their camp, she heard his full-bellied laughter ring out into the desert wasteland.

Raaikat had been amused at the comments from his European visitors about picking up goat and dog droppings in the camp. He put away his baking and took the foreigners to see one of many large "Scarab" or dung beetles that were rolling enormous balls of goat dropping into their underground abodes. "Kyk heir is die 'Misstamper.' Hy maak ons tuin mooi skoon.[9] Dan kry hy 'n lekker mis geskenk as hy al die mis opgetel het,"[10] Raaikat said with a very serious look on his face. Lisa was the only visitor who understood the Afrikaans language that he spoke and burst into peals of laughter at his words. Raaikat kindly explained that the farm was a healthy system and that here on the dunes, everything worked in perfect harmony with nature.

Raaikat was the ultimate trickster both in his words and his work as an artist. There was always a twist and a delightful gold thread of humour in everything he said and did. His words often left people wondering and savouring his stories and parables for years afterwards. These words were always memorable, a beautiful offering of connection and healing. There was much laughter and chatter over breakfast that day, with all of Lisa's companions talking excitedly with Raaikat and his Bushmen friends about the dung beetle and other curious desert creatures. Charlie described her experiences traveling along the Nile in Egypt and spoke with awe about the sacred Egyptian Scarab

---

7 Nut Coffee or rough ground, strong coffee
8 Ash bread
9 Look here is the dung beetle. He cleans our garden beautifully.
10 Then the Scarab beetle gets a big reward for picking up all the dung.

beetle and how it was known as an ancient symbol of rebirth and fertility and of the endurance of the human soul.

Lisa remembered how Raaikat was dancing beside the fire, a tobacco joint dangling from his lower lip, when she presented him with the gift of a kikoi blanket. He had been partially crippled when he was struck by lightning as a young boy and had been left with only one functional lung as a result. Then later in his life, he contracted Tuberculosis, which ravaged his remaining healthy lung. Raaikat knew that his condition and health were very fragile, but he was determined to live his remaining days to their fullest.

"Ai Lisa, dankie,"[11] he said, smiling. "Jy gee vir ons n baie mooi geskenk. Dis asof jy een van ons eie family stam is. Meskien moet ek darrem n tweede vrou vat. Wat dink jy daaroor Anna?"[12]

Lisa threw back her head and laughed, "Ag, dear Raaikat, you're up to your tricks again."

She knew that Raaikat lived unconditionally and fully in the realm of all possibility. Lisa also knew that he had made similar astonishing proposals to Charlie, Sissy, and a few of their international lady friends and sponsors. Although the Bushmen are polygamous, as many African tribes' folk are, she understood his proposal to be a symbolic statement of unity and extended familial protection—not merely a proposition. Raaikat was a refined, wise, and gentle soul who was accepting of his weakened condition and impending death. In his unique way, he was telling his friends in the plainest language that he knew how numbered his days on earth were and how much he cared. In bringing them into his family hearth, he was showing that he would always be close in spirit to protect and guide them through difficult times.

He and his kin were the people of the Eland. Many Khomani,

11 Thank you
12 You have given us such beautiful gifts—and have become as close as a family member in our hearts. Perhaps it is time that I consider taking a second wife. What would you say to that, Anna?

of the original way, were undoubtedly the blessed and the meek that Jesus Christ had spoken of.[13]

In the time that Lisa had got to know the Bushmen, she'd realized how the essence of the Eland was exactly as early Christians had described, the essence of Christ or the Logos—a mythic, eternally gentle, unconditionally loving, and compassionate presence. Many Bushmen possessed these qualities and those of natural, inner humility, and peace. This was especially true of those Bushmen who followed the pure shamanic path. Raaikat Blinkman was one of these, a true leader, a born prophet, healer, and artist of the Khomani San.

Raaitkat went about his daily farm chores, frequently chuckling and commenting that the English ladies would all find it much more comfortable under the huge "Witgat" tree, sitting on their comfortable "wit gatte," which politely means, "comfortable European behinds." For the three days that they stayed on the farm, all four women spent most of the hot afternoons under the shade of this wide and magnificent Shepherd thorn tree, chatting to one another, telling their stories, cooling themselves down with water spritzers, and sipping cool drinks while preparing their evening meal.

That day, Lisa, Anna, and Sissy sat riveted, listening while Charlie told them the details of how she had spent several months as a prisoner in a Somali jail cell. Charlie's beautiful blue eyes and English rose complexion made her a compelling storyteller, even more so because her story was her very own experience. It was made even more shocking because she had so narrowly escaped being incarcerated and forgotten in this African prison for the rest of her life.

"It happened in the early 1980s. I was invited by a crew of

---

13 Mathew 5:5. "Blessed are the meek: for they shall inherit the earth. Blessed are the pure in heart: for they shall see God. Blessed are the peacemakers: for they shall be called the children of God. Blessed are those who are persecuted for righteousness' sake: for theirs is the kingdom of heaven." And from Psalms: 37:11. "But the meek shall inherit the earth."

experienced yachtsmen on a sailing trip from Monte Carlo in Monaco to Cape Town. They all knew the route past Eilat in Israel and through the Suez Canal very well. We chose a good time of the year to set sail. The sea was beautiful, and everything was going well. We had just rounded the horn of Africa when the motor on board the yacht began to splutter and give trouble," she said. "The crew needed to anchor the yacht in sheltered waters to repair it, and we were anchored for some days off the coast of Somalia while the engineer worked. It was such a long wait in the hot sun, and the sea in the bay off the Somali coast was so enticing. Most of the crew, including myself, had jumped off board into the azure seawater to cool off, and I decided to swim to shore with the other crew members.

"I was eager to meet the British archaeologist and his team, who we knew were working on a fascinating and ancient prehistoric dig just off the coast near where the yacht was anchored. I became so absorbed in talking with the chief archaeologist that I hadn't noticed the arrival of a military jeep with several AK47-bearing soldiers. Unfortunately, the Somali official posted nearby had spotted us with his binoculars. The chief army officer immediately accused us in a very angry voice of being on Somali soil illegally. It was so foolish of me to imagine that nothing serious might happen. Of course, I didn't have any papers on me to prove who I was, and they wouldn't let me go back to the yacht to get them.

"Although the archaeologist testified to my innocence, I was still detained and accused of espionage. The yacht crew was ordered to leave immediately or face arrest, and I was driven away in an army land rover to a prison camp for Somali women in Mogadishu. I was left there to rot for almost four months. The Somali soldiers stripped me down to nothing and took all my clothing and possessions away, and I was made to wear the traditional African wrap that most Somali women wear. I never saw my jewelry or clothing again. Then I was put into a crowded cell filled with female Somali political prisoners. We could not speak to one another because of the language difference and because any form of communication was strictly forbidden in these cells. If we spoke, or even tried to use sign language, the wardens simply didn't bring us food that day. And of course, the meals were so spartan anyway. Most of the time, we were given a pot of maize porridge and gravy to share between us. Incredibly, it was these Somali women prisoners who taught me the meaning of sharing with dignity. They were so courageous, so gentle and kind, and it was these soulful women who gave me the strength to keep going throughout the nightmare of my imprisonment. All of them were women who had been silenced and punished for challenging the Somali regime. They all wore the Hijab veil, and all that was visible was their beautiful, expressive, dark eyes.

"Amazingly enough, we women all accepted that the only way we could converse was through our eyes. But, somehow, we understood each other. A few Somali women were young mothers and had been allowed to keep their babies with them. I suppose this was because many of these babies had been born in prison and needed to be breastfed until they were old enough to be separated from their mothers. I was there and helped with the delivery when one of the Somali mothers gave birth to her child. Every day after the midday meal, they would sit on the bare earth with their babies resting on their legs and begin the daily routine of massaging their children. It was incredible to witness how these proud and dignified women found ways to communicate their love, continue their lives, and extend tender motherly care for their children even while faced with the terrible conditions of their imprisonment. The time I spent in this Mogadishu prison was one of the most liberating experiences of my entire life. I was so used to all the luxuries, my fine clothes, expensive food, and a beautiful home. In fact, I had left my entire existence behind on that beach on the coast of Somalia. Within a few hours, I was reduced to nothing. My entire past had been stripped from me, even my name and identity. At that point, I did not know whether I would ever be rescued, if anyone knew where I was, or if I was still alive. But I remember those golden African evenings, watching the flight of the graceful blue cranes over Mogadishu as they sailed free across the skies. These beautiful and sacred African birds were my inspiration to keep hope alive in my heart. 'Oh God, free me from this living hell' was my silent daily prayer.

"Eventually, the British Archaeologist, who I had been talking with before I was arrested, flew back to London and appealed on my behalf to have me released. I will never forget the day when I was told I could leave and how a tall, noble-looking Somali woman whom I had befriended came to me. She touched my heart with her fingers and then touched her own and looked deeply into my eyes as if to say, 'Please don't ever forget us! Please tell the world about us and our plight in Somalia.' Later that day, I was taken away from the Mogadishu prison in an army jeep and put onto a private aeroplane bound for Johannesburg, South Africa—and home." She took a deep breath and closed her eyes.

"Charlie, your story leaves me breathless," Lisa said with deep compassion. "Isn't there anything that can be done to help these courageous Somali women?"

"I don't know, Lisa, and to tell you the truth, I feel too afraid even to want to find out after what I have been through in that terrible Mogadishu jail," Charlie said quietly, her beautiful blue eyes filling with tears. "So many have said, I ought to write my story down and have it published. But I really wouldn't know where to start. The desperate situation in Somalia and the thrall of war that has spread right across Africa feels overwhelming to me. Once I start telling my story, the voiceless faces of these soulful, hopeless, and brave Somali mothers all begin to cloud my vision. There is just so much suffering in Africa today. It simply feels too much for me to write about, too much to bear. And there are so many children who suffer because of oppression and starvation in a land that, before colonization, was rich in culture and abundant resources. I suppose in some ways, I am afraid that by writing about my experience, I will endanger my life and that of my family."

Lisa reached out and touched her friend's gentle face and smiled into those sad eyes that carried so many memories and heartbreaking stories for the women of Africa.

The group of friends had all been so absorbed by Charlie's story that they had forgotten about the flies and how hot it was, even sitting underneath the Shepherd's tree in the deep shade. It was so hot that any perspiration or moisture on their clothing evaporated within a few minutes of its appearance. Later that afternoon, Raaikat, Surrikat, and his friend Haasie arrived in their donkey cart and dumped a sack of spiny, ripe, "Nara," or gemsbok cucumbers, at their feet. "Hierso," he said with a big smile. "Dit sal julle baie koeler laat voel."[14] He and Oom Haasie began cutting some of the ripe fruits in half. Lisa found the wild cucumber taste refreshing. It was juicy, like a melon, although the texture was slightly starchy and tasted more like a banana. Raaikat explained that they had harvested the wild crop growing in the desert dunes just down the road from Blinkwater. "Hulle sal baie beter proe as hulle op die vuur vanaand gebak is." He and Oom Haasie explained that the "Gemsbok cucumbers" would taste so much better roasted in the fire. They explained how their pips and skins could also be ground into a tasty meal.

It was a colourful, wild vegetable supper that the little group ate that night. As Raaikat, the Bushman, strummed his off-key tunes on his old guitar, everyone felt sleepy, full, and content. The African sun had sapped the energy of all three of these European women, and they were asleep even before the moon arose.

The next day, Anna drove her friends to meet Bosjan Blinkman, the appointed leader of the Khomani people. Bosjan was Raaikat's half-brother, and they shared the same father, Old Oupa Opstaan. The old Bushman had worked with the Human Rights lawyers in their bid to find the Khomani people a piece of land where they could hunt, keep goats, and live traditionally. Old Opstaan, their

---

14 These will make you feel a lot cooler.

leader, had died with this long-held hope coming to fruition. He had been a wise and fair leader in his time. When he died, Bosjan Blinkman had taken the role of leader of the Khomani people.

Anna explained the very complex lineage of the Khomani and, more specifically, the Blinkman family. She told us that Raaikat was an older son of Oupa Opstaan, destined to be a leader and an elder of the group, but that his crippled and damaged lungs had always been a severe setback. When Raaikat was struck by lightning as a child, he nearly died. The experience brought him back from the edge of death, and after that time, he was never the same. Raaikat was a walking miracle. His people knew that he was living on borrowed time and didn't have the physical strength that politics and negotiations would require. In fact, Raaikat had no stomach for politics. He hated government officials and often said of politics, "Politiese goed is net 'n gejaag na geld.[15] Bly altyd in die middel wereld!"[16] He would advise his friends in his wise Bushman manner.

Raaikat was a man, alive in more ways than average people would ever understand. He lived in this "middle world"—a crossover point between the spirit realm and life—and he saw details and subtle nuances that very few people could see. When Raaikat met Ian once on a visit that he and Anna had made to Cape Town, he pointedly remarked, "Hierdie man is 'n ware wit boesman."[17] Raaikat was not only a leader through his lineage, but he was also a born leader with a keen sense of observation and deep wisdom. He could relate stories in the manner of a true Bushman and had the talent to convey prophecy and humour into exquisite jewel-like paintings and drawings. He captured the hearts of everyone he met without doing or saying very much at all. It was just his natural warmth and presence that drew people to him.

Raaikat and Anna were the silent leaders who led their

15 Politics are just the pursuit or "desire for" money.
16 Stay in the neutral world.
17 This man is a true white Bushman.

community as spiritual shepherds by leaving their gentle, beautiful message of peace and healing, indelibly stamped on everyone's hearts. The two would often have to take their meagre food supply and share it with the Khomani children and families in desperate need. They were the clan mediators, and Anna was often kept busy negotiating with the Khomani leaders on behalf of many family members.

Bosjan Binkman and his family stayed on the outskirts of Witdraai in a straw bale building built in the style of a skerm, but big enough to be a gathering place and home to a large family group. His home was affectionately dubbed "Rooi Dakkies" because it looked like a red roof or shelter. When Anna arrived with Lisa, her friends, and Raaikat, many of the Khomani and riverbed folk were already congregating around a communal fire. They chatted to some of the group while Anna went to sort out her farm rental. Lisa sat down next to the fire on an old straw bale and exchanged a few words with Oupa Bosjan about the Khomani land claim. She noticed that the Bushman leader did not easily hold eye contact with anyone. Lisa later heard that he had allowed this grant land to be rented out to Khoikhoi or "Mier" livestock farmers. And although Oupa Bosjan had been instrumental in the negotiations for the land restitution grant in 1999, in many ways, he had broken the agreement to keep the land sacred for Khomani tradition and culture, thus selling his people out of the promise of freedom that the land grant had initially offered them.

As they drove away on the back of Anna's bakkie, Lisa was left thinking about Oupa Bosjan Blinkman and his family and feeling saddened by the predicament of the Khomani Bushmen. She thought about their wild and beautiful, multicultural, and cosmopolitan country, South Africa, and about leaders like beloved Madiba Nelson Mandela. Voices were often silenced because they spoke a truth many were not ready to hear. Along the road, they stopped to buy a few curios from the dusty loincloth-clad Khomani Bushman craftsmen. Lisa purchased a tiny ember holder carved out of bone from one of the smiling roadside traders to take with her as a memory of those precious few days in the Kalahari. She also bought a beautifully carved walking stick for Anna to give to Raaikat as a gift of gratitude for their stay.

Lisa sat in the front of the truck beside her friend Anna as they drove back onto the dirt road to Twee Rivieren. "These Bushmen traders are the 'Riverbed children,'" Anna fondly described the people they had stopped along the road to meet. "Many of them are of mixed blood, Nama, and Khomani folk." As she drove, Anna explained the background history of the Riverbed Kids.

"There have been many families divided because of intermarriage with the local Nama and Griqua tribe's people. Unfortunately, the descendants of these mixed marriages have been left out of the land grant for the Khomani. This divide has created further problems for the 'Riverbed kids' because it forced an ever dwindling population of Khomani Bushmen to keep their bloodlines 'pure.' The result has been intermarriage, family conflict, and even incest," she said with sadness in her gentle brown eyes. "Of course, there were further ramifications because the children of this racial conflict have been left deeply traumatized, abused, and sometimes even abandoned."

After a few days in the company of my Khomani friends, it had become clear to me that the challenges affecting the Bushmen were too complex to be resolved by a few outsiders. Like Anna and Raaikat, I could see that the only real solution would be a 360-degree change in the entire global mindset. I knew that the few remaining groups of Bushmen left in the Kalahari would be doomed to extinction unless attitudes and understanding towards ancient cultures changed. The gradual disappearance of the original people, of their culture and precious indigenous medicinal knowledge, was indeed a tremendous loss to the world because their understanding of the balance and the interconnection between nature and human existence was something so unique, pure, and refined.

From my interactions with the Bushmen, it was evident that their cosmology had a profound practical wisdom to it. It was heartbreaking to see how civilized nations looked on with apathetic sympathy as one of earth's oldest living human races rapidly became extinct. And this, because the rest of humanity had not yet joined the broken strings of understanding how it is that our civilization, industry, technology, and land development have caused the Bushman's demise. It is this very same disconnection from nature and from our sense of self that has brought our world to the brink of extinction. In these tumultuous times, we have become like a ship without any moral compass, rudder, or sails. My time with the Khomani people highlighted the fact that nature and our entire human existence were in peril. And that we would continue to teeter at the edge of survival unless we chose to rekindle respect for ancient cultures, natural wisdom, our environment, and all living creatures. This, to me, was the powerful, unspoken message of the Bushman people.

Sissy and Lisa were sitting at the back of the bakkie with Raaikat, who was happily puffing on a large joint. It was scorchingly hot as they drove back along the dusty road to Twee Revieren and entered the gates of the Kgalagadi Transfrontier Park. Everyone was ready to buy an ice-cold drink and plunge headlong into the lodge pool. "Ons is hier, ons is hier, kry n bier," they chanted playfully as they rounded the dusty corner.

As they all sipped cool drinks, Raaikat and Anna shared a tender memory about a Khomani relative, "Ag ou Blikkies!" Anna shook her head, smiling nostalgically. "He was a sensitive soul, a brilliant artist, and visionary," she said, describing their friend. "Sadly, he succumbed to alcohol addiction, as many of the Bushmen hunters and trackers had. Blikkies frustration with the Khomani situation was terrible. His enormous sense of futility was because the Khomani were no longer allowed to hunt freely on traditional land. When the Kalahari Gemsbok National Park was first proclaimed, the Khomani had been prohibited from entering this area, their original hunting territory. Then, when the Botswana game reserve amalgamated with the Kalahari Gemsbok Park in the 1990s, the entire reserve was fenced off with electric fencing to stop poachers. It was long before conservation policies had been reassessed to address the exclusion of First Nations people and the mistake that dispossession of those who historically occupied the land had been. As a result of these old game reserve conservation policies, the traditional Bushman hunting and gathering practices were no longer a sustainable way of life. Everything that had ever meant anything to him and his people had been made illegal. He, Blikkies, a once-proud hunter and brilliant tracker, had completely lost his identity. In a world where money and power rule everything, he had become a worthless, penniless game poacher and therefore a criminal," Anna shrugged.

"Blikkies had resorted to desperate drinking forays. He lost his sense of purpose and his will to live. Toward the end of Blikkies' life, he had been apprehended by the police on suspected charges of breaking into the Game lodge bottle store, but the police had no evidence. The local farmers, officials, and police hated Blikkies. They had marked him because he was wild and because in his drunken rages, he often berated local white communities for xenophobia, racism, and mistreatment of the Bushmen people."

Raaikat and Anna laughed at the memory as they shared an anecdote about Blikkies.

"One day, he had climbed up to the top of the Witdraai cell phone tower, as drunk as a lord," said Anna, smiling. "And then he stood there swaying precariously for hours, shouting abuse at the local Boere.[18] 'Ja, dit was omdat Blikkies kan sien hoe onregverdig die saak was. Dis hoekom hy altyd so dronk verdriet geword het.'" Raaikat pointed out that these drunken

18 A colloquial term for police officials and white farmers

ravings were Blikkies only outlet for the unspoken truths he kept hidden in his heart. Truths like who the real culprits of poaching in the reserve were and about the terrible disrespect that the Bushmen people endured daily.

"Ja!" said Anna nostalgically. "It was not long after this incident that Blikkies was found dead in the bushveld, on the Lodge grounds. He had been shot in the back by the police as he ran from his assailants. It was a sad loss and testimony to the complete lack of understanding between the local farmers and the indigenous Khomani people." Anna had smiled wryly as she shared their story.

Lisa couldn't help thinking about Ian and his many confrontations with fishing inspectors and police because of Crayfish and "Perlemoen" poaching.[19]

Many "Cape Coloured" or Khoikhoi fishermen who had historically and traditionally been fishermen by trade had also had their independent livelihoods curtailed because of the Conservation Fishing quota system. Nature Conservation organizations put this legal fishing quota in place to protect the extreme depletion of fish stocks by fleets of industrial trawlers in South African waters. This quota system favoured the commercial fishing industry and not independent local fishermen. Perhaps the saddest part of this story was the fact that so many "dispossessed" Cape traditional fishermen had resorted to poaching, petty crime, and drug dealing as a means of survival and to quell their sense of futility. It is these poachers and fishermen who found themselves being used as a smoke screen for the international drug cartels. It was this very same

---

19 Abalone or "Perlemoen," as it is commonly called in the Western Cape Province of South Africa, is an edible mollusc of warm seas with a shallow ear-shaped shell lined with mother of pearl. In recent years, Abalone from South Africa have been poached almost to extinction to supply a steady demand for this delicacy to the Asian market. The word Perlemoen is an Afrikaans word that derives from its description and use. "Perle," meaning "Pearl" and "Moena," meaning "sweetheart" or "lover."

sense of purposelessness, futility, and worthlessness that the Khomani Bushman hunter, Blikkies, had suffered.

The stay with Anna and Raaikat Blinkman was brief and over too soon. They had spent almost a week in the desert, and time had flown by. No TV, hardly any cell phone reception, no clean clothes or mirrors for glamorizing themselves with. Their involvement with the community and with one another was fulfilling enough. By the time the week was over, Lisa's lips were parched and chapped from the heat. She asked Anna for some vaseline to soothe them. Raaikat had just chuckled and muttered in Afrikaans, "Gaan kyk eers in jou eie hamelsak in."[20]

By now, Lisa was used to the rich symbolism and meaning that the Khomani imbued into their words, and she did not take Raaikat literally. But sure enough, when Lisa checked her handbag for anything vaguely soothing to put onto her skin, she found a small tin of "zambuk," a camphor-based soothing ointment. Raaikat smiled and spoke about how in the Bushman culture, a person carried their own "Hammel sak" or skin gathering bag. This referred to the bag that each person carried to gather and share whatever they came across in their day. The word had a double meaning. The Bushman hammel sak is the bag that carries the identity or personal belongings of each man or woman. Symbolically, the hammel sak represents to the Bushmen the life force, soul purpose, and responsibilities of an individual. The meanings vary and have many rich connotations.

Lisa was aware that Raaikat was making a very cutting observation about what her future held for her and that she needed to look carefully at her life. Her relationship with Ian was still not resolved. Raaikat had seen her heart. He knew Lisa still hoped for Ian's healing and that she wanted to give her lover a second chance to find himself, his purpose, and direction again. It was true, Lisa had a tough decision to make when she returned home.

20 Go and look in your own handbag.

HAMMELSAK

My hammelsak is so swaar
Prop vol,
Met alles wat ek nou dra
Dit voel asof die sterre en die maan
binne in my hammel sak geklim het
Ek dra almal saam
En buig
Met vreugde in my hart
Want my volle sak
Sal almal
Kan volmaak
My hammelsak is Leeg
Of ten minste dink ek so
En nou as ek na binne kyk
Is daar niks wat my angstig laat voel nie
Daar is net een ding daarin
iets wat sin maak
Van lewe
Dit laat my hart klop
Dit hou my aan die gang
Ek steek my hand in my sak
Om hierdie enigste ding te vind
Maar as ek daardie ding
Probeer vas hou
voel ek dat daar niks is om aan te klou
Dan sien ek
Ja dis waar
My hammelsak is leeg
En die werk is klaar!

(English translation)

My Gathering bag

My gathering bag is so heavy
It is full of everything that I carry
It feels as if the stars and the moon
have climbed inside my bag
I carry the cares of everyone with me
And I bend with joy in my heart
Because my full bag
Can fill every stomach
My gathering bag is empty
Or at least that's what I think
And now when I look inside
There is nothing to make me feel afraid
There is only one thing inside
that makes sense of life
And makes my heart beat
It keeps me going
I put my hand into my bag to find this special thing
But when I try to grasp it, there is nothing left
And I see, it's true
My gathering bag is empty
And my Life's work is complete

CHAPTER 6

A SECOND CHANCE

Life is often bittersweet. It is comforting to be encouraged, but much harder to let go of the past. Emotional baggage has first to be seen for what it is—lessons, experience, nothing more. Once you gain this insight, beautiful gifts are unlocked, and you can move on unburdened by the clutter of the past. These are life's precious secrets, available to all who seek them. Introspection is the key for those brave enough to dive deep and explore the soul. But yes, it does take courage!

When she arrived at the Adderley Street bus terminus in Cape Town, Ian was waiting for her. Lisa felt annoyed and embarrassed, but she was not surprised. He had left so many urgent messages, telling her that he wanted to meet and speak with her as soon as she returned. On the bus trip home, her girlfriends had planned a last dinner together at Charlie's flat, and Lisa was invited to join them. But when they saw Ian waiting there, her friends had looked at her knowingly and squeezed her hands.

As she got off the bus, Ian walked towards her quickly and took her bag. "Sorry to surprise you like this, Lisa," he said, beaming with mystery and excitement.

"But, but… Why are you here, Ian? I didn't expect this at all," Lisa said, looking completely bewildered.

"Ah, but I have got something special to tell you." Ian smiled his mischievous smile.

"But I don't want to leave my friends yet, Ian. I've just got back from a wonderful time together with them, and Charlie has invited us all to share a meal with her at her place tonight. You're welcome to join me and tell me about your news on the way there?" she said, feeling flustered and trying to keep her balance.

"I've simply got to tell you this privately, Lisa," Ian exclaimed excitedly. "Something incredible has come up! It's so amazing, so wildly beyond all imagination! And when you hear what it is, you'll understand why I've been waiting to share it with you for so long. I know it's sudden and that I'm asking a lot of you, but please give me a chance. Let me take you out for dinner tonight, please," he said insistently.

Eventually, Lisa relented. "Alright, Ian. If you will take me straight home afterwards," she said, closing her eyes and quietly sighing as she agreed to go with him. Ian whisked her away before her women friends could take up any more of her time. They all knew that they would see one another again, but Ian's eagerness, intensity, and insensitive manner had made her feel empty and hurt. It felt as if all the wonders, shared memories, and laughter of her trip had been eclipsed the moment that she stepped off the bus.

I knew then that I should have said no and told him the truth. But "if only's" are like butterflies in the wind and are very hard to catch. When I was a younger woman, I was an idealist and a dreamer. And like so many young women, a part of me desperately wanted a happy, stable relationship and a family. But I was trapped in a vicious cycle. One where I loved Ian, but in my heart, I knew that I would never change him. I already knew that I couldn't live with him because of his challenges. The truth was, I was also in denial. I was still looking for love in the wrong places and for the wrong reasons and hadn't yet realized the power I

*had, as a woman, to steer my own life uncompromisingly in the
healthiest direction, no matter what.*

That evening over dinner at a restaurant beside the crashing ocean, Ian took Lisa's hand and shared his life-changing secret. "Lisa, do you remember Uncle Otto? We had dinner with him once or twice at this same restaurant. Well, while you were away, I had a phone call from my wealthy friend's attorney. He told me that Uncle Otto had been suffering from liver cancer. Apparently, very few knew that he was suffering, and he never mentioned anything to me. He passed away recently at his home in Switzerland. According to his attorney, he has no family or children and has left his entire South African estate to me." Ian paused for a moment and took a deep breath. "Do you realize what this means, Lisa?" he asked, taking her by the hands and looking at her intensely. "It means that once the estate has been wrapped up, I can offer you a home and a comfortable life. I will be able to buy a fishing boat of my own, and I will become a millionaire many times over. Things will be different for us now that I have money coming to me, I promise you," he said with delight sparkling in his sea-green eyes.

Lisa was very quiet. She didn't know what to say. But she could hear the voice of reason and truth inside her whispering, *Only truth, love, and kindness will change everything, not money.*

"Why so quiet? What are you thinking, my beauty? Aren't you happy? Now we can get a home of our own, beside the sea or wherever you want to. You can paint to your heart's content. I expect the estate to be wound up and the inheritance will probably be paid sometime in the coming year. Then I'll be free to fish and write, and we can be together again without all the financial stress. In fact, without many worries at all."

Lisa felt tears well up inside her, but she tried to hide them from Ian. She knew that his problem with addiction was extremely serious—so serious that he would have to really step up to show that she could trust him again. "Wow!" she said with genuine astonishment.

Ian leaned forward and kissed her. "I love you, Lisa."

Lisa smiled at him through the tears that brimmed in her eyes. Maybe, just maybe, things could be better between them. Lisa was willing to hope.

It was a spring day, just after a rain, and all the forest was alive with bird calls and other insects and creature life. Crystal raindrops collected on leaves and fern fronds, hanging pendulously, waiting to drop onto the forest floor. The damp moss squelched under their feet. Lisa had gone for a forest hike looking for mushrooms with Ian. As they trudged along the green path, he spoke passionately about doing creative work encompassing his love of writing and nature. It was the right kind of day for open hearts, and Ian had shared the reason for his suffering and his deep sadness about both his parents.

"My Dad was such a loving father," he said in his slow drawl. "But Dad and Mom could never understand that I just needed to be myself and follow more creative pursuits. It was as though they just didn't see me or my talents at all. I felt as if they just didn't care about me enough. The things that I excelled in, like creative writing, water sports, biology, and fishing, held absolutely no value to them. My Dad believed creative careers weren't profitable. I was pressured into a world that I didn't fit into and ended up feeling disappointed. I wasn't the son my father wanted, the high achiever, the academic, the mechanical engineer, the rugby player, the army officer, or model son. I'm just a fisherman at heart, and I love the sea."

They were hiking through a beautiful fern and moss-filled forest clearing. Lisa had stopped walking at that point, and she sat down on a moss-covered log in the dappled sunlight.

"Ian," she said, looking up at him standing beside her. "You already have everything you've ever hoped for. There is no reason on earth that you cannot follow your dreams and be exactly what your soul most longs to be. Spend time really listening to what your heart is telling you. The answers are in here, not outside of yourself and certainly not in your past or in the bottle." Lisa looked up at him smiling, and added. "Your future is golden if you will only follow your heart and not allow all those misgivings to take up space in your head."

Along a path that leads us to vistas where we strive to see
Up along a path my love and me
Not close to edges but straight up high
Surefooted, circling to the mountain top
That trail, past brush
that grabs and stings our calves and slaps our thighs
Ducking under and over rock
The mountain is chanting to us and yet solitary
Vistas for the soul, prayer for the mind
Sons and daughters, a million years… buckets full of tears
We sit around this beauty, you and I
The world we gaze at our feet—laughing and talking as we do
Talking about high highs and low lows
Side by side we sit
Attraction without ages
You, me, and a mountain

Time rolls by, and quickly, the landscape changes. One decision,
a long-held desire made manifest, and everything changes again,
expands, and becomes richer and fuller than you could ever
dream.

Ian was making good progress on the 12-step Alcoholics Anonymous program. Sometimes he would come over to Lisa's flat after his group sessions and tell her about the many surprising people he had met who, regardless of their station in life, were all like him, battling to come to grips with alcohol addiction. "Lisa, these people make me feel like a human being again," Ian said one evening, "I've been three months now without a drink, and I'm not missing it. In fact, I'm feeling better than I've felt in years."

As his head cleared, Ian began to feel more confident and willing to interact with work and socially. Soon, his desire to dream again and express his creativity began to manifest as excitement. "I want to be involved and to make a profound difference in the world, Lisa. I've always loved writing stories and have wanted to share my knowledge about our oceans with children," he said, smiling at Lisa. It didn't take long before Ian decided to self publish a book about the sea life around their part of the South African coast. It was to have been the first of a series of children's books, written by Ian and illustrated by Lisa, with beautiful, simple water colours. They used colourful characters and local names to bring their story to life. The Fisherman named their first book, *Peter and the Magic Dolphin,* and it was not surprising that this heartfelt children's story won a national award and was later published for many children to enjoy. Ian designed his own letterhead and logo for his book series. It was a beautiful and simple message. Two words, written between two leaping dolphins. "Show Love," it said.

Manager at a Fancy Hotel

Ian was a fisherman at heart and always would be, but he knew he needed a steadier form of income than from fishing, poaching crayfish, and seasonal home maintenance. Something that would challenge him and give him a future to invest in. Ian had already applied as a manager at several hotels in the Cape Town area. "I'm going to blow you away, Lisa," he said on the phone one day.

"One of the top five-star hotels here on the Cape Peninsula coast has selected me, and once I've finished my training period, the sky's the limit. I'll have an inheritance and an incredible career. Perhaps we will even end up having our wedding at this seaside hotel someday, my beauty," Ian chatted to her happily on the phone, telling Lisa all the details of his experience. He was feeling as pleased as punch with himself.

The job required him to wear a dress suit and tie to work every day. Ian had pulled out all the stops to buy his manager's uniform, and Lisa had accompanied him to the outfitters in Cape Town to have the suit fitted perfectly to size. He tried on his smart black woolen dress suit and strutted around the shop, glancing at himself from time to time in the shop mirror. This was a whole new Ian. At last, he was on the road to healing his shattered self-esteem and bettering his life. He was shining, proud of himself, and so happy. The work at the Hotel would initially involve six weeks of intensive training to manage and oversee the restaurant kitchens. He would be working long hours for five days of the week and often until very late at night. This was Ian's ultimate test, and perhaps if he had been further down the road with the 12-step AA program, the training at the Hotel might have served him well. Management and staff were not allowed to drink alcohol at their workplace, and they were given three decent meals per day at the hotel. It was challenging work, and he was on the run for most of the day. The weeks and months passed peacefully, with Ian waking up early and working hard at his new hotel job. Everything seemed to be going well.

It was late one night when Lisa awoke to the sound of Ian's vehicle parking outside her flat. She heard his footsteps on the stairs outside, and the next moment, he stood at her door. Lisa remembered feeling a sense of foreboding. She hadn't wanted him to come over that night because she had been busy until late doing intricate work for her next exhibition, and she needed the creative space to focus. Ian had arrived fully clad in his dress suit, and she could see that something was wrong by the look on his face. "I've just walked out of the job at the Hotel," he said bluntly and parked himself down wearily on Lisa's bed. "I'm not going back to work there again. I've just had enough of working such long hours for next to nothing when I really don't have to. I know this is an internship opportunity, but I just don't like the vibe there. I don't enjoy the clients or the managers. They are all a bunch of toffee-nosed, pompous idiots."

It was one o'clock in the morning. Lisa was still feeling dazed and half asleep. Ian was clearly distraught and needed comfort. She felt disconcerted by Ian barging in on her, but her nurturing side overrode her grumpiness. She smelled the faint but distinct trace of spirits on his breath. Had he been caught drinking at the Hotel? Was he telling her the truth? She dismissed the thought, made him a cup of coffee, and let him talk. After a while, she suggested that he sleep on his decision, but Ian was adamant that he would never return to work at that hotel again. "I'll find another seasonal restaurant job equally as good and better paid and one where I won't have to put up with all that stupid hotel protocol," he said. Lisa felt devastated by his decision. It had been such a wonderful opportunity to get this management position with one of the Cape's top hotel groups. He had come such a long way on this healing journey, and he was just getting started with this new and responsible life.

"Of course," she responded. The fact that he had a lot of money coming to him was a factor working against his progress. Ian felt that with cash in his bank in the years to come, there would be no need to try to find permanent employment. She knew that if he gave up on his healing process now, it would be a very long downward slide. One that she was utterly unwilling to live through again.

Lisa listened to Ian with a gut-wrenching feeling in her stomach. Tears stung her eyes as the realization dawned on her that he had never wanted to be anybody's employee. He was a wild man, a Fisherman and an urban or "white Bushman," as her Kalahari Bushman friends Anna and Raaikat liked to call him, and he would never conform in any way. That night, as she watched him speak about the hotel's people and staff, it seemed to her that he was describing a space landing on another planet and his encounter with alien beings. Beings who, by his description, were so different and whose behaviors were so unlike his that he felt every moment spent in that environment would be utterly unbearable. And all this from a man born into an affluent home. One who grew up with parents, siblings, and friends who lived their daily lives soaked in an environment of South African prosperity and well-being.

Lisa couldn't help wondering what had made him react to working as a corporate hotel manager. Was it the environment, and because it simply wasn't the career for him, that he didn't fit the mold and had a different set of values than most who worked there? There was no doubt that Ian would have begun a very successful career and done very well for himself. The reaction of the hotel Director to Ian's decision to leave was to invite him into his private office and to offer him insider information about how hopeful the hotel board had been at the outset of his internship with them. The Director told him that within the week, they intended to offer him a full salary and an extremely responsible position. But Ian was too blinded by his objections and inner turmoil to care.

Perhaps you could say that this was the hand of fate. Perhaps you could say that the Fisherman had an important spiritual destiny to fulfill. One that took him deeper and into far darker places than many choose to go. However, it still left me wondering why he had such deep internal conflict. What lay beneath his sense of rejection and belief in unworthiness? Why that strong sense of envy for others who were successful? The unconscious "demons" and the ever-looming shadow of failure that haunted him. Ian

*was a golden soul, handsome, capable, bright, well-educated,
employable, and so good with people. I couldn't help asking the
obvious questions, "What happened to the Fisherman? What had
changed his perspective on life and affected his attitude like this?"*

*It was a question that would haunt me for many years to come.
And it was only much later that I found out exactly what had
happened to Ian. It was long after I had surrendered the search,
once I was older and wiser. It took me to know myself through
all the challenges life presented in the years that followed. I wish
I had known and understood more then. The truth is, it takes
suffering to crack open our hearts and to allow the golden light of
understanding to shine forth and guide us home to love.*

At the Bottle Again

Ian found another job. It was just a seasonal job, but with a
brand-new up-market restaurant on a Cape Town wine estate. It
was a beautiful restaurant situated on the slopes of the Constantia
mountains, under the old Cape oak trees, and he seemed very
happy working there. Ian was busy throughout the summer
months. And it gave Lisa the creative space that she needed to
prepare for her next Art exhibition.

It was soon after he had started his new job that she discovered
quite by accident that Ian had begun drinking again. He had
arranged to meet Lisa for supper after work at a quaint cafe just
down the road from an art gallery opening. The exhibition was
held at a studio gallery just off Kloof Street in Cape Town. Lisa
arrived early, intending to wait for Ian, but the art studio was
already packed with champagne-toasting Capetonians. It was too
full and too noisy, and Lisa felt jostled and very much out of place.
She squeezed herself through the crowded room to look at the art
on display. She loved the work. Each one of the oil paintings she
saw was sensitive and filled with light. Exquisite landscape work
evocative of the Cape fynbos and of ocean storms. She found
herself wanting to leave the crowded atmosphere and return to

appreciate the exhibition when it was quiet and she could enjoy it in peace. Lisa slipped silently out onto the shadowy pavement. The streets were so much cooler and quieter at that time of the evening, and she immediately began to relax. She wandered slowly up the road, admiring the interior decor window displays, and stood marveling at the colours of Table Mountain and Lions Head Peak in the warm glow of a twilit sunset. As she crossed the busy Kloof Street junction and approached the street cafe, she caught a glimpse of the Fisherman's van parked outside. Lisa was almost an hour early and had been expecting to order some coffee and wait for him. Instead, Ian was already there, sitting smoking, waiting for her in his vehicle. He looked up suddenly as she approached. His face changed and darkened when he saw her. There was a flurry of movement, and Lisa saw him rapidly cover something up and put it underneath his seat. Lisa walked around to the driver's side of his van. "Hey, I didn't expect to see you here so early," she said, smiling. "Come on, let's get a bite to eat at the cafe?" she asked, as he leaned over to open the passenger door to his van. Lisa climbed in and reached over to give him a hug, but Ian flinched and pulled away. She could sense the tension in him. It felt like wild electricity in the air.

There was a bottle of methylated spirits on the dashboard, and the smell of strong alcohol on his breath. Lisa's brow furrowed instinctively. She looked pointedly at him, and Ian became instantly defensive. "No need to get into a panic, Lisa. I was just cleaning my windscreen while I waited for you," he mumbled. "It's the smell of meths," he said, lighting up another cigarette.

"Okay, Ian. I'm hungry and in need of a coffee or a sandwich. Can we grab a bite together?" Lisa asked lightheartedly.

"I'm tired, Lisa. Let's just go home. It's been a long day," he said with a voice as heavy as lead. She knew that pattern of behavior all too well, but she kept quiet. Ian was silent all the way home. As they drove, her heart began to feel heavier with questions. As soon as they arrived, Ian parked on the roadside and immediately went upstairs for a shower without speaking to Lisa. As she got out, she quickly put her hand underneath the driver's seat in Ian's van and felt the slippery coolness of glass. It was a bottle of brandy. She pulled it out and brought it with her. Upstairs in the flat, Lisa put on the kettle and took out some mugs to make tea, then went through to the bedroom where Ian was sitting in bed, scrolling through messages on his cell phone.

"I found this underneath your seat, Ian," Lisa said with a wry look on her face and put the bottle down on the bedside table. It was obvious that he was avoiding her gaze. "I slipped up for a moment, that's all," he mumbled. Ian put his phone down on the bedside table and turned over to go to sleep.

The Fisherman's Shanty

The Autumn rains had returned. Her friends Raaikat and Anna Blinkman were coming to Cape Town for an exhibition of his artwork. "Ons nooi jou in vir hierdie vergadering, Lisa,"[1] Vetkat smiled his golden and wide toothless smile at her with a hand-rolled cigarette hanging from his lip. Lisa felt her heart swell with pride at being a part of such a special display of artworks by Raaikat and other Bushman/San South African-inspired artists. The exhibition was to be held at a coffee shop come art gallery, beside the sea in Kalk Bay. It was the perfect venue with wide open spaces and natural light on the walls, which contrasted the bright, pure colours of the Khomani San Art.

After his recent drinking incident, Ian tried hard to make it up to Lisa. He stepped up to support her and helped to have her work framed and delivered to the gallery. On opening night, he was there, looking handsome and dapper in his best corduroy jacket. Ian stood back, watching her closely and sending her knowing smiles whenever she looked his way. He knew that Lisa didn't like crowds and was particularly shy when it came to Art dealers.

---

1 We invite you to participate in this exhibition, Lisa.

"Who is the artist of these sensitively painted rock art pieces?" asked a burly man with a mustache and strong German accent. Lisa's work had caught the eye of a prominent Art dealer from Cape Town. "Wunderbaar! Wonderful reflections of South African San art, Lisa. I absolutely love your work. You are a most talented young woman." The art agent boomed and immediately bought all her most valuable pieces. Ian silently reveled in Lisa's creative success and world. In those peaceful days, he would adore her, bringing her bunches of wildflowers, freshly picked, bright pink Watsonias from the slopes of Table Mountain, and bright golden orbs of Leucospermum, the pincushion Protea. Lisa would smile, pick up her brushes, and soon beautiful artworks inspired by his indigenous floral gifts would pour out of her soul.

On the surface, and in public, everything seemed to be going well between Lisa and Ian. But in other ways, Ian's behaviour was still confusing and disturbing. His adoration for her so often translated to insecurity, extreme possessiveness, and insensitivity. "Ian!" she would burst out sometimes. "You've got to give me the creative space I need, if you want this relationship to flourish." But Ian was still too stuck within the old South African male chauvinist pattern to accept her boundaries or really listen to her. There were far too many inconsistencies that caused tension between them, and he was still in deep denial about the severity of the PTSD behind his drinking. What was most concerning to her was the fact that Ian was so possessive. He wasn't just jealous or protective of her in a tender, masculine sort of way. He was often scary, controlling, and abusive, especially when he drank. Not long afterwards, Ian decided to quit the AA program. "I won't need it anymore, Lisa. I'm managing fine without group support," he said with finality. This should have been enough warning for Lisa.

The next night was Lisa's birthday, and the Fisherman had invited her to come dancing. A fresh evening mist had enveloped the bay, and the gold lights of ships shimmered magically on the ocean through the haze. They shared a beautiful candlelit dinner, and then Ian took Lisa by the hand, and they danced until the early hours of the morning. It was one of those peaceful autumn nights, the same time of year when they had first met several years ago. Afterwards, they left the restaurant and walked hand in hand down to the beach together. The Fisherman leaned his broad back against a salty granite rock, and holding Lisa gently in his strong arms, he sang to her in that deep, crusty voice that she had always thought sounded like whale song.

> *"Whichever way life goes, I will always love you.*
> *However our love flows, I will always love you.*
> *No matter if you stay or go, I will always love you*
> *I will always love you; I will always love you."*

Somehow, the sea song made everything feel magical between them again, like it had been when they met. They made love with the sound of the ocean surging on the shore. They had always loved each other with a deep soul love, borne of great compassion and understanding. On this night, every touch and every kiss felt as though they were saying goodbye to one another. As if they both knew without word or explanation, that destiny was about to change both of their lives completely.

It was at this time that Lisa had a vision of a beautiful young girl who appeared in her dreams. The child had a wise, cherub-like face, framed with blonde curls and alight with the deep sea, blue eyes that gazed intently into hers. "Where is my father?" she seemed to be asking. When Lisa awoke, she knew unquestionably that this had been a vision of her own child, her own beautiful daughter of the future. And the question that her daughter was asking was prophetic of the sacrifice Lisa would have to make if she were to conceive the Fisherman's child.

Exactly a fortnight after my dream, I knew that I was pregnant again. All the signs were there. A part of me had desperately longed for this child and a family of my own. The other part conflicted with the truth, the reality I knew that I'd have to face if I were to stay with Ian. The Fisherman was not ready for parenthood, and neither was he ready for this, a pure soul relationship between us. It was simply too intense, too challenging, and immense. The reflection between us demanded emotional and spiritual growth and commitment to release everything that limited us and kept us both stuck: every belief, every excuse, and all the dependencies. Meeting Ian and being together had been an initiation for us both. As hard as I had fought to keep the flame burning between us, I also knew that accepting his challenges had almost destroyed me. Neither of us was ready for this. In the deepest part of my being, I knew that I would leave the Fisherman. And that I would have to raise this child alone, as best as I could without him. Gradually, this inner knowing became a deep acceptance in my soul.

She tried one more time to win him over, but it soon became apparent that it was pointless. Ian had relapsed and was drinking heavily again. He would arrive at her flat late at night, with the fiery smell of brandy on his breath, and Lisa would immediately recoil.

"What's the ma'rra, Lisa?" he would slur blindly.

Lisa's eyes would fill with tears of disappointment. Her heart ached to see him like this.

"Ian, why are you doing this to yourself? Why?" She implored with her whole heart. "We both know that this was a second chance for you to get the healing that you've so desperately needed. Please don't give up on us now!"

Ian would immediately retaliate. "There you go again. Mona Lisa. Moaning and criticizing again! I'm not in the mood for this conversation." He'd pick up his bag and leave.

In those days of hope and disappointment, there was nothing more that I could do or say. I had already done it all, said it all. I knew why he had given up and opted out of society, and I didn't blame him. I didn't fit into this world either, and it had stopped mattering to me. In those precious few sober months together, sharing our hearts on the beach or in the small hours of the morning, we had spoken about not fitting in. Ian was a star, a burning sun, inspiring me on this subject. "Why would anyone bother trying to fit into this cruel, patriarchal, insane world?" he would exclaim passionately. "I'd rather be a trendsetter and fit 'out' than fit in." And I would feel so proud of him for daring to be different. Except Ian couldn't shake off the sense of shame he carried with him everywhere. He drank because of it, because he believed that he was a disappointment and a failure and that nothing he ever did was good enough.

No matter what I did to show Ian I believed in him, he had stopped believing in himself and simply would not take the steps to self-empowerment. He was still so blinded by deep trauma, anger, and denial that he could not listen or understand what I was trying to show him. My maternal instincts took over, and a whole new life began with my baby at its center. Nothing and no one would ever step in the way of motherhood and what needed to be done. Life would be about my child and me, from that time onward: a Lioness mother and her Lion cub.

I am beginning again
Beginning to wax like a new moon
I am beginning again
Can I begin?
Dare I start?
Where do I start?
Who would care if I did?
If I stand up and carry on going?
Would you?
Why should I pick myself up from the dirt and
sludge of shame?
And poke my head out and see
What possibly lies ahead
Why when all that has come to pass
Has disappointed, hurt, and broken me?
Still, I am beginning again
A tiny plain start
A Future Vessel
a single hope
a flame to
Light the dark
Who would care if I did?
Why I would
I would care again
Who would change or what would be
If I begin again
If I begin again
If I begin to dream again
Everything begins again
in the end

CHAPTER 7

GOODBYE TO THE FISHERMAN

I knew that I was by no means ready, but I was already well on my way to discovering what it would take for me to be a mother and a single-earning parent. Everything that I was doing flew in the face of acceptable family tradition—my choice to leave the Fisherman and carry this child, to become a single mother, and to continue to be true to myself as an artist and as a woman.

Lisa saw him one last time on the beach. He was sitting on the grass overlooking the sea, smoking, and looking angry and uncomfortable. It felt as if they had already had this conversation, as if he knew what Lisa had come here to say. There was none of the usual warmth and tenderness between them, and Lisa could see by his body language that Ian didn't want to be there. The conversation immediately grew heated when she brought up the issue of addiction and the fact that she would not accept a future that included his lifestyle.

"Ian, there's something that I think you should know," she said after a long silence. "I'm pregnant again." Ian said nothing, but she could sense through his coldness and discomfort that this was not something he wanted to hear. "I don't think either of us wants to go through what happened the last time," she said quietly and truthfully.

Ian sounded like a trapped animal. "So exactly what do you expect from me, Lisa?" he said, taking a long draw of his cigarette. "Why do you want to have a baby now, for God's sake? You might want that life, but I don't," he spat back at her. "Do you really expect me to change to become the person you want to suit your life? Haven't we been through this before? I told you that it's my choice to live the way I do, underneath the radar. It's my choice to continue this lifestyle, and if you want to know the truth, I don't ever want to change. I'm going to drink, smoke, and have the freedom to do whatever I choose to do, no matter what. And I'm not going to live by your standards of normal or with society's fucked-up rules and laws. You're never going to stop me or change me." Ian stubbed his cigarette out on the ground furiously in front of him. "You know, Lisa, if you really did love me, you would understand and accept that." He got up, turned his back, and stormed off as he would always do whenever there were difficult issues to settle. Lisa knew that he was, in his way, utterly right about this being his choice and his journey. But what the Fisherman was not yet ready to accept was that his choice spelled an inevitable splitting of ways for them both.

Lisa sat there for an eternal moment, staring out at the stormy, wintry ocean. She felt emptied of all feelings as if all the breath and life had suddenly been sapped out of her. She was floating, completely body-less and without the desire to do, think, or say anything. She had no idea how long she sat there—perhaps half an hour, perhaps an hour had passed. Then she heard herself softly murmuring the words that formed the only reasonable thought inside of her. "Dear God, what would you have me do now?"

Slowly, Lisa stood up. "You will carry on. You must carry on!" she heard the quietness in her heart and soul say silently. She closed her eyes. "I will!" she said under her breath and then turned to go.

Lisa pressed ahead with her exhibition plans for the National Arts Festival, using the time away to reflect on her work and values. As her pregnancy progressed, she began to feel more sensitive and extremely directed. She didn't miss Ian at all in the days to come and began to have fun on her own again. Once she'd closed her art exhibition for the day, she went out into the streets of Grahamstown to enjoy the festival. She bought tickets to see shows, went to see other exhibitions, shopped at street markets, and ate festival food. In many ways, Lisa wasn't alone. She could feel the presence of her child growing in her womb. There were certain sounds and smells that she simply couldn't deal with, so Lisa relaxed and adapted to being fully present to her pregnancy. It felt good to be independent again, regardless of not having a car. She was working so hard to save enough to buy a decent vehicle, and she was almost there. Every painting sold was another step closer to her goal.

The Fisherman sent her one last text message on her cell phone. "Lisa, I know you still love me." It was a message that went unanswered. She didn't contact him again. Unwavering and with courage fixed on the future, Lisa walked into single motherhood and into the unknown. She kept a tiny flame of hope burning against all odds that he might come back, but along with her hope came a strong inner knowing that if he did, the reality of his addiction and abusive behaviour would accompany him like a shadow and with it, his violent rage. Lisa knew that the Fisherman would not keep his word, nor would she ever be able to trust him with this child of the future. Not in his current condition, and definitely not with her in this delicate stage of pregnancy and motherhood. Her decision was firmly made, and there was no going back. It was this firm resolve that made her commitment to single parenthood seem much easier than she knew it would be. She knew that the financial load that most parents could afford would be far too heavy for her alone. Lisa also knew that she would be left scrambling for a foothold into that world, somehow trying to make ends meet where they would not.

A Psychic Named "Buzz"

On her return to Cape Town, Lisa's friend Debbie phoned and offered her a flight to Johannesburg. "Lisa, you're freaking out. I know that you're facing an enormous challenge, but just take a breather, girl. Get away, get some perspective, and come and stay with us," Debbie suggested. "There's somebody I would like you to meet while you are here. He is a Spiritual Healer, and I believe that this man could help you considerably with what you have been through and will have to face in the future." Lisa knew Debbie and her husband Frank well. They had bought many of her paintings throughout the years. She gratefully accepted their offer and took the flight to Johannesburg.

The mysterious man that her friend wanted her to meet was a well-known South African psychic, therapist, and counselor named Buzz Everest. Frank and Debbie had visited him several times during their marriage. He lived in a quiet leafy suburb of Johannesburg on the edge of Delta Park, quite close to Braamfontein spruit. His home was a cool, green sanctuary, surrounded by shady willows and Jacaranda trees. Buzz was sitting on a garden bench, waiting for her in the shade of the trees, when Lisa arrived. He took one look at her and read her shattered energy field. "Aha, you're here," he said simply, looking at her with his piercing gaze. He made Lisa comfortable in his warm therapy studio, then immediately began using Reiki healing techniques on her. Lisa lay on the padded massage bed in the softly lit room and watched the bird-like man flit around her as he gathered and cleared the many layers of dark, negative energy from her aura.

Lisa had not given Buzz any details at all about her situation. Nevertheless, he had intuited her pregnancy and picked up immediately that she had been in the atmosphere of somebody who drank spirits and smoked marijuana. As he moved around her, he pointed out the various blockages and the sticky, dense energy around her body. Lisa could smell sage and other herbs burning in a bowl to clear her aura. Buzz was using the smoke to "smudge" with, in the same way that Bushmen and African Sangma's used these herbs to cleanse a person's energy field. As Lisa lay quietly, she heard the repeated, clear, high-pitched tone of a Tibetan crystal bowl sounding gently to raise her vibration. It was quiet in the room for a while, and Lisa lay there slowly drinking in the sense of light that had replaced the heaviness of her heartbreak. Buzz let her relax for a while, just breathing in and out slowly and listening to the delicious sound of waterbirds singing in the garden outside. Then he helped her to sit up gently and drink a glass of water.

"We are finished here for now," he said with a gentle smile. "I've removed quite a hefty load of dark energy from your entire auric field. You should start to feel a lot better, although I'd imagine you will feel quite lightheaded for a while. I hope you've arranged a lift home."

Lisa smiled weakly. She was feeling rather strange. It was as though she were bouncing instead of walking on the ground. "Come and sit over here with me for a moment. You are going to need some firm guidance for your situation from what I can see." Buzz pulled out a chair for her and chatted with her gently about the reality of her circumstances.

"Lisa, while I worked on your energy field, I picked up that you have recently undergone a situation of extreme conflict," Buzz said solemnly. "It seems that this has involved your partner and may be affecting your family as well. My dear, you are going to have to become very realistic about what you are facing presently," the old man said earnestly. "You must realize that this is no ordinary situation. Your partner is an addict, I take it. I picked up severe alcohol abuse, which makes this situation even more sensitive, and I can see that you have been in a dangerous position, one where you literally could not move left or right without your partner controlling you. Given your choice to be a single parent and the severe psychological challenge your ex-partner faces, it would be better to prepare yourself with a very solid legal protection document," Buzz paused to let the import of his words settle with Lisa.

Lisa looked up, astonished by his words. She knew that her choice to leave Ian was necessary, but she hadn't yet fully understood how critical these steps were for her safety, well-being, and the health of her unborn child. Buzz continued. "A legal interdict will enforce that the father of your child undergoes the full process of safe access, with the consultation of social workers to monitor his level of sobriety."

At the time, the councilor's advice had seemed daunting, but Lisa fully understood the implications of her situation. What Buzz told her that day was true. Ian was an extremely possessive and aggressive man, and she knew she would need to protect herself and her child immediately. Lisa's leonine mothering instinct kicked into full action.

She went through the court system feeling utterly nauseated. The whole business of going to the state family violence protection court in Cape Town and waiting for hours in dank corridors to see the magistrate felt unreal to her. Eventually, it was all done, and the interdict was granted and sealed. There was such a wonderful sense of victory and relief once the paperwork was cleared. Lisa was entirely on her own now. She had accepted that this was to be a solo journey for her child and herself. And although she felt utterly daunted at the prospect of single motherhood, she was also covered in the golden glow of early pregnancy and the hopes and dreams she had for her child.

Within two months, she had found a beautiful sunny flat quite close to the seaside in a quiet and safe suburb of Cape Town. Her flat looked out onto the vast Atlantic Ocean. It was perfect. Lisa felt supported and surrounded by caring friends and family members. Moving into her new home was a wonderful steppingstone, and for the first time in a long while, she felt a warm sense of herself. She had found a cocoon of safety for both her and her baby. The flat was already furnished and had rose-patterned curtains for the glass sliding doors that opened onto the sea. Lisa was blissfully happy here. Her creative and fertile imagination had found a space to regenerate and grow.

The next step was a leap of faith. It came as an opportunity from an unexpected source. A friend of the family was going abroad and had suggested that Lisa put in an offer to buy her almost brand-new car. It was a plain white Ford, comfortable and reliable, so Lisa took the chance and paid the deposit immediately. Everything seemed to be falling effortlessly into place. An international client had commissioned her to paint a large frieze of rock art for a considerable fee. Exhibition and gallery sales kept on raining in. She had always been conservative with money, and in this way, she kept her savings account filling up in preparation for the months when her baby would be born and when it would be less possible to focus on work. In between paintings, she used her time well to keep her body healthy. She walked and swam and stretched and rested as much as she could. And she fed her craving for her favourite foods like nuts and berries and fresh vegetables. The initial nausea of morning sickness slowly melted away, and she was left with a glowing sense of well-being.

Winter came and went, with routine check-ups with a warm and highly respected gynaecologist. On one of these early visits, she had the wonder of seeing the ultrasound pictures of her unborn child. On every screen, her tiny little child would pop her head up and raise her open hand as though she was waving hello. The last of these shots showed her child kneeling in a prayer position on the floor of her womb.

The days went by quickly as Lisa's body rounded and smoothed out like a waxing moon. She was at peace with her pregnancy. Everything seemed to flow now, gently and gracefully, to their destination—to the birth of her child.

The Fisherman's Child

One winter morning, Lisa was reading the village newspaper on the couch in the sunshine when she saw a notice posted about a community gathering in the local Hout Bay town hall.

"Come and join the Imagine Cape Town discussion, folks!" the newspaper article said. Lisa decided she would attend; after all, she had nothing to lose. The local town hall was filled with people from all walks of life, all of whom wanted to contribute meaning and value to the community. Khoikhoi Rastafarians, Hout Bay churchgoers, Buddhists, Rotarians, nature lovers, animal lovers, African men and women from the local Imizamo Yethu township, paramedics, police officers, business owners, and other members of the public were present. The meeting was directed by a most unusual woman from the United States of America. She was the very first Anglican minister ever to be ordained into the church. Reverend Cindy was introduced briefly to the crowd and then took the floor. She explained that hugely positive social and global change could be possible in Cape Town within vulnerable local communities. She spoke enthusiastically about how individual members could harness the power of imagination and work collaboratively to bring about such change. Once Reverend Cindy had spoken, the local folk were separated into groups that addressed various skills and talents. Lisa found herself among creatives, artists, performers, and writers. At that point, she had no concept or desire to put any of her talents or ideas into the pool for discussion, but as she listened to the group leaders, a seed began to grow in her soul.

The day after the Imagine Cape Town discussion, a powerful vision came to her to direct a Christmas Narrative production as street theater for the whole community of Hout Bay. She telephoned the imagination program convener and suggested that they meet. A lively South African woman named Marie listened to Lisa's suggestion and immediately agreed that they should plan a meeting at the convener's home in Hout Bay.

Lisa arrived well prepared for the meeting. She had made sketches and written a basic script to illustrate her ideas.

"Here it is." Lisa laid out her vision on the dining room table at her host's house. "This is the script that I have envisioned and written. The project is centred around a contemporary Christmas narrative entitled 'The Fisherman's Child.'" She took out the sketches, notes, and some hand-carved wooden Khoisan puppets and showed them to the Imagine Cape Town team. "I have been inspired to write a play which comprises several vignettes. It's a straightforward, impactful story based on the 'Holy Nativity,' except here, Mother Mary, Joseph, and the Christ child are of Khoisan origin. The Nativity is set in the local fishing community and in contemporary times. The play will require a children's dance group, a children's choir, and musicians. I realize that this is a very courageous project for anybody, let alone a pregnant artist." Lisa smiled and laughed and the Imagine Cape Town team smiled with her.

The Imagination convention team, led by Reverend Cindy, had a brief conversation between all the conveners. Lisa's drawings and ideas were discussed and finally accepted.

"Lisa," Marie said, looking at her in admiration. "We all love it! The concept, the script, and the community-bridging potential. We are behind you all the way." Marie smiled while the small group gathered, Reverend Cindy, and Lisa's host all nodded with enthusiastic agreement.

It was September when she began planning the nativity. Lisa felt that she was being lifted and carried throughout the days of preparation, as she gave her time and focus to this community-building project. She had no idea where to begin, let alone who she should approach to help bring this production to fruition. She was introduced to the production team for a local community dance program that raised funds to teach disadvantaged street children. Lisa drove out to Hout Bay and met the young dancers and their instructor at their studio at the Hout Bay Harbour. She was also introduced to a violin and cello program for disadvantaged children. All these incredible pieces of the puzzle seemed to fit so naturally and effortlessly together. Lisa's tiny baby seemed to thrive on the social interaction and positive vibes of collaboration and was growing healthier and stronger in her womb every day. The Christmas play rehearsals came and went. The Imagination team and local Rotarians helped Lisa pay for refreshments, logistics, and taxi fare so that all the township musicians and dance crew could practice together at the planned venue. As Christmas approached, lights were put up on the biggest fir tree in the village square. It was here, underneath this magnificent evergreen tree, beside an old, shipwrecked trawler that the children rehearsed their performance. Gradually, the Nativity grew into a magical production.

Finally, the evening of the performance arrived. A huge crowd of Hout Bay locals gathered to watch and sing Christmas carols. The children of the Imizamo Yethu Township Choir were positioned together under the old fir tree beside the violin and cello orchestra. The dancers and children were dressed in their costumes and ready, waiting in the wings to take the stage in front of the old fishing trawler in the town square. The violin ensemble started to play. Candles were lit. The Christmas sermon was said, and without any further direction from Lisa, the angelic township children began to sing and share the message of Christmas. The magic of the acoustic violin and the children's choir floated across town, in the starlight and moonlight and under the old fir tree. The children danced on the cobbled village street where all could witness the birth of a Khoisan Christ child into the heart of their fishing community. The simple performance was breathtaking, poignant, and sweet with innocence—it was the kind of evening that no one could ever forget. Then just as suddenly, the magic was over. Slowly, all the musicians packed away their instruments, and the children were fed with slices of warm pizza from the nearby pizzeria before being taken home in a taxi. Gradually, the crowds drifted away from the village square, leaving Lisa the last to leave the town square.

After the festivities had ended, I stood in the empty village square with my heart open wide, savouring the feelings of contentment and joy. I placed my hand on my swollen belly and whispered to my unborn baby, "Well, this was our very first Christmas together, my darling one." And I smiled wistfully, closing my eyes and wishing with all my heart that the Fisherman were standing beside us. "I'm here," I felt her presence say to me, and my own heart answered, "Yes, I know my child, and little did anyone guess that it was you who were my inspiration. And that you are 'The Fisherman's child.'"

It is easy to fall in love
In love
where you burn with a million questions
Like candles
The answers beckon
Will you love them too?
It is easy to fall in Love
to keep falling
into infinity
That's not so easy
for we are afraid
of what we are
It is easy to be in Love
With you
Out there
Unsure, unaware
But me
Would I still be in Love

If I could see myself
Merge with you
Sat Chit Ananda
If I could see myself in you
Would you guide my soul
To a million answers
Would your eyes speak like candles
burning with the questions
Your soul yearns to learn
Or as the sleeping world does
Shall we forget to wake
shall we fall yet forsake
our souls searching
The expression of eternity
All our love
Yes, it is easy
to fall in love again
but to be alive
in Love, to be in Love, in Love
hmm, that takes something
hmm that takes love

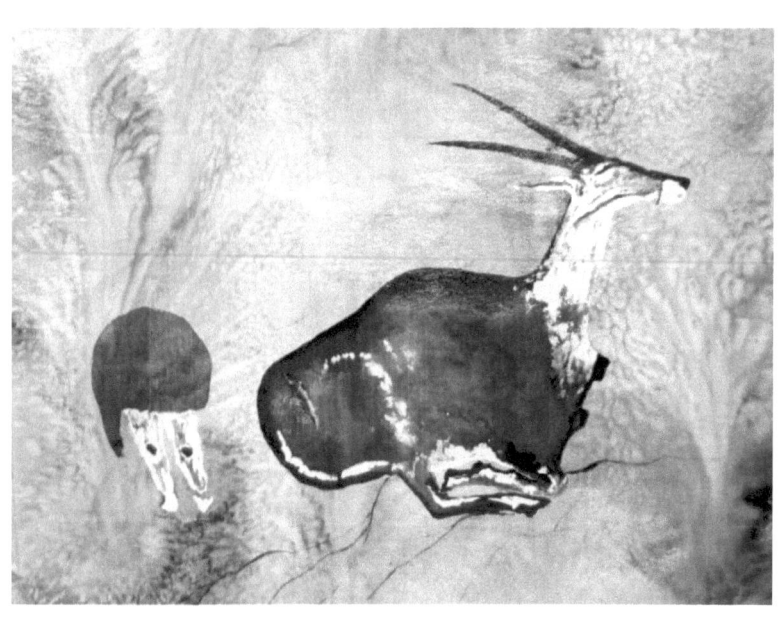

CHAPTER 8

The Fisherman's Child is Born

A thousand kisses deep, skin softer than a peach,
colour of peace, child asleep.

*Life is about cycles, rhythms, and ever-deepening. Do we ever
really complete these cycles? Or do they just become deeper and
wider as we evolve and finish one revolution of our life after
another? I had already been through several cycles in my life,
career, and in relationships with those I loved. Each time a
relationship ended, I felt shattered and rejected. But this time,
it was different. It was over—completely and forever. This cycle
was over! I had learned a painful lesson. That nobody can change
another unless and until the other is ready. I would not allow
myself to look back and hope for a repeat of the things that had
happened between me and the Fisherman. The terrible shock
waves that were the after-effect of having a relationship with an
alcoholic had been so intense. The new cycle seemed so different
from any other in my life, and it had only just begun. Gradually,
I felt the strength and courage return and rebuild within my
heart. I had widened my world and stepped into a new and more
peaceful rhythm. The reality of becoming a single mother was*

yet to dawn on me, and many old family patterns had yet to be addressed. One of these was my habit of carrying emotional responsibility for others and overcompensating to mask my hidden sense of worthlessness.

I knew that I was by no means ready for motherhood, but I was already well on my way to discovering what it would take to become a single parent. Everything that I was doing, my choice to leave the Fisherman and carry this child to term, my choice to become a single mother, flew in the face of most South African family values. This offset the old patriarchal, Calvinistic, and judgmental attitudes about women who divorced or went out on their own as single parents. I had grown up within a family and a community that considered those who challenged traditional family values to be "disruptors," controversial women of questionable morals and standards. All too often, children of single parents were regarded as the offspring of unstable backgrounds. Traditional families were reluctant to entertain children with struggling single parents and so-called "broken homes" for fear that they might introduce perspectives that contrasted too differently with their own. For me, all that mattered was that I would be there for my child with all the love and commitment that I was capable of. I knew that no parent would ever be perfect, no matter how much financial stability there was. And from my experience growing up in an affluent family, I knew that the more money, pressure, and distraction there was, the less quality time and love there often was, too. Although I expected South Africans to be conservative in their values, still, it took living a life that was challenging to the maximum to discover just how parochial and conservative my own family and community could be.

One evening, Lisa turned on the TV and caught the beginnings of what seemed like an interesting movie. It was a romance, her favourite. She wrapped a blanket around herself and curled up on the couch to watch. The story described an angel who had chosen to live on Earth and how he had fallen in love with an Earthling woman. Suddenly, Lisa was filled with the image of the angelic child of her vision. A little girl with cheeks as soft as a peach. It was the very same child that she had seen in her dream before she fell pregnant. At that same moment, Lisa knew without a doubt that her child would be a girl and that she would call her daughter "Kathleen"—after her beloved grandmother.

She often felt the presence of the Fisherman when she was alone. She still wore the whalebone necklace that he had made for her. But he never came to her, not then and not in the days that were to follow. He was caught between sobriety and a netherworld where all things were lit up in phosphorescence and where life merges with the spirit realm. Slowly, the Fisherman faded beyond this story, leaving the taint of strong spirits and glowing dust on everything he touched. Like a Cheshire cat with its wide grin, the Fisherman disappeared from Lisa's life.

Lisa grew round and ripe like the full moon. February came, and she saw the whales more often. Fish clouds swam past her windows when she woke. The constellation of Pisces arrived, and her soft, tender, peach blossom daughter—the child of their love—was born.

This is where the story *really* begins—from dreams into waking, from innocence and naivety into motherhood. On a hot South African summer night, without very much complaint and with more of a gentle coo of pleasure, Lisa's daughter arrived, healthy and glowing, shining with all the love her mother felt for her. And as anyone who truly knows the journey of a single mother, into a life where every thought and act determines the way things blend, as mother and daughter.

Lisa woke up the next morning in a comfortable hospital ward bed. The early morning sunlight had begun pouring its golden rays between the cracks of the curtains, and already the hospital ward was bathed in a warm, golden glow. The entire ward was filled with roses and flowers of every kind from her family and friends. There was no sound, but she could sense her child's presence. Lisa opened her eyes and blinked. Next to her bed, lay her daughter in a cozy, white cotton blanket.

She was looking at Lisa, with her baby blue eyes, in that all-embracing and penetrating way that was so much a part of her nature. In this moment of silence, tears began to form in Lisa's eyes. This tiny, healthy baby was a soul that she knew well and loved. Baby Kathleen seemed to be smiling with every cell of her body, aware of and seeing her mother looking at her. It was as if she already knew her Mother and that she was wordlessly celebrating their reunion. Tears of joy flowed down Lisa's cheeks, unchecked as she lifted her child tenderly and gently from the crib next to her bed and held Kathleen close to her heart.

I am round like the moon
Everywhere
No part of me is unwhole
The outside world
Has an empty place
That has been awaiting you
And my round full body
Holds you in readiness
To come into
This heavenly space
Out of thought
And seed
And growth into
Life on Mother Earth
Welcome to you
Great soul
Child
Of the New Dawn

There was a time when Lisa hated the Fisherman so much. She cursed him with a woman's vengeance, with the powerful curse of an angry mother. "Strip him and take away his false power and pride," she uttered the curse at the mountains before she knew what she had said. Every shadow, every glimpse of him was not only reviled but feared. Until one day, there came a day when she felt his shadow melt into the bush that lined the street. "Come out, Fisherman," she called, facing her bitterness and fear. "It's time for you to see the child you sired." A stillness followed and then a stir, and slowly out he came. He wore a salmon pink women's jersey over his fishing pants and boots. The pink woolen knit was decorated with pretty roses. This was a most unusual contrast, but not entirely out of kilter for him.

By then, their beautiful, fair-haired baby daughter was a few months old and was already very aware of her world. Lisa lovingly scooped her daughter up into her arms and offered the bundle for the Fisherman to hold. "This is our child," she said simply.

He took her onto his chest and looked down at her with wonder in his eyes. In the minutes and seconds that followed, the Fisherman held his child and stared. His little daughter looked back at him with the sweet innocence of her baby smile, her tiny, fat fingers playing with the knitted roses on his chest. Then, the Fisherman drew in his breath—a deep and inward sound, as the innocence of heart to heart caught him completely unaware. He could not shut out his child; he could not keep her out. He could not pretend that she was not his. He saw and felt the kinship in the beat of his heart next to hers. She was his as he was hers, and his heart began to melt. His bearded face softened with his smile, and his tears began to fall. "Oh, my heart," he said, looking over at Lisa. "She has opened it, and it hurts."

Lisa looked upon the two of them. The union of a natural father and his only child. She knew that the journey was his and had to be hard-won by him and by him alone. Yes, he was Kathleen's father by blood, but he had so much inner work to do to truly be a father.

This Fisherman had things to say to Lisa that she needed to be true. She needed to see the practical stuff done now and to meet their real needs; the money to be well spent on what their daughter needed and not on his addictions anymore. She had been too badly scarred by the pain of living with an alcoholic to be blind any longer. These storms were not for a little child, a beautiful daughter such as this. The anger caused by insecure and shame-filled emotions did not belong here in a baby's world. Lisa looked at him with a long, measured look. "Perhaps, Ian, by now you know the need. We have spoken often and at great length about this. You are her father, but it is your choice," she said softly, taking their child from him. Her beloved daughter did not look back at all. She didn't know her Dad then and had only felt an immense comfort to be in his arms and to smile into those deep, sea-blue eyes and at that craggy face.

As Lisa turned to leave, she heard his whale rumble of a voice. "Tell me, what did you call our child?" he asked. "Kathleen," she answered.

"Ahhhhh!" he exclaimed with eyes closed.

"Lisa-Kathleen," he smiled, eyes brimming with tears. He shouldered his canvas bag and left.

I have waited for you for countless years
Come to terms with my fears
You are not coming home
Because neither you nor home exists
Only my desire for you and home
And my belief in the lack of you
And the lack of home
My faith in waiting
The Waiting Game
Is over

"Game over"
I admit defeat
I will never win
you will never come
And home will never be
While I play this game
And so, I have started a New Game, Voila!
One in which I am the Game called Love
The operator and the creator
I decide
No more waiting,
I am home
And the rules are Love
What I desire becomes my experience
I Follow my bliss
And so it is, and so it is

CHAPTER 9

CAMAGU UBABA VUSAMAZULU

Sawubona is an isiZulu African greeting that means, "We see you. We care about you. Our ancestors and our ancient lineage honour you." Sawabona is about humanism. It is an invitation to deep witness and presence. We invite each other to recognize, communicate, and explore the possibilities of how we can help each other in this space where we are meeting. Here, no one is above another. We are all chosen. The ancient way starts with Sawubona and becomes true service to one another. By seeing and hearing one another, we are shedding light in our lives. A light that brings us all into existence.

For the first weeks of baby Kathleen's life, there were praying mantises flitting around them everywhere. It was warm in March with long, sultry evenings and beautiful sunsets lingering in the sky for hours. Often, Lisa noticed three tiny green mantises that would settle at the edge of her baby's crib at night, one at the head of her crib and two at each end. Lisa could feel the spirit of the Bushman people gathering around her to protect her as she went through this difficult passage of early motherhood alone and without the natural support of a family.

At first, Kathleen was a quiet, easy baby to care for. Lisa was breastfeeding and caring for Kathleen naturally, and her milk flowed easily. But after a while, without any support, Lisa began to feel run down. There was no one around her to give her any time to rest. She tried everything to keep her breast milk flowing, but without enough deep sleep, the problem became worse. Baby Kathleen wasn't getting enough milk. Within days, her child became anxious, and colic set in. Lisa began feeding her milk formula to give herself time to replenish. There was something that Lisa could do. She drove her baby and herself to the nearby fishing village in Hout Bay, where some time ago, she had met a caring and very capable woman named Miriam. Khoikhoi women like these were rare pillars of strength within their communities, especially Miriam and her Church Elder Sister, Eve. They lived in one of the original fishing cottages overlooking Hout Bay Harbour. Miriam was ironing in her kitchen with an enormous pile of clean washing beside her when Lisa arrived at their tiny house in the fishing community. She recognized Lisa immediately.

"Ag sies tog, and who do we have here?" she asked, peering through her glasses at three-week-old baby Kathleen. Lisa sat down at the kitchen table and chatted to Miriam while she did her ironing. The gentle, full-bosomed Khoi woman put the kettle on the hob and made a strong, sweet cup of Rooibos[1] tea for Lisa. Baby Kathleen gurgled and seemed peaceful and content in Miriam's company. She was completely calm and quiet for a change.

"I really could do with some help looking after Kathleen," Lisa said, looking up at Miriam. "I can see that I need a little time to rest, get on with work, and build up my strength. Being a single mother has already been a tough journey."

"Ek weet dis so, Mevrou Lisa. Om enige moeder te wees is dit baie moeilik as daar nie help is,[2] I will come and help you twice a week," Miriam said with a gentle smile.

"Oh, thank you. I am so grateful," Lisa said as she stood up to go. She knew that Miriam was the kind of woman she could completely trust with her child.

The dreams started to come back again once Lisa had begun

---

1 Red bush
2 It is very difficult to be a mother without support.

to catch up on sleep and regain her strength. At first, she dreamed about Raaikat and Oom Haasie. The two Bushmen had arrived at her front door in an old, battered car and left a letter on her dresser. The letter was written in clear, penciled script and said that the Bushmen folk missed her company and would like to meet baby Kathleen. The dream kept on recurring for about three nights in a row. It was around the same time when Raaikat's wife, Anna, arrived from the Kalahari to visit her family in Cape Town. Lisa had gone to fetch her friend from the bus station, and that night over supper, she spoke about the dreams she'd been having with Anna. She smiled her slow, deep, Khoi smile, looking at Lisa with her beautiful, hooded eyes. "Maybe you have to listen to the call if your heart pulls you to do so," she said thoughtfully.

"I can't leave home now, Anna. Not with Baby Kat still so small and vulnerable," Lisa answered her. "But if I ever do get back to the desert, I would like Raaikat and our Khomani friends to do the sacred star ceremony for Kathleen and to teach her about Great Spirit and the Bushmen ancestors. I feel that this is something that must be honoured. It would mean that you and Raaikat would become Kat's spiritual Godparents, Anna."

The slender, dark-eyed Anna smiled and silently nodded, looking with deep affection at little Kat. "Dit sal 'n groot plesier wees,"[3] she said softly. Lisa knew that both Anna and Raaikat could not have children of their own.

"Lisa," her Khoisan friend said after some thought. "The Great Prophet and Sanusi, Ubaba Vusa Amazulu, has been asking us for some time if they could come and visit our home. He would like to journey here and meet with the Khomani elders while he still has strength. He is almost 90 years old, and I know how strongly he feels that the old traditional ways should not be forgotten. Before he dies, he would like to travel to the Great Kalahari Desert to meet with those Bushmen who remain. He has often said that those Khomani Elders who still have a heart

---

3 That would be a great pleasure.

for this path should gather and tell their stories together before they are all lost to the wind."

Baby Kathleen was only a few months old at this time. Lisa held her on her lap and smiled into her baby's sparkling sea-blue eyes. "Kat, what would you say to the journey of a lifetime, in an aeroplane to meet the Great African peacemaker and author Vusamazulu?" Kathleen gurgled and smiled a toothless smile at the two women friends as they sat outside chatting.

"Anna, do you think that my dream has to do with this gathering, perhaps? I suppose we could make a phone call to his wife, Mama Martha, and ask if she and Baba Vusa would like us to arrange their transport to the Kalahari. I must speak with Mama soon to tell them of the birth of baby Kathleen, and I will mention this gathering. If they are both keen to have this meeting in the Kalahari, then perhaps it is time to set the wheels into motion."

Her Khoi friend, Anna, laughed at Lisa's enthusiasm. "Ag jurre, Lisa, jy's altyd so vol blydskap vir die hele blerrie wereld.[4] Do as your heart shows you to do, but make sure you and little Kat are well looked after. Look after your energy. You're going to need it in the years to come," she said, giving her friend a look of hope and encouragement.

Baba Vusamazulu was born in 1921, in Zululand, to parents of mixed Zulu and Bushman (KhoiSan) descent. He was taken away from his mother's home while he was still a young boy and sent to a mission school far away. As Vusa grew older, he contracted a mysterious and untreatable illness, which in Africa often is an indication that one has been called to a spiritual path. When he came of age, his maternal grandfather called him back home to Zululand to take up his calling as an initiate "Sanusi" or Oral Tradition Keeper of ancient AmaZulu history. After extensive training as an African Sangoma, Diviner, and Story keeper with his grandfather, Baba Vusamazulu went to work in Johannesburg for the thriving African curio market. Not only did he serve to

---

4   You're always so full of the joys of life.

identify and describe African curios, but he was also employed to find these precious artifacts in many parts of Southern Africa. Soon, his knowledge of African tradition and heritage came to the attention of the Professors of Archaeology and Anthropology at the Transvaal Museum. They encouraged Vusamazulu to write a book of African history and mythology, describing the African legacy. Among the highly initiated, it was forbidden to break the Oral Tradition Keeper's vow of secrecy. However, Baba Vusa had taken a personal oath to be an agent of peace and to build a bridge of understanding between all racial groups in Southern Africa.

His commitment to writing this book[5] was inspired by the tragic and untimely death of his newly betrothed. She was shot accidentally during the Sharpeville riots in 1960. Vusamazulu's grief at her loss knew no bounds, and the young Sanusi swore an oath that instead of avenging her death with blood, which was the traditional Zulu way, he would spend the rest of his days writing books and creatively educating the people of Southern Africa. His work from that time onward was utterly dedicated to peace and an end to racism. Baba Vusa's book of Ancient African Prehistory was published in the late 1950s and was banned only a few years later by the South African Apartheid Government. This was mainly because the African legends and history that Baba Vusa had written, radically contradicted the accepted South African history books of the time. His was the first collection of African Prehistory and historical information that any black South African author had ever published.

Baba Vusamazulu continued his work educating South African people about their true heritage. He was commissioned to build a cultural museum called Kwa-Khaya Lendaba in the heart of Soweto township, Johannesburg. The museum was burned down and destroyed in the 1970s, and Baba Vusa and his family had to flee Soweto. Later, he built another Cultural Village Museum outside Mahikeng in Bophuthatswana. Every African culture was

---

5 *Indaba My Children* by Credo Vusamazulu Mutwa

represented in its entirety here, complete with enormous cement sculptures of the Great Gods and Goddesses of African mythology. Unfortunately, this amazing labour of love, his lifetime work, was also burned to the ground, and yet again, Baba Vusa had to flee his home for safety. In 2005, Baba Vusa and his wife Martha went to live on the outskirts of the town of Kuruman. Here he spent his last years giving talks to visitors, imparting the profound wisdom and legacy of Ancient Africa, and building a center for the education and healing of those who have HIV and AIDS.

When Lisa was still in her early twenties, she decided to find this great African historian, Sanusi Baba Vusamazulu, and meet with him, even if it was to be a brief encounter. Lisa diligently saved up her pennies for a bus trip to Mafikeng where Vusa and his wife were living at the time. She walked the long and dusty African road to see this Great Man at his home on the banks of the Lotlamoreng dam, just outside of the town of Mafikeng. Lisa arrived at her destination on foot, carrying armfuls of gifts, fresh fruits, vegetables, nuts, and even medicinal plants that she had collected from the river that fed the Lotlamoreng dam. By the time she arrived at the settlement, she was dusty and footsore. The entrance closest to her destination was a small gate in the high electric fence which was decorated with the horns of a Wildebeest. The gate was kept traditionally for Sangomas and healers. Lisa was completely unaware of this and had already walked a long way barefoot in the hot African sun. She found the gate open and went in.

Baba Vusa's first wife, Celia, was waiting for her at the doorway of the Great wife's hut and smiled warmly when she saw Lisa. The old Sangoma greeted her with ceremonial blessings, taking her into her hut to receive her gifts with a thankful heart.

"Lisa, your name is Lisa?" she asked in her mellow, round, and gentle way. "My husband, Vusa, is expecting you this morning. He is busy with the preparations of the inauguration celebrations for this traditional village. My daughter and the young initiates will take you to meet him in a while but first, let us get to know one another."

Celia looked deeply into Lisa's soul and smiled, and then she took Lisa by her hand and began to read her palm.

"Lisa, would you like me to tell you some more about your future? Perhaps you have a yearning to know what is to become of our beautiful country and how you can help bring about peace and prosperity to our people," the old lady spoke slowly and clearly, nodding with her whole upper body. She closed her eyes, and breathing in deeply, she paused and nodded again.

"Yes, you, Lisa, are a bringer of change. An intelligent woman and one that will submit to no man. Your soul was born for a very great purpose, and this is what has brought you here today!"

Celia was wearing the red, black, and white cotton shawl of a High Sangoma around her shoulders, and she held an intricately beaded and decorated wildebeest tail. She occasionally waved this about her body to keep the flies away. It lent her an air of mystery and authority.

"My dear, I do have good news and bad news to tell you. Would you like to hear what it is I have to say?" she asked in her slow and steady way.

"Yes, thank you, I would," Lisa said with dignity.

"Very well, then I will tell you." The old woman drew in her breath with her eyes closed again. "I see a great path laid before you—an extremely difficult path with many challenges that lay upon your road. But you have a gift, Lisa. As they say, the pen is more powerful than the sword and I see that you are a woman of great tenderness and kindness. The path of peace is your chosen way. And I see that you will be successful in almost everything you do. You are born lucky, Lisa. You are born under a constellation of lucky stars, and you are protected and guided in your work on this earth." The old Sangoma stopped and closed her eyes. "But Ma'am, the road ahead will not be easy for you. I see that you have a free and wandering spirit. And because of this you will not complete any formal studies. Therefore, it will be a difficult path for you to tread on your own. You will be without the shelter of any institutions or established schools behind you. God will be with you and guide you so do not fear." And with that Celia looked at her and smiled.

She spoke with Lisa for a while, directing her to approach the honoured Sanusi Baba Vusamazulu, with head and knees bowed and to clap her hands in the customary African way of respect. Then she called one of the younger initiates of the village, her daughter Nomthunzi, to take Lisa to Baba Vusa's own kraal,[6] where she was to wait for him.

Lisa walked with the young sangoma down the dusty path towards the cultural village.

"Have you seen the beautiful work of my father, Baba Vusamazulu yet?"

Lisa shook her head. "No, I haven't."

"Then come, I will take you and show you his living museum." Nomthunzi shone her wide, gentle smile at Lisa. They stepped inside an enclosure that was built out of clay and a woven lattice of strong branches. Once within, the magic of a reconstructed Nguni kraal was laid out for all to see. Nomthunzi led Lisa from hut to hut to show her the beautifully constructed living exhibits. Each of the villages and huts were representations from the different tribes of Southern Africa. Lisa found The Zulu Chiefs kraal particularly fascinating. Everything down to the tiniest detail was included on the display, from leopard skins to beautifully made sleeping mats, wooden and clay eating utensils and exquisitely beaded artifacts. They walked from village to village comparing the cultural details of one tribal village to another. The last living exhibit that Lisa was taken to see was the sacred enclosure that was built around a huge shady acacia tree.

"This is the Chief's meeting place, Ma'am Lisa. It is where the elders used to meet and hold 'Indaba.' It is here that all the wise

6 Home

ones meet to discuss important matters on behalf of the entire village."

Lisa was looking down on a well-swept natural earth area surrounded by high mud clad walls. She could imagine the scene well. The old wise "Induna" or African Chief, seated on his carved wooden throne and encircled by a gathering of his royal advisers.

"Let me take you to meet Ubaba Vusa now. He will be ready to see you. He has been very busy finishing an enormous cement sculpture of the legendary Goddess Amarava. He and his work team are almost finished now with preparations to open the Lotlamoreng Cultural village, and his time is very precious. But I know that he is looking forward to meeting you."

Nomthunzi took her to the little brick house where the great man lived and bid her goodbye.

After a brief wait, Baba Vusamazulu arrived. He was covered in cement dust and had concrete on his hands and his workman's apron. He washed his hands and removed his apron. He was wearing a pair of enormous but ordinary, denim workman's overalls and sat humbly upon a kitchen stool beside her. He was an extremely large man but despite this was abundantly energetic and generous with his time. Lisa quickly became aware, as the Great Sanusi spoke, that she had no need to ask any of the questions that she had carefully prepared for him. He seemed to address each of the questions that she held silently in her heart. That day, Baba Vusa spent the entire afternoon talking with her, telling her the ancient and sacred stories of Africa that were kept secret for those who were to be initiated in the African way.

"Madam Lisa, has anybody told you the ancient African stories, these sacred stories that hold many secrets for the initiated Sangoma? More especially the story about the origin of our moon and the planet Mars?" Baba Vusa asked in his slow and respectful Zulu voice.

"No Baba. I have not yet heard many of these stories," she replied with a smile.

"Ah, well then, let me tell you the most beautiful and fascinating story of all about how we, humans came to exist on Earth. Did you know, Ma'am Lisa, that a very long time ago, the heavenly body that we call Planet Mars used to be a wonderful and verdant planet, teeming with life, rivers and animals and populated with people who looked very much the same as we human beings do. Well, it is for a very good reason that this planet got its name. You see, the people who inhabited this land were constantly at war with one another. In fact, so hell bent were these people upon fighting one another that eventually they destroyed almost all life upon their planet. This is the reason it was named 'Mars' after the Greek God of war. The ancient story that comes down to us through time tells of a long and terrible, bloody war that almost entirely decimated the population on this once beautiful planet. Eventually, only a few of the strongest people remained as survivors of a terrible plague that had been released as biological warfare to extinguish the population.

"It happened that one of these survivors was a Priestess, a powerful woman and an exceptional healer. In her journey to find the remains of her clan, this beautiful woman came across a fatally wounded man. He was clearly a warrior and was still wearing the battle attire of the enemy. She stopped in her tracks and realizing he was still breathing and alive, she bent down, lifted the great warrior's head and administered a few drops of her restorative healing potion to him. Then she made a fire and stayed by his side until he was well enough to walk with her to safety. In this way she was able to save this great man's life and restore him back to full health. These two people, male and female, helped one another to restore their strength, and rekindle something that was so rare and had been almost completely forgotten on this war-torn planet. Love! The beautiful medicine woman had shown compassion to a man who not long ago she would have considered an enemy. Love and hope had been reborn between these two people. Very rapidly the healing and beautiful emotions of love and compassion were spread among all the remaining Martian people. And because of this, renewed hope for a possible future life on another planet was born. Together the survivors of Mars were able to escape their hellish, ravaged and war-torn planet. Together they searched until they found the last remaining egg in the nest of a giant Martian eagle and set about hollowing it out and preparing the interior for the voyage to Earth. It is this Martian space vessel, which was left in Earth's orbit, that is known to all earth beings as the Moon.

"Once the egg vessel had entered the Earth's atmosphere and was close enough for the survivors to disembark, they were able to float from the giant vessel into the sea and make their landing on earth that way. These first people who arrived on earth from Mars, were called 'The Healers or Sangomas'. They were a powerful and very wise race and were strictly forbidden to harm any living creature on earth. And it is from these early times, from the survivors of Mars that we human beings were gifted the all-healing arts, using sound, light and singing and the application of plant medicines." Baba Vusa told Lisa many of the traditional Zulu stories that day. Then when the dusty evening light began to filter through the windows of his little house, Lisa bid Baba Vusa farewell. As she was preparing to leave that evening, Baba Vusa turned to her and said in a humble, almost pleading tone, "Ma'am Lisa, please, may I ask you to do whatever you can to help us save the children of this generation in Africa. Teach them to respect their own culture, their true history, the precious natural heritage of Africa and this sacred planet, Mother Earth."

This conversation was to be the beginning of her friendship with a profoundly wise teacher. A friendship that was to develop steadily throughout many decades to follow.

Several years later, the gentle Celia, Baba Vusamazulu's first wife, succumbed to cancer and the Great Sanusi had to continue alone with his work to bring about peace in South Africa. Eventually, Baba Vusa remarried an exceptional woman, a senior nurse and powerful Sangoma named Martha. Over the years that

Lisa grew to know them, Baba Vusa and Mama Martha became her great friends and Baba Vusa remained a source of wisdom to Lisa right until the end of his life.

A Telephone Call from Ubaba

Baby Kathleen was almost four months old when the call came. Lisa picked up the receiver and heard the crackling line of a long-distance call. It was Baba Vusa's daughter, Nomthunzi, on the telephone.

"Gale Boga,[7] Mama Lisa." She heard the young voice with a strong Tswana accent.

"It's me, Nomthunzi. How are you?"

"I'm well, thank you, how lovely to hear from you," Lisa said smiling.

"Ma Lisa, Our Father, Ubaba Vusa, has asked me to call you. He would like to speak to you. Would you please hold the line for him? Thank you, Ma Lisa. God bless you and goodbye." There was a moment of silence and the sound of footsteps approaching. She could hear a strong African voice in the background.

"Siyabona, Ma'am Lisa." It was the familiar, gentle voice of Vusamazulu. His was the slow accented Zulu of a highly respected Elder. Lisa was surprised to hear from the old Sanusi.[8] Baba Vusa insisted on using the respectful title, Madam and Sir, when addressing people.

"Camagu, Baba Vusa. How are you and your family?" she asked respectfully.

"We are old, Ma'am, and suffer all the maladies of old age, but considering this, God has blessed us, Ma'am. Thank you," he answered in his humble, almost apologetic manner.

"Baba Vusa, what is it that has brought you to call me this morning?" she asked.

"Madam Lisa, we have heard that you would like to arrange

7   Greetings
8   Prophet and History keeper

a journey to meet with the Khomani Elders in the Kalahari. Both my wife and I feel that this would be a highly auspicious journey and that the coming month of July is a particularly powerful time for this work. The journey would be even more blessed, Ma'am Lisa, if you would accompany us as our friend. You are a mother of a newborn baby and therefore your company would make this journey even more of a blessing to us all."

Baba Vusa spoke very clearly and with a radiance and depth of humility that is rarely heard among ordinary people in South Africa.

Lisa paused. Her breath had caught in her chest as the Great Sanusi made this request of her. She was awed that this great man felt the journey to be of such importance that he had called her.

"Yes, Baba Vusa, I too have had dreams and the signs to tell me that this is a very auspicious time and an important quest to make. I hear that you have not been well recently and respect how strongly you and your wife feel about this meeting. I will make the necessary request for funding from the United States. And if it is possible, Baba Vusa, I will immediately telephone your family to let you know."

"Ngiyabonga! Thank you, Madam Lisa. We would be very grateful," Baba Vusa said in his quiet and measured voice.

When Lisa put down the telephone, her hands were shaking both with awe and excitement. To have been offered the honoured opportunity to travel with this Great Teacher, Baba Vusamazulu, was more than she could ever have hoped or dreamed of.

Lisa immediately wrote a detailed email to Dr Fiona Lewinsky, a wealthy American Anthropologist, who had created an international trust fund for the First Nations around the globe. Fiona had already given considerable assistance to First Nations in Africa, especially to the Masai in Kenya and the Khomani people here in Southern Africa. Lisa told Dr Lewinsky of the request from the Great Sanusi to meet with the Kalahari Khomani people and elders. She promptly received a brief and positive email in response, to go ahead and do the necessary groundwork for the journey.

Lisa was still feeling tired to the bone as a new mother, but this was such an inspiring adventure, and she understood that Baba Vusa had a powerful and vital message of hope for the Khomani people. She was determined to keep the momentum flowing and plan for this auspicious date to become a reality. Her general health had suffered with lack of deep sleep, and she had eventually been to see a homoeopathic doctor about treating her condition and the flu that she simply could not shake. Lisa's mother was concerned about her health and about Lisa traveling alone with her four-month-old baby. Thankfully her doctor had some prior knowledge of African history and knew of Baba Vusamazulu's work in Southern Africa as a national hero and peace bringer. Her doctor graciously offered to talk with Lisa's mother on her behalf.

"My dear," he said gently addressing Lisa's mother, "A journey with a Holy Man of Baba Vusa's caliber would be a very special opportunity and if I might add, would be incredibly healing for both Lisa and her little one. Simply to be in his presence would bring your daughter and granddaughter such peace and renewed health."

Eventually, Lisa's mother began to see things from a calmer and softer point of view. And gradually she and Lisa's family give her the support she needed to prepare for the journey to meet Baba Vusamazulu and his wife, Martha.

Lisa caught an aeroplane from Cape Town airport to Oliver Tambo International in Johannesburg. This was to be Kathleen's very first flight. Her sea-blue eyes were alight with joy and adventure. "My little Kat," Lisa spoke gently with her baby daughter. "We are going on an aeroplane together and it's going to be so much fun. You will love it, I know you will. We will be able to see the clouds from up there. It's magical and exciting to be in the sky." Lisa had packed carefully and was prepared for all events.

She timed everything well and baby Kathleen was ready for her next feed when she settled into her passenger seat. Very soon, little Kat was lulled to sleep by the thrum of the aeroplane engine.

Lisa was met at the airport in Johannesburg by her old friends, Debbie and Frank, and taken back to their Craighall park home. It was early winter and very cold up in the Highveld. Both Lisa and baby Kat were tired after the excitement of the aeroplane trip. Her friends prepared a simple warm meal, and they shared supper beside the fire together that evening. Lisa went straight to sleep in preparation for an exciting and busy day ahead. She had planned to have one day in Johannesburg to finalize plans and to book a vehicle with enough space to afford both the Great Sanusi and his wife Martha some comfort on their travels into the heart of the Kalahari. The vehicle was to have been delivered safely to her friend's home, only, there had been a delay with the bank transfer from the sponsors in America. This left Lisa in a very difficult position. The journey absolutely had to go ahead as planned. There was simply too much invested in this trip to reschedule or cancel now. She had to act fast and decisively. After calling her Dr Fiona Lewinsky's office in the USA to confirm that payment had been sent, Lisa took all her own savings out of her bank and transferred these to the travel account to pay for the vehicle rental, fuel, and additional traveling costs. At last, they were on their way. Lisa packed the Toyota Ventura ready for an early start and with Baby Kat safely strapped into a car seat, she headed out of Johannesburg towards Rustenberg and the Magaliesberg mountains to meet Baba Vusamazulu and his wife. As she arrived at the gate on the dusty farm road where the Great Sanusi lived, she heard the soft electronic "ping" of a bank notification on her cell phone. The international transfer of funds for the sacred journey had arrived at the perfect time.

Bound for the Kalahari

The two venerable old people were waiting for her on their stoep[9] in the morning sunshine. Baba Vusa was wrapped in the warm, royal blue shawl of a High Sanusi, and his second wife, Mama Martha, was wearing a warm woolen jacket over her many multicoloured necklaces of traditional beads. The Old Sanusi wore his ceremonial jade and copper necklace and carried the holy staff topped with the bronze dove of peace. Their faces lit up with huge smiles when they saw the hired vehicle pull up on the grass in front of their home. Lisa got out to greet both of her special friends respectfully and to introduce baby Kathleen to them. Mama Martha wasted no time and immediately disappeared inside to fetch their luggage.

While they waited, Baba Vusa showed Lisa a rambling bush that was growing right next to their front door. The plant had a pungent smell and was bedecked with bright red flowers. "This, Ma'am, is the wonderful medicine plant that we Zulu's call 'unwele.' The scientists have named it 'Sutherlandia Frutescens.' But most African people simply call it Cancer bush or 'Kankerbossie.' I have already gone to a great deal of trouble introducing this powerful 'Grandmother herb,' to the world as a cure for many maladies including cancer. My wife Martha and I have used this medicine in the treatment of those who are suffering from the terrible plague, the HIV virus." Baba Vusa broke off a small sprig and gave this to Lisa to taste. "Do you see how bitter it tastes, Ma'am?" Baba Vusa asked her. "It is the bitterness of this African herb that makes the medicine so powerful. It is a strong blood cleanser." Baba Vusa took off his thick-lensed glasses and began polishing them. "It is our hope that we can find the right health medicine company to introduce this beautiful plant to all South Africans as a support for HIV and cancer and many other blood-related diseases," the Old Sanusi said, nodding his head and gently smelling the leaves.

9   Veranda

Soon Mama Martha arrived outside with a friendly African gentleman who was carrying their bags. She introduced the tall gentleman to Lisa as Thembelani, their traditional African helper and companion. They loaded the bags into the back of the Ventura, along with Lisa's luggage and some grocery shopping to take with them on the journey. Mama Martha happily climbed into the back of the car with Lisa and baby Kat. And Lisa gratefully gave the wheel to the gentle Thembelani, who was also Baba Vusa's driver. Then they settled back after all the tension of preparation to enjoy the journey.

From Magaliesburg all the way into the Northern Cape, the Old Sanusi sat telling fascinating stories to everyone in the vehicle. Snippets of the history of the region and beautiful African tales about great leaders once past. Dense bush and wide acacia trees gave rise to red soil and thorny scrub as they traveled deeper into the wilderness of the Kalahari. They stopped every now and then to stretch their legs and to buy refreshments at roadside farm stalls. Dry biltong,[10] fruit and sparkling water for the Old Sage, Baba Vusa.

At four months old, Kathleen was as good as gold on the first part of the journey, but as they traveled further, little Kat began to feel anxious, and very car sick and she began to cry. Lisa comforted her child, breastfeeding her in the back of the vehicle as they traveled. They had entered the dry lands of the Northern Cape, and here, even in mid-winter, the hot African sun beat down on them relentlessly as they drove through the desert landscape. Even with the air conditioner on, little Kat felt as uncomfortable as they all did. The big Zulu Sanusi and his Tswana wife, Martha, filled the vehicle with their presence and their physical bodies and even though Lisa had taken dampened towels to cool and shield them from the burning midday sun, it was still uncomfortably hot.

"We call such children, 'isingane zenxabano,'" Lisa heard Baba Vusa say quietly in the front of the vehicle. "This means a child

---

10 Dried meat strips

born of conflict." The old man's voice sounded sad as he spoke these words. "Too many African children are born into the conflict of poverty and war-affected homes. Too many families have been broken through drug and alcohol addiction in Africa. The ancients say that men should look at women in a sacred way. They should never put women down or shame them in any way. When we have problems, we should share with them openly seeking their counsel. A woman has powerful intuition, and she has access to another system of knowledge that few men develop. She can help us to understand. We must always treat her in a good way."

When I heard that, my heart began to crack with the painful truth of Old Vusa's words. Of course! My daughter had been so sensitive from the very day of her birth. She had immediately picked up any vibration of conflict, even in our family home. Little Kat seemed to know whenever there were feelings that were not harmonious in our peaceful sanctuary. Of course, I knew what this wise old healer was saying was true. And although I still loved the Fisherman, our child had been born into the tearing apart of the relationship between her parents. Ian was not there when Kathleen was born. Only my mother had stayed to support us throughout this time. The Fisherman had gone back to live in his world, and I had walked on carrying our baby in my womb alone. The old African wise one's words struck a deep chord within me and as we journeyed into the heart of the Kalahari, I turned my head towards the window and quietly let my tears well up and fall while my child slept at my breast. I felt exhausted and very much alone. All of this, the sense of not having the support I desperately craved, the emotional burden and a deep inner weariness, had caught up with me. I wept silently as the Kalahari landscape whizzed by us on the national road. The African Elders I was traveling with knew very well how hard the road was for single mothers. Mama Martha, Baba Vusa's wife, raised three children on her own. Too many African women have had to walk this path as a matter of survival. Too many African fathers have had to leave their families as migrant workers to work on the gold mines near Johannesburg or on contract for farms, dams, irrigation schemes or roads. And far too often these African men never came home. There were also far too many young African girls who followed their glamorous lovers to a life in the city where often their hopes were dashed and their lives ruined when they were left pregnant, with nowhere to turn but the streets. The whole African continent and in fact, the entire world, had never seen a time such a time as this before. It was a time when family life had been split asunder and where single mothers everywhere struggled to raise their children alone, without family or a father.

My child was a blessing, and I never lost sight of this fact. Kathleen was so alive and beautiful and such joy to all who met her. But the circumstances of her birth and the inner conflict that I suffered because of it, still brought me a sense of pain and grief. Even so, knowing this and my life circumstances, this dignified and great tradition keeper and healer, Baba Vusa Amazulu, had chosen to travel with me and my child. In Africa, it is highly auspicious for a Holy man to travel accompanied by a newborn baby. It was said to bring rain, protection and other great blessings. Among many ancient traditional peoples of the world, newborn babies were the greatest blessings of their people and the closest link to God because their hearts were still so pure and innocent. This was the Ancient African way, and I felt enormously honoured to be a part of it.

The drive was long, but the travelers were all filled with a sense of joyful anticipation. They made two stops along the journey. One in Kuruman, the ancestral home of Mama Martha, to buy sacred crystals to give to Anna and Raaikat Blinkman. And then to overnight at the farm homestead of Jan Bosman, a veteran explorer of the Kalahari and an intrepid hunter of his day. Their farm was not far from Kuruman and a perfect place to rest after the heat of the day's drive. The two Elders, one an Afrikaans farmer and hunter and the other a historian and Sanusi, met for the first time and sat sharing the secret stories of Africa and talking until late at night.

The next day, they left the Bosman's home for Upington and the Twee Rivieren area where Raaikat and Anna Blinkman and many of the Bushman elders were awaiting their arrival. This part of the journey was much cooler, and Little Kat was quiet all that day. They finally arrived at the Blinkman's new home in the little town of Welkom, just as the sun began to set over the red sand of the Kalahari Desert. Raaikat had been waiting for them at the gates of their home. "Welkom, Welkom, Welkom!" he yelled joyfully when he saw the dusty Ventura, arriving with the Great man sitting in the front passenger seat. Anna and Raaikat helped Baba Vusa and Ma Martha to get out of the vehicle. There were more Khomani hands ready to take out the luggage and get everyone settled in a comfortable place for the night. A wonderful crackling fire awaited them along with a chorus of greetings from community members who had all gathered to welcome the famous guests. There were hugs, kisses and handshakes all around. Baba Vusa was led to the place of honour beside the fire and given a warm bowl of soup. Anna had prepared a big pot of steaming hot bean and vegetable soup for dinner. Mama Martha was treated to a gentle massage to soothe her travel-weary legs. After supper, "Mammie" and "Pappie" Vusamazulu were led to Anna and Raaikat's own bedroom, which had been converted to fit the occasion. Lisa was so tired that she asked to be shown to her bed, and then she curled up contentedly to sleep with little baby Kat beside her.

The next day, Anna and Lisa worked together to make some breakfast for all their visitors. Lisa tied Baby Kat onto her body with a soft blanket while she was working. The old people were still asleep, and Lisa was anxious that Kat should not wake them. But of course, as soon as she was hungry, Kathleen began to bellow, and the whole house awoke to the smells of steaming hot African mealie meal porridge and scrambled eggs.

An African Ritual Cleansing Ceremony

All that morning, the womenfolk had been busy preparing to make a small ceremonial fire inside the house. They were using aromatic, fragrant wood; branches of the "kameeldoring" and "rosyntjiebos" trees were added to the more precious woods to keep the fire burning. Then Anna arrived carrying a bowl of mphephu[11] and scented Kalahari Desert herbs to scatter onto the coals. She explained to Lisa that the Khomani women were preparing a sacred cleansing fire and that the smoke from this fire would help release baby Kathleen from her difficulties with colic and anxiety. Then Mama Martha took Kathleen from her mother and gently unwrapped the blanket from around her. They carefully undressed her, and the Khomani women began to gather closely around the ceremonial fire, chanting and singing in rounds, clapping and stamping their feet softly. Anna poured a small bowl of fragrant liquid over the fire, and then Mama Martha passed baby Kathleen through the midst of the scented smoke to cleanse her and clear the spirit of conflict that affected her child. Together, they sang a soothing Khomani ceremonial song as they performed this cleansing ritual. The rhythmic singing kept baby Kat calm all the way through the fire ceremony. Mama Martha and Anna took some camphor salve and sweet oil and mixed some of the sacred wood ash into it, and with this, they both began to rub little baby Kathleen from top to bottom. The Khomani women all showed Lisa how to massage her child. "Do you see how we do it, Mama? Massage the stomach from inside out, in a circular motion from left to right. Rooi Laventel en Kamfer olie,"[12] Ma Martha said. Little Kathleen seemed startled by the ceremony and the smoke, but she loved all the attention, the massage, and the wonderful feeling of

---

11 Wild African sage
12 Lavender and camphor oil

communion between the women, which seemed to have quieted her. This incredibly gentle cleansing process had helped to calm her. When the women finished bathing and massaging Kathleen, Lisa could feel how peaceful and relaxed her baby daughter was. There was none of the tautness in her limbs and neck muscles. She was calm and smiling with her beautiful baby smile. Kathleen never suffered from colic again after that day. And Lisa couldn't help thinking, "If only our mothers and maternal elders still had this knowledge to share with their daughters. We have gained so much that is necessary from technology and modern medicine, but we have lost so much of the 'Grandmother' wisdom that womenfolk and midwives of all cultures have always passed on from one generation to the next."

There was so much that she could learn from these Khomani women. All these natural remedies that were still very much in use. Despite the ravages of poverty and alcoholism within the community, the women kept these matriarchal secrets closely guarded. Perhaps it was simply because the bushmen had always valued their children as the most precious gifts of life within the family. But there was another aspect to this keeping of sacred knowledge that gradually became clearer for Lisa as she spent more time with Khomani mothers. These women were the acknowledged "keepers of the hearth." The Khomani women's role of keeping the family and the children safe and healthy was well established and respected. Women worked together to care for their children, to feed, nurture, and clothe them. It was the womenfolk in a Bushman band who gathered wild vegetables, roots, and fruits to cook and provide the staple diet for the family. The womenfolk kept the campfire burning and built the little "skerms" or shelters for the family to sleep in. And most importantly, it was the women who understood childbirth and all the little details that make for happy and healthy children. This was true not only of the Bushmen folk but among women of all the traditional tribes of Africa, there existed a powerful connection, the bond between mothers and a mother and her children. It is this strong physical connection that an African mother has to her child and the easeful sense of belonging that has made the children of Africa so grounded and physically at ease with the world. This sense of being forever rooted or connected to one's mother and homeland has allowed African people to return, both to themselves, their culture and values, and to their village of origin, for nurture and renewal.

For the few days while she was there, Lisa was completely accepted by the community, and she was treated as one of them. The Khomani women showed her many of their favourite ways of treating babies and children using inexpensive remedies and salves for the relief of earache, colic, breastfeeding issues, teething, and other stress-related problems. She was shown by example how wonderful it was to be a mother in a loving and supportive community. During their time in the Khomani village, Lisa's child, Kathleen, was passed from one gentle Khomani adult to another. Even Baba Vusa blessed baby Kat with a kiss on her forehead and a short chat on his lap. Ma Martha, of course, was the grandmother of all grandmothers and gave so much wisdom where being a mother was concerned. It was wonderful to see how, even amid difficulties and though seriously affected by negative external influences, by alcohol abuse, lack of resources, diaspora, and conflict within the community, there was still a spirit here which allowed the respect and support of mothers and children to be present. This so radically contrasted with the suburban, city world Lisa had come from, where the spirit of community was too often absent. Where, too often, distance separation breeds indifference and an extreme lack of connection. And where lack of empathy, respect, and support for mothers, the elderly, and the less advantaged becomes evident.

Gathering of the Khomani Elders

The day of the Khomani Elders' arrival came. No telephone

calls had been made, and neither Anna nor Raaikat had openly discussed this meeting with the community. When the time came, the Elders simply arrived, knowing that this was what they needed to do and where they needed to be. They came from afar in the Kalahari to meet the renowned Sanusi and African spiritual leader, Baba Vusamazulu.

Before the meeting began, there was an encounter with one of the younger members of the Opstaan family. Domkat had been a sensitive and talented artist until addiction to the demon drink began to get the better of him. Domkat had arrived that morning, smelling of spirits, and was obviously quite hungover. He had stopped off on the way at the local shebeen, which was fatal, for Domkat and Anna caught him red-handed in their home stealing money to buy more liquor. Since their arrival in the little town of Welkom, both Raaikat and Anna had decided on a very firm policy regarding their home and property. There had been a fence erected, and a lock was put onto the gate for just such an occasion.

The Khomani Elders watched while Anna very firmly but gently guided Domkat to the gate and told him not to come back or disturb the meeting. This, Lisa realized, was the only way the leaders in the community could successfully deal with alcoholism and the resulting behaviour. As Raaikat put it so well, "Om net nee te se!"[13] was the only answer.

As this significant meeting of Elders began. First, Baba Vusa and Mama Martha blessed the space where all were to congregate. At this sacred blessing ceremony, they were given a beautifully carved walking stick by the Khomani community. The respected old ones, in turn, gave sacred crystals and gemstones to the elders to represent the sacred knowledge and power that was being shared. Only those who truly understood and genuinely wished for the continuation of the sacred ways came to this meeting, and slowly the Blinkman's home filled with all the Khomani Elders,

---

13 To just say no!

from both near and far. There was such a wonderful spirit among the small crowd that gathered in a circle in the Blinkman's yard.

Baba Vusamazulu, the Old Sanusi, sat outside under the shade of a huge acacia thorn tree to protect himself from the full sunshine of the Kalahari Desert. Raaikat and the Bushman Elders had begun to gather around him. Some squatted on the red dirt of the outside yard, and others had found crates or chairs to sit on. Baba Vusa had begun to talk with them and was animated in the sharing of one of the old Zulu tales about the origin of the Bushmen race. His strong African voice resounded across the red dust of the little Kalahari town.

"Amarava, the beautiful Mother of all Nations, escaped from 'Udu,' her ugly half-blood suitor and ran away. And in her wild desperation to escape him, she fell over the edge of a cliff that cut into the mountainside. Down, down, down, she tumbled, desperately grabbing at small shrubs and rocks to break her fall until she reached the bottom and lay there unconscious. Badly wounded and close to death, she was rescued by a strange, giant lizard-like people who were one of the most ancient races to inhabit the Earth and who disappeared long before the human race as we know it, was born. When Amarava awakened from her unconscious state, she found herself lying in a cave on a comfortable bed of leaves, being tended to by these most intelligent of all beings, the Giant Lizards or Frog people as they were sometimes called. This is how it happened." Baba Vusa spoke in a slow and animated way that drew his listeners to come closer. *"Amarava, the mother of humanity, was cared for and protected by these strange lizard-like beings. She lived with these creatures for a very long time and soon grew to trust and even love her protectors, as her own tribe and family. Eventually, Amarava was impregnated by one of the Lizard people and she gave birth to the 'yellow-skinned ones,' who as you know are called the 'Mutwas' or the little people—the Earliest Bushman and Pygmy races of*

today. These yellow-skinned people multiplied and became the most skillful hunters. Their mother, Amarava, taught them many of the gentle arts hoping that her children would grow up to be as wise, kind and nurturing as their Lizard parents. She taught her children how to make medicine from plants, trees and minerals to heal their people when they were sick. How to play the bow harp and the little thumb piano that we Zulu's call the 'mbira.' But they soon learned how to fashion the hunting bow and arrow to suit their cunning. Soon the Mutwas had perfected their craft to such a level that they turned their hunting bows on the Lizard people. Only a few of them escaped and fled underground through holes in the mountains. Many succumbed to the yellow-skinned people's arrows and their species was almost completely wiped out. Amarava was grief-stricken when she discovered what had happened to her Lizard friends. And she left the valley where she had lived for so long, leaving her yellow-skinned children to fend for themselves. This was, as Zulus knew it, the beginning of the ancient Bushman line."

Baba Vusa's story resonated deeply with the Bushman Elders. The gentle healing power of his voice had drawn them to listen even more closely. It was clear that these ancient stories held a thread of truth for everyone present. Those like Baba Vusa, who were the keepers of the ancient wisdom stories, were highly respected as custodians of Earth's ancient memories. It was almost as though while he spoke, the wisdom of his story traveled down into the earth and through the bare feet of the Elders who gathered before him. They had many questions for Baba Vusa that day. He seemed tireless in answering these with respect and good humour. Ma Martha and Anna constantly brought water and refreshments to the Khomani Elders and menfolk sitting in a circle around the Old Sanusi. Baba Vusa spoke to them of the encroachment of the modern lifestyle, the loud electronic music that has drowned out the gentle sounds of the Mbira[14] and the bow harp that so beautifully blends with the sounds of the desert. He spoke to them about the great healing of the Bushman trance dance, and he reminded them that to keep this alive for the Khomani people was to keep the heart of the world beating. The menfolk could hear the women chanting, clapping, and singing in the background as Ma Martha laughed with them while singing a traditional Khomani Bushman song.

Then Baba Vusa began to talk with them about the change that had started to happen to their bodies since the Khomani relocated from the hunting territories that used to be their home.

Oom Haasie, the Khomani herder, had been sitting on his haunches, rocking and quietly listening to the Old Sanusi speak. And every now and again, he would utter a sound in agreement that so closely resembled the lowing of cattle. "Mmmmmm, mmmmm," he nodded his head and body in accordance with his sounds.

A very small but clear, almost birdlike, intelligent voice from the group of Elders spoke out. It was Oupa Piet-Jan, one of the few Khomani trackers who was employed by the Kgalagadi Transfrontier Park. "Baba Vusa," he said, addressing the Great man respectfully. "Almal van ons heir, weet,[15] that even before 1999, when the Kgalagadi Park was proclaimed in Botswana, this once free land was made completely off limits to all bushmen communities and hunters. The change of life from the hunting and gathering way to living in these terrible squatter camps has had a very bad effect on our people's health and lives. The exclusion of the Khomani people from their original homelands, sacred watering places and natural food sources has created terrible heart-sore and suffering within our Bushman communities. Some of our people used to live further South, but now they have even been pushed out of their homes by farms and the development of

---

14 Bushman thumb piano
15 All of us gathered here know.

game reserves. And now our people have lost all access to their land, water, freedom, and independence. The Khomani people were useful only for their hunting and tracking abilities during the SADF 'bush war,' and now they cannot keep up with these modern changing times. Today, most of our people make their living working on farms or by selling handcrafted artifacts to tourists along the national road or at Game reserves. We cannot go hunting, and it is no longer possible to look for wild foods surrounding the squatter camps because the environment is already damaged by overuse. And we are not permitted to look for our favourite wild foods on other people's land or in the park. In the past, Baba, our Bushman groups used to live in the wide, open places of the Kalahari. This helped to keep wild plants and animal life healthy and in balance. Our old ways ensured that when wild foods or plant medicines were collected, there would always be enough left behind for the animals to eat and reseed. The Khomani way was to live in harmony with the seasons, with nature, and with other living creatures, so that we would all survive even in the middle of a drought. But now the old ways are disappearing. Our heartlands, our families, and everything we value is broken, and we the Khomani people are becoming sick and dying, Baba Vusa."

Baba Vusa listened to Oupa Piet-Jan and nodded. "It is true what you say, Oupa," he said. "Our people of the great Zulu nation have always honoured the traditional ways of the 'Mutwa' people. In Africa, we have looked up to the Bushmen, who were known as the rainmakers and the breakers of drought. Your people have been very much admired and respected for your abilities to live closely with nature and understand the secret ways of the Great Mother Earth. It has been a great injustice forcing the Bushman people to leave the land of their heart and soul. These lands of their mothers and grandmothers and their great grandmothers before them. And you have all been left here to breathe this poisonous asphalt from the dusty tourist road. To eat this dust and whatever may come your way so that your Bushmen children and the generations of the future will all forget the knowledge that is your special heritage. I was just a boy growing up in the mountains known as the Drakensberg. I remember well how, after the decimation and enslavement of the Bushman people, the few families left would hide anything that identified them with their ancient cultural origins. They no longer practiced their rain magic or their healing trance dance. Their ancient languages were no longer spoken, for fear that someone might overhear them and carry them away. Their valuable traditionally beaded aprons and skin 'kaross' coverings were no longer made or worn. Traditional medicines were very rarely collected or used, and the places where natural plant foods could be found were all forgotten. Most of the San medicine men were hunted out and killed because the invading settlers mainly wanted the women and children to work for them.

"When I was a boy growing up in Zululand, we did not yet know about these modern foodstuffs that now all African people must eat to survive. White bread, refined mealie meal porridge, and the biggest problem of them all, which has been the introduction of refined sugar to the African diet. I have suffered from sugar diabetes for many years, because of my diet and lifestyle. I never knew of these problems when I was a youngster. I grew up eating traditional African foods, stamp mielies, millet, wild herb stews, and my mother's best pumpkins. But when I went to live in the city of Johannesburg, we began to drink fizzy cool drink, as if it were water, and lots of fried and fast foods, never realizing the damage that this would eventually cause."

Every head was turned in his direction, listening to him intently. "Now look at my health. I have suffered tremendously because of this change in our traditional way of life. You must all try to keep to your original and traditional ways of eating as much as you can. Teach your children about the wild foods and try to grow vegetables, pumpkin, and mielies in your gardens, if you can. And be aware of the dangers of introducing sugar, refined meal, and flour into every child's diet and as a staple in every home. Sugar is the silent enemy that has crept into all our lives. It is this modern commodity that has opened the door wide to the problem of sugar addiction, diabetes, and eventually alcohol abuse."

The gathering of men seated around the Great Sanusi all murmured among one another in agreement, and some shook their heads gravely at the truth of his words.

Then Baba Vusa spoke about something very close to the Bushman's heart. He leaned closer to the menfolk seated with him and, speaking in low tones as if to exclude the womenfolk from the conversation, he said. "Fathers and Grandfathers, please teach your young men to always uphold respect for your womenfolk and for the important role that mothers play in the home. Of course, we all love spending time with our women. The African continent boasts some of the most beautiful women on this earth. Even those who, like me, have reached such a venerable age, have a great appreciation for beautiful African women, and I too, have had to constantly discipline 'Old John Thomas,' my own manhood. Of course, it is good to be a proud husband and to have many children. The greatest blessing of all is new life in the family. But I would ask you all to consider carefully the consequences of disrespecting a woman and the reality of bringing fatherless and unwanted children into this world."

Baba Vusa paused for a while to let the Khomani elders feel the importance of his words. "Friends, in these uncertain times, we all face an invisible enemy. They say it has come about as a plague that will attack our people, killing many of us in the future. Some say that this plague has been man-made in a laboratory. Humanity has not yet learned the truth that is behind all of this. This enemy the doctors have called HIV and AIDS syndrome." Baba Vusa took off his glasses and mopped his sweating brow with his large handkerchief. "Friends, we must always be on our guard against this invisible enemy. Take care of your wives and children and do not bring this terrible disease into your families and communities, I beg you, please! The only way that you can be sure of this is by remaining faithful to your marital spouse and not straying. We must set our families and our young people a good example regarding the sacred flower of our love. Keep this flower alive and well in your marriage and in your homes, and do not bring these diseases of infidelity into your family life. This will only allow for the risk of HIV and AIDS to enter the doorway of your homes. I pray that you may all be spared the terrible suffering that this disease has brought to our beloved African nation." Baba Vusa paused and shook his head. There were tears running down his cheeks as he spoke with the Elders about the effect of AIDS. Baba Vusa himself had known the sadness of losing his own child, his eldest son, to the disease of AIDS. He wiped his cheeks, and after a while, he continued.

"We African people are all having to change and adapt. Nowadays, we must send our children to schools to get a good education. Our children must be well prepared to meet the future, my friends." Baba Vusa nodded wisely. "They must know how to read and write and how to understand what is happening in our world so that our children, our future generations, can begin to reclaim and heal our world again and to live in the ways of our forefathers. But African Elders should not forget that once they were the ones who taught the youth everything, they need to know about how to live with and respect the desert. Do not forget your role as wisdom keepers, the sacred guardians of memory and teachers of our people. Teach your children the wisdom of their ancestors. Always remember that the past is the mother of the future. You will have to remind your children often that the future will only belong to them when they embrace their own traditions and past with reverence and respect. Africa is and always has been the richest resource on the planet. It is no wonder, Honourable Ones, that we African people have been subjugated throughout the ages of colonization by those who used these resources to enrich themselves. Our children should not forget about their sacred connection to this land and to one another. Because if they do, they will also forget how to value themselves. We must remember this and teach our children to be proud of our African heritage." Baba Vusa paused and looked deeply into the eyes and souls of each of the Khomani elders gathered there.

The elders murmured softly among one another, nodding and shuffling their feet in the soft, red sand.

"Always remember, my friends, that the Mutwa or Bushman race is a very ancient and sacred race. Yours is a bloodline that leads directly to the heart and soul of our greatest African Ancestors. You alone stand as the guardians of our sacred knowledge. Ancient knowledge that is so rapidly disappearing and becoming forgotten. This knowledge about Grandmother plant medicines and how to prepare these, how to understand the weather, how to make rain, and how to live in balance with the earth and all its living creatures. Your race is rapidly dying out now and taking with it all this precious understanding. It is of great importance that you see yourselves, the Khomani people, for who you truly are, an ancient, sacred, and valued race. Khomani Elders therefore hold an enormous responsibility to teach your children and your grandchildren about who they are and about the value they must share with a rapidly changing world."

They spoke long into the evening when the dusty town had begun to settle and when a large three-legged pot of stew was put onto the fire to cook. Slowly, the Elders began to leave. Some stayed and ate with Raaikat, Anna, Martha, and the Great Sanusi. But eventually they were all gone and the day was over. Baby Kathleen was already asleep after a very busy and exciting day. Mama Martha had fed her some of the gravy and soft porridge from the stew pot, and Lisa's little one had closed her eyes contentedly and drifted away into dreamland.

Everyone in the group was content and tired. The bright

Kalahari stars shone with magical intensity on the little dwelling that night, as the Old Sanusi and his friends shared their meal and took their rest.

Homeward Bound

The next day, the Ford Ventura wended its way back towards Kuruman, where Mama Martha had built her own homestead on the edge of a rural township. Here they were greeted by Martha's daughter, Nomthunzi, and all her grandchildren. Lisa and Kathleen were welcomed as their honoured guests at their township home. When morning came, Ma Martha arrived with an enamel wash basin filled with steaming hot water and a fresh towel for Lisa to bathe with. The dignified Grandmother stood in the doorway and addressed Lisa as she washed and dressed baby Kathleen for the last leg of the journey back to Johannesburg.

"Mama Lisa, we have been given some very bad news. At the time when Baba Vusa's firstborn son contracted HIV, we also began treating many of our people with traditional medicines for this terrible disease. We are still treating many of these patients on our farm in the Magaliesberg. It is necessary for us to treat those suffering with healthy food and our medicines every day. They must be near us at this time so that we can help them. Unfortunately, Baba has just been told to leave our work with HIV patients on the farm. This is no longer a place where our people, the sick and dying, are welcome to receive treatment for such illnesses. We have therefore had to make a strong decision and have agreed that we will stay here in Kuruman. Baba Vusa is arranging to hire a large truck. Thembelani will go to pack up our home in Magaliesberg next week. I feel thankful and blessed because Kuruman is my very own ancestral home. At last, we are returning to a place where we are welcome," she said with a note of sadness in her voice.

"Ah, Mama Martha, this is very sad news indeed," said Lisa, shaking her head. "Do the people in the Magaliesberg not understand the good work that you and Baba Vusa are doing there?"

"No, Lisa, they do not," she said, "Baba Vusa has said I should not be concerned about what people say, about our healing centre and our work with HIV patients. He says that people fear what they do not understand. That it is their fear that makes them behave as they do."

They had their last breakfast together before Lisa set out on the road back to Johannesburg. As Lisa sipped her cup of coffee, Baba Vusa sat with baby Kathleen on his knee. He smiled through his thick-lensed glasses at her child and said, "You know Ma'am Lisa, there is a delicate, blue flower that grows on the slopes of a mountain in Zululand where I grew up. This flower was known to me as 'Tuliswa.' From now onwards, this little child will always be known to us as our special 'Tuliswa,' the flower of Zululand."

Lisa smiled with gratitude at her two special friends. "Thank you, Mama Martha and Baba Vusa. It was a great honour to travel with you," she said respectfully.

"May the blessings of the warm African sun always shine upon you," Baba Vusamazulu said to her as she climbed into the Ventura and took her leave. Lisa waved farewell to the two African healers as they faded into the dusty distance outside their Kuruman township home.

When at last I sat in the aeroplane with little Kat fast asleep on my lap, watching the golden sunset light the clouds, I thought back on the profound miracle that this journey had been. I was exhausted but filled with a sense of profound peace and fulfillment to have been a part of this sacred experience. It was beyond all imagining, that a humble South African woman like me could have helped make possible this sharing of precious knowledge, of hope and love among the Khomani Bushmen in the Kalahari.

Listen to the whispers in your heart
In your soul
Listen to the child with radiant words
to fill the hole
Listen sweet listener
Listen as you speak
Listen as you think your thoughts
before you turn the other cheek
Listen to your loneliness
Listen as you pray
Listen to the ache within
That's begging you to stay
Listen to your heart's great story
Although you think now, it's too long
Although you'd rather not be burdened
with your own soul's sorry song
Listen to those around you
The echoes of your life
Listen to the sounds and symbols
that show the way out of your strife
Listen to the ripples and the patterns
of the waves you make
When you toss a careless pebble
into the depth of being's sacred lake
Listen to the tenderness that flows from
Our mother's breast
And know that all she does
is teaching us to give our best
Listen to her trembles as we burn our forests down
Listen to the crisis we have reached in every home and town
Oh, Listener can you listen with the heart that we all share
Can you listen and not be tempted

to taint words with your fear
Listener can you listen to the future that I speak
Can you hear and help to find
the solution that I seek
When you've heard the truth within
reflected so within your heart
Listen to the way it touches you
within that painful part
You may share your pain or keep it
For it is your choice alone
Or you can listen to the whispers
That point to the healing
Of Earth, our sacred home

CHAPTER 10

THE FISHERMAN'S DAUGHTER

Bubble blower
She whistles them into existence
the bubble blower on the lawn
she dances with the wind
and the bubbles float out of her delight
a little wand in her hand
She is the creator of magic
in her fairy princess world
working with the breeze
She lines the sky with her magic
casting spells on trees
and birds and grass
little planets glide by and sail upwards
reflecting the rainbow worlds
then burst sparkling their contents silently
the whistle breath within each bubble
carrying its soft magic to soothe hearts

On a happy spring day, Lisa and the Fisherman's child were out walking. Kat, taking in the scenery in the pram with her usual happy smile and chatty, baby voice. In the heart of the small village, there was a small park beneath the milkwood trees. Here and there, a few park benches and a children's play area with swings, a slide, and a beautiful hand-crafted wooden climbing pen. It was perfect. Simple but magical fun and such a happy outing for the day. Here she could sit and watch her child play and push her on the swings while singing nursery rhymes and their special songs.

What Lisa didn't know was that the Fisherman often passed that place and was quietly sitting at the entrance to the park, rolling a cigarette and watching her and their beautiful, fair-haired child. As Lisa and her little daughter walked hand in hand down the steps from the park, he came out to greet them. Lisa lifted her head as she felt his presence.

"The two of you make such a beautiful picture," he said, smiling.

Lisa stiffened and instinctively drew her daughter closer to her. There was no one around to protect her, and she did not have her cell phone with her on that day. She could smell the alcohol in him from where she stood. He'd been drinking heavily. "Ian, don't think that you can simply be involved in our lives without addressing your issues. You have so much work to do before you can be responsible for yourself, let alone a child," she said, looking at him with her direct gaze. "You know exactly what I am talking about, so do not imagine that I will soften now."

The Fisherman stood still and regarded them for a while. Then he moved forward, took Kathleen into his arms, and held her tenderly. Then he turned and carried her gently over to his van. Lisa did not panic or react to her child's screams. She moved calmly towards his vehicle and saw him sitting inside, cradling his child and looking at her face.

As Lisa approached, the Fisherman looked up with round and desperate eyes. "Lisa, I can afford to take care of her. I can take care of you both now. I know I'm just a simple Fisherman, but I have a house near to the ocean and a boat. I know what you must be going through on your own. You don't have to struggle anymore when I can offer you both a comfortable life," he said, pleading with Lisa.

She stood in front of the Fisherman, stunned. A part of her longed to believe him, wanted with every cell in her body to be embraced and supported. But the mother's wisdom in her knew that what he said didn't add up; it just didn't feel right. Kat was crying now and wanted to go back to her mother. Her little arms were reaching out for Lisa. She leaned forward and gently took her child away from the Fisherman. "No, Ian. This is not about money or a house or having the wealth to afford anything your heart desires. This is about a precious child, our daughter, and how she feels and what she needs. She is what matters most now. You still don't get it, do you? Your scary behaviour, your drinking, your moods. No matter how much money there is, that's not the home to offer a child like ours. Only you know what you must do. No one else can do it for you. The question is, do you really want to be a parent and a father? Because if you do, it's you who will have to step up and take responsibility, address your pattern of addiction, and realize what must be done for yourself!"

Lisa turned away, holding Kat tightly to her beating heart, her tears stinging her eyes. She bent down, buckling her little girl into the pram, and walked away from the Fisherman. Away from his offer of a home, from all his promises, a family, and his love and protection. Away from the possibility that she might ever know this for her child and herself.

Gwyn's Surprise

Little Kathleen was just over a year old when Gwyn, the Fisherman's mother, contacted Lisa. She had heard nothing from Gwyn for all this time. Her dreams told her that there had been a departure and that their family home had been sold. In her vision, she saw their friends and Ian's family from abroad, gathering at the beautiful old homestead in Higgovale, and afterwards, the lovely old Cape Dutch house had been left standing empty.

Gwyn telephoned when she next visited South Africa from Australia.

"Oh, hello, is that Lisa?" asked the soft, genteel voice on the phone. "This is Gwyn, Ian's mother. I hope you don't mind me calling you out of the blue like this. I know it must come as a great surprise to you."

Lisa caught her breath and took a mental step back. "No, not at all, Gwyn. It's lovely to hear from you. How are you?" she answered simply.

"Oh, I'm fine, fine," Gwyn replied carefully. "But you do know, Lisa, that we have had to sell our beautiful home in Cape Town. The cost of upkeep was just too much for me, especially with the home rates and taxes rising the way they are. It is such a shame for the children that I couldn't keep the family home, but there you have it. I did my very best to keep it as long as I could," Gwyn told Lisa in a chatty voice.

"I'm sorry to hear that, Gwyn. I know how much you loved your home and how much you love Cape Town," Lisa answered kindly. "Where have you moved to, if I may ask?"

"Oh, we have sold up pretty much everything," Gwyn said sadly. "My eldest son flew in from Australia to help us pack up the house and get things organized. I moved to Sydney to stay with my family last year," Gwyn replied. "Of course, I do miss my son, Ian, and all of my Cape Town friends, but I have come to accept that it is a brand-new chapter of my life, and of course I am privileged to see my Australian grandchildren growing up." She paused.

There was silence on the phone for a moment. Lisa didn't say anything. She waited until Gwyn was ready to broach her about the reason for her call.

"Lisa," Gwyn spoke softly now. "Some mutual friends of ours from Cape Town arrived in Sydney and came to visit me while on holiday. They showed me some lovely photographs and told me that you gave birth to a child a year ago. I hear that she is a beautiful, healthy daughter."

"Yes. Ian and I conceived a child, and I named her Kathleen," Lisa answered as honestly as possible. "I'm so sorry that your son did not tell you the truth about her birth, Gwyn." She paused and took a long breath. "It has been essential to my well-being as a mother to put the past behind me. At least for now! These things regarding Ian may change in time, and I really hope that they will."

"Yes, yes. I completely understand, Lisa," Gwyn said sadly. "Would it be okay if I came to see you and my granddaughter—I mean, Kathleen—before I return to Australia? I would be so happy just to see her and to take some pictures to show my family back in Australia," she said graciously.

"Yes, of course, Gwyn, you are welcome. Why don't we both meet at my home for tea on Saturday? You do remember the address, don't you? I would be glad to see you, and you will be delighted with young Kathleen. We can chat a little more then," Lisa said gently.

Gwyn sounded tired and sad when she said goodbye and put the phone down.

Lisa was glad she had kept the doors open to Ian's family, and although she felt rather tense about the meeting, she was happy for Kathleen's sake that she would grow up with the love and support of both her grandparents.

It was lovely to see Gwyn. She arrived wearing a crisp linen dress and an orchid pinned to her lapel. Her hair had been recently styled and cut, and she looked like the perfect Cape Town gentlewoman. Lisa, too, had dressed herself and Kathleen for the occasion. They looked lovely in their soft cotton skirts and T-shirts. Lisa had always retained her natural gypsy spirit. She and her young daughter were so utterly different from both Gwyn and Lisa's parents in this regard. Gwyn sat outside on the garden patio with a cup of tea on her lap, watching, fascinated by her granddaughter. Kathleen was so alive and so involved, talking with the fairies and busily doing things in the garden. It was lovely to watch her making fairy homes and playing on her own independently, happily fetching and carrying gifts of nature for all the adult company.

As the afternoon drew to an end, Gwyn sighed with contentment. "Thank you, Lisa," she said. "This has been a very special day for me. I will be able to go home knowing what a beautiful granddaughter I have." She smiled and blinked back the tears.

Lisa smiled, too. Neither of them had said much about Ian. "Lisa," Gwyn looked at her directly as she stood up. "Do you think there is any hope for a reunion between you and Ian? He would want to know that." Lisa reached out gently and touched the older lady on the shoulder. "No," she said simply and shook her head.

"Then I wish you the greatest courage and respect for your decision to bring Kathleen up on your own. I take my hat off to you, Lisa. I lost my husband before my children completed their schooling, and I had to make ends meet. It's tough being a single mother. And you will have to manage all of this on your own." Gwyn paused and shook her head sadly. "Lisa, are you aware that my son has come into a lot of money through inheritance?" Lisa nodded her head. "Yes, I do know, Gwyn."

"Well, legally speaking, Ian should at least pay you a decent amount towards maintenance to help you along the road with Kathleen," she said matter-of-factly. "Please don't quote me, but I happen to know that he will be inheriting approximately twenty million shortly. Of course, if I were you, Lisa, I would find a decent attorney to represent your case, so that you can claim financial support for Kathleen as soon as possible." The old lady bent down beside her chair and picked up her handbag. She turned to thank Lisa and then walked slowly towards the door. "Goodbye, my dear," she said kindly. "And goodbye, dear little Kathleen. Look after yourselves and keep well. I hope to see you again someday."

"You're always welcome, Gwyn," Lisa said kindly. "If you do come back to South Africa, come and spend some more time with Kathleen and I." Lisa stood on the roadside waving goodbye with little Kathleen on her hip. Her little daughter smiling her partly toothless smile happily, waving to Gwyn, along with her mother.

Lisa had taken the advice given to her by the Fisherman's mother, Gwyn, regarding Ian's inheritance. After some consideration, she found an affordable lawyer who advised her on how to go about claiming a monthly maintenance payment for Kathleen's education. However, Lisa knew Ian very well. She understood the way that he saw things. Right from the beginning, she hadn't wanted to go this route. It had always just seemed more peaceful and simpler to do everything on her own. In Gwyn's mind, it was a cut-and-dry case of making a legal claim, but Lisa knew that Ian would never concede. He was too strong-willed and lived too far off the radar to ever be governed by the law. Nevertheless, she set the legal proceedings in motion and dutifully showed up at the courthouse repeatedly until finally the magistrate ordered a monthly maintenance payment to be set in Ian's absence. But the Sheriff of the court never managed to track Ian down to serve the court order, and the monthly maintenance cheques were never paid. It had all been a fruitless waste of time, exactly as Lisa had thought.

The Messenger Bird Named Cancer

The first two years of motherhood were the most physically challenging for me on my own. I spent most of the time on my own with Kathleen, with little glimmers of adult interaction here and there. Not long after the visit from Gwyn, I had a dream about an old friend, a Jeffrey's Bay surfing legend named Dragon Gold. The tall veteran surfer appeared wearing a long white and blue cotton caftan, and his bearded face was full of care. He showed me the African buchu plant. "To cleanse and heal," Dragon said with his kind eyes, and pointed to my womb. "Take care of yourself, Mama," he smiled and then vanished from the dream. In the days to come, I was left thinking about Dragon's message. My bones ached from weariness, and I knew that I was on the physical edge of exhaustion. The unceasing demands of looking after an energetic young child, working, and the pressures of keeping the wolf from the door had begun taking their toll. There was no extra income to pay for medical treatments, supplements, or healthy foods to help with the healing process. I had begun to lose a lot of weight and was feeling extremely fragile, and there were black circles underneath my eyes. By the time I began to use the buchu tea, the condition had already progressed. An herbalist from the area offered to make up a course of sutherlandia, buchu, and aloe-based medicine to help clear the infection. Deep in my heart, I knew that the condition was very serious and that I may need medical intervention. I made an urgent appointment to see the same gentle, generous-hearted Gynecologist who was present for the birth of my baby.

"Doctor Rishad, the stress that I have been under recently has been beyond comprehension. I haven't been looking after my health at all since Kathleen was born. It's just been so difficult, and there has been far too much financial pressure to carry on my own," Lisa sighed. Her doctor nodded kindly. "Yes, this condition is clearly your body's response to stress, my dear. All these factors play a role in your overall health, especially when it comes to one's womanhood," she said simply. This beautiful and insightful Muslim woman had recently returned from completing her Holy "Hadge" pilgrimage to Mecca during the most torrential rain recorded in recent history. While Doctor Rishad chatted about her experiences in Mecca, she did a thorough examination, took a smear, and did a few blood tests. Soon the test results came back. Lisa had early, stage two cancer.

She had always been a pragmatist, and there had only been one way that she had ever dealt with illness. She knew that she needed to immediately minimize her stress and get as much rest as possible. When little Kathleen got home from playschool, they would eat a healthy lunch and then Lisa would lie down with her little girl and read her stories until they both fell asleep. How her child loved hearing stories. It was telling stories in song and in books that fired her child's young imagination. The stories Lisa told Kathleen helped them both to make sense of a world where they were often alone. It populated their thoughts and imaginations with lively mythological beings. Sea creatures, mermaids, and fish that could fly and talk. Kat most loved to hear the stories that Lisa would invent while she sat with her mother on the beach. Stories kept her entertained in the most challenging of circumstances while sitting in waiting rooms at the hospital and in shopping malls, driving long distances to places in the heat of the African midsummer. "Mommy, tell me another story of your heart," her child would insist. Kat was happy and, in another world, born on the tongue of her mother's imagination.

It was the cancer that made Lisa decide to pack up all their belongings and move away from the city, far from all that they had known and far away from the Fisherman. She was running towards her healing, to a place where she and Kathleen could live a simpler life. Once she had made up her mind, there was no reason to stay. She threw a few bags of essentials into the back of her car and drove over Sir Lowry's pass, onwards, past the Swartland mountains, and far away into the Tsitsikamma forest. There, Lisa found an affordable, peaceful place for them both to live in a small farm village called Hankey, at the foothills of the Baviaanskloof Mountains. This fertile valley was once inhabited by the Go Aquasub, Khoikhoi people, as well as Saartjie Baartman, a beautiful young Khoi woman known for her historical significance. In the 1800s, Sara Baartman, became an indentured Khoi slave, working in the house for a wealthy Cape Wine producing family. She was taken to London by Dr William Dunlop, where she was put on show in Piccadilly Square as entertainment for the British public. Dr Dunlop had promised that after a year, he would give Sara her freedom and that he would bring her home on the same ship that she arrived on. Sadly, Dr Dunlop had not kept his word and had sold her to a Parisian medical scientist. Sara Baartman eventually died in Paris of syphilis, tuberculosis, and pneumonia. Her body was kept in Paris at the Musée de l'Homme[1] to support racist theories about people of African ancestry. Once Nelson Mandela became President of South Africa, he formally requested that Sara Baardman's remains be returned to her homeland for burial. And in 2002, her body was eventually returned to her native home, in Hankey, where she was buried on the hilltop for all to visit her grave.

It was in these beautiful, lush green farmlands surrounding the Gamtoos River where Lisa began to heal her body, mind, and soul of the cancer that had taken root in her womb. Thankfully, she had caught the cancer early, and there were plenty of treatments available to heal herself naturally. She kept in constant contact with her Gynaecologist and followed a strict cleansing diet which included lots of spring water, Papaya, yoghurt, and lots of fresh farm produce. Lisa also took herbal remedies daily, especially the powerful, bitter herb called Sutherlandia (Cancer bush) that Baba Vusa had shown to her in the Magaliesberg, the strong cleansing Aloe, and the Bulbines that grew in abundance around the Eastern Cape mountains of Hankey. She knew that she could not afford to let the infection spread or allow the cancer to survive in her body, and so she surrendered completely and utterly to the process of her healing.

That small, tight knot of fear and anxiety in my solar plexus would sometimes spread until it threatened to completely engulf me. At times like these, I would wake up in the dim light of dawn and stand outside, quietly surrendering in prayer. "Oh God," I would whisper through my tears. "I know that you would never have given me this beautiful child only to take my life. Please show me what I must do to heal myself. Whatever it is you want me to be and do, I will do. I offer the rest of my life to your service and to the service of humanity. Help me to restore my health!" I prayed ardently. And miraculously, within a very short time, I knew exactly what I had to do.

1 Museum of Man

The process of healing cancer is never a one-dimensional focus. It is always multifaceted and many-layered. My journey to healing naturally required the fullest attention to every single detail of my present reality. I began to really listen to my body and to what my body needed. I rested more, slept deeply, and took natural medications to relieve the nausea and pain. I grounded more and allowed my body to relax as often as possible. I knew I had to look to the future and allow the release of anger as a part of my healing process. The advice given to me by the psychologist several years ago regarding compassion and forgiveness played a vital part, and I forgave my father without even thinking about the need to do so. The healing process itself led me to the place of struggle and inner conflict. I saw myself sprinting like a Bushman hunter, away from the emotional pain that my father's behaviour had caused. And then I pictured him on his deathbed. In my vision, I saw myself turning back, just in time to stand beside my father and show him forgiveness and love. With that one single inner movement, I felt an immediate release. Just a few tears fell, but I felt a powerful shift within my body and soul. Somehow, I knew that from that point on, this cancer would start to heal. There was no more fear after that. My appetite began to return, and my strength began to build again. Still, I continued to take the cleansing herbs and do all that I could to heal my compromised immune system. As I began to get stronger, a powerful desire grew inside me to see the face of my mentor and spiritual father, the African sage, Ubaba Vusamazulu.

At that time, Baba Vusa, too, was recuperating from a serious illness. He had suffered from a heart attack and almost died in the ambulance on the way to the hospital. Had it not been for his wife Martha's nursing skills and her being there to resuscitate him with the "kiss of life," he would certainly have passed away. The Old Sage was still extremely frail and was recovering at their home in Kuruman. Lisa began to collect traditional African gifts to take to him. Sacred clay oxides, beads for traditional adornment, natural crystals that she had found in the mountains, candles blue, white, and red for an African traditional ceremony, and the most precious gift of all, a very sacred artifact that she had been asked to return to Baba Vusamazulu. It was the very same exquisitely beaded Sangomas Wildebeest tail switch that had belonged to his first wife Celia. This was the same precious artifact that had been lost when Baba Vusa's home was ransacked and burned down during the Bophuthatswana riots when he and his family had fled to the Magaliesberg.

Lisa understood that she was preparing for a holy pilgrimage of healing.

Miriam, the kind Khoisan woman from the Hout Bay fishing community who had been Kathleen's nurse, immediately came to help her when she heard that Lisa had cancer. She spoke to Miriam of her decision to visit her teacher, Baba Vusamazulu, for a few days. "Miss Lisa, you must go if it is time. I understand that these traditional things are the matters of God and of healing," Miriam said. She agreed that she would stay and look after Kathleen for a few days while she was away.

As soon as she felt strong enough to take the journey, Lisa drove the distance to Kuruman. She made an overnight stop on the farm of her Aunt Sherry and Uncle Ben, near Kimberley. The previous night had been extremely hot, and Lisa woke to find that massive thunder clouds had begun to gather. Her concerned Aunt Sherry suggested that she stay with them until the next day when the rain had cleared and it would be safer to drive, but Lisa decided to head off into the thunderstorm. The rain did not arrive until evening. It began softly and then started to bucket down just as she reached Kuruman. She drove through the lightning and torrential rain into the townships, arriving at the doorstep of her friend's home, in rivers of muddy water that ran through the streets. The astonished Baba Vusa and Mama Martha were standing outside in their dressing gowns with torches in their hands to welcome her when she arrived. Mama Martha immediately shuffled through to her spacious kitchen and very soon had the kettle on the hob. She chatted sleepily to Lisa as she brewed a steaming, hot cup of tea, offering her a pile of warm blankets and showing her where she was to stay that night. Then she bid Lisa a good night and padded back to her own bedroom. Lisa drifted off to sleep to the sound of the pouring rain, drumming on the corrugated tin roof of Martha's home. It was a strangely comforting sound and even more so because she had arrived safely at the home of her dear friends on this stormy night.

When Lisa awoke the next morning, Baba Vusa and Mama Martha were already up and waiting for her in the sitting room of their house, with anticipation. The rain was still pouring down, but more gently as Lisa dressed and prepared. She gathered up all the gifts that she had carefully collected to bring her friends. Somehow, Baba Vusa already knew that there was something extremely sacred that she had brought back to them. Lisa was shocked to see how ill Baba Vusa had been. He had lost a lot of his previous weight, and his face was drawn and pale, but he was waiting for her, watching every movement as she made the offering of her ceremonial gifts. When Lisa finally unveiled the ancestral relic, the ceremonial Wildebeest tail belonging to his first wife, Celia, Baba Vusa, caught his breath.

"Ma'am, how did you come upon this sacred artifact? Who gave this to you Ma'am?" he asked sharply, barely containing his anger.

"I was given this to return to you by a friend who knows you well, Baba. It was found after the Lotlamoreng, Mahikeng raids, and recognized as yours. And it was passed on through this friend who, at one time, helped you to design and build a traditional African temple."

"Ma'am, forgive me for my strong emotions, but I had thought this holy relic belonging to my late wife, Celia, was lost to me forever," Baba Vusa said, shaking his head sadly.

"Baba, I have been honoured to bring this valued artifact back to you and perhaps to restore some faith and peace in your soul again," Lisa said softly, sensing that the old man was upset and tired and needed to go to his private rooms and rest.

In those short moments together with Baba Vusa, I felt the intensity of his sorrow and the depth of the betrayal of the African traditional way that he stood for. This sacred Wildebeest artifact was a powerful and symbolic object given to the highest of the African Sangomas or healers for ritual purposes. It had been taken from his family home in Mahikeng, at a time when there had been so much political upheaval in Bophuthatswana. It was also around this time when the Great Sanusi had been terribly betrayed, tricked out of the royalties and copyright of his own book about Ancient African History and sadly, when Baba Vusa had lost his dear wife, Celia, to cancer. The return of the Wildebeest tail artifact had brought back all these memories in a great wave of sadness. I felt the old man's deep emotion, grief, and wrath rise as he held this memory in his hands. Even then, I knew that the sadness that had come upon him was largely caused by the terrible racial tension in South Africa. In this beautiful land, where small things could instantly spark suspicion and misunderstanding. I remembered feeling the full emotional charge of collective rage that surged through the African High Sanusi at the terrible acts of betrayal, corruption, and injustice in Southern Africa. I knew that all I could do at that time was to hold peace in my heart and continue my friendship and loyalty to Mama Martha and Baba Vusa—no matter what. It was this very loyalty and the unconditional love I felt for them that had forged the strong bond of affection and trust between myself, Mama Martha, and Baba Vusamazulu.

Lisa spent one more day with her friends before preparing for the long drive back to her child in the Eastern Cape. It was a Sunday. She had woken early to join Mama Martha at her church gathering. Martha was speaking openly with Lisa as they drove along the dusty township roads about the deep grief and sense of betrayal that her husband Baba Vusa still carried in his heart. As they arrived at the simple, corrugated shanty church that morning, Lisa saw a rose bush growing in the red soil of the churchyard. How miraculous to find that it was a peace rose—the most perfect symbol to give Baba Vusa to heal his broken and betrayed heart.

As she drove homeward to the Eastern Cape the next day, she thought about her precious daughter Kathleen and the promise that she had made to God during her healing, to offer the rest of her life in service of humanity. Within four months of her cancer diagnosis, her journey to see Baba Vusa and the move to the Tsitsikamma, Lisa was in full remission, and her natural vitality began to return.

Raaikat to the Stars

One day, Lisa was hanging out her washing in the garden when she heard her phone ringing. She dashed inside just in time to catch the phone call. It was Anna, her Khoisan friend from the Kalahari.

"He's gone, Lisa," she said through her tears. "Raaikat passed away peacefully on Friday night."

"I'm so sorry, Anna," she said with genuine care in her voice. "How have you been coping throughout all of this? I hope you're taking good care of yourself. Raaikat would have wanted you to. You know how much he loved you and had faith that you would carry on his sacred work as a custodian on behalf of the Khomani people."

"I know, Lisa, I know. It's just going to be very hard now without him," Anna said.

They had all known that Raaikat did not have much time left.

He had known for a long time that he was going to die, and he had prepared Anna well for his passing. Before Raaikat died, he had bought Anna the little house in Welkom that he had dreamed of. His artwork was now both in print and in the form of a book.

Anna spoke of his traditional Bushman burial and how his body had been wrapped in Lisa's soft Kikhoi blanket and then stitched into a Blesbok skin. They buried Raaikat in the most sacred and respectful way possible, laying his body in a "foetal" position, facing the rising sun. Sacred burial stones were placed on top of his grave site, and a strong Rosyntjiebossie wood "skerm" of latticed branches was erected over the grave site to protect his burial from scavengers.

"Lisa," Anna added. "Our American friend and sponsor, Dr Fiona Lewinsky, will be coming to South Africa with a whole group of her friends to pay homage to Raaikat's life and to visit the grave site. She has asked whether you and little Kathleen would like to accompany them. All expenses will be paid."

"Of course, we would love to, Anna. Raaikat and you are a part of our family. It is very important that we can be with you at this time," Lisa replied.

"Thank you, thank you so much, Lisa. We will all be glad to see you and little Kat again," said Anna. Lisa could hear the gratitude and strain in her voice.

Kathleen was two years old when they traveled to the red dunes of the Kalahari again. Dr Lewitzky had hired a small bus for the international guests, which took them all from Cape Town along the West Coast of South Africa and through the little town of Springbok, in the Namaqualand, then east to Upington and the Orange River. Fiona had hired a cameraman to film the highlights of the journey. She had also brought with her a group of interesting friends from all walks of life. Lisa found herself talking with an elderly Black American gentleman of Egyptian heritage. He was an astrologer and educator and had brought schooling for the black communities alive in Harlem by creating a library full of alternative and exciting books. The school had flourished because he had found a way to teach mathematics by teaching astrology and quantum physics. However, the Government education board had eventually shut his school down, and his library had been burned to the ground. Doctor Kanya, as they called him, looked exactly like an Egyptian scribe. Tall, intelligent, and full of natural respect for all the indigenous cultures of the world. Doctor Kanya had a mystical understanding of all things pertaining to the ancient civilizations of Egypt and the Ancient world. Lisa found it interesting to listen to him, and little Kathleen, too, was fascinated by his stories.

It was very hot when they arrived, and the full summer sun blasted the North American visitors. Lisa met up with Anna at the Twee Rivieren campsite where a chalet had been booked for each group. As they hugged each other, Lisa saw that her friend's loss was still an open wound in her heart. Anna was joined by all the Bushman people, Ouma Lys, the women, and the Khomani children. Lisa had brought along with her some handmade puppets that she planned to tell Bushman stories with. There was a huge fluffy lion, and some lion cubs, a meerkat, and a bumblebee. When the children saw these soft puppets, they went berserk with joy, pretending that they were lions and animals, laughing and tumbling in the Kalahari sand together. Little Kathleen and the Bushman children played for hours on the dunes with these animal puppets.

Night fell and Lisa gave each of the children a handful of firelight sparklers. After dinner, musical instruments were brought out—a conga drum and a penny whistle. Lisa lit the sparklers and handed one to each of the children. They held their sparklers aloft and ran around the fire, making spark patterns in the deep velvet canopy of night. Lisa began to tell the story of the origin, the birth of Mantis, the first Bushman... An African Sangoma began to play the congo drum, and Doctor Kanya breathed an air of the mystical into the story with eerie sounds of his penny whistle. The audience was spellbound.

They were all transported back to the beginning of time, where the spirit of Raaikat sat in their midst, watching and holding his beloved Anna by the hand. They were all one. The story brought them to a place of sweetness together. When the first Bushman, the Mantis, licked the honey that dripped out of the tree, they all felt the sweetness of life, and the African Sangomas began to ululate in unison when the Mantis greeted the sun, the earth, and the heavens.

These were the memories and jewel-like treasures that Lisa planted in her beloved child forever. The day had been hot and very full, and little Kat was so tired that eventually she curled up at her mother's feet in a soft springbok skin blanket that Anna had wrapped over her shoulders. She was sound asleep even before the golden full moon appeared in the night sky.

Early the next day, Lisa took little Kat by the hand and walked along the dusty path to the place where the Khomani encampment was situated. Just outside the Khomani camp was Raaikat's grave. Lisa could see the new branches of the grave "skerm"[2] around the burial mound in the distance. Grandmother Lys appeared walking towards them with her graceful, dignified gait. "Hello, Ouma Lys," Lisa greeted the old Bushman Elder respectfully. "Ai, Muvrou Lisa. Soek julle twee die begrafnis plek van my klein seun, Raaikat?"[3] she asked.

"Ja, ons loop maar om hallo te se. Raaikat was Kat se peetpa, En hy is nog steeds baie speciaal vir klien Kat."[4] Kat was watching the conversation and had not understood that their beloved Bushman friend had passed over. Lys and Lisa watched as little Kat tried to climb into the burial hut but couldn't. "Mommy, where is Raaikat? He's not here?" she asked with her serious little face concentrating on trying to look inside the burial skerm.

Lys and Lisa looked at one another with a sad smile. And

---

2   Shelter
3   Are you looking for the resting place of my nephew, Raaikat?
4   Yes, we have come to pay our respects. Raaikat was Kat's Godfather, and he is still very special to little Kathleen.

then Lys said, "Hy's weg, my engel. Hy is nou hemel toe." Lisa bent down to explain this to her little daughter. "Kat, our friend Raaikat was very sick and has died. This is his resting place now."

"No, Mommy, no!" little Kat cried, trying to dig a deep hole in the sand to get underneath the burial shelter to Raaikat. "Let me get him, please let me get him out. He mustn't die, he's our friend," she said, weeping and digging with all of her strength.

Lisa picked Kat up and carried her to the place where Oupa Haas, Lys, Pietkat, and all Raaikat's relatives sat under the shade of a tree. Oupa Haasie took little Kat onto his knee and showed her the great canopy of the sky. "Kyk nou my klien Kat. Hier is waar jou Peetpa is. Ou Raaikat is nou saam met ons. Maar hy is hoog waar die sterre in die hemel skyn,"[5] he said gently to her, drying her tears with his dusty sleeve.

Little Kat understood very well and this simple teaching from one of the Bushmen was to be the beginning of Kat's deepened understanding of how connected we all are to the galaxy and all of life.

That night, they sat around the Bushman fire in honour of Raaikat and Anna and ate their favourite foods. Roosterbrood (coal baked bread), chicken, potatoes, and onions, all cooked on the "braai" coals. The Khomani children broke off chunks of hardened and salty sand from the edge of the desert pan and were busily carving little sand toys for their new friend Kat. The children played these simple games until the sun went down.

It was sad to say goodbye to their new Kalahari Bushman friends, but the bus was leaving for Cape Town that morning. The next stop would be "Traveller's Rest," Pakhuis Pass, in the heart of the Cederberg mountains. This was Lisa's favourite haunt, and she had been asked to take the international visitors to see the ancient Khoisan rock art. It was here in this remote area of Southern Africa that the rock art of the Khoisan people was most

---

5 Here is where your Godfather is. He is with us, but he is high up there in heaven, where the stars shine.

prolifically found. These rock paintings varied widely in quality and subject matter, from majestic, shaded rock paintings of Eland to small monochrome red-ochre figures of hunters, dancing figures, family groups, and antelope. Each of these paintings was delicately depicted and exquisite in its detail.

Baviaanskloof Mountains

When little Kat was still small, it was easy to travel with her to these sacred places, and Lisa took Kat everywhere she went—on excursions, to exhibitions, and even to do mural painting work. But as Kathleen grew older, she needed more stability and young playmates of her own. Lisa made the decision to send her daughter to a play school in the nearby village. They were living in the heart of a farming community in the Baviaanskloof mountains, and little Kat had started pre-school among the orange groves of the Gamtoos valley, along with the local Khoi and Afrikaans farmer's children.

What was so uniquely beautiful about living in a rural environment was the freedom and space that Kathleen had to grow up in. She was a naturally expressive and friendly child. And whenever she smiled, her eyes would light up with sunbeams, and her whole body would smile along with her face. Little Kat knew her own mind very well. She knew what she loved and what she didn't. Lisa gave her plenty of space to explore and create in the magic of nature and the safety of her home environment.

For a time, they lived in a great sprawling farmhouse in the heart of a friendly neighbourhood where there were lots of children of Kathleen's age growing up, too. The house had a huge garden filled with rockeries, groves of banana and indigenous flowering trees, and best of all, a beautiful back garden with a swimming pool. But the greatest attraction for little Kathleen was her playmates. It was completely unimportant to Kathleen that she was an English-speaking child in the midst of an Afrikaans-speaking community. She loved her friends and wanted nothing more than to fill her home with friends. One day, Kathleen, in an adventurous mood, went to the pantry, helped herself to a strawberry lollipop, and with her Fischer toy wind-up radio on her shoulder playing at full volume, she danced down the wide farm street and kept dancing until she arrived outside the home of her favourite young friend. Lisa was busy in the kitchen while Kathleen went on this journey of discovery. She was almost four years old, an intrepid explorer and adventurer, with a heart filled with curiosity and love. Lisa soon noticed the silence and realized that her child had disappeared. Her heart stopped with panic at the terrifying thought that Kat had been kidnapped. An hour later, the message arrived from one of her neighbours to say that Kathleen was safe and playing happily on the trampoline with their young daughter.

Lisa and Kathleen had been so privileged to live in a safe neighbourhood like this one. Not far away were the most gorgeous camping sites along the Gamtoos river, exquisite lily pools to swim in, and places where one could go exploring into forested mountain kloofs. Here in this magical place of natural beauty was where Lisa had found refuge. She was constantly haunted by financial difficulty throughout the years while Kathleen was growing up. She had absolutely no steady form of income in the farmlands. She still had her painting career, but living so far away from the city had its disadvantages. There was no market for her work, especially living in the middle of nowhere in the Baviaanskloof mountains. Lisa was teaching art to children at the local primary school, which provided her with a small salary. The Summer tourist season in South Africa was the only time when steady income would stream in. For the rest of the year, Lisa and Kathleen simply had to tighten their belts and survive somehow. There were many good things about living in a farming community. People were more down-to-earth and solid. Food was rarely expensive, especially if you were buying from the farmers' co-op. Whenever Lisa's coffers would dry up completely and she couldn't think of anything else to do to feed Kathleen and herself, she would take her child by the hand, and with a rucksack on her back, they would go exploring the farmlands after harvest season. There were always navel oranges and naartjies left in the citrus groves, butternuts, "soet patat," green beans, and abundant mulberries in the trees growing on the banks of the river. Somehow, their cupboards and food bowls were always filled to overflowing.

An icy wind blows down from the Baviaanskloof mountains
We are prone, hidden in our pile of blankets
Our neighbours, conscious only of the muffled house life
Daily routine, some coming and going
Visitors enter our door and leave before nightfall
Quick footsteps on wooden floorboards
Laughter, shouts, and urgent calls
Then silence
We are warm together, she and I
Hidden in our pile of laughter
The snow falls thinly above us on vanishing peaks
We comfort ourselves
With small things
Seeds flung from trees in gardens
Words and song and laughter, like wine
Which flows on and on until the sharing ends
Naturally, we all need air and space
Thin sheets of snow air, sneak under our doors
Through windows left open a crack
We shelter together, she and I and our dog
In these last days
She says, "I want to stay here forever in this house"
But we both know the time will come
And we must go when the snow has gone
We must enter and leave just like the steady stream of visitors
That comes for warmth and company
We must move on, she and I
When the snow has gone

Rosaline's Supper

Lisa met a good Christian woman named Rosaline during their time living in the Baviaanskloof mountains. She was a powerfully built Khoisan woman, with the typical steatopygia[6] of her race. Lisa had got to know many of the local township folk through her community development work, but when she met Rosaline, the daughter of the local Pastor and her mother Sana, the doors to the heart of the Gamtoos Khoisan communities began to open.

Rosaline lived with her husband in a small, tin shanti, built into the red clay soil of the mountain. Their house was not far from the church, and if you walked up the winding dirt track through all the scrap and jazz of township life, you would soon reach the home of the Pastor. These beautiful Khoikhoi mountain people were Rosaline's family, and soon they became family to Kathleen and Lisa, too. The fact that these were Khoikhoi and Xhosa folk and Lisa was of Celtic origin didn't seem to matter to Rosaline and her kin. They loved her in a plain and genuine way, as they would love their own blood. When there was no money, no food, and nobody else to turn to, Lisa would drive to the home of Rosaline and her mother, Old Sana and her husband, Pastor Johannes. Here, Lisa and little Kat would always find warmth, love, and acceptance. Often, they would join the family for their simple rural church services. And afterwards she would hear the voice of old Sana say, "Lisa, wat eet julle twee vanaand?" Then she would shuffle off to the kitchen to return with a small packet of chicken and vegetables for them both.

One day, Old Sana sent a message to invite Kat and herself over for a braai in their yard. "Kom eet 'walkie talkies' saam met ons vanaand," said the text message on her cell phone.

"What on earth are walkie-talkies?" asked Lisa, laughing to herself and shaking her head. But her affection for this kind old

---

6 Large behind

matriarch and her friend Rosaline warmed her heart, and she sent a message back that they would be there that evening. That afternoon, Lisa took her little daughter to the township across the valley from where they lived. They stopped outside the Pastor's house on the dusty mountain street. The children were playing outside with an old soccer ball. Rosaline and her family were all sitting outside on plastic crates in the twilight, next to a huge bonfire. Pastor Johannes was playing Hymns on his old guitar. Everybody was singing and clapping joyfully along with the Afrikaans' songs. Pastor's granddaughter, Poppie, took Kathleen by the hand, and they went to play with their dolls while Lisa joined Rosaline's family around the fire.

"Ons is besig om 'n gebedsoptog te beplan. Ons sal baie bly wees as julle kan saam met ons stap,"[7] her friend Rosaline told her. "We are praying for peace and prosperity in our little community. We will pray for an end to the terrible problem of division between the farming community and us coloured folk who live alongside them, that there can be peace and understanding between our separate communities."

"We also pray for an end to the problems with drugs and alcohol in our township," Pastor Johannes said.

"And after the prayer march, we would like to hold a Christmas party for all the community children, in the Baviaanskloof park down by the river," said Rosaline, handing Lisa a freshly baked, still warm "as brood rolletjie."[8]

Soon, the Pastor's wife, Ma Sana, arrived carrying a large three-legged black pot filled to the brim with the famed "Walkie Talkie stew" to put onto the braai fire. The lid was on tightly, and the surprise for Lisa was yet to come! She stopped when she saw Lisa and smiled warmly. The Pastor's son, Marco, put down his battered guitar and took the black pot from her.

---

7 We are busy planning a prayer march and we would be grateful if you would join us, Lisa.
8 Coal baked bread roll

Ma Sana wiped her hands on her apron. "Hello, Lisa," she exclaimed with a wide, toothless smile. "Baie dankie dat julle twee gekom het."[9] Lisa followed Rosaline and Ma Sana inside their humble home to the kitchen, where she was busily cutting, peeling, and making generous bowls of potato salad and "boontjie slaai"[10] for the entire family gathering. Rosaline explained that the big get-together was because of the arrival of their missionary friends from Namibia. Ma Sana chatted to Lisa about the planned Prayer march. "Ons moet 'n opstog lisensie nog kry, Lisa,"[11] Old Sana had said. "Pastor must plan this prayer march properly otherwise we will all be stopped from gathering and celebrating. Nothing must prevent the power of this beautiful Christmas event from going ahead," Rosaline said with enthusiasm. There was much excitement and planning that night among the Pastor's friends and family, and even the children were excited because they were all going on a ride in a big old "karretjie" donkey cart, down the winding mountain road into the town to a beautiful park on the Gamtoos river. Here on the banks of the river where Sara Baardman and her people used to meet, dance, and celebrate was where they, too, would all gather to dance, feast, and celebrate for Christmas.

Supper was ready, the candles and paraffin lamps were lit, everyone present sat around the fire and bowed their heads while the Pastor led them in saying grace in Afrikaans. Then their simple meal was served. Little Kat and Lisa were presented with a truly African meal that night. Mielie pap with "Tomatie sous"[12] and the feet and heads of chicken or "Walkie Talkies," as they call them here in Southern Africa. Lisa politely accepted one but found the delicacy far too rich for her to eat. The family gathering, the soet patat, "boontjie slaai" and "asbrood rolletjies" were so enjoyable and the sense of communion and joy so strong that night, that

---

9 Thank you both for coming to join us.
10 Bean salad
11 We must get a permit to gather on public ground.
12 Homemade tomato gravy

this humble African meal and the occasion remained one of the most generous and memorable that Lisa and Kat had ever had.

Hamburgers at the Surfer's Pub

Lisa would often take Kathleen down to the sea to visit her friends—Dragon Gold and other South African surfing legends who lived in Jeffreys Bay—where some of the best surfing was to be found. Little Kat loved swimming in these warm waters and in the lagoon nearby, and they would sometimes stay overnight with a friend who had a beach house overlooking Seal Point at Cape St. Francis.

During long winter months, the beach house was often left unoccupied, except for a young Cape Khoisan maid named Donna. Lisa knew the family and their servants well, and they were welcome to stay overnight whenever they drove down to the sea. Donna was always happy to see them both again. She would chat with Lisa at length about her life in the Paarl mountains near Cape Town, growing up within the Khoisan community. "Ai, Lisa ek verlang so aan my Perelberg mense,"[13] she would say with a sigh.

One night, on the spur of the moment, Lisa decided to take Donna and little Kat out for hamburgers at the local beach pub restaurant in Cape St. Francis Bay. It was getting cooler in the season and Lisa had dressed her daughter up warmly. Their Khoi friend, Donna, was so thrilled to be going out at night that she dressed herself in her favourite new outfit for the occasion: A bright red trousers suit and pink beret that beautifully complemented her high cheekbones and dark curls. The three girls were a colourful company: Lisa and Kathleen, the two gypsy girls, and a Khoi woman, all wearing wide smiles. Little Kathleen was so excited! She didn't get taken out for dinner that often, and this was a wonderful experience for her. Her hair was brushed until it shone, and she wore seashell clips in her hair. All three were holding hands with little Kat in the middle as they entered

13 I miss my own people in the mountains of Paarl.

the pub. They were offered the best table in the house, overlooking the ocean from a comfortable window seat.

The small village lights began to sparkle, catching on the ocean and echoing as the waves cascaded onto the beach. Donna and Lisa both ordered a glass of white wine, and little Kat had a strawberry milkshake. She was in her pink phase. When Kat was still very little, everything but everything had to be pink. They sat sipping their drinks contentedly, chatting until one of the men at the bar looked in their direction. He stood up and came over to say hello. It was Frank, a local surfer and a good friend of the owners of the beach house. Lisa greeted him warmly. He smiled at Donna and Kat and went back to the bar where his friends were drinking beer together. The three were so content with their own company. Donna chatted away in both Afrikaans and English, and little Kat joining the conversation with her incessant questions, "Mommy, what's that?" and "Mommy, look at my drawing and why is that," and a million other small but necessary reasons to be heard and simply loved. Lisa had given Kat a drawing book and a pack of pencil crayons, which she took with her everywhere they went. Kat was busy now in the candlelight of the restaurant table. Her head bent low with concentration on her latest drawing of a mermaid. Life was such an adventure for this fantastic, alive little human being.

The hamburgers arrived with a special mini burger and chips for Kathleen. The restaurant began to fill up. Shortly after, a local guitarist arrived and plugged into the stage audio equipment. Soon, the local pub was a hive of activity and fun. The musician was playing and singing and some of the restaurant locals were dancing. Lisa took Kat by the hand and led her onto the restaurant dance floor with Donna. The three of them were having a wonderful time, laughing and dancing, until eventually, Little Kat was almost asleep on her feet. As Lisa walked back to the table, the waiter approached with a smile. "Your bill has already been paid, Ma'am," he said. Lisa caught her breath. "By whom? How?"

she stammered. "You have a secret admirer," said the manager. Lisa smiled and glanced over at the bar where her benefactor sat drinking beer. It was Frank. She smiled her thanks, blew him a kiss, and waved goodbye.

The three of them walked out onto the sandy street and got into her car. All the way home, Lisa couldn't help thinking about the many miracles, the many unexpected acts of kindness and magical things that had come about to help her along her path as a single mother. Every time she began to doubt that she had done the right thing to bring this beautiful little child into the world, another miracle would happen. Lisa was young, healthy, strong, and alive. Clearly, the Universe was on her side, helping her to make her way forward for the sake of her daughter. She climbed the stairs at the beach house, with her sleeping child in her arms and sighed with contentment as she tucked her sweet peach of a daughter tightly into bed.

A Christmas Family

The years passed, and Kathleen grew up into a thoughtful, sweet, and intelligent child. She was independent and very sociable. Above all, Kathleen loved Christmas time the most because it was a time when all her friends and family would come together, relax and share stories, enjoy braais, and celebrate the year. It was the magic of Christmas tradition that she loved, and it was made even more special by the sharing and family time that her soul craved. Each Christmas, they would take the annual "trek" back to Cape Town to spend a few weeks with Lisa's parents. Kathleen would help her grandmother wrap presents, bake cinnamon biscuits, and decorate the Christmas tree. "Mom, how many more days until Christmas?" Kathleen would wake up every morning and ask. Lisa would take Kathleen on the traditional expedition to find the perfect "fir" tree in the forests that grew on the slopes of the Cape Mountains. They would pack a small picnic and a wood saw in a bag and drive to the foothills of the mountains where the forest pines grew. Here, they would hunt until they found the right tree to cut down and decorate for Christmas. Kathleen would usually spend her time in the forest gathering pine gum that would run from the tall pine trees in the South African summer heat. "Look, Mom, I have found amber," she would say, holding out the sticky blobs of pine resin in her hands.

There were Carol singing outings to the beautiful botanical gardens of Kirstenbosch with her Granny and all her cousins. Movies and surfing on the beach with friends. Then Christmas day would arrive in a flurry of excitement, and Kathleen would wake up at the crack of dawn to open her presents. Christmas dinner would be laid out on the table. Grandma would set to work carving the Christmas ham, turkey, and beef. And then everyone would arrive, and begin drinking champagne, eating nuts and chocolates and sharing their gifts. The family would join the Christmas feast around the table together, and everybody would put on their party crowns, pull Christmas crackers, and tell Christmas jokes. The children at the far end of the table would tease each other, and for a while, Kathleen would have her heart filled. Her family together, all to herself.

If Kathleen had had one wish in her life come true, it would have been this: to have her family gathered close to her, not just on holidays, but throughout the year. The fullness she felt during these moments lingered on in her heart—a wish for togetherness, comfort, and belonging, enduring far beyond the festive season.

Love ripens and opens
the blossom full is ready to burst
all petals open for you
When the day cools
and nobody comes
I wait but don't hear that special footfall
I don't feel your soft skin brush against

I miss seeing your happy face
and love closes again
to protect that tender heart
while my petals cool
Waiting for you to come and visit again
but you are gone
years and years pass
the flower waits
and dies
and the river carries her petals to another land
her heart seeds start again
ripening growing waiting
knowing
while the cool river time rushes endlessly past
and one day you come down to the river
and see her in her new form
I've been waiting for you
in the heart of the flower
You see
what you have been looking for
We have both been searching
for that cool wide love
To carry us home
where we belong
just to be me
and you to be you

CHAPTER 11

PASSING ON THE TORCH

"If a culture rejects the sacred, it rejects the elders.
If it rejects the elders, it rejects the welfare of its youth.
You can't have one without the other."
—Malidoma Patrice Some'

Lisa found a small, one-bedroom cottage on the banks of the Keeurboom's river estuary. Although small, it was a safe and beautiful home for Kat and herself and exactly what she could afford. Lisa spent her time outdoors in the garden planting a vegetable patch, painting, and preparing her art classes for children. She found a stand of bamboo and river reeds growing near the river, and with these, she built a small playroom for her daughter on the terrace of their cottage. Then Lisa planted granadilla creepers along the bamboo walls so that the granadilla would offer both shade and its abundant fruits. It was a magical and happy space, and Kathleen loved her homemade play area. Kat grew up running and playing with the lambs and calves on the farm meadows and with the local Khoi farm workers' children, combing the beaches of the Tsitsikamma for shells and exploring the forests with her mother.

At that time, I was living on the barest minimum income. It was often hardly enough to feed myself and my daughter. I could just afford to pay for our little home and Kathleen's school fees, and, by the grace of God, we seemed to always have enough to eat. When the guava trees were in season, I would take a basket, and with little Kat beside me, we would gather guavas, make puddings and preserve to share with friends. When the tide was low, we would gather mussels and make delicious seafood rice paella. I planted a vegetable garden which produced an abundance of tomatoes, salad greens, beans, marrows, potatoes, and carrots, and when we went for our walks together, Kat on her bicycle beside me, we would collect wild mushrooms, nettles, cress, and water blommetjies[1] to turn into stew. In earlier years, I had learned how to collect medicines from the wild, and so I showed my daughter which plant juices to put onto her skin to heal cuts and bruises, as well as how to make medicinal tea to cure a sore stomach or cough. Kathleen grew up in a wonderful and imaginative world, where nothing was impossible, and creativity was the magic that made all one's dreams come true. This was a world where lack had no place at all—where gratitude for good friends and abundance had first place. A sweet and joyous world where even as we buried our beloved old dog, Baloo, there were still magical memories to take with us forever.

It was during this golden time with her young daughter that Lisa had another sacred dream. In her vision, she saw the Old Sage, Baba Vusa, had been severely paralyzed by a massive stroke, and it gradually became clear that he had passed away. In her dream, she saw how Baba Vusa's body was lovingly prepared and laid out for burial in all his ceremonial finery. He was surrounded by his wife Martha, his family, and many holy people who had congregated to attend his funeral. She saw herself standing respectfully beside his coffin, and as she stood witness, Baba Vusa

---

1 Water lily pods

took a breath, and life began miraculously to flow into him again. His eyes opened, and he saw her smile and held out his hands to her. She helped him to his feet again and was surrounded by a sense of celebration, with many people dancing, ululating, and singing with great joy.

Lisa had been having these prophetic dreams ever since she could remember. She had grown to expect that she would soon hear from friends and family members when she had such dreams. And sure enough, a few days afterwards, Mama Martha sent word to Lisa that they would very much like to visit her and little Kathleen on the Tsitsikamma coast. Mama Martha had been suffering from the exhaustion of caring for her husband and living within the confines of township community life that was often extremely harsh, fraught with violence and superstition. Both she and Baba Vusa desperately needed a seaside holiday with good friends and as far away as possible from the troubles they had recently experienced. It was just as her dream foretold. Baba Vusamazulu had recently suffered from a stroke that affected the entire left side of his body. Ma Martha felt that the rest, Lisa's friendship, the sea air, and sea medicine would do them both good.

Just a little way down the road from Lisa's farm cottage lived a kind and neighbourly family whom Lisa had befriended. The wife of the farmer was a Tswana-speaking woman named Emily, who, over time, had become her closest friend. Lisa immediately went to see Emily and told her about her dream and the request from these eminent people. Emily made her a mug of tea, and the two women sat for a long time together discussing the matter. "I don't have the space to offer our great friends, Em. The cottage is simply too small. Where will we sleep and how will I cook all the meals our friends will need?"

Her practical friend Emily offered Lisa a bedroom for Kat and herself in her own home and promised to help Lisa with bringing traditional African home-cooked meals over to Lisa's little farm cottage for Baba Vusa and Ma Martha.

The day of Baba Vusamazulu's arrival came. A beautiful place for the two older people had been prepared where they could rest and recuperate in peace. Lisa had filled their tiny home and space with beautiful things. Bowls of delicious fruit had been set out, and a glass vase filled with bright Lourie and forest bird feathers decorated the entrance. Her home was such a humble place to offer these venerable guests, the great national hero Baba Vusamazulu and his wife Martha, but the old couple had decided that they would rather be among humble friends and company at this time than accept the hospitality of affluent strangers.

The Old Man Vusamazulu was well over 90 years old when he and his wife made the long journey to the Cape to visit. The Great Prophet, author and Sanusi suffered from sugar diabetes and had been ill many times before, but this time was different. Regardless of his weakened state and the obvious effects of the stroke, he still wore his holy ceremonial cloak and the heavy bronze and jade necklace around his chest, and he always kept his sacred staff with a bronze dove on the top close to him. Always, the Old Seer walked with the Ancestors, and more so now that he drew close to the crossing point of his life.

Once again, Lisa had been offered financial help from her American friend and sponsor, Dr Fiona Lewinsky—enough to cover the costs of transport, groceries, and fuel for these important guests. On the day of their arrival, Lisa, little Kat, and Emily's family lined the farm road waving South African flags as the car carrying their special guests arrived. Emily and Lisa had prepared and laid out a feast for Baba Vusamazulu and his wife. All their neighbours arrived bearing gifts of food and drink. Chairs were brought from her friend Emily's home so that all could sit and listen to this grandfather of Storytellers share the tales of Africa. Although the great man was exhausted after a full day's travel, Baba Vusa, the Great Zulu Father, spoke on and on into the evening, telling animated stories about the Great Kings of

Africa like Dingaan and Mzilikazi until daylight had completely faded from the sky. And then, with some effort, Baba Vusa stood up and raised his sacred staff to the heavens.

"Who will tell the stories when I am gone," he said with sorrow. I felt Baba Vusa's heart flame reach out to ignite my own. In that one apparently ordinary moment, my heart knew the answer. "I will." I realized I was born to protect this sacred legacy. The truth of our African past. At that moment, I knew that becoming a guardian of this legacy was my calling. That moment was the passing on of the torch for many light bearers.

The truth is, our calling does not originate in the external world. It is our souls that are constantly calling us to our life purpose. This calling is built into our very cellular structure and coded into our DNA as the blueprint of our lives. We are each like a single puzzle piece in a gigantic multidimensional puzzle, each of us embodying a unique piece that completes an aspect of the entire picture. So, when this Great African Sanusi gave voice to his sorrow, he was speaking of his search for these missing pieces of the puzzle. His question, "Who will tell the stories when I am gone," was about finding those who would fill his place as a guardian, custodian, and story keeper of Ancient African history and truth, long after he had passed on.

Lisa was born in Johannesburg into an ordinary middle-class South African family and was neither African by race nor descent. She was a humble artist, a mother, and an ordinary woman with only her goodwill, sincere love of Africa, and her friendship to offer. Yet in that instant of respect and love for her teacher, she knew beyond all outward appearances, and beyond all that was intellectual or academic, on a purely soul level, that she was called to this task. Baba Vusa had known this through all the years that they had been friends. Throughout her entire life, everything she'd ever believed in, everything that she had come to understand about South Africa, her own life story, the disintegration of natural family values, and the African traditional way, had set her on a quest for truth. This was beyond any personal request. It was her own soul calling. Everything she held sacred was given meaning by this call to share the precious heritage and traditional history of Africa with our children.

When the stars began to twinkle above the rural homestead in the Tsitsikamma, Baba Vusamazulu and his wife Martha bid everyone goodnight and returned to Lisa's humble cottage to sleep.

Their guests blessed Lisa with their presence for just over a week. Many people came from the towns and outlying areas to see the Great Sanusi, but the Old Seer was very tired and not feeling well at all. He slept most of the time and awoke only to prepare himself to meet groups who had come to see him. Lisa took her old friends to see the forests and to collect mphephu[2] and other sacred herbs along the forest lanes. She also took them to the sea, where Baba Vusamazulu could look out at the Great Mother Ocean and speak to the whales and dolphins in the mysterious language of a High Sanusi. When Lisa asked if he would like her to bring him some sea water to bless, he smiled mysteriously and softly replied, "The sea is already swimming in me." The language he spoke was of a deeply connected soul. One who truly could feel the cetacean creatures singing their deep ocean story to his heart. He raised his old arms to the sky, holding the symbol of the ancient Ankh[3] to the oceans and to the sky in blessing.

The next day, Baba Vusamazulu heaved his heavy and crippled body out of bed, knelt on the floor, and began to pray in earnest for the rains to come to the drought-stricken Eastern Cape and to Southern Africa. Before long, the first raindrops began to fall.

Just before they were ready to begin packing to leave for their home in Zululand, Baba Vusamazulu had yet another mild stroke.

2   Wild African sage
3   Symbol of all Life

This time, Lisa was ready and fully prepared. She had listed all emergency numbers on her cell phone and ensured that she was ready for all eventualities regarding her guests' well-being. It was late at night while everyone was still sleeping. The rain had already begun to pelt down on them, and the farm roads rapidly became waterlogged and almost impassable.

"Mama Lisa, Mama Lisa, come quickly, help me please," she heard Vusamazulu's wife Martha urgently calling her. "Baba has fallen and had another stroke. He needs to go to the hospital." Lisa immediately called the emergency ambulance services while Mama Martha packed a few of their essential things into a bag. When the ambulance arrived, it was pitch dark and the rain was pouring down so hard that the cottage roof had begun to leak. Lisa watched as the ambulance turned slowly onto the dirt road to the farm, splashing through all the mud in the early morning hours. The medical attendants entered their cottage and gently loaded and carried the unconscious old African sage on a stretcher through the coursing rain. Thankfully, the ambulance was an emergency overland vehicle and could easily navigate the flooding river to get Baba Vusa to the nearest hospital just in time to stabilize him. He was in safe hands for the while. His wife, Martha, went along with him in the ambulance and stayed beside him until she knew he was out of danger. When she returned to Lisa's cottage, the sun had begun to shine through the rain clouds again, and the rain had turned the green farmland into a wide and beautiful vista of blue. The rivers were overflowing, and the farm roads were muddy and almost impassable. Mama Martha slept until she was well rested, and then she joined Emily and Lisa for a chat, a good laugh, and a cup of tea on Emily's farmhouse stoep.

After a week in hospital, Baba Vusamazulu was strong enough to be discharged.

"We must return to bless your home, Mama Lisa," Baba Vusa said to her. And despite Martha's objections to his weakened condition, Baba Vusa had Lisa bring them both back to her cottage for the night. Lisa had already arranged for a well-equipped, comfortable ambulance to fetch the Old Sanusi and his wife the next morning and drive them all the way back home to Kuruman in the Northern Cape.

That night, the old sage was restless. Lisa brought him a bowl of soup, but he ate very little.

She and Grandmother Martha had just finished their own evening meal when Lisa heard sounds at the entrance to the cottage. The old man stood, swaying precariously in the doorway. His enormous African body, framed by the light behind him.

"I heard voices outside. Where are you, Sthandwa?"[4] the old man asked.

His wife, Martha, was exhausted. She sat outside in the garden, wrapped in her blanket, enjoying the balmy autumn evening.

"I'm coming inside just now, Vusa Sthandwa sami."[5]

Lisa stood up and took the old man gently by his arm, leading him inside the cottage, back to his bed. She helped him to sit down and take the slippers off his swollen, old feet. Then she lifted both his legs and covered him with a warm blanket, sensing the trauma in his body, the confusion of thoughts, ebbing and flowing like a storm in his mind.

"Close your eyes and rest now, Baba Vusa, close your eyes. I will stay here with you and sing you to sleep." Lisa sat down on the bed beside him and began to hum the tune of a traditional African lullaby. The old man closed his eyes slowly, and his body began to soften and relax. As she sang, Lisa found the words of the lullaby coming back to her.

Thula thul, thula baba, thula sana,
Thul'ubab 'uzobuya ekuseni.
Kukh'in Khan- yezi, zi-holel' u baba,
Zim-khan yi sela indlel'e ziyak haya,

4 A Zulu word for "darling"
5 Vusa my darling

Sobe sik hona xa bonke be- shoyo,
Be-thi bu- yela u bu-ye le khaya,
Thula thula thula baba
thula thula thula sana
Thula thula thula baba
Thula thula thula san

Quiet my child, quiet my baby.
Be quiet, daddy will be home in the dawn
There's a bright star that will lead him home,
the star will brighten his way home.
The hills and stones are still the same my love
My life has changed, yes, my life has changed
The children grow but you don't know, my love
The children grew but you don't see them grow

She sang the gentle African refrain on and on until the old man was fast asleep.

In the morning, the Great Teacher, Baba Vusamazulu was already awake when she brought them coffee.

"Ngiyabonga kakhulu,[6] Mama Lisa. Your singing brought me peace last night, and my tired old body has rested and healed. From now on we shall call you, 'Nomngoma' which means, 'The Mother of Song.'"

Before the old couple left the Tsitsikamma, Baba Vusamazulu blessed her home and herself and her daughter, Kathleen.

"Mama Lisa, we will not be traveling much in the future," said the Old Man slowly. "This may very well be our last visit. I shall return home now to spend my last days at my wife's home

---

6 Thank you so much

in Kuruman in peace. Please Ma'am, look after your child well. Always remember that you are an artist and a deeply spiritual person, and you will need a very special and holy place to live. Teach the children to respect and honour the sacred places of Africa and to honour the Great Spirit Unkulunkulu in these holy places. Teach them to remember the ancient ways!"

Lisa looked at him respectfully and quietly nodded.

"Please, Ma'am, I ask you respectfully. You must write a book. A truly great book about Africa and its people. The world must know about what is happening to the children of this continent. Without you and others like you who will speak out, our children are destined to become the 'Lost Generation.' Ma'am, please do everything in your power to save our African Grandchildren from this terrible fate. You must write this story and many other stories, too, so that they will remember the path that their African ancestors once trod."

Mama Martha smiled with care in her eyes at her husband. "Baba is right, Lisa. The children of our time have forgotten their legacy. They have lost all respect for their elders, for nature, and for our Ancient African traditions. They have fallen into the trap so many children have, and they sit all day watching TV or playing games on cell phones. It is as though the children have forgotten how to play together outside anymore."

Baba Vusa had taken off his thick-lensed glasses, and Lisa could see the tears falling from his eyes. "The children do not understand that our traditions have long been here for their protection. The past is the mother of the future. The schools here in South Africa do not understand this, Ma'am. And our children are being educated in a way that does not encourage them to respect their traditional heritage. So many times, I see children learning things at school about our own African history. Facts about our greatest leaders that are incomplete and utter rubbish, Ma'am. These school history books are misleading, and our children's minds are being skewed by the misinformation that they are being taught as part of the curriculum. They are turning away from their own traditions and families because of it. Our African people are no longer proud to be African anymore. They have become ashamed of who they are, of their parents, grandparents, and great grandparents. These children should be taught the kind of history that has been recorded by African people. Well-researched information and not biased facts about our history and traditional ways. We need friends like yourself, Ma'am, who will restore the pride and dignity of our African nation. If our young people continue the way they have, addicted to technology, drinking at the shebeens, abusing their women and each other, spoiling our beautiful land, and leaving our old ones to suffer and die, the future will become very bleak for all of us, Madam Lisa. We must remember the ancient ways and respect will be restored in this land and far beyond."

Lisa bowed her head. "I promise to honour you and do whatever I can that is best for the children of Africa. Thank you, my dear friends, for blessing my child and me with your presence." She smiled gratefully at Baba Vusa and Mama Martha.

The old Sanusi bowed his head in farewell.

With that, he and his wife Martha departed her home, leaving the spirit of peace and gratitude behind them.

KIRSTENBOSCH BOTANICAL GARDENS

Miracles are never where we expect them to be
If we wait, they come to us
In places like this
Bright Garden of Contemplation
Floral treasures which cluster
Like gemstones in Aladdin's cave
We wish, and are transported instantly
Over lawns, under milkwood
Through forest and vlei
Deep into glades and deeper still
Within ourselves
The Summer Agapanthus herald us
Swaying on long and graceful stems
Blooms blue and indigo, violet and purple
Are temples of pollen
For beetles, butterflies and bees
Each floret is so precise in pattern and design
The Agapanthus sings her praise
In heavenly chorus
To our Master Architect
To the granite mountains above Cape Town
To the sky a breeze with life
To the winds Southeast and stormy
And to the sun, our gold Cape sun.
Little feet and children's happy hands
Explore and touch and climb
The gardens knowing trees
Decades and even centuries old
Their branches hold our children
The soil and soft turf

Have replenished tired souls
Broken spirits lifted, healed
And nurtured
With each draught of beauty
From the cup of Suikerbossie protea
The flame of Strelitzia
Ericas, dandelion, velvet scented geranium
Love inspired and coloured with the sweet song
Of Cape Robins, doves
The crickets and cicada's hum
And in winter the storm comes and steely cold
The garden holds us still
Hibernating are those seed thoughts
Waiting for the colours of the Sun.
Out of our sleep
We come to the garden and are blessed
With sense and unfurled fronds
With tree shadows that evoke memories
With fallen leaves that scatter our doubts
Again, and again we return
Our footsteps we retrace
Into this gentle valley we go
To seek a miracle and unveil its face
For although so few would admit to such
We all still hope for Magic
And although we bow to the urban rules
It's the Garden and Nature
Which provide
God's
ultimate
Hat trick

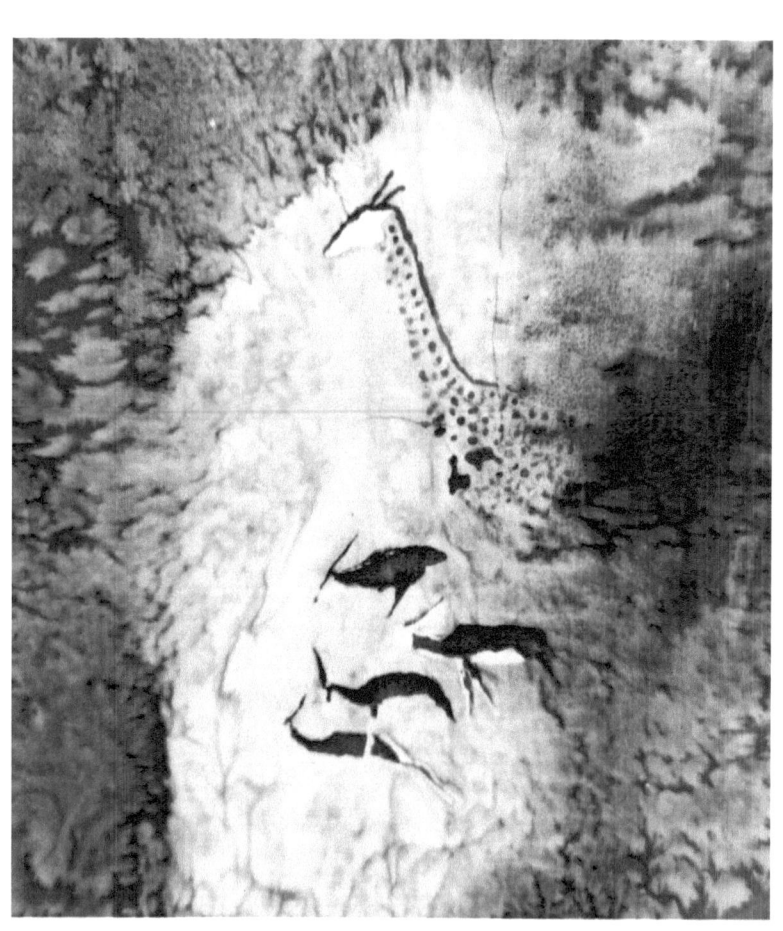

CHAPTER 12

SURFING IN THE GALAXY OF LIFE

With tears, I released him back to the Great Oceanic Mother,
where he belonged. The "Wildman," the Fisherman that he
always was. His soul was released from separation as he was
carried through time and space on the back of a giant sperm
whale, surfing in the galaxy of life.

Soon after, Lisa received an offer to work at the Kirstenbosch
Botanical Gardens in Cape Town. It meant moving back into the
city again, changing schools, and making new friends. At least Lisa
still had her family living in Cape Town, and Kathleen was happy
because she would have her beloved grandmother living nearby.

Lisa was aware that unseen angels had drawn her to leave
their humble, beautiful home on the Garden Route. Perhaps it
was the hand of the Master Weaver of Life itself. Lisa accepted
the position at Kirstenbosch Botanical Gardens as an assistant
coordinator and designer. Her daughter, Kat, was placed at a
primary school nearby. It didn't take long for Kathleen to
discover that she had to fit into a very different and constraining
public school system. Neither mother nor daughter fitted into a
cosmopolitan city world.

At first, people who met them didn't know what box to put Lisa and Kathleen into. In the world of labels, titles, and social ranking, they were not even considered. Kat was a child of the wilderness; she had been to the deserts of the Kalahari and had sat with Great African elders and with the Bushman people. She had never known about a holiday overseas nor owned an electronic toy.

Lisa didn't have a smartphone or drive a flashy car. Society and family, which should have been their safety net and their tribe, seemed to have changed completely. They no longer fit in, nor were they accepted into its fold. Within about a year, they both had become outcasts of the mainstream city world and extended family where they were supposed to belong.

Lisa's intuitive navigation system kicked in and began directing their focus away from family dynamics or anything uncomfortable or the opposite of their happiness. Her job at the Kirstenbosch Gardens was a grace. These beautiful gardens, situated on the slopes of the Cape Mountains, were a sanctuary for Lisa and her child. On weekends, she would pack a picnic and take Kathleen with her to explore and enjoy the magic of this tranquil natural environment. Only her own dear mother's love was left, surviving like a candle burning in the wind, harbouring her granddaughter and her child, in the knowledge that at some stage, Lisa would find her place here or that they would eventually leave Cape Town.

The process of letting go of Cape Town and their family completely took almost three years. In that time, Kathleen grew from a freckled young child into a unique, strong, and vibrant young woman. They learned the profound lessons of letting go of what they had to, and then they left the beautiful mother city again. They were "on the road" mother and daughter—gypsies and homeless, except they didn't have a mobile home to sleep in, as the Fisherman had done. Perhaps their sojourn to the city was about unfinished business. It was a difficult, sad, and tangled time.

Inevitability was a huge part of this chapter of their lives. Kat was already eight years old when they arrived in Cape Town. She had asked to see her father, and Lisa had tried to find him, asking everyone who knew of him for his whereabouts. Ian's own family had also tried to contact him, but he never answered his phone. The only sign of him she ever found was someone she thought was the Fisherman. A homeless man wearing a Khaki jacket like his—a burned-out shell of a human being, lying in a crumpled heap asleep—but she couldn't be sure it was him. The man she found was a broken human being, motionless on the beach with his green jacket hood covering his head. Nobody was home. The steel gate of this man's heart was shut tight against this life for good.

It had been years since anyone had seen the Fisherman. His mother had been searching for him high and low. No telephone calls, no letters, and no communication. It seemed that he had been lost for many years. Lisa had heard no word from him ever since Gwyn, the Fisherman's mother, had gone to live in Australia. He had vanished from the surface of this earth, leaving little or no trace of himself behind. Some thought that he worked as a handyman at a local seaside backpacker, but they couldn't be sure. The handyman never disclosed his real identity. They only knew that he drank heavily and often slept on the beach. The Fisherman's mother had gone home to her family in Australia with a broken heart, believing she had lost her son.

Kat was around ten years old when the news came. It was almost Christmas, and Lisa and Kathleen had been staying with her mom. It was evening, and they were on holiday. The feeling of Christmas was in the air. They had been to the beach, and as Lisa arrived home, she heard the telephone in the house ringing. Ian's mother was calling to say that her son, the Fisherman, had passed away on the beach. That night, rainbows, double-banded, triple, and more, glistened in the evening sky. People stood on rooftops, taking selfies and rainbow photos with their cell phones. Little did they know of the story behind the life of a Fisherman—a white

Bushman who was, in these moments, leaving the planet with a completely open heart.

Lisa felt the weave of life give a little and then break through as the realization sank in. Her heart dropped heavily like a stone. She listened to the sound of his mother weeping on the phone, on the other side of the world. Lisa said little, yet enough to share her deep regrets and sympathy. Through the heavy waves of her shock, she listened to this fragile old woman trying to stay coherent while expressing her plans to come to South Africa for his funeral.

Ian's family had asked Lisa to identify his body at the government morgue. Perhaps it would have been best not to, but it had felt right and complete to do so. It was closure for her and, although a difficult decision, one that she felt compelled to make. It gave her a chance to bless him and to say goodbye. When she got there, she was surprised at the strength and courage that she felt. The government official led her through the mezzanine into the back of the mortuary. There he was, behind a thick glass-plated window. His tough, stocky form showed clearly beneath the body bag covers. When they opened the canvas, Lisa found it very difficult to recognize the form presented. Only his face was shown under the mortuary covers, and this was so changed it was difficult to be sure because the body had already been exposed to the hot South African sun. He looked like a sea creature, a merman who had been washed up on the land. His body had already begun to deteriorate, and much of it looked like the sea-green kelp on the rocks where he loved to fish.

His relatives and family decided to have him cremated immediately. Lisa was glad about the decision because no mother should have to see their child that way, let alone bury them. It was better that Gwyn remembered him in the fullness and prime of his life.

The funeral was held on the beach where the Fisherman was found. A motley crowd was gathered beside "Leopard Rock" at the beach parking area. A few homeless people had also arrived to honour their departed friend. Lisa collected Kathleen from school and drove to where his family was having the funeral.

All that Kathleen could think of at the time was having a little piece of her father to hold onto. "Mommy, please, could you save some of his ashes." But when Lisa gently asked Gwyn, Ian's mother, to please keep some of the ashes, the old lady was so lost in her grief that she flatly refused. Kat was standing within earshot with her mother when she heard Gwyn's words, "What on earth would possess you to want his ashes? There could be something recognizable in there, and you wouldn't want that!" The full shock of realization hit Kathleen like a freight train. Her father was gone forever. She had been refused and rejected, and now absolutely nothing of her father remained. Her sorrow and the pain in her young heart knew no bounds. The little girl began to run across the beach, as far away as she could get, as far as she could go, until she had climbed up the highest dune at the furthest side of the beach. And there she sat, digging a hole in the ground in hopeless desperation, trying to bury the wound of deep rejection, hurt, and disappointment that had opened in her all over again.

"Kat, Kat, it's okay, Kat," Lisa called hoarsely, running across the windswept beach. She climbed the steep, grass-tufted dunes and eventually found her daughter sobbing in the sand. Lisa knelt beside her weeping daughter. Gently, she took her child into her lap and spoke words of comfort, rocking her and stroking her hair.

"Alright, my darling, alright, you're alright," Lisa murmured to her daughter, as she held her and rocked her in the sand on the dune. "Your father's spirit is still alive. He lives on. He lives in you, my precious child. You and your beautiful being and body are closer than any ashes or possessions that your father could ever have left behind."

"But Mom, Mom," Kathleen sobbed helplessly. "I only wanted a tiny, little bit, just a tiny bit of my dad, to keep—that's all." Then she buried her head in her mother's bosom and cried on and on.

Lisa held her and let the tears of loss, longing, and emptiness flow.

"My darling, I know that what you were asking for was fair, and I understand how hurt you are feeling today, Love. But, please, try to understand that no one can take away the fact that you are the Fisherman's special child. So come on and dry your tears. You have so much to be proud of. Let's both get up and stand up tall. I'm taking you to a restaurant nearby to get a lovely cool drink!" Lisa took her young daughter by the hand and dusted off all the sand. Slowly, they walked back along the beach together to the nearby beach cafe, where they sat quietly, side by side, sipping their ice-cold drinks. It was all over. There was nothing left to hope for now. Nothing more that could be done. Her child had every right to feel this pain and cry.

"Why didn't you try harder to find Dad? We could have found him and saved him Mom, I know we could have. He was probably right here all the time, and I never even got the chance to know him or hear his voice," Kat sobbed.

"Kathleen, love, there was nothing more we could do. You will understand this more as time goes by," Lisa said gently, looking into her daughter's puffy red eyes. "I know you want him here, but remember—you will always be the closest living legacy there is to him. After all, you are his only living child."

Lisa and Kathleen made their way back to where the funeral gathering had been. The few tramps left hanging about met the mother and her daughter at the car park.

"They have gone inside to have a meal at a fancy restaurant," said one.

"Ja, we were not invited," said another man with a shrug and a gravelly laugh while winking at Kathleen. "You could come and join us at the beach pub if you like. We will treat you to a pizza and a beer," he said, smiling at the Fisherman's daughter.

"Are you my dad's best friend?" asked Kathleen, looking up at the tall man with dreadlocks in his hair.

"Ja, we were all your father's friends a long time ago. Always used to fish with him, but now we are not welcome to his funeral," said the white Rasta tramp, Pete, with a cynical laugh.

Lisa's daughter warmed to this man. She felt no revulsion, nor did she feel that he was different in any way. Kat accepted him as her dad's friend. "We can join you," she said with a sweet smile, and the homeless man looked at her with love. She hadn't judged him at all.

They were instant friends, this innocent child and the man from the street. She slipped her smaller hand into his grubby, calloused hand and the two began to have a deep conversation about her father the Fisherman, and his life. In many ways, this homeless man helped the Fisherman's child to put things in perspective and to deal with the pain of her loss.

"You know Ian was a cut above the rest of us, don't you? He was always organized, well-dressed and clean, and a good fisherman. Ian taught me how to fish like nobody else could. He was a good friend to me, Lisa," Pete said, wiping his tears on his sleeve. "We had a disagreement some time ago, and I hadn't seen him for quite a while. You see, Ian was a naughty one. He started to mess around with some hardcore drugs. I warned him about it once. I told him nothing good would come of it and that the law would catch up with him eventually. But it was no use. I was right. He was caught poaching and smuggling and that's when he lost everything. You know Ian. Man, he was a 'Harde Kop,' that one," Pete said, shrugging his shoulders and shaking his head.

On that day, Pete had taken a soggy matchbox out from his well-worn pants, and as she left the pizza restaurant, he handed Lisa the box and said, "Here, Mommy, it's for her. I gathered up some of the ashes when the old lady wasn't around. She can keep them and do whatever she wants with them. So, don't be a stranger when you see us on the street again, okay? Cool." He leaned over and brushed the young girl's peachy cheek.

◈

My Love is safe within the
heart of time
No coarse or vain intention
can spoil its gentle shine
My name and your name are set together in the stars
And so, I seek no more on earth for you
But smile inwardly towards your heart

Message in a Bottle

It took a long time for Lisa to come to terms with what had happened. The Fisherman's death had come as an enormous shock to her. His death was symbolic in many ways. It was the end of a cycle and a completion. Lisa had no one with whom she could relate her experience, so she began writing. She wrote letter after letter to the Fisherman. She filled a bottle with gifts from the sea, with a lock of her hair, and put these into a beautiful bottle with the letter to Ian. Then she corked the bottle tightly and threw the message far out to sea where the Fisherman used to go catching crayfish at night.

The Letter

Ian, I remember how drunk and lost you used to get. I remember how you would search every memory and story I told you for mistakes, holes, and reasons to pour your shame and pain into. I remember the smell of powerful fire water, and smoke on your breath and skin when you would return hungry for my warm embrace at night. I remember how you would make me feel when you could only think of liquor and the next quick fix before you had even looked at my face or remembered why or that you were here. I remember all those challenging moments juxtaposed with the eternity of soul and the poetry of us sitting together on a rock with limbs and hands entwined. I remember all the tears, and the doorways where I stood, having to set you free to choose alcohol or me. I remember, I remember, I remember, our little girl born at the same place where we met, and the sweet and aching heart as I waited and hoped that someday you might realize what it all meant and come home.

I remember the vaults of tears and the years of hopes and disappointments as I dropped down, down, down to the earth where you had crossed over, leaving your body behind for good. All those windows were kept open just in case you returned, but all for nothing. Fisherman, you were trapped in your own nets, entangled in a web of history, pain, and loneliness—unable to cut yourself free of the trap of disillusionment that deadened your very soul. Addiction to alcohol. We were both the losers in the end, and all that promised love was blown away like sand footprints in the wind.

But I carried on, keeping one foot in front of another. We have our child, our beautiful daughter, to forever remind us of our shared love. And when I look at her, I see you. I see your sea-blue eyes, and I see the deep, deep care. And to tell you frankly as plainly as I can, I miss you, Fisherman. I miss everything that we did. Nature walks, the long, long talks, our secret spaces, and the dreaming that we did together. Many hopes and dreams. So many lives within a few years. We could have had it all, my special soul—there was no end to the vast adventure that life had in store for us. We were given a perfect hand of cards. We could have had our perfect ocean home where we watched dolphins swim in their wide arc into the horizon. We could have created family life, so simple, a dance of lovers and our young child together, blending all our energies and creativity. We could have shared so much of what we had. Our great love for one another could have touched the four corners of this world, Fisherman. But instead, the road took you on another way back home, leaving me to live out our wild and exotic dreams alone. I know why you left me and understood your fears, but even after so much time, a place within me longs for the exquisite nature being that was you.

I remember how one New Year's night, I was mourning you. I wept and wept an endless river, a waterfall, rapids, and streams of tears. So many, many years. Ten years and more of waiting for you to magically heal and come home to us once and for all. But you never did. All my prayers went unheard, unmet, and unheeded. Every seed of love that I had ever poured into your broken soul had been for naught. All the windows and doors in my soul left open for your return, for nothing now. Your beautiful daughter is forever fatherless after all my hopes and dreams—forever shattered.

I wept, rooted to the spot of weeping, and all time became tears. I was utterly lost in that timelessness of sorrow—no more life. The line is broken now, and only emptiness is left where you once were. I sat there, coming to terms with loss, in a strange place, in the middle of nowhere—yet everywhere with you. You died here at the beach in this seaside village. Your heart gave in; it broke. No, it exploded with all the love so long contained. All the anger, rage, frustration, alienation, and betrayal suppressed for so long. Not even your lips would speak about this love and longing to be reunited with our family again. Two souls who hungered to be together, kept apart by the very thing that separation caused, this false sense of alienation, an identity based on victimhood, of succumbing to addiction instead of accepting the heart's true longing to be loved. To be the love, the good, brave, beloved father to our child. Yet, this very thing that joined us, the freedom and will to choose, kept us apart in the end: just pride and egocentric thought, which manifested as isolation and did our child no good.

If I could put time in a bottle and put your realization into that bottle, too, maybe that would have been the last time you ever drank. The poison you smoked and the pain-relieving numbness you injected into your veins would all simply disappear, and the vision of your life, your love, the mother of your child, our baby in my arms, would reveal itself so clearly.

I rocked myself in my sorrow, the tears staining my dusty face. Forgetting time, the people there, forgetting all but this. This road sign, this place marker of your departure and me remaining on this earth. My tears were not shed in vain; my tears were heard, shame-free, with not one tear shed in fear, only from love and with the release and abandon of a true African mother. I wept as only a mother of this soil can. I wept for the soul who, in this lifetime, suffered so much unnecessary pain and depravity instead of love. A soul who chose a path of darkness that I could not and would not follow. A path that took you step-by-step, further away from me, from those you loved and who loved you in return.

With tears, I released you back to the Great Oceanic Mother where you belong. The wild man, the Fisherman you always were. Your soul was released from separation as you were carried through time and space on the back of a giant sperm whale— surfing in the galaxy of life. This lovely child and I, our child of love, will walk the paths you and I once trod together, the natural paths of life. In the deepest part of space and soul, I feel you here, treading quietly beside us, bringing calm and gentle balance to our arguments and moving things the way you always could. Showing me how to drop the line and keep still, dance the way and catch that fish, write that book, and create the work. To be a master craftsman in a flash by entering into the quiet space of work, playing and dancing with the energy that made magic come your way. By staying true to my nature and walking the freedom way, sharing the love, and answering only to God, I keep the vow and will always remain true to you and our child.

I remember how there was mist in your eyes as you spoke when you told me the truth about what had happened to you so long ago. You shared your heart with me so often, and I completely understood. Throughout these years, I've slowly pieced together why you fell apart and remembered all the jagged bits you shared of your shattered heart.

You spoke about your first love, a beautiful young girl named Maria. The child of an impoverished family, she grew up on the streets of Woodstock in Cape Town. Maria's mother took care of them in the best way possible, given her circumstances. She was a street worker. She and her family shared a tiny two-bedroom flat that overlooked the busy city street. She drank heavily and used any pain-relieving drug that she could get, smoking weed, taking uppers, downers… whatever she could sell to make a living. Maria knew nothing else. You spoke so honestly about how you loved this lovely, wraith-like girl; how you tried to help her and give her a taste of a better life, but how you, too, were eventually dragged into her shadowy lifestyle. Helplessly, you watched her turn to prostitution to support her addictions.

Through the beautiful Maria, you entered a world you didn't know or understand—a twilight world where people seldom return. An underworld where people of the night moved and traded their illegal wares. Underage girls, sex, nightclubs, hard drugs like pink heroine, white pipes (mandrax), and crack cocaine. Prostitutes and their pimps woke up as the rest of the world went to sleep. They spiked up and went out on the town. And no matter how hard you tried to keep Maria from the world that she came from, eventually, she returned to the twilight, and you followed like a bleating lamb into the dark night. At first, you tried to work as a bouncer outside the nightclubs where she used to go, hoping to protect her, but it was useless. It was only when she left you that you were able to get out and return to the salty shore and ocean that you loved so much.

Fisherman, you often spoke of how it pained you to think about her because you knew how much of yourself you had lost. You had been stripped of everything, including your dignity and, more importantly, the very essence of who you knew yourself to be. You almost sacrificed yourself to save the girl you loved but, in the end, you had to let her go and save yourself. Maria saved you by turning you away from a world where you did not belong.

However, the experience left you feeling like an outcast in every world you'd ever known, from your own world, your family, and from friends who had watched you fall. Your fishing friends and the deep-sea fishermen that employed you to join their crew did not see you for years and when you did come back, you were marked by your addiction. The pain was so deeply etched into your face for one so young. Doors closed to you, Ian, and you had nowhere else to go for your survival but to the sea.

Eventually, your mother turned to professionals for help when you began the downward slide. First, it was the rehabilitation clinics where they admitted you to break the addiction pattern. But your pattern of substance abuse was so severe that it impacted everything, every part of your life, including your entire family. Most could not deal with your addiction and turned their backs on you. You were alienated from every form of support you knew and grew more withdrawn and alone. Eventually, you were incapable of finding or keeping any job at all. You hit rock bottom and took to the streets of Cape Town, eating from dustbins and lining up in queues of homeless people outside the St. George Cathedral for the daily soup kitchen handouts. Then you would swing your canvas backpack over your shoulder and walk from the Gardens in Cape Town, up the steep slopes of Table Mountain and over the saddle between the Lion's head, down to the sea, and into the bay.

Here you would spend the quiet evenings at the ocean, waiting for nightfall so you could begin catching the prize crayfish that lived deep in the rock pools on the coastline where you grew up. It was also here that you felt closest to your father, that warm bear-of-a-man who taught you how to fish and handle a fishing boat. Your dad's memory kept you alive throughout those dark years. You clung to him in those moments when you felt life was simply not worth living anymore.

"My son, you can do anything if you just put your mind to it! Just apply yourself. You have the talent," your father always used to tell you. Whenever things were tough, you and your father would spend the afternoon messing about on fishing boats or fishing off the rocks on the coast near your home. And even if you came back completely empty-handed, both of you would be feeling so elated that you would often arrive singing and laughing with the joy of sharing. Ian, I know how you missed your father desperately after he passed on. You told me once how, on the one hand, you were glad that your father had not been around to see you slide the way you did. You knew it would have broken his heart. And on the other hand, how you longed just to spend one more afternoon, one more day, fishing in the company of this wonderful, warm, friendly man. It was here at the edge of the rocks on the Atlantic coastline, where you felt closest to your father.

In these quiet moments, sitting beside the sea, you would reflect on deeper childhood memories. You remembered all the happy moments tadpole fishing with your friends, and then the haunting, dark memories would come flooding back and make you want to run away. Those memories of being four years old, playing with your friend in an old Cape Dutch mansion with long, dark corridors. Again and again, your deepest memories brought you to that shadowed place you always tried to avoid—a place defined by experiences that no child should ever have to endure. The scars left behind by those memories continued to shape your inner world, casting long echoes over your journey forward. You knew even then that what happened was abuse, but as a child, you could not erase the memories from your mind. That dark and dirty stain was a secret part of you that wouldn't go away. The memory haunted you, no matter how much alcohol you drank to erase the shame and pain, it percolated into every corner of your life, making you seem melancholy and setting you apart from your friends. Eventually, this painful experience changed and overwhelmed you so much that you didn't know how to make things right again or bring it into the light of day, how to make it leave you in peace. Where to begin again without these shadows and memories occupying your life?

Then one day, in desperation, you simply blurted it all out in a flood of words. And I listened to you in deep silence and respect, carefully considering how you must have felt to carry this terrible burden and suffering with you for all those years. Finally, I looked at you, saying as gently as I could, "Ian, you were an innocent child. You did nothing wrong. Those you speak of committed a crime by doing what they did. Take the weight of shame off your shoulders. You have your life to live and so much to look forward to. Don't allow those memories of the past to take hold of your life. Lift the burden from your heart and give the shame back to wherever it came from because it does not belong with you."

You smiled and shrugged at my words. "I guess I had not thought of it that way, Lisa, thank you." Tears were in your eyes. I smiled back at you with all the tenderness and love I felt.

A Purple Haze

Half dream half asleep
A lingering Medi-World of Life
Between Worlds
Here I can touch the ones I love
Without the pain of life's vicious issue
Deep and beautiful Love
I'm steeped in Love like a bath
Sleep, I am beyond anxiety and pain
Present and beyond all presence
I am with God inside out
folded within this multi-petaled flower
I am asleep
Perfect and purple
A veil of disbelief made real again
Dream of an amazing world quite natural

As extension of our terrestrial dream world
And we can take these dreams into our waking world
We choose and, in our dreams, we are the chooser too
We awake into the purple haze of sleep
A World of dreams
A little death
No different from the illusion we call real
except what we choose to believe is obvious
Yet we die in dreams
And awaken from a coma in our lives
We choose, we believe, we perceive
The Universe inside our hearts

CHAPTER 13

Searching for Belonging

Belonging shapes our identity, influences our choices, and gives
wings to our dreams, especially when we are young. There is
nothing more valuable to a child than the sense of belonging—to
feel a part of a family and to take pride in that connection.

The Fisherman's child was very angry for a long time after her
father's death. She felt sad, alone, and disappointed at his loss, and
that the opportunity to really know him was gone forever. She was
angry at Lisa for making choices over which she had no control.
For the choice her mother made to love her father, a man who she
would never know. Kathleen and Lisa were both deeply affected
by the Fisherman's passing. They were experiencing shock in
ways that left them both feeling frozen and empty. The worst part
was that there was nobody in their family or friendship circle who
understood what they were going through. They were together
in this but completely alone. At first, Kathleen had terrible
arguments with her mother and then began to withdraw out of
anger. Not even the school social worker and child psychologist
knew how to support Kathleen through this delicate time. It was
testing to the maximum for Lisa to maintain her own balance and
not let the sense of devastation and grief she felt affect her child.

The beginnings of her teenage years were tumultuous and confusing. Hormonal changes spiked her already fragile emotional landscape. By the time she was 12 years old, Kathleen was utterly convinced that she would never fit in anywhere and that everything that had ever gone wrong in her life was her fault or ultimately her mother's fault. She felt undeserving, unworthy, and angry at her mother, her family, and the world because she had lost her father. The golden times when she was small seemed to fade and crumble into dust with the disappointment that she felt. The hope that both Kat and her mother had silently carried to see the Fisherman alive and well had been dashed forever. Kathleen started to withdraw from her school friends and to feel painfully, excruciatingly different. Her wonderful, shining, healthy body, glowing skin, and sparkling sea eyes began to dim with disappointment and anger. Kathleen, who had always been so innocent, lovable, confident, and connected with both family and her peers, gradually became a shadow of herself.

And on top of it all, the family home had become a target for robbery. Lisa's aging mother was extremely vulnerable to crime, and the Cape Town gangs knew it. She could not afford the electric fencing and sophisticated security systems that most affluent homes now had, and their home had been robbed many times before. This time, she and Kathleen were there when the gangsters hit. They came in over the back fence and through the darkness. That night, Lisa heard a sudden, piercing shriek of terror coming from the kitchen garden. It was her mother screaming for help. Lisa leaped up and ran to her assistance. A group of five dark-clad and balaclava-hooded Tsotsi's[1] had forced her mother to the ground. They were busy searching for gold jewelry and valuables, forcing her wedding ring off her finger and her watch from her arm. They took her cell phone and ordered her old mother in muffled voices to show them where she kept the family safe. Lisa stood framed in the light of the kitchen door. "Leave my old

---

1 Thieves

mother alone!" she commanded in a firm voice. "Where is your respect for the elders? Now do what you came here to do—and quickly!—the Armed Security guards will be here in ten minutes." Then she helped her mother up and brought her inside. Kathleen was sitting crumpled up on the corner of the sofa, crying with fear. "They'll be gone soon, love. Don't worry," Lisa said, putting her arms around her daughter to calm her. In five minutes, the gang vanished into the darkness with their knives and pangas[2] leaving the whole family shaken.

After the home invasion incident, Lisa knew that she had to move herself and Kathleen out of their present environment and into a safer and more nurturing space. They needed a home of their own again. It was time to move on with their lives. Her mother had already put their lovely seaside home on the market, and it was just a matter of time before her family property would be sold. For the past two years, Lisa had felt trapped between doing what was best for Kathleen and the hostility of her two younger siblings. Her brothers were both married and had never understood Lisa's solitary path, nor what she stood for. They admired her for her adventurous life and her achievements as a professional artist. However, they did not understand her reasons for continuing the social upliftment work that was so important to her. Lisa's mother understood, but she, too, was caught in the middle of both worlds, wanting the best for her daughter. The success and the financial independence that Lisa had enjoyed before single motherhood had claimed her.

Kat saw her mother in stark contrast with this materialistic world and longed for the acceptance of her family and her teenage peers. She felt her father's death to be the last blow of his rejection of her and took her rage and frustrations out on her mother. At times, the teenage warrior would come out in her, and she would roar at Lisa, "Why did you have to choose my father? Couldn't you see that he was an absolute idiot, an alcoholic, and an asshole?

2   Machete knife

Why do I have to suffer for your mistakes, Mom?" Lisa would stop everything and simply listen while Kathleen sobbed and poured all the venom of her shame, anger, and disappointment out onto her.

Before Ian had died, Lisa had done everything she knew possible to restore some vestige of Kathleen's legacy—the gifts of her daughter's paternal line. She did her utmost to contact Ian, and when he didn't respond, she went to see the Police Inspector near where he had lived. Lisa knew that he had bought a fishing boat and a beautiful home on the beachfront near Betty's Bay. Kathleen might never know her father, but Lisa felt that her daughter deserved to know the security of a good education and the promise of a golden future in her chosen career. Lisa fought the good battle to have a part of the Fisherman's wealth paid into a Trust fund as maintenance for Kathleen. But her attempts to reach the magistrates and authorities who could help her were met with complete apathy and often scorn. It felt as if there were an iron wall between herself and the law—this very same institution created to protect and represent the vulnerable and those who needed legal assistance. No matter where she went or whom she spoke with, nobody seemed to care. Finally, she was told by the regional Police Commandant that Ian's assets had been seized and frozen to pay a criminal fine for illegal poaching and drug dealing. His house and fishing boat had been sold by the liquidators of his estate. Lisa remembered getting back into her car that day and driving away feeling empty and alone. "If the legal institutions of this country won't help with a legitimate claim for child support, then who will?" she asked the wind as she drove back along the beautiful Cape coastal road.

TABLE MOUNTAIN

Hoerikwaggo (Huri! Oaxa)
Mountain of the Sea
Mother of all Mountains
Altar to the stars
I greet you
Here in my place
I shall never forget you
Table Mountain!
Beautiful Mountain of the sea
You fed my emptiness
You gave me heart water
When my soul was dry
And I shall never forget you
Beautiful Mother
You carried me
In your wild garden wake
When I believed I would never walk
You made me crawl from flower to flower
Doing what I had to do to get through the day
When words
no longer were the way
Mother, Mountain, strength, love, multitude

Hoerikwaggo
I Greet you
And I will meet you
Here where I stay
Mountain of the sea
Woman at the tip of the world
The sunset and sunrise

meeting in one place
No need to conquer
Only to stand in worship
Mother Mountain of the sea
Hoerikwaggo!
Hoerikwaggo! Hoerikwaggo!
Rise and meet the sun
Rise and meet the day

Cape Town held no further pull for Lisa. There had been too many painful memories and not enough understanding or kinship to tie Lisa and her daughter to her family. Lisa took Kathleen out of primary school in Cape Town and moved to the Hemel and Aarde mountains in the Cape Overberg. There she began to homeschool Kat.

At first, Kathleen was happy just to have a break from the school routine. It was a good break that gave Kathleen and Lisa a chance to reconnect again and just hang out the way they always used to. The farm cottage Lisa had found in the Hemel and Aarde valley was built on the slopes of a beautiful mountain kloof where one could walk to a waterfall, and swim in the river and farm dam. A little higher up the kloof was a cave that the mountain bushmen of the region had once inhabited. The area was covered with Bushman stone tools and the droppings of wild game, wild buck, dassies' or rock rabbits, baboons, and sometimes even leopards. The farm had been owned by Dr Van De Post—a Doctor of Political Science and an extraordinary academic and confidante to former South African President F.W. De Klerk. It was here on this beautiful farm that the vision to bring in a New South Africa had unfolded. These visions planted the seeds of hope and ultimately became the plan to hand over the South African Presidency to the leader of the ANC, "Madiba" Nelson Mandela.

It was the eve of Kathleen's thirteenth birthday and a special time, as it was her coming of age as a young woman. She and Lisa had made it a very special occasion. Lisa bought her daughter gentle, feminine gifts, soaps and bath oils, a pretty pair of sandals, and beautiful things to wear. Then she packed a delicious supper into a small backpack and took Kathleen for an evening walk up to the Bushman cave just behind their home. There, they lit a small fire. While Lisa was preparing their meal, Kat walked down to the nearby stream to fetch some water. Suddenly, Lisa heard Kathleen yell with surprise as she ran back up the hill, wide-eyed. "Mom, you should have seen it!" she gasped. "About twenty of the young baboons were leaning down over the edge of the cave looking at me and making weird throaty noises at me. It was so scary."

Lisa began to chuckle softly. "Supper is ready, love," she said, handing Kat a paper plate with salads, fresh home-baked bread, and a sizzling hot piece of boerewors sausage. The baboons soon disappeared higher up into the mountain kloof. The chacma baboon troops usually find safe shelter on the upper slopes of the mountain where they settle to sleep as the sun goes down. Kat and Lisa ate in silence, watching the full moon slowly rise above the kloof. Then they put the fire out, covered the ashes carefully with sand, lit their torches, and took the mountain path back to their little farm cottage nearby.

Sadly, their stay on this farm was not to last. The Van De Post family decided to move back to the Hemel and Aarde valley within that year and by that time, Kathleen was ready to go back to school.

The barking of baboons woke Lisa in the pre-dawn light. She realized that she had been shivering with cold and pulled the covers tighter around herself. Her beautiful cottage bedroom was built out of the local mountain rock and although it made all the difference with keeping the place cool in summer, it was very cold in winter. She wrapped a blanket around herself and padded into the kitchen to put the kettle on for some coffee. There was a tiny glimmer from the embers left in the fireplace after last night's fire, and scattered on the coffee table in front of the fireplace were a couple of local newspapers and estate agency leaflets. Lisa had been combing the newspapers for some months now, hunting for a home that would suit them both. She had circled one of the agency ads in the Overberg newspaper. It was a rambling old rose cottage in the farmlands, very close to Hermanus. Lisa took her steaming mug and a bowl of rusks over to the coffee table and stoked the fire a little by adding a few small pieces of wood, then began to write her thoughts and feelings into her journal. She pasted the ad for the cottage beside her journal entry. *Always so much to consider, so much to bear alone,* she thought to herself.

Later that day while she was preparing lunch, she heard the phone ring. "Hello, Lisa speaking," she said, wiping lemon juice off her hands with a tea towel.

It was an international call and the connection was terrible— it was difficult to hear the speaker at the end of the line. The troop of farm baboons just happened to be in the garden that morning. Some had even jumped onto the cottage roof and were making a tremendous noise, thumping and barking and screaming at one another. "I'm sorry, could you hold the line for a minute, please? We have a troop of baboons outside making an awful ruckus," she said to the caller as she closed the cottage back door. There was relative peace once more. Enough that she could hear the pucker British accent on the end of the line.

"Good day. This is Michael Ingram, curator for the special art collection at Buckingham Palace. We are looking for the artist of the beautiful Khoisan rock artwork that was presented by Nelson Mandela during the time of his inauguration. Are you she?"

Lisa put her hand onto her heart. "Oh, my goodness. The San painting I did of the cave of Eland. Is that the one?"

"Yes, Madam. President Nelson Mandela commissioned this painting in 1995 and gifted this work to the British Monarchy. I would like your permission to have your beautiful painting placed on exhibition at the Royal Summer collection at Buckingham Palace."

Lisa was speechless. Her? A humble South African artist who simply loved Khoisan rock art so much. "Thank you, Sir," Lisa heard herself say quietly. "I would be deeply honoured."

"Good, then I will have my assistant send you all the necessary paperwork and a curator's guide to this year's art collection. And, may I add," said the British gentleman with amusement in his voice, "I so enjoyed hearing the sounds of the wild from Africa," and he proceeded to chuckle. "It is so rare that we experience such things here in London and I must add, it was a breath of fresh air for me. Thank you, my dear. Goodbye."

He put the phone down, leaving Lisa completely breathless at this turn of events.

It wasn't long before she had made up her mind. She had to keep on with her work.

Lisa found a place for Kathleen at a Montessori school where she knew her daughter would find the right support for her middle school years, and they moved into the little rose cottage in a village nearby.

Even though she was earning an art teacher's salary, Lisa struggled to find her feet financially under such enormous pressure. The expenses were simply too much for her on her own. Her mother had stepped in to help with Kathleen's school fees, but very soon this created tension among her siblings. To add to this pressure, the economic situation had begun to deteriorate rapidly in South Africa. Lisa had always been a very independent and successful artist. She'd always had a positive, refreshing outlook on life, but this crazy political and economic situation had very rapidly started to affect her own life and the lives of so many that she knew. Protest riots had begun all over the country because of the dramatic rise in the cost of living. And even here in this little coastal town, local protesters from the townships threatened to burn down municipal buildings and set fire to the mountainside if their basic needs were not met. Many African people were still living in abject poverty without water or sanitation. Too many families were still living in corrugated tin shacks, which leaked when it rained and hardly kept the weather out at all. Some had very little hope of employment or any support for their families.

Kathleen had been at school when the worst of the protest riots broke out. Township protesters had put burning tires and blockades out on the road and then set fire to the mountains. Lisa was on her way by car to fetch Kathleen from school that day when the fires were lit at every entry and exit point to the town. She had managed to get through on the farm road she usually took before it was closed, and the mountainside set alight. To add to the situation, it was the hottest and driest time of the year in the Western Cape. The intensity of the fires only made it worse. Police cars with blaring sirens sped up and down trying to manage the chaos. Fire engines and helicopters were deployed. The people of the Overberg Mountain and coastal areas had never seen such havoc and confusion as this before.

Eventually, Lisa managed to get through to Hermanus and then was forced to join a long, slow-moving line of cars traveling along the alternate road into the town. Many parents, just like her, were on their way to fetch their children from school. The smoke pall was extremely thick that day. Police sirens were blaring; emergency rescue vehicles and fire engines were all racing from place to place through the traffic. By the time Lisa arrived to collect Kathleen, the flames on the mountains had already burned dangerously close to her daughter's school. No more than half an hour after Lisa had driven away with Kat safely in her car, the wind turned, and a heavenly downpour of rain began to fall. Torrential rain continued to put out the protest fires all throughout the night. It was a miracle, a blessing, and an answer to many prayers. Without the rain, the flames and sparks would no doubt have leapt from the trees and burned right across the town.

So many South African families had been affected by the economic downturn, high inflation, high cost of rates and taxes, and the rising cost of living. That same year, Lisa's mother had become ill with a rare heart disease, and her move to a smaller, more self-contained home became necessary. She had eventually sold their beautiful home on the Cape coast and moved into a retirement village that was closer to hospitals and local shopping centers. At first, Lisa had driven into Cape Town with Kathleen several times a month to see her mother and bring her flowers and whatever she needed. Very often, her older brother, Mark, would be there looking unwelcoming and unwilling to let anyone else but the doctors come near. Lisa stayed only long enough to see her mother and for Kathleen to give her beloved grandmother handwritten poems and flowers, and then they would drive all the way back home again.

Eventually, the stress of living on too tight a budget and never knowing where the next pennies were going to come from began telling on Lisa. She felt a wave of depression crash down on top of her in a tsunami of despair. It was so hard to find a decent job in a small town. She tried hard to keep going, teaching art to children, painting for exhibitions and galleries, and baking delicious shortbread and cakes for the local farmers' market every weekend. Lisa found work wherever she could, even helping on wine farms in the area, doing basic administrative tasks. She did whatever she could to keep bread on the table and the roof over their heads. Lisa's siblings blamed her difficult financial situation on her depression and an inability to work with others or keep lasting friendships and relationships. It was all projection. Neither of her siblings had ever been close to her or Kathleen, and they simply could not understand her situation as a single mother. For whatever their reasons, they couldn't connect the dots. Their own financial difficulties stemmed from the very same high cost of living that she and all South Africans were facing. "Well, if you were not so Goddamn lazy, and constantly sponging off of Mom, you might have achieved more financially, academically, or professionally," Mark would say in his bland accusing tone. "You cannot hide behind your situation as a single parent of Kathleen forever, you know." This could not have been further from the truth and spoke of her brother's own insecurities and fear for the future. The whole family knew how successful Lisa had been before she became a mother. It was obvious how her situation as a single parent had changed all of this. There were no more expensive holidays or international exhibitions. And there was absolutely nobody else to help her take care of her daughter. To take Kat to school, fetch her, care for her, drive her to sporting events and play rehearsals. There was only Lisa. She was a homemaker, breadwinner, gardener, mother, father, confidante, cook, cleaner, storyteller, nurse, psychologist, taxi, and more. But somewhere way beyond all of this, she was also a woman with needs of her own. And at times, it all became too much for Lisa. She felt overwhelmed, drowning in financial responsibility and in desperate need of emotional support. Instead of reaching out with compassion, her family grew increasingly cold, critical, and intolerant of her and Kathleen. Lisa understood that they had been used to her independence and strength and simply didn't know how to deal with her now that she was facing a difficult time.

"Hmph. You're nothing but a poor white, looking for a free meal ticket," were my brother's caustic words to me. That one single sentence made me feel so terribly crushed. Why on earth would I want to remain in contact with family members who were so heartless and indifferent? My psyche was shattered by cold disregard for my child and my motherhood. The scars that were left by thoughtless, cruel words opened old wounds in my heart and ripped deeply into the vaults of my already fragile sense

of self. Kathleen, too, had been deeply cut, and the wounds of rejection in her young heart began to rankle again.

Silently, I longed to fill the space the Fisherman had in my heart. I had tried to kindle relationships, but the truth was, nobody would ever fill that place. I had been privileged to know what very few experience in a lifetime. The love of a soul, so like myself. A mythical, magical, timeless soul. Despite the Fisherman's inward struggle and his issues with substance abuse and addiction, we loved one another in a wide, real, and accepting way. Through knowing the Fisherman, I had learned to understand that there was a great difference between love and compromise. I would not be fooled.

Lisa was grateful for this solid old farmhouse where she could quietly heal and hide from the world. The farm cottage was one of the oldest homesteads in the Overberg region. It had extremely thick brick and mortar walls and was wonderfully cool in summer. The ceilings and floors were solid wood, and the rooms could be closed off for warmth in winter. The homestead garden was old and rambling and hadn't been cared for in many years. Lisa spent her days at home gardening, planting vegetables, and painting. Soon, the trees and vines began to bear fruit, and the old Wisteria creeper and wild roses began to bloom in abundance. She was content for a while, but she knew that she needed more than this. She needed company of her own kind. A soul tribe and a home where she and her daughter could simply be themselves. But where would they go? Not overseas, that simply wouldn't feel right. Lisa had thought about life in England for her and her daughter. But the thought of leaving the heartbeat of Africa and living so far away made her heart ache, and she would wake up with tears in her eyes.

Gradually, the answer came to her in the early summer breeze.

Lisa had made some good friends in the mountain areas of Hermanus. A conservationist and his wife who managed a private nature reserve often invited them over for walks, events, and evening braai's. On one of these occasions, Lisa was relaxing with a book in the sunshine. Kathleen had just been for a swim in one of the crisp mountain pools. She sat down quietly beside her mother and looked out over the sea.

"It's time to leave here, Mom!" she said.

Lisa knew exactly what Kat was saying. Kathleen, the child of her twin flame. No one else knew her as completely as her daughter did.

"Yes, I know Kat," she said, looking at her and nodding. "We are gypsy folk, you and I, your father was, too," she smiled. "And yes, it is time that we left this place. We'll be shown our next home. We always are," she said softly, touching the whale bone pendant that hung around her neck.

In the quiet spaces of my soul
Is Joy
Joy and ecstasy are born in silence
Silence is the meeting place of hearts
It springs out of steadiness
True focus and being well-lit
By investigation, knowledge, courage, caring and sharing
community, resourcefulness and
Peace
Silence is the change
the world needs
What do you do with brokenness
Do you do anything with it at all
But sit with it
It is broken
You could glue the broken bits together
If you could find them

But the broken bits too are broken
And what do you do with that?
Soul sits and looks on
Broken and broken and broken and broken
what else is there but
peace, gentle at the end
What else is there really?
What else is there
How do you start again when
all you expect is to be broken again
Broken is all I ever knew
Broken everywhere, heart pieces, dust in the air
My blood, dust, so broken
Who would do anything
with the shattering nightmare of sound
Who would interfere
who would stop, put their hand out… to help, to share
New, renew, that's what to do
A plant survives in the darkness
A new life survives in dust
A little bit of moisture and lightness
is enough, that is enough
All the brokenness needs is just a little bit
of love

CHAPTER 14

FOLLOWING THE PULL
OF THE WIND

The price we pay for authenticity is often the highest price of all.
Yet truth and love are the very essence of our souls.

Lisa followed the pull of the wind.

She packed up her home again, selling everything they did not need, putting everything they owned into storage. Then, with only the lightest and most essential possessions, herself, Kathleen, and their two wolf dogs in the back of her battered old car, they drove away towards another new beginning.

"Lisa, you and Kathleen must come and stay here on the farm with me for a wee while, just until you've found a place of your own," her kind Scottish friend had offered. Morag lived on an old sheep farm in the middle of nowhere, deep in the heart of the forest on the Garden Route. She was a true flower child and a gypsy. Both Lisa and Kathleen loved living where life was so simple and gentle and where at last Lisa had the support of women friends and the companionship of like-minded people. Gradually, Lisa began to feel at peace again and more alive than she had in a very long time. Slowly, she began to get the sense that she was truly home. Home to where she and the Fisherman had spent their happiest times together. Home to where she could simply be herself!

Kathleen, like most young girls her age, wanted to be part of a group of youngsters. So Lisa let her go along to summer concerts, learn to ride a quad bike, and to enjoy just hanging out with young friends on the beach. There were frequent teenage arguments between Kat and her Mom about boundary setting then. Lisa knew the realities of a world that was no longer safe or healthy for youngsters. She knew there was plenty of time for Kathleen to experience all the excitement that being a teenager entailed.

It was New Year, 2020, in South Africa. They had forgotten all about the problems they had left behind, but this wonderful peace was soon to be shattered. 2020 was a crazy time when everything was turned upside down and nothing made sense anymore. Soon, world news broke. Her Scottish friend, Morag, described how a new type of influenza had been spreading like wildfire in China and how news reports described people dying of what was being called "The Bat Flu."

It can't last, Lisa thought. But it did. Suddenly, everyone was being told that they were at risk of contagion and that the whole world was to be shut down. But the mountains, streams, and forests, the oceans, whales, and animals continued being wild and free, and she and Kathleen did, too.

While the world went into lockdown and everybody stayed at home, her life seemed to speed up. Significant events began to happen one after another and happened incredibly fast. At first, Lisa felt like Alice in Wonderland, falling down a rabbit hole, watching while so many lost their businesses and their loved ones. Life changed overnight. The entire human population across the globe turned inward and had only their families or themselves to connect with. So many took their business online that within a matter of months, meetings, shows, and gatherings were all hosted through the internet. Lisa's work with children and her art exhibitions for the season had either been canceled or suspended until the following year. There was only one thing left for Lisa to do. She began to take art commissions and to sell as much of her work as possible online.

Then, in April of 2020, Lisa received an unexpected email. It was from a dear friend in India, urgently requesting that she send in her proposal for an Environmental Education grant. This was an aspect of Lisa's social upliftment work that she had always longed to focus on but had never had the financial means to do so. Within a miraculously short space of time, she was awarded this grant to teach awareness of African heritage to less advantaged school children. The opportunity had come just in time to support Kathleen and herself through one of the most tumultuous times in human history. A time when so many were unemployed and struggling to survive. At last, Lisa had purpose again. Not only was this Environmental Education Grant a life-saving blessing, but it was also exactly the kind of work that most fulfilled her soul.

The early part of the year in 2020 was a very strange time. So many of her elderly friends were ill. There was something in the air. One by one, the news of their deaths began to arrive. The first message of bereavement came in just before the lockdown began. It was from her respected friend, the African Grandmother, Mama Martha. "My dear, Lisa. It is with great sadness that I share the news of our dearly beloved Ubaba Vusamazulu's passing. He left us peacefully yesterday in the early hours of the morning. We know how much you loved Ubaba and we wanted you to know."

The passing of this Great Teacher had been perfectly timed. He died in the Kuruman hospital on the very same morning before all the craziness of the "Bat Flu" began.

Lisa clearly remembered the last words that she had seen her teacher, Baba Vusa, deliver to the world on a televised documentary. He was sitting in their garden, outside his Kuruman home, addressing his daughter. "My child, as you know, I have given my entire life to bringing peace to the people of this land. Throughout the years, I have written many books. I've shared this message in many feature documentary films, and I have traveled widely and spoken with many, many people across this globe in my quest to enlighten and unite the leaders of nations, but it seems that nobody wants to listen to the message of a living Holy Man. I have offered fair warning about the dangers that humanity is facing today, yet still they make mockery and call me a wizard and a grotesque, stupid, fat black ape who doesn't know what the hell he is talking about. I have begged and pleaded, and I have done my best to inform the world about the reasons that we are facing such troubled times. Even my own Zulu people ignore me and carry on blinded by this falsehood, forgetting everything that is sacred to Mother Africa. Can they not see how they damage their own land? Do they not heed the cries of Mother Nature, calling us to come home and live in harmony with her? Not to sell their souls for all the artificial rubbish we are encouraged to buy. I am too old for this work now, and I am ready when the Great Unkulunkulu calls my name. If they do not wish to listen, they will have to bear the consequences of their foolishness. This whole nation can go to hell as far as I am concerned."

With that statement, Baba Vusa stood up and the interview ended abruptly. Lisa broke into a wide grin, chuckling uproariously for a long time afterward. It was so like the Ubaba Vusa she had grown to know and love. During the first days of lockdown, Lisa sat quietly remembering the sense of joy, freedom, and wisdom that he had passed on to her throughout almost forty years that she had known him. She celebrated his release from physical suffering, lighting ninety-nine sacred candles in honour of Baba Vusa's profound spiritual work during almost a century of life.

When the next phone call came, Lisa was prepared.

She heard her older brother's flat and sarcastic voice at the end of the line. "Hi, Lisa. Just to let you know that Mom has taken ill and is in hospital. Her doctor suspects that she may have this COVID virus. Apparently, quarantine protocols prevent all family members from visiting patients in the hospital. So unfortunately, we can't go and see her at all."

Lisa felt instantly alarmed. "Oh, poor Mom. How is she doing? Any news from the doctor yet?"

"Actually, Mom is no longer any of your concern, Lisa," her brother snapped at her sternly. "You cannot visit her, and please don't try to contact her or bother her in any way. You have caused enough trouble in this family already. In fact, the whole family thinks that it was her worry regarding your financial situation that has made her so ill. All your life, you've insisted on being controversial and disrupting our lives with your liberal ideas. I heard a rumour recently that you flatly refuse to take this COVID vaccine and that on top of everything, you are working in township schools. For God's sake, Lisa, just stay away from the family, please. We don't want you to bring any contagion into our homes or to infect Mom. We have all decided, in the light of current circumstances, that you and your child will be cut off from any future financial assistance. Mom has been far too generous with helping you out of late, and we feel it's time that you stand on your own two feet," her brother said gravely. "Look at it this way, Lisa. Kathleen is your problem and not ours. As far as we are concerned, you've brought this difficulty upon yourself. Frankly, the whole family feels the same way. Nobody wants you or your negativity around, especially at such a critical time. You are no longer welcome to contact us or to visit any of us any longer."

Lisa didn't reply to her brother's accusations. The phone call had made her feel nauseous. There was a huge lump in her throat, and she could barely speak. She quietly and simply wished them all well and said goodbye. What else could she say in answer to such a one-sided view of things? She was guilty of nothing but being herself and making the choice to raise a child on her own. She had been generous with helping her brothers and had never asked anything of them… except love and belonging. Her mother's help with Kathleen's school fees had ignited a family war and triggered the accusation that she was incapable of being a decent mother. It made her feel extremely heart-sore to know that her family felt that way about her. Her brother knew that she and her mom had always shared so much, particularly their love of nature and painting. Of all her family, her mom recognized her daughter's vision, spiritual inclinations, and the unique path she had chosen.

Lisa sighed and closed her eyes in resignation as she put the phone down.

I remember the tremendous upwelling of sadness that I felt at the time of this separation from my family. My frustration at these misunderstandings and my desperation at the unnatural family rift. The cruelty of such a situation would not only affect me but also Kathleen, in terrible and profound ways. At the time, Kat was only 14 years old and desperately needed belonging, the warmth, acceptance, and embrace of her extended family. She felt torn and conflicted because she loved and longed for her family so much. Our rejection from them, in her young mind, had been my fault. I had been completely cast adrift by my own blood relatives at a time when we both most needed them. And Kat felt she was right to blame me. I was her mother, and it was my responsibility to keep the peace, be compliant, and the bridge for her to her place of belonging. Instead, I had not only burned her bridge of connection to her father but also to her beloved grandmother, uncles, and aunts. No matter how gently I would try to explain, the extreme conflict that the situation caused Kathleen made her extremely volatile. Kat and I had several heated arguments about what had happened until I realized how pointless it was. The more I tried to connect with Kathleen, the more it became impossible to approach her. Kat knew that Uncle Mark and the family wanted to put her into a boarding school and remove her from my care. She didn't want this to happen, and yet she was extremely angry with me. Everything had become so confusing for my young teenage daughter. Kat had trusted me to stand by her, to mend relationships and make everything alright again, but this time it simply wasn't up to me. I could not save her father nor was I able to mend the relationship between my family members and me. It would take time for Kathleen to understand these dynamics and the responsibility that each member of our family had to own their behavior. I had no choice but to turn my attention towards those with whom I had felt real belonging.

I had been privileged to become a part of a sacred community with other like-minded souls across the world. These people were my spiritual tribe. They were a friendship circle that over time, had become a family of sisters and brothers. Many of my friends had known Baba Vusamazulu and Mama Martha personally. I remember feeling an uncanny and inexplicable sense of joy, release, and freedom during this time. So much could and would have been very different for a vulnerable single mother had it not been for the full support, love, and understanding of my international friends and allies. I could only feel tremendous sadness and compassion for my siblings and extended family. Their decision to cut me off during a time of global crisis could have broken me completely, but instead, their decision had erased them from our world and brought us into a totally different paradigm. My mother described my new world as a paradise, one in which I existed far away from toxic attitudes, in peace and prosperity, with beauty and warmth surrounding Kathleen and me.

Regardless of the family's decision to exclude Lisa, she took Kathleen with her to visit her mother once she was sent home to recuperate. These were unpredictable times, and she didn't know when next they would be able to see one another again. Her mother was overjoyed to see her grandchild and daughter. You could see the happiness radiating from her wrinkled old face. They spent the afternoon sitting outside in the sunshine just as they always had, drinking tea, chatting, and catching up on the news.

"How are you feeling after all that chaos, Mom? Wow, I must admit, I was petrified for your sake," Lisa said, looking at her mother with wide eyes.

"Oh, it was a terrible time, my darling. I'd caught bronchitis and had been coughing for quite some time. It wasn't a serious problem but because there had been a flu scare in the retirement home, my doctor sent me to get some routine tests done at the local hospital. I was shocked when they immediately admitted me to a quarantine ward just in case I might have this virus. The atmosphere in the hospital was so tense that you could have sliced it like butter. There were some medical staff who seemed sensible enough, but you could see that the doctors and nurses were on edge. I suppose at the time they were facing a global medical crisis. All the patients were being shoved and shunted around amid the panic, and we were not treated with much consideration. The nurses were very kind to me in the ward, but you could see that they were scared. The hospital staff all had to wear those white hazmat suits when they walked inside the quarantine wards. I felt as though I was living inside the worst nightmare possible. Honestly, it was like a science fiction movie," her mom chortled.

"Eventually, the nurse came in to tell me that the test results had returned as 'false positive' and that I could go home. I was so relieved. She gave me a small plastic container of antibiotics and other pills and said that I had to take every single one of them before I could leave the hospital. Of course, me being my cheeky self, I asked if my specialist, Dr Stanford had prescribed them because I know how strict he is with this heart condition. He would never allow me to take certain medications that I might react to. The nurse disappeared down the passage and returned accompanied by a very officious-looking doctor who told me these medications were compulsory protocols for all patients suspected of having the virus and that I had no choice but to take them all before I could be discharged. Oh, I did my best, but my old body wasn't having it. The next thing I knew, I threw up and went into shock. Shortly afterwards, I had a minor heart attack and lost consciousness. I woke up the next day with all those tubes stuck in me. Dr Stanford said that they had given me the wrong medication. Ah, well. At least I made it out alive, Lisa, and I'm still clear-headed and healthy enough to get along," her mother laughed softly brushing the incident aside.

Lisa looked at her mother with compassion. "Oh, Mom," she said softly and squeezed her hand. "You really have been through hell and back, haven't you. Well, at least, you needn't worry about Kathleen and me. Do you remember my telling you about the application and my hopes to be awarded an international grant for my work with disadvantaged children?" Lisa quietly asked her mother. "Well, a miracle has happened. The Environmental Education proposal I presented a few months ago has been accepted and all my social upliftment work will now be completely funded from now on. My special African friends, Baba Vusamazulu and Ma Martha so often appealed to me to help the children of Africa remember their traditions and heritage. Well, after all these years, at last, this is possible." She smiled happily as she shared her good news. "It's incredible how prayers are answered in God's perfect time! Mom, I am so relieved, for both Kathleen's sake and mine."

"Congratulations, my girl. Honestly, you deserve it!" her mother said, smiling at her with pride. "You've always been so independent and resourceful. Don't worry about what the rest of the family has to say about you. I'm not so easily fooled, love. There's a lot of silly nonsense and jealousy in this family, I'm so sorry to say. Especially concerning you and the fact that you are a single parent. Forgive them, my child, they do not understand. Thankfully, you have risen above it all in your usual independent way," her mother said, smiling at her with pride. "My darling Lisa, I have become so frail and susceptible to all these bugs going around now. Please be strong for me and look after your daughter as best as you can. We never know what tomorrow will bring. Remember that I love you both, no matter what."

Six months later, Lisa's mother was back in ICU on life support. Her doctor did not know whether she would survive it this time. Lisa drove down to Cape Town to be closer to her mother. Nothing had changed. Her presence still clearly rankled her family, especially her brother Mark. He couldn't prevent her from being there to visit her mother, but if she did happen to see him in the foyer or outside the retirement home, he would not greet her or exchange any words of kindness, and she did not expect him to. Lisa could see that her presence annoyed him. He was extremely distraught and as always, he lashed out, blaming her for her mother's condition. The last words she remembered her brother roaring at her in front of her family and young teenage daughter were words of anger that had slashed at her heart. They were unkind, cruel words. Words that were meant to utterly break her heart and wound her so deeply that she would never want to come back again. He stood there, blocking the light from the entrance door of the nursing home.

"Lisa, be aware that we have cut you off from this family entirely. And if you ever bother us again, we will take your daughter away from you and have you locked away in a psychiatric ward."

I could still feel the gut-twisting slam of his words as they hit me like a cold, concrete object. For a long time afterwards, I felt the numb, absolute finality of his statement. There was no longer any way through with my brother. His heart had become stone cold. It was sad, it was petty, and it all felt so wrong. Although these harsh words had touched me at my most vulnerable point, I wasn't fazed by my family's antagonistic attitude. My spiritual journey was my life. It had always been my survival and my heartbeat. I knew this to be yet another, even deeper and more profound level of initiation. In fact, I'd always known that there would come a time when I would be presented with a decisive parting of ways. This time, it was my brother's heartless words that were a clear road marking to this transition.

There was a painting that Lisa remembered that had always hung in pride of place in their family home. It was a picture her father had inherited from his grandfather, of a beautiful Scottish sailing ship. *It must have been this painting and the legends of the British Naval Officer, her great-grandfather, who inspired my father's love of the sea so much,* she had often thought.

Many years ago, before her father's passing, Lisa had introduced Baba Vusamazulu, the Great Sanusi, to her family. Baba Vusa had listened deeply to her father's conversation about his research on the ocean currents. Afterwards, he had given him the Zulu name, "Indoda Yamanzi," which means "Man of the Waters." She smiled wryly with the realization that the dysfunction in her family was simply an old pattern playing out again, just as it had in her childhood. It was all just a distortion of the natural flow of love in a family. As she felt her brother Mark's terrible wrath arrive in yet another emotional storm, she remembered her father, "Yamanzi" and the image of the Scottish sailing ship crashing through the storm waves flashed through her mind. Then Lisa smiled with the understanding that all storms eventually passed. If the old sailing ship could survive such enormous ocean swells, so would she.

Like a candle guttering in the wind, her mother continued to live. Her mother's frail, genteel existence remained as the only semblance of love that had been her family. From now on, Lisa was completely on her own. She could not, nor would she ever wish to face such cruelty and humiliation from her family again. Certainly, she would never expose Kathleen, her daughter, to such unkindness again. Her world had become clearly divided, and there was no going back.

Once her mother was home and had recuperated sufficiently, Lisa and Kathleen video-called her. "Mum, no matter what happens, we will always love you," Lisa said to her over the phone, smiling inwardly at the memory of the Fisherman's song. "And even if circumstances prevent us from seeing one another, we will meet here in our hearts whenever you want to." Lisa's mother had smiled gently, touched her heart, and closed her eyes. Lisa could see the unconditional love her mother felt, radiating on her beautiful, frail, old face.

"Whichever way life goes, I will always love you.
However our love flows, I will always love you.
No matter if you stay or go, I will always love you
I will always love you; I will always love you."

Love is like the mists that roll in from the sea
they completely engulf the land and the land absorbs
the mist
Then it's gone
we are separate once more
longing always for the mists
the cool, dripping particles of water that cling to our hair
drip from our cool wet faces, permeating our clothes,
cool wet, life entering our atmosphere
a respite from the dry harsh wind of reality
Love is the mist of memory that makes you long at every
waking moment for the touch and smile of that little child
the one you bore and nurtured and cuddled
it makes the bond Unbreakable
by every human or inhuman device
Love is the mist that permeated and
became another soft bark ring of the tree trunk
ever-present now to mark the story of how love entered in
It is the love of a husband, a lover, a troubadour
ever singing your praises in his work
becoming so engrossed in excellence
of his love song

and the glamour of his job that he forgets…
His muse, and takes the inanimate associated
with the song as his companion
amen
Love is in striving for one's ideal
for love in the "ever after," a kiss which lasts forever
a flower which fades not
and only lives in our imaginations
to comfort the dry rasp, we often feel
in our daily striving for love and happiness
Love is the Soul mate we have met and not forgot
the hands we have held
and clasp anon
the head that rests on head
Simple we are one
with what we are
and enter thoughts and mind and heart
of one another with ease
like mist
And the Greatest love of all,
is peace and understanding, acceptance and the
unconditional love of the enlightened
Those who for years and years
have been despised and persecuted
simply because they're different
and possess self-mastery
So Great is this Love that joins
the mists, the sun and the earth itself
in its movement towards new life and
a new and even stronger
Love

THE MISSING CHAPTER

"When a woman speaks the truth in a dysfunctional family, she is
punished for breaking the spell."
—Hannah Fraser Moore

As you become more aware of the global situation, of
worldwide diaspora, the dissolution of the nuclear family and
how deeply this has affected children, your eyes begin to open
to the startling reality of just how many single parents, homeless
children, and broken, dysfunctional families there are all over the
world. Lisa was aware of how much she had taken on alone. She
often felt as though she was fighting her way through the sand
blast of a coastal storm, and in many ways, she was. For Kathleen
to come first and to be safe emotionally and physically, Lisa had
to stand up and fight tooth and nail for her daughter's sanctity.
She knew with certainty that she had to do this to protect the very
values that kept Kat safe. There was no question about it; her stand
and her courage were a lifeline in a severely dysfunctional world.
She had to be brave. There was only God, her mother's instinct,
her love, and her ability to see reason and keep her child's feet on
a natural healthy path. In fact, there was no one else in her family
who supported her home-based values. Her light alone would
have to see Kathleen to the other side of her teenage confusion.
It was an immensely confusing time for all people, and especially

for youngsters. During the COVID years, Kat felt pressured and controlled to comply with school regulations. She hated wearing a mask all day while she studied and having to keep distance from her peers. It was the very opposite of the freedom that she had grown up with. Lisa knew she had to keep praying, holding on to clarity, and asking wherever she could for support.

A soft wind was blowing that evening. Lisa loved to feel the elements. She made time as often as she could to just listen to the wind blowing and the birds chattering. She could hear Kathleen talking to her friend on the phone from the other side of the house. And then her daughter's cat-like, soft-padded footfall caught her by surprise.

"Mom, what's for supper? I'm getting hungry." She smiled at her mom.

"Okay, would you like to eat now, Kat? I have already made a salad and stir-fry. Let's heat up the wraps together, love." Lisa got up from her desk and drifted into the kitchen, still thinking about her last call with her mother and the two days of unearthly silence that had followed the frail old lady's sedation in hospital. "Come on, Kat! Let's get this party started. Will you help me with the cutlery and plates please, my poppy?"

Lisa switched on the stove top and began to heat the already sautéed stir-fried vegetable strips and chicken. "Mom, stop checking your phone all the time." She heard Kathleen's voice through the haze of her concern and thoughts about her mother's present health crisis. It was a lot more serious than her doctor was willing to say. He had been so brusque about her mother's condition. "I cannot see her unless her chest has cleared. There is no point in any further operations unless she is strong enough to recuperate," he had stated in a matter-of-fact manner. Her mother had survived each crisis by sheer strength of will. Her mom's sisters saw her during visiting hours and had written to Lisa.

"She's a lot better but she is very tired. Her physical strength is failing, my child," her aunts said kindly.

"Mom, don't burn them," Kat said, snapping her out of her deep reverie again. "Perhaps I should help you to toast the wraps, Mom. You're clearly just not with the program this evening," Kat said kindly.

Lisa looked at her daughter and smiled, handing her the pan.

"You're right. I'm not, Kat," she said, collapsing into a kitchen chair.

"It's your Granny, love. Things are not going well, and I just don't know if she has the strength to fight this anymore. I have always been very honest with you, Kat. When we went through to Cape Town two weeks ago to see Gran, I realized how sick she was. You remember how I sat with Gran? Well, it was at this point that I realized that she desperately needed to be taken to hospital. Kat, we can only hope that Gran has the strength because God knows she has certainly been through enough physical discomfort, pain and suffering over the years."

"I know, Mom. I already know that Gran is going to die soon. Don't worry about me please. It's not Gran being so sick and dying that makes me sad, Mom. It's the entire family and this horrible situation that has stopped us from hardly ever seeing Gran anymore. I hate this family, Mom. I wish I had never believed them in the beginning." Her daughter's gray-green eyes flashed with anger as she spoke. The light was fading fast. Lisa could see the gold red ball of sunset just over the field. The beautiful chestnut farm horse they were taking care of was grazing nearby, highlit in the golden light of sunset.

"Oh, Kat, no don't hate them sweetheart. Don't fill yourself, your precious heart with their pain, love. Forgive them. It's not your fault or your stuff to deal with. It is theirs, you see." Lisa reached out and took her daughter's hand in hers.

"No, Mom, you don't understand. They hate you." Kat had tears in her eyes. "I never told you, but my cousins, Aunt Liezel and Uncle Jim have been reaching out to me to join them whenever I go on holiday to my friends. They tried to get me to join their family chat group not so long ago. But when I did, it all felt so wrong because you weren't included and they never for a moment considered how I might feel with them running you down in front of me like that. Eventually I just left and to tell you the truth, I never want to be part of their exclusive family club again. Even my cousins are not innocent, Mom. They really are not. They always pretend that they are when they are with you and me but when you're not around, they run you down so badly. It's so wrong to just let the 'dissing' happen when you're not even there to defend yourself. Mom, you haven't even done anything to deserve it."

Lisa sat listening to her daughter with her heart on fire. She took a deep breath and sighed. "Well thank heavens we live here in this beautiful, tranquil place and we don't ever have to be a part of their world if we don't want to. It really doesn't matter what they say, Kat," Lisa said, biting into her stir-fry and wrap. "Wow, this is delicious, eat up darling. I know your Gran would love to see us while she's in hospital. It has always cheered her up so much to see your lovely face." Deep within her, a wise and knowing voice was speaking, telling her to prepare. That the reality of her mother's impending death was close.

There was a strangely tight feeling in Lisa's chest. She knew it was coming. Not the inevitable fading of life but the complete division that, too, was inevitable. She tried to push it all away for a while. To pretend that the softness that was her mother's heart had worked its magic. "Just maybe, maybe my brother could be different. Perhaps Mom is right, he is softening and maybe there is hope that he will listen and we can talk. Please God let it be true." She felt her spirit yearning for the change that she so hoped for. Lisa remembered with a smile the happy time she and Rose had spent with her mother so recently. It felt like yesterday when all three of them were huddled up together on her nursing home bed, laughing and talking and looking at her mother's lifetime of drawings and paintings that she had filed neatly in two ring binders. Kathleen was entranced by her grandmother's exquisite depictions of the fairy world. All these drawings were illustrations for various books about nature that her mother had so hoped to see published for children someday.

"Ah, my darlings. These drawings are precious only because you love them. Please Lisa, take them and look after them, won't you. Remember all the joy we shared together, painting and looking at flowers. And if you ever have the chance to and want to have these stories published, you have my blessing, my child," her mother said with all the love in the world.

"Thanks, Mom. I will. I would love to see your stories published someday." Lisa smiled into her mother's warm brown eyes.

Whenever they were with Lisa's mom, everything felt so happy again. They both felt that warm feeling of belonging, the privilege of those who have family members who really love and understand them. Lisa was so privileged to have a mother who naturally shared so much with her and who adored her daughter, Kathleen. Occasionally her brother would come around and bring a completely different conversation and mood with him. Neither Kat nor Lisa felt any affinity with him anymore, although she respected his ways. It was always her mother who would be there with her arms held open wide and who would walk them to the gate when they left Cape Town for their home in the Garden route—no matter how ill she felt and whatever the weather, rain or shine.

"We'll come again soon and visit you, Mom," she said as they drove away that day. But it was the last happy time they'd had together, and the last time she saw her mom alive.

Lisa heard her cell phone beep and checked the message that flashed onto the screen. *We have had a meeting with Mom's Doctor. She is failing fast now and has been put onto morphine. It is possible that she may not even last the night,* her brother Mark wrote in his bland way.

I knew it, she thought. A part of her longed to be at her mother's side. The other part of her knew the truth. Nothing was different for the rest of her family and at a time like this, even if she drove like hell to get there before her mom took her last breath, it still wouldn't change a thing. Her mom was leaving, and her family were all going in their own direction, too.

Later that day she went to the sea and found herself standing in the waves up to her waist, clothes and all. In one instant she knew. A roar of loss erupted out of her soul. "Mommmmmmyyyyyyyyyyy, MOM don't go, Mom. Please don't leave. I love you Mom," she found herself sobbing and calling out into the ocean's depth.

It was all over.

When she got back into her car and checked her cell phone, she saw precisely at that time when she had felt her mother's spirit depart her body, her brother had called to say that their mother had passed on.

My Mother's eyes
solve mysteries in an uncomplicated way
tell stories about rainstorms, forests, bats
and the choice she made to stay

They're deep, deep pools of mysteries
Listening and curiosity
Like distant stars where new worlds are
Her wisdom a part of her beauty

My Mother's eyes speak to your soul of nourishment and love
about fountains of clear water
tears and rivers of a woman's sorrow
About silent suffering and the patience that hopes for a dawn
tomorrow
My Mother's eyes are calm
She lives for every day
gathering each moment as the magic unwraps an unexpected fay

they transport you into her world,
Her wonderful kind of world
The same but somehow different
Through her gentle eyes
A Heaven
A new dimension
And my Mother's way

Kat and Lisa held one another through this time. Lisa came and snuggled up with her daughter in her bed. They bought nonalcoholic strawberry pop and went out for a sumptuous breakfast at a fancy hotel. Then they took their only friends with them to the forest for a fireside memorial ceremony.

It was a very special time. Nothing would prevent them from honouring Lisa's mother's memory. No threat of family division could ever obliterate the love that both felt for Lisa's mother.

Kat wasn't sad about her Gran. She felt too proud to be the granddaughter of such a special and beloved grandparent. There were too many good memories of her not to smile and feel at peace about her Gran's death.

The memorial service in Cape Town came and went without any mishap. Only the most wonderful, gentle people from Lisa's life growing up in Cape Town spent time with the two of them. Some of these wonderful mentors had gone to great lengths to buy gifts to give to Lisa. She couldn't help but feel so blessed and so loved by her friends and community.

And then they were home. Back to normality again, except everything was different now. Now the soft wind held her mother's smile. Now the little frog in the kitchen held memories of her mother telling her how rare it was to ever see a ghost frog. Now every morning she would awaken to the sounds of *tap tapping* at her bedroom windowpane as a small female Cape Robin with a golden, orange heart would be peering in at her. Every single morning, she would kick start her day with these thoughts about her mother and her mother's exuberance about nature. "Nature is always your best teacher," her mother would say, pointing with her wooden walking stick at some distant tree or flower. "Someday your daughter is going to thank you with all her heart for bringing her up so close to nature and in such an exquisite part of the world, Lisa. You just stick your chest out, hold your head up high and be proud of yourself, my girl." She would nod and enthuse at all of Lisa's stories and forest escapades.

Not long after the passing of her mother, Lisa got sick. It was a mild case of pneumonia. She felt so tired and weak most of the time. For three solid days Lisa slept and slept, hardly getting up at all except to use the loo and to drink a little bit of tea. Kathleen was wonderfully gentle and kept the kettle singing and made food for everybody, their cat, dogs and horse included, while Lisa drifted in and out of sleep. Friends called around and brought her something delicious to eat. She got up, wrapped in a duvet, and went to sit beside the fire with them for a while. Once the meal was finished, she felt the tiredness washing over her again and she was soon asleep. Lisa was too ill even to drive Kathleen to school. Her daughter had to call her school friends and keep up with her school projects and studies at home for a while. They had fun, Kat and her, but Lisa was grieving, and you could see it.

After a few days of rest, Lisa was feeling a bit better. Kathleen came into her bedroom with a cup of tea. "I don't know if I should show you, Mom, not with you feeling like this," she said, holding out her cell phone to show her mother a message.

"Read it to me Kat, love," Lisa said brightly.

"I don't think you will want to hear this when I read it, Mom," Kat said, looking quite concerned. "Well, here goes. 'Hi Kathleen, it was great to see you at the memorial service, my dear. Please would you kindly give your mother an urgent message from the family. You see, she has wrongfully taken possession of your grandmother's art and is about to be charged for it. All my mother's possessions belong to the inheritance trust. In fact, Kathleen, if you were a part of this and refuse to assist, you too will be charged. This is just a heads-up, dear girl. Tell your mother to return the artwork and anything else she has stolen immediately or face criminal charges. Thanks. Uncle Mark.'" Lisa felt the whiplash of shock jettison towards her, but she dodged the impact with a carefree laugh.

"Good God, Kat!" she said, shaking her head. "That about takes the cake!" She released a long sigh and ended up coughing her lungs out. The next day she took Kathleen to the local craft market and bought them homemade chocolates and warm chicken pies. They explored the vintage stall and found some sweet silver jewelry to go with Kat's new dress.

When Lisa felt a little stronger, she and Kat planned a trip to a very special place in Wilderness. It was in a wooded part of the river estuary called the Fairy Knowe. Kathleen had prepared a special ceremony for them both, one that she was so eager and proud to tell her mother about. "Mom, I think we should do this. According to an old Fay folk tradition, if there are people in your life who hold ill feelings towards you, then the only way that you can break the spell or curse is by making a symbol for these people and burying them in the soil forever. That's exactly what we need to do, Mom. We need to bury the family for good."

"Wow, Kat! That's quite strong, love. I have never heard of such a simple ritual before. Perhaps we should do it, together, I mean?" Lisa looked at her child with a solemn expression in her eyes.

"Sure Mom, I'd really love to go to Fairy Knowe again. I'll get the stuff ready for the Scottish ritual."

They walked barefoot together down the wooded lane. The turf was so soft and springy underfoot that it was a pleasure to walk it. The birds were singing in the indigenous yellow wood trees nearby as they passed. And they were almost at the end of the forest trail when Kat spotted a clearing where a small bracken frond waved in the breeze. "Here, Mom. We will bury the family here. Let's start with Gran," she said, taking some watercolour-painted slips of paper out of her pocket. She knelt and wrote each family member's name on the paper scrap with a pencil. Then she leaned forward and uncovered the earth closest to the bracken frond. "Here is where we bury my Gran, Mom," she said with finesse, pushing the paper deep into the dark loam. "And here around Gran we will bury all of Grampa's family and Uncle Mark, my cousins, and Aunt Liezel." She pushed each scrap deep into the soil. "This last one is for Grampa and Gran's friends who just don't get it, Mom, the ones who buy into the cruel, nasty nonsense and who have excluded us. I'm going to bury them all, too." And she scooped up the soil at the edge of the clearing and threw the paper into the soil. "There, it's done!" she said, kneeling in front of the fairy burial space.

"Not quite yet, Kat," Lisa said, kneeling beside her. "We need to sing them a prayer in the true Scottish way. Do you know any Gaelic prayers?"

"No, Mom. I only know the basics like, 'Tha an t-aran math.' That means the bread is good," she said with a wry smile.

"Well then, 'Tha an t-aran math' it will be, my Kat," she said and held her daughter's hand while they chanted the simple burial prayer over their beloved family and friends.

"That's such a lovely prayer, Kat. You know, if anything were to happen to me, when I get old and weary and die one day, will you put these special words onto my grave, darling? You can carve them into a tree or make a plaque to put in the garden. It's a magical and holy phrase, and it brings heaven into our midst, doesn't it?" She squeezed her daughter's hand and stood up in all her Gaelic glory.

"Stand tall and hold your head high. Be proud of yourself, my girl." She heard her mother's words echo in her heart.

It was many, many years later, Lisa's autumn-coloured hair had slowly become as white as snow. Time seemed to have slowed to a standstill. Lately, she spent her days in the garden talking with her plants. When the call came, she was outside, planting snowdrops and bulbs for spring. She could hear her cell phone ringing softly inside the cottage. Lisa put down her trowel, wiped her hands, and walked into the kitchen. She picked up her phone with surprise. The number on the screen showed that the caller was her daughter. Lisa hadn't seen or heard from Kat since her daughter left home. She felt breathless as she answered the call.

"Hello," she heard herself whisper.

"Mom… is that you?" It was Kathleen. Her silvery voice was wracked with deep sobs of despair.

"Yes, Kat, I'm here. Are you okay, love?" Lisa asked softly.

"Mom, I'm so, so sorry." Lisa could hear her daughter softly weeping on the other side of the line. "I understand now how I hurt you. And I know that I broke your heart. Mom, I was still so young and really couldn't deal with what was going on at the time. I so much wanted to be a part of a family and to have a normal family life of my own. I know you were the only one who ever stood up for me, despite what everyone was saying about you and what I said to you. You weren't perfect, but nobody is. I'm so sorry. I wish I could take it all back now, but I can't. Will you ever forgive me? I'd like to come home and spend some time with you. I really need you now, Mom." She heard Kathleen intermittently sob and pour out the words.

"Kat, you know I'm here whenever you need me, love," Lisa said with as much strength as she could find in that moment.

"K, thanks, Mom. I'll send you a text and let you know when I am on my way," Kat mumbled through her tears. "And Mom…?"

"Yes, Kat," she answered.

"I love you," Kat whispered before clicking off the line.

"I know, Kat, and I will always love you," Lisa replied softly to herself.

Dawn chorus—Change's song
Frogs, doves, night jars, Piet my vrou and cars
What does the night hold
That tomorrow which turns into today. What does prophecy in the
dove coo and echoed birdsong say?
"We're going to just love you. We're going to just love you. Always
and forever, always and forever, always and forever."
And the forest shrike's sweet note strikes, "with pleasure, always and
forever, always and forever."
And the forest shrike sweet note strikes, "with pleasure, with pleasure
and joy and plenty of life, happiness and joy."
"We're going to just love you; we're going to just love you." Say the
doves in between. A mouse bird trills. "Just believe it. You can see it.
You can feel it. Just feel free inside you, you'll see!
Believe it is in you, it's in you."
Piet my vrou says, "Let it grow, let it go, let it grow, let it grow."
A forest dove and friends chorus,
"You! We're going to just love you;
we're going to just love you."
"Let it grow, let it grow," Dove says. "It's easier with God, it's easier
with Love. Let it grow, let it grow."
The white eyes chorus, "For sure, of course it's so. Y'see how easy?"
A car swishes by on the tar. "Nnnnjaaaaar—who cares
a dove echoes, we're going to just love you,
we're going to just love you."

Epilogue: Return of the Fisher King

This epilogue comes from a beautiful dream I had. A dream that has brought great healing. A sense of belonging and the soul reunion of the Fisherman, his child, and me.

The red ochre-stained piece of bone was palm-sized. It was smoothed with wear and weathered by the salt and sea, as graceful and elegant as a woman but as strong and sturdy as a man. The image engraved onto its surface was of a whale. It was a gift from the Khoi ancestors and the Fisherman who had once loved her.

Time had passed. Their world had slowly started to go back to normal. Lisa often took Kat and their two wolf dogs for walks on their favourite beach near Buffalo Bay. It was one of those exquisite still mornings when the sea was covered with swirls of ocean foam and mist. Kathleen was sitting on the beach, happily chatting with one of her friends on the phone. Lisa was walking down the beach when she saw a man appear out of the mist, from the rocks where she had first found the whale amulet. Lisa was gazing at the sea, lost in thought, when she spotted him. A strong, stocky-looking man, wearing a deep chocolate brown sweater, just like the one Lisa had knitted for the Fisherman so long ago. And he carried an old canvas fishing bag.

Lisa focused on the apparition and started to frown with incredulity. *It looks so like Ian, but it couldn't be the Fisherman,* she thought. As he approached, she saw his familiar jaunty walk and that stoop to his shoulders which seemed more pronounced now, much more resigned. She saw that he had grown older. His thick blonde hair was streaked with grey and was receding around his temples. She also saw a deep sadness and humility etched onto his face and in his eyes. He stopped a short distance in front of her and smiled at her face with recognition and compassion. Gently, he lifted one of his calloused, worn hands to touch the whale bone amulet at her throat. "So, you still have the amulet, my beauty," he said in his throaty, quiet way and then gathered Lisa into his wide embrace.

"My Lisa, it's alright, I'm alright, I am alive," he said softly into her ear as the deep sobs began to well up within her. "Here, sit down, listen, and I'll explain everything to you."

They sat talking on the beach for a very long time, in the same way that they always had. The Fisherman told Lisa his story while she listened and then shared her heart, too.

They walked back along the beach to the car park. Ian opened his fishing bag and took out the keys to his truck. "Just a minute," he said with a secretive smile. The Fisherman reached into the interior of his vehicle and took out a small rectangular wooden container from the glove compartment. "Here, look!" he said simply, handing her the small wooden box. Lisa carefully opened the box and stared at the object inside. It was a familiar-looking old bottle wrapped in a piece of soft cotton cloth. "H-how did you find this?" she stammered, gently lifting a beautiful, weather-beaten bottle out of the box. It was her bottle. The bottle that contained the letters she had written for Ian and had thrown into the sea all those years ago.

"It was old Pete, the Rasta fisherman who found it, down there in the bay where I took you fishing once. He kept it and gave it to me not long ago when I went back to look for you, Lisa."

"That's incredible!" Lisa gasped, shaking her head in disbelief. "But, I still don't understand, Ian," she said, looking at him steadfastly. "It's as though you've returned from the dead. I was there at the mortuary. I saw you."

Ian shook his head. "No, Lisa. It wasn't me that you saw. I can't explain what happened, but there was a terrible misunderstanding. Years ago, I took a contract to do trawler fishing off the island of St. Helena and along the west coast. Almost all the inheritance money I had was confiscated by the state. You see, I was caught poaching kreef and abalone and running drugs. I had no choice. I joined the SA Marine deep-sea fishing crew and left this place with all its terrible memories behind me. I was on legal probation and received psychiatric treatment for PTSD," he said, briefly closing his eyes. "It's taken me a long, long time to return to myself again. But I kept seeing your face and the face of our child. And it was… simply, everything we shared, my love for you both that brought me back. You touched my heart and showed me that there was another way, a more courageous, loving, and caring way. I never forgot you."

Lisa looked at him quietly for a long moment. "Ian, where were you for me, for our daughter when she needed you? And when I needed you, through all those difficult years? How are you going to explain that to Kat now?"

Ian smiled gently. "All I can say is that while I was in treatment, I changed. I'm still me, but the anger has gone, completely. I understand now that it was all me, my choices entirely, that took me to the streets. There was no one else to blame. I was so broken that I couldn't be there for you, as much as I wanted to... My addiction took me right down to rock bottom, where I had to choose death or love. It kind of feels like I've been given another chance at life and to make it right by you and Kathleen, if you know what I mean," he said. "While I was at sea, I made up my mind that I would find you, no matter what it took, and even if you and Kat didn't want anything to do with me, I would at least try to help take some of the financial load from you. So, I started studying. I applied to study Marine Biology about fifteen years ago while I was still working on the boats off St. Helena Island and was accepted. As you can see, this is my work now." Ian indicated his vehicle and the equipment he was carrying. "I was posted here to the Wilderness area recently. You see, I am an asset to the Marine team because of my background. Apart from doing detailed analysis on the impact of ocean pollution on cetaceans, I also monitor poachers on this entire stretch of coast."

She could see that the Fisherman had changed. It was as plain as day. He was healthy, fit, sober, and present. He was the Ian that she had fallen head over heels in love with. The Lion man that she'd dreamed about. Lisa looked at him, smiling in sheer disbelief, shaking her head again, breathless and speechless with the impact of the moment.

This time, it was the Fisherman who led the way. "I'm so sorry. I was blind, Lisa. Will you ever forgive me, for all I have done and left undone? For leaving you alone with Kat?" He looked at her in his quiet, forever way and when she didn't answer, he said, "I know it's the stupidest question. What's done is done. We can't change the past now. We have both learned an immense amount and grown into incredibly strong people. I realize how much you have been through on your own and how terribly hurt you have been. Could you ever consider me as a friend to you both?" Lisa felt herself beginning to shake inwardly, crying with joy and laughing at the same time. It had been such a long, hard, lonely battle without Ian's support. All the pain and anguish melted instantaneously, and all the emptiness was filled with his words. It had been sixteen long years since they had last seen one another, and she had thought that she would never see him again. He was dead, as far as she knew.

Kathleen had been watching them from Lisa's car, and somehow, she felt drawn to be there. Slowly, hesitating, she walked over and stopped to look at him.

"It's Ian, Kat. It's your father," Lisa said simply. The Fisherman's child stared at him with a look of disbelief, then contempt and smoldering resentment in her eyes, and she began to turn away, but the Fisherman moved instinctively and instantaneously towards his beloved daughter. He caught her with the kind of grace and agility that comes from a heart filled with many, many years of longing for reunion. With a father's tenderness and care, the Fisherman bent down and took her gently by the hands, looking at her and speaking life into her angry, wounded heart. "Even though you believed I did not, I have loved you so much throughout all those empty years." Lisa heard a snatch of the conversation, a sentence here or there, floating on the gentle evening breeze, as the Fisherman poured out his heart and remorse to his only beloved child. And then she was there between them, hugging, weeping, forgiving and laughing, all three, smiling with joy, relief, and love.

They were finally home together.

And the whales rejoiced.

I love you in ways only you know
My love wider and deeper than the oceans and heavens above
Your eyes are my eyes, what you see I see
Your mind is in me and mine in yours
Your brave forgiving heart makes me your brave heart
Your courage and truth make me find mine
Your body, your existence I embrace
My soul finds fulfillment
that only you can offer and understand
Where I am empty, lost or confused
You console me and steady my thoughts
In you I am me

Acknowledgments

I wish to express my heartfelt gratitude to my publisher and author mentor, Jane Astara Ashley of Flower of Life Press. Her unwavering professional guidance, steadfast friendship, and continuous support were invaluable throughout the journey of completing this book. Jane's encouragement, wisdom, and belief in my vision enabled me to move through each stage of the process with confidence and clarity.

I am also deeply thankful to the many gifted international authors I have had the privilege of meeting through Flower of Life Press. This remarkable sisterhood of women, united by their dedication to creative expression and personal growth, has honoured, accompanied, and encouraged me along my path of soul excavation. Their presence offered both inspiration and reassurance, and I am particularly grateful to authors Mari Dreamwalker, Sherry Marriot, Crystal Steinberg, Stellar Fairbairn, and many others. Their kindness, attentive witness, and warmth created a nurturing and sacred space where we could openly share our truths. In this environment, we experienced profound personal and collective growth by supporting one another's voices and stories.

My heartfelt thanks also extend to fellow South African star seed traveller and co-author of Kalahari Rainsong, Belinda Kruiper Regopstaan. Her willingness to share her wisdom, insight, and deep understanding of the Khomani Bushman people has been an extraordinary gift.

Finally, I would like to offer my deep acknowledgment to the Honourable Viginia Mutwa, wife of the late, great African Sanusi and traditional wisdom keeper, Baba Credo Mutwa. Her tremendous love and magical friendship over the years have been a true blessing in my life. Viginia's presence, guidance, and generosity of spirit continue to inspire and uplift me.

About the Author

Sarah Alissandra Nomngoma is a poet, writer, and artist of the soul. Her work reflects qualities of the mythical that are so intrinsic to life on this beautiful African continent. She was trained in Archaeology and Fine Arts at the University of Cape Town. She later continued her research into San culture and the Rock Art of Southern Africa, weaving these elements into her work. Her paintings have been exhibited widely in South Africa and internationally in New York and London.

Sarah writes about the human experience, focusing on Motherhood and her deep connection with Mother Gaia. She has valuable memories of her time with the Khoisan people, deep in the Kalahari desert, listening to their stories and to those of many Great African leaders and healers.

She presently lives on the beautiful Southern African shores of the Garden Route where she paints, writes, and directs a children's Education Program called the "Ubumama Outdoor Classroom Project." Ubumama has recently been awarded the South African National Parks Kudu award nomination for environmental education.

Look out for future books by this exciting new South African author.

Learn more at: **https://ubumama.co.za/**

VISIT US AT

www.floweroflifepress.com